IF ENGLAND WERE INVADED

WILLIAM LE QUEUX

D0108947

ABBOT PUBLIC LIBRARY
235 Pleasant Street
Marblehead, MA 01945

This edition first published in 2014
by the Bodleian Library, Broad Street, Oxford, OX1 3BG

www.bodleianbookshop.co.uk

ISBN 978 1 85124 402 7

Introduction, compilation and notes to this edition
© Bodleian Library, University of Oxford, 2014
Originally published in 1906 as The Invasion,
by William Le Queux, London

All rights reserved

No part of this book may be reproduced, stored in a retrieval
system, or transmitted in any form or by any means, electronic,
mechanical, photocopying, recording, or otherwise, without the
written permission of the Bodleian Library, except for the purpose
of research or private study, or criticism or review.

Cover design by Dot Little
Text designed and typeset in 10 on 12½ Monotype Joanna
by illuminati, Grosmont
Printed and bound by Page Bros, England

British Library Catalogue in Publishing Data
A CIP record of this publication is available from the British Library

CONTENTS

BOOK III   THE REVENGE

INTRODUCTION

THE BATTLE OF DORKING, a short story by George Tomkyns Cheney published in 1871 as a serial in *Blackwood's Magazine*, was the first example of a genre of novels known as "invasion literature". It was prompted by the swift and sensational defeat of France, a major European power, in the Franco-Prussian War. Cheney was an officer in the Royal Engineers, and his story was meant to alert the public to the threat that military and technological developments posed to a state unprepared for modern war.

The Battle of Dorking was unusual in that it envisaged an invasion by Germans (the enemy was not in fact named, but they spoke German). It was not Germany, however, but France that was the perceived threat to Britain and her Empire, and France (with her ally Russia) was the usual enemy in the most notable examples of the genre published before 1903. For output and success in the genre, no one in the Edwardian era could outdo William Tufnell Le Queux. Le Queux was born in Southwark in 1864, the son of a French draper's assistant and his English wife. The *Dictionary of National Biography* states that his own accounts of his early life are "unreliable" as once he became well known he wove an air of mystery around himself, posing as a spy, adventurer and criminologist. His *Who's Who* entry listed his recreations as "revolver practice, skiing in Switzerland, the study of Egyptology and criminology" and "experiments in wireless telephony".

Le Queux seems to have made his early living as a journalist in England with local newspapers, though he claimed to have worked in Paris. He seems to have given up this work to concentrate on writing melodramatic thrillers as well as various short stories and articles. He churned out novels at an average rate of five a year, beginning with *Guilty Bonds* (1890), a story about Russian nihilists. The ingredients of many of his books were often quite similar, and usually included exotic foreign locations, debonair heroes, beautiful heroines and wicked (usually foreign) villains. His works were very popular and by 1898 he had become one of the highest paid writers of fiction.

Le Queux became chiefly known for his contribution to the "invasion literature" genre. In this he worked with Alfred Harmsworth, later 1st baron Northcliffe, the newspaper owner and pioneer of popular journalism. It was Harmsworth who commissioned Le Queux's first such work, "The Poisoned Bullet", published as a serial in *Answers*, and subsequently as a book, *The Great War in England in 1897* (1894). The introduction to the work neatly expresses the purpose underlying such novels:

> In writing this book it was my endeavour to bring vividly before the public the national dangers by which we are surrounded, and the absolute necessity which lies upon England to maintain her defences in an adequate state of efficiency.

The work ran to eight editions from July to December 1894, and in the preface to the ninth edition in March 1895 Le Queux equated this success with the British public having heeded his dire warnings. The enemy was still at this stage perceived to be France, with her ally Russia, and although Britain eventually triumphed in the Great War of 1897, she had been forced to endure the Russian capture of Birmingham and Manchester, and "terror on the Tyne", including the destruction of the High Level Bridge in Newcastle, before the foe was finally vanquished.

In 1900 Britain stood in "splendid isolation", with no European allies. She was also embroiled in a war in South Africa against the Boers that would require 450,000 men to bring it to a successful conclusion. With her forces so committed, the spectre of a sudden invasion by the French loomed in the thoughts of political and military thinkers, and "invasion literature" received a new impetus. Titles appeared such as *The Sack of London in the Great French War of 1901* (London, 1901) and *Seaward for the Foe, by Headon Hill* (London, 1903).

But by 1903 a new threat was emerging. The very fact that France seemed to pose the greatest menace to British security, and was Britain's greatest imperial rival, tended to push the two countries into negotiation, emerging in the *Entente Cordiale* of 1904. By now the German threat was beginning to worry politicians as the Kaiser embarked on a massive naval programme which would challenge Britain's maritime supremacy. Erskine Childers's 1903 best-seller, *The Riddle of the Sands*, caused such a stir that the British Admiralty actually commissioned an inquiry to see if the scenario suggested by Childers of a sudden descent by the Germans on pre-arranged landing places on the East Coast was feasible. The Naval Intelligence Department decided that it was not, and indeed there is no evidence that Germany ever seriously considered an invasion, although elaborate plans had been drawn up in 1896 before being abandoned as impracticable.

Nevertheless, Lord Roberts and Harmsworth, who became Baron Northcliffe in 1905, continued their crusade to awaken the British public to the perceived threat, and from 1905 Le Queux took a decidedly anti-German position. In his own account of his life, *Things I Know about Kings, Celebrities and Crooks* (1923), he claimed that he discovered a huge network of German espionage in Britain in 1905, and toured the south-east of England in search of likely landing places, receiving advice from Lord Roberts, the former Commander-in-Chief of the Forces and an advocate of compulsory military service. Northcliffe now commissioned another sensationalist serial, *The Invasion of* 1910, published in the *Daily Mail* in 1906. Again, the work was published as a book the same year, and once again Le Queux explained his purpose to his readers in his preface:

> The object of this book is to illustrate our utter unpreparedness for war from a military standpoint; to show how, under certain conditions which may easily occur, England can be successfully invaded by Germany; and to present a picture of the ruin which must inevitably fall upon us on the evening of that not far-distant day.

The book was to become Le Queux's best known work, and was promoted by many and satirized by others. It was translated into twenty-seven languages and sold over one million copies. A German version appeared, with a different ending.

The scenario of the novel, and the points it is trying to put across, are explained in an exchange in the first chapter:

"The Germans evidently laid their plans with great cleverness. Their spies, already in England, cut the wires at a pre-arranged hour last night," declared Fergusson. "They sought to prevent this gentleman from giving the alarm by shooting him. All the railways to London are already either cut or held by the enemy. One thing, however, is clear—fleet or no fleet, the east coast is entirely at their mercy."

"Well, if what you say is the actual truth," exclaimed Sir James, "to-day is surely the blackest day that England has ever known."

"Yes, they should have listened to Lord Roberts," snapped his lordship.

The naval chapters in the book were written by H.W. Wilson, a journalist and naval historian who later wrote a thirteen-volume history of the Great War, published by Northcliffe's Amalgamated Press between 1914 and 1919. The first volume was used to justify the British war position and to encourage men to enlist.

A constant theme of Le Queux's and others' writings was the presence of a network of German spies and a "fifth column" that would sabotage communications to aid the invasion. In 1908 Lord Roberts had warned the House of Lords that there were 80,000 Germans, mostly trained soldiers, working in hotels and railway stations in the United Kingdom, who would be there to support an invasion. Although many ridiculed these preposterous ideas at the time, this only served to encourage the "scaremongers" to make further efforts. The effects in some quarters of the relentless campaigns of Northcliffe, Lord Roberts and their supporters can be seen in British reactions when war broke out in 1914. Andrew Clark, rector of Great Leighs in Essex, recorded a number of spy scares in his diary, though he himself remained sceptical. It so happened that his village was right in the centre of the imagined battles of Royston, Harlow and Chelmsford in the Invasion of 1910. Indeed, in Le Queux's account, German forces fired on the British from Great Leighs Wood. On 26 September 1914 Clark recorded that the chief of the Special Constables, Sir Richard Pennefather of Little Waltham,

plumes himself that he has caught a spy. An elderly woman, with a strong German accent, selling lace at Little Waltham, was arrested by his order. ... This is probably the lace seller who caused great alarm to the Tufnell household at Langleys, Great Waltham. She made ... most minute enquiry as to the number and character of the rooms in the mansion and as to the age and habits of all its inmates. The Langley people imagined she was a militant suffragette, planning an incendiary outrage.

On 20 October Mrs Sargeant, wife of the gardener at Lyons Hall, told of a German spy at the Boreham end of the village. He was seen drawing plans of the roads, and was reported to two troopers of the Bedfordshire Yeomanry from the camp at Terling. They interviewed the "spy" and noted that he had a foreign accent, and sent two soldiers out on bicycles to arrest him. It transpired that he was an Ordinance Survey reviser (they were very active during this period of planning for large-scale military manoeuvres), but no villagers could be made to believe that he was not a spy, and that his OS map was not a "blind", until "the Little Waltham policeman passed and certified his honesty and official status".

Sir Richard Pennefather's enthusiasm eventually brought him some ridicule. On 29 October Clark noted that Pennefather had the Special Constables of Little Waltham, the "grocer, butcher, baker and other comfort-loving citizens ... out as patrols, night by night". He describes Pennefather as an "amicable but fussy, ex-Paymaster of the Metropolitan Police, very full of terrors from spies prowling about to blow up bridges and cut down telegraph poles".

The spy scare was not confined to the localities. At the Cabinet meeting on 4 August 1914, the day war was declared, Lewis Harcourt the Colonial Secretary noted in his journal that "there are many German spies here now and have been for a long time: we have full evidence against them and shall seize them at once."

The truth was that just twenty-one real German spies were arrested on 4 August 1914, and their activities had already been discovered by British intelligence. However, the government received thousands of reports of imagined acts of espionage, with some local authorities being only too willing to believe anything. Despite a lack of any real evidence of spying activities among Germans living in the United Kingdom, in May 1915 the government decided to intern "enemy aliens" for the duration of the war. It was also in 1915 that the theme of secret plots, espionage and counter-espionage received its most famous expression in John Buchan's book, *The Thirty-Nine Steps*. This too had begun as a serial, in *Blackwood's Magazine*.

Perhaps, then, there is a lesson to be drawn from Le Queux's book. It is not that we should be alert to the presence of covert agents in their thousands waiting to subvert the country on behalf of the enemy – it is the (unintended) message that one should not believe everything one reads in the newspapers.

In 1912 the Gaumont Cinematograph Company planned to make a film of *The Invasion of 1910*, under the title *The Raid of 1915*. There were to be alternative endings, a British and a German victory. When the film was finally released in October 1914 a real war with Germany had begun. The film was released under yet another title – *If England Were Invaded*.

MIKE WEBB

PREFACE

"I sometimes despair of the country ever becoming alive to the danger of the unpreparedness of our present position until too late to prevent some fatal catastrophe."

This was the keynote of a solemn warning made in the House of Lords by Earl Roberts. His lordship, whilst drawing attention to our present inadequate forces, strongly urged that action should be taken in accordance with the recommendations of the Elgin Commission that "no military system could be considered satisfactory which did not contain powers of expansion outside the limit of the regular forces of the Crown."

"The lessons of the late war appear to have been forgotten. The one prevailing idea seems to be," said Earl Roberts, "to cut down our military expenditure without reference to our increased responsibilities and our largely augmented revenue. History tells us in the plainest terms that an Empire which cannot defend its own possessions must inevitably perish." And with this view both Lord Milner and the Marquis of Lansdowne concurred. But surely this is not enough. If we are to retain our position as the first nation of the world we must be prepared to defend any raid made upon our shores.

The object of this book is to illustrate our utter unpreparedness for war from a military standpoint; to show how, under certain conditions which may easily occur, England can be successfully invaded by Germany; and to present a picture of the ruin which must inevitably fall upon us on the evening of that not far-distant day.

Ever since Lord Roberts formulated his plans for the establishment of rifle-clubs I have been deeply interested in the movement: and after a conversation with that distinguished soldier the idea occurred to me to write a forecast, based upon all the available military knowledge—which would bring home to the British public vividly and forcibly what really would occur were an enemy suddenly to appear in our midst. At the outset it was declared by the strategists I consulted to be impossible. No such book could ever be written, for, according to them, the mass of technical detail was far too great to digest and present in an intelligible manner to the public.

Lord Roberts, however, gave me encouragement. The skeleton scheme of the manner in which England could be invaded by Germany was submitted to a number of the highest authorities on strategy, whose names, however, I am not permitted to divulge, and after many consultations, much criticism, and considerable difference of opinion, the "general idea," with amendment after amendment, was finally adopted.

That, however, was only a mere preliminary. Upon questions of tactics each tactician consulted held a different view, and each criticised adversely the other's suggestions.

One way alone remained open—namely, to take the facts exactly as they stood, add the additional strength of the opposing nations as they at present are, and then draw logical conclusions. This, aided by experts, was done: and after many days of argument with the various authorities, we succeeded in getting them in accord as to the general practicability of an invasion.

Before putting pen to paper it was necessary to reconnoitre carefully the whole of England from the Thames to the Tyne. This I did by means of a motor-car, travelling 10,000 miles of all kinds of roads, and making a tour extending over four months. Each town, all the points of vantage, military positions, all the available land-ing places on the coast, all railway connections, and telephone and telegraph communications, were carefully noted for future reference. With the assistance of certain well-known military experts, the battlefields were carefully gone over and the positions marked upon the Ordnance map. Thus, through four months we pushed on day by day collecting information and material, sometimes in the big cities, sometimes in the quietest and remotest hamlets, all of which was carefully tabulated for use.

Whatever critics may say, and however their opinions may differ, it can only be pointed out, first, that the "general idea" of the scheme is in accordance with the expressed and published opinions of the first strategists of to-day, and that, as far as the forecast of events is concerned, it has been written from a first-hand knowledge of the local colour of each of the scenes described. The enemy's Proclamations reproduced are practically copies of those issued by the Germans during the war of 1870.

That the experts and myself will probably be condemned as alarmists and denounced for revealing information likely to be of assistance to an enemy goes without saying. Indeed, an attempt was made in the House of Commons to suppress its publication altogether. Mr. R.C. Lehmann, who asked a question of the Prime Minister, declared that it was "calculated to prejudice our relations with the other Powers," while the late Sir H. Campbell-Bannerman, in a subsequent letter apologising to me for condemning in the House a work he had not read, repeated that it was likely to "produce irritation abroad and might conceivably alarm the more ignorant public at home."

Such a reflection, cast by the late Prime Minister upon the British nation, was, to say the least, curious, yet it only confirmed the truth that the Government are strenuously seeking to conceal from our people the appalling military weakness and the consequent danger to which the country is constantly open.

To be weak is to invite war: to be strong is to prevent it.

To arouse our country to a sense of its own lamentable insecurity is the object of this volume, which is somewhat compressed from the form in which it originally appeared, and that other nations besides ourselves are interested in England's grave peril is proved by the fact that it has already been published in the German, French, Spanish, Danish, Russian, Italian, and even Japanese languages.

WILLIAM LE QUEUX

R

Speaking in the House of Lords on the 10th July 1905, I said :—"It is to the people of the country I appeal to take up the question of the Army in a sensible practical manner. For the sake of all they hold dear, let them bring home to themselves what would be the condition of Great Britain if it were to lose its wealth, to forfeit its position". The catastrophe that may happen if we stile remain in our present state of unpreparedness is vividly and prettily illustrated in Mr. Le Queux's new book which I recommend to the perusal of every one who has the welfare of the British Empire at heart.

29. Nov: 1905

Roberts. F.M.

BOOK I

THE ATTACK

CHAPTER I

THE SURPRISE

TWO OF THE MYRIAD of London's nightworkers were walking down Fleet Street together soon after dawn on Sunday morning, 2nd September.

The sun had not yet risen. That main artery of London traffic, with its irregular rows of closed shops and newspaper offices, was quiet and pleasant in the calm, mystic light before the falling of the smoke-pall.

Only at early morning does the dear old City look its best; in that one quiet, sweet hour when the night's toil has ended and the day's has not yet begun. Only in that brief interval at the birth of day, when the rose tints of the sky glow slowly into gold, does the giant metropolis repose—at least, as far as its business streets are concerned—for at five o'clock the toiling millions begin to again pour in from all points of the compass, and the stress and storm of London at once recommences.

And in that hour of silent charm the two grey-bearded sub-editors, though engaged in offices of rival newspapers were making their way homeward to Dulwich to spend Sunday in a well-earned rest, and were chatting "shop," as Press men do.

"I suppose you had the same trouble to get that Yarmouth story through?" asked Fergusson, the news-editor of the *Dispatch*, as they crossed Whitefriars Street. "We got about half a column, and then the wire shut down."

"Telegraph or telephone?" inquired Baines, who was four or five years younger than his friend.

"We were using both—to make sure."

"So were we. It was a rattling good story—the robbery was mysterious, to say the least—but we didn't get more than half of it. Something's wrong with the line, evidently," Baines said. "If it were not such a perfect autumn morning, I should be inclined to think there'd been a storm somewhere."

"Yes—funny, wasn't it?" remarked the other. "A shame we haven't the whole story, for it was a first-class one, and we wanted something. Did you put it on the contents-bill?"

"No, because we couldn't get the finish. I tried in every way—rang up the Central News, P.A., Exchange Telegraph Company, tried to get through to Yarmouth on the trunk, and spent half an hour or so pottering about, but the reply from all the agencies, from everywhere, in fact, was the same—the line was interrupted."

"Just our case. I telephoned to the Post Office, but the reply came back that the lines were evidently down."

"Well, it certainly looks as though there'd been a storm, but—" and Baines glanced at the bright, clear sky overhead, just flushed by the bursting sun—"there are certainly no traces of it."

"There's often a storm on the coast when it's quite still in London, my dear fellow," remarked his friend wisely.

"That's all very well. But when all communication with a big place like Yarmouth is suddenly cut off, as it has been, I can't help suspecting that something has happened which we ought to know."

"You're perhaps right, after all," Fergusson said. "I wonder if anything has happened. We don't want to be called back to the office, either of us. My assistant, Henderson, whom I've left in charge, rings me up over any mare's nest. The trunk telephones all come into the Post Office Exchange up in Carter Lane. Why not look in there before we go home? It won't take us a quarter of an hour, and we have several trains home from Ludgate Hill."

Baines looked at his watch. Like his companion, he had no desire to be called back to his office after getting out to Dulwich, and yet he was in no mood to go making reporter's inquiries.

"I don't think I'll go. It's sure to be nothing, my dear fellow," he said. "Besides, I have a beastly headache. I had a heavy night's work. One of my men is away ill."

"Well, at any rate, I think I'll go," Fergusson said. "Don't blame me if you get called back for a special edition with a terrible storm, great loss of life, and all that sort of thing. So long." And, smiling, he waved his hand and parted from his friend in the booking office of Ludgate Hill Station.

Quickening his pace, he hurried through the office, and, passing out by the back, ascended the steep, narrow street until he reached the Post Office Telephone Exchange in Carter Lane, where, presenting his card, he asked to see the superintendent-in-charge.

Without much delay he was shown upstairs into a small private office, into which came a short, dapper, fair-moustached man with the bustle of a man in a great hurry.

"I've called," the sub-editor explained, "to know whether you can tell me anything regarding the cause of the interruption of the line to Yarmouth a short time ago. We had some important news coming through, but were cut off just in the midst of it, and then we received information that all the telephone and telegraph lines to Yarmouth were interrupted."

"Well, that's just the very point which is puzzling us at this moment," was the night-superintendent's reply. "It is quite unaccountable. Our trunk going to Yarmouth seems to be down, as well as the telegraphs. Yarmouth, Lowestoft, and beyond Beccles seem all to have been suddenly cut off. About eighteen minutes to four the operators noticed something wrong, switched the trunks through to the testers, and the latter reported to me in due course."

"That's strange! Did they all break down together?"

"No. The first that failed was the one that runs through Chelmsford, Colchester, and Ipswich up to Lowestoft and Yarmouth. The operator found that he could get through to Ipswich and Beccles. Ipswich knew nothing, except that something was wrong. They could still ring up Beccles, but not beyond."

As they were speaking, there was a tap at the door, and the assistant night-superintendent entered, saying:

"The Norwich line through Scole and Long Stratton has now failed, sir. About half-past four Norwich reported a fault somewhere north, between there and Cromer. But the operator now says that the line is apparently broken, and so are all the telegraphs from there to Cromer, Sheringham, and Holt."

"Another line has gone, then!" exclaimed the superintendent-in-charge, utterly astounded. "Have you tried to get on to Cromer by the other routes—through Nottingham and King's Lynn, or through Cambridge?"

"The testers have tried every route, but there's no response."

"You could get through to some of the places—Yarmouth, for instance—by telegraphing to the Continent, I suppose?" asked Fergusson.

"We are already trying," responded the assistant superintendent.

"What cables run out from the east coast in that neighbourhood?" inquired the sub-editor quickly.

"There are five between Southwold and Cromer—three run to Germany, and two to Holland," replied the assistant. "There's the cable from Yarmouth to Barkum, in the Frisian Islands; from Happisburg, near Mundesley, to Barkum; from Yarmouth to Emden; from Lowestoft to Haarlem, and from Kessingland, near Southwold, to Zandyport."

"And you are trying all the routes?" asked his superior.

"I spoke to Paris myself an hour ago and asked them to cable by all five routes to Yarmouth, Lowestoft, Kessingland, and Happisburg," was the assistant's reply. "I also asked Liverpool Street Station and King's Cross to wire down to some of their stations on the coast, but the reply was that they were in the same predicament as ourselves—their lines were down north of Beccles, Wymondham, East Dereham, and also south of Lynn. I'll just run along and see if there's any reply from Paris. They ought to be through by this time, as it's Sunday morning, and no traffic." And he went out hurriedly.

"There's certainly something very peculiar," remarked the superintendent-in-charge to the sub-editor. "If there's been an earthquake or an electrical disturbance, then it is a most extraordinary one. Every single line reaching to the coast seems interrupted."

"Yes. It's uncommonly funny," Fergusson remarked. "I wonder what could have happened. You've never had a complete breakdown like this before?"

"Never. But I think—"

The sentence remained unfinished, for his assistant returned with a slip of paper in his hand, saying:

"This message has just come in from Paris, I'll read it. 'Superintendent Telephones, Paris, to Superintendent Telephones, London.— Have obtained direct telegraphic communication with operators of all five cables to England. Haarlem, Zandyport, Barkum, and Emden all report that cables are interrupted. They can get no reply from England, and tests show that cables are damaged somewhere near English shore.'"

"Is that all?" asked Fergusson.

"That's all. Paris knows no more than we do," was the assistant's response.

"Then the Norfolk and Suffolk coasts are completely isolated—cut off from post office, railways, telephones, and cables!" exclaimed the superintendent. "It's mysterious—most mysterious!" And, taking up the instrument upon his table, he placed a plug in one of the holes down the front of the table itself, and a moment later was in conversation with the official in charge of the traffic at Liverpool Street, repeating the report from Paris, and urging him to send light engines north from Wymondham or Beccles into the zone of the mystery.

The reply came back that he had already done so, but a telegram had reached him from Wymondham to the effect that the road-bridges between Kimberley and Hardingham had apparently fallen in, and the line was blocked by débris. Interruption was also reported beyond Swaffham, at a place called Little Dunham.

"Then even the railways themselves are broken!" cried Fergusson. "Is it possible that there has been a great earthquake?"

"An earthquake couldn't very well destroy all five cables from the Continent," remarked the superintendent gravely.

The latter had scarcely placed the receiver upon the hook when a third man entered—an operator who, addressing him, said:

"Will you please come to the switchboard, sir? There's a man in the Ipswich call office who has just told me a most extraordinary story. He says that he started in his motor-car alone from Lowestoft to London at half-past three this morning, and just as it was getting light he was passing along the edge of Henham Park, between Wangford village and Blythburgh, when he saw three men apparently repairing the telegraph wires. One was up the pole, and the other two were standing below. As he passed he saw a flash, for, to his surprise, one of the men fired point-blank at him with a revolver. Fortunately, the shot went wide, and he at once put on a move and got down into Blythburgh village, even though one of his tyres went down. It had probably been pierced by the bullet fired at him, as the puncture was unlike any he had ever had before. At Blythburgh he informed the police of the outrage, and the constable, in turn, woke up the postmaster, who tried to telegraph back to the police at Wrentham, but found that the line was interrupted. Was it possible that the men were cutting the wires, instead of repairing them? He says that after repairing the puncture he took the village constable and three other men on his car and went back to the spot, where, although the trio had escaped, they saw that wholesale havoc had been wrought with the telegraphs. The lines had been severed in four or five places, and whole lengths tangled up into great masses. A number of poles had been sawn down, and were lying about the roadside. Seeing that nothing could be done, the gentleman remounted his car, came on to Ipswich, and reported the damage at our call office."

"And is he still there?" exclaimed the superintendent quickly, amazed at the motorist's statement.

"Yes. I asked him to wait for a few moments in order to speak to you, sir."

"Good. I'll go at once. Perhaps you'd like to come also, Mr. Fergusson?"

And all three ran up to the gallery, where the huge switchboards were ranged around, and where the night operators, with the receivers attached to one ear, were still at work.

In a moment the superintendent had taken the operator's seat, adjusted the ear-piece, and was in conversation with Ipswich. A second later he was speaking with the man who had actually witnessed the cutting of the trunk line.

While he was thus engaged an operator at the farther end of the switchboard suddenly gave vent to a cry of surprise and disbelief.

"What do you say, Beccles? Repeat it," he asked excitedly.

Then a moment later he shouted aloud:

"Beccles says that German soldiers—hundreds of them—are pouring into the place! The Germans have landed at Lowestoft, they think."

All who heard those ominous words sprang up dumbfounded, staring at each other.

The assistant-superintendent dashed to the operator's side and seized his apparatus.

"Halloa—halloa, Beccles! Halloa—halloa—halloa!"

The response was some gruff words in German, and the sound of scuffling could distinctly be heard. Then all was silent.

Time after time he rang up the small Suffolk town, but in vain. Then he switched through to the testers, and quickly the truth was plain.

The second trunk line to Norwich, running from Ipswich by Harleston and Beccles, had been cut farther towards London.

But what held everyone breathless in the trunk telephone head-quarters was that the Germans had actually effected the surprise landing that had so often in recent years been predicted by military critics; that England on that quiet September Sunday morning had been attacked. England was actually invaded. It was incredible!

Yet London's millions in their Sunday morning lethargy were in utter ignorance of the grim disaster that had suddenly fallen upon the land.

Fergusson was for rushing at once back to the *Dispatch* office to get out an extraordinary edition, but the superintendent, who was still in conversation with the motorist, urged judicious forethought.

"For the present, let us wait. Don't let us alarm the public un-necessarily. We want corroboration. Let us have the motorist up here," he suggested.

"Yes," cried the sub-editor. "Let me speak to him."

Over the wire Fergusson begged the stranger to come at once to London and give his story, declaring that the military authorities would require it. Then, just as the man who had been shot at by German advance spies—for such they had undoubtedly been—in order to prevent the truth leaking out, gave his promise to come to town at once, there came over the line from the coastguard at Southwold a vague, incoherent telephone message regarding strange ships having been seen to the northward, and asking for connection with Harwich; while King's Cross and Liverpool Street Stations both rang up almost simultaneously, reporting the receipt of extra- ordinary messages from King's Lynn, Diss, Harleston, Halesworth, and other places. All declared that German soldiers were swarming over the north, that Lowestoft and Beccles had been seized, and that Yarmouth and Cromer were isolated.

Various stationmasters reported that the enemy had blown up bridges, taken up rails, and effectually blocked all communication with the coast. Certain important junctions were already held by the enemy's outposts.

Such was the amazing news received in that high-up room in Carter Lane, City, on that sweet, sunny morning when all the great world of London was at peace, either still slumbering or week-ending.

Fergusson remained for a full hour and a half at the Telephone Exchange, anxiously awaiting any further corroboration. Many wild stories came over the wires telling how panic-stricken people were fleeing inland away from the enemy's outposts. Then he took a hansom to the *Dispatch* office, and proceeded to prepare a special edition of his paper—an edition containing surely the most amazing news that had ever startled London.

Fearing to create undue panic, he decided not to go to press until the arrival of the motorist from Ipswich. He wanted the story of the man who had actually seen the cutting of the wires. He paced his room excitedly, wondering what effect the news would have upon the world. In the rival newspaper offices the report was, as yet, unknown. With journalistic forethought he had arranged that at present the bewildering truth should not leak out to his rivals, either from the railway termini or from the telephone exchange. His only fear was that some local correspondent might telegraph from some village or town nearer the metropolis which was still in communication with the central office.

Time passed very slowly. Each moment increased his anxiety. He had sent out the one reporter who remained on duty to the house of Colonel Sir James Taylor, the Permanent Under-Secretary for War. Halting before the open window, he looked up and down the street for the arriving motor-car. But all was quiet.

Eight o'clock had just boomed from Big Ben, and London still remained in her Sunday morning peace. The street, bright in the warm sunshine, was quite empty, save for a couple of motor-omnibuses and a sprinkling of gaily dressed holiday-makers on their way to the day excursion trains.

In that centre of London—the hub of the world—all was comparatively silent, the welcome rest after the busy turmoil that through six days in the week is unceasing, that fevered throbbing of the heart of the world's great capital.

Of a sudden, however, came the whirr-r of an approaching car, as a thin-faced, travel-stained man tore along from the direction of the Strand and pulled up before the office. The fine car, a six-cylinder "Napier," was grey with the mud of country roads, while the motorist himself was smothered until his goggles had been almost entirely covered.

Fergusson rushed out to him, and a few moments later the pair were in the upstairs room, the sub-editor swiftly taking down the motorist's story, which differed very little from what he had already spoken over the telephone.

Then, just as Big Ben chimed the half-hour, the echoes of the half-deserted Strand were suddenly awakened by the loud, strident voices of the newsboys shouting:

"*Dispatch*, spe-shall! Invasion of England this morning! Germans in Suffolk! Terrible panic! Spe-shall! *Dispatch*, Spe-shall!"

As soon as the paper had gone to press Fergusson urged the motorist—whose name was Horton, and who lived at Richmond—to go with him to the War Office and report. Therefore, both men entered the car, and as they did so a man jumped from a hansom in breathless haste. He was the reporter whom Fergusson had sent out to Sir James Taylor's house in Cleveland Square, Hyde Park.

"They thought Sir James spent the night with his brother up at Hampstead," he exclaimed. "I've been there, but find that he's away for the week-end at Chilham Hall, near Buckden."

"Buckden! That's on the Great North Road!" cried Horton, "We'll go at once and find him. Sixty miles from London. We can be there in under two hours!"

And a few minutes later the pair were tearing due north, turning at last into the handsome lodge-gates of Chilham Park, and running up the great elm avenue, drew up before the main door of the ancient hall, a quaint many-gabled old place of grey stone.

A few moments later the breathless journalist faced the Permanent Under-Secretary with the news that England was invaded—that the Germans had actually effected a surprise landing on the east coast.

Sir James and his host stood speechless. Like others, they at first believed the pale-faced, bearded sub-editor to be a lunatic, but a few moments later, when Horton briefly repeated the story, they saw that, whatever might have occurred, the two men were at least in deadly earnest.

"Impossible!" cried Sir James. "We should surely have heard something of it if such were actually the case. The coastguard would have telephoned the news instantly. Besides, where is our fleet?"

"The Germans evidently laid their plans with great cleverness. Their spies, already in England, cut the wires at a pre-arranged hour last night," declared Fergusson. "They sought to prevent this gentleman from giving the alarm by shooting him. All the railways to London are already either cut or held by the enemy. One thing, however, is clear—fleet or no fleet, the east coast is entirely at their mercy."

Host and guest exchanged dark glances.

"Well, if what you say is the actual truth," exclaimed Sir James, "to-day is surely the blackest day that England has ever known."

"Yes, they should have listened to Lord Roberts," snapped his lordship. "I suppose you'll go at once, Taylor, and make inquiries?"

"Of course," responded the Permanent Secretary. And a quarter of an hour later, accepting Horton's offer, he was sitting in the car as it headed back towards London.

Could the journalist's story be true? As he sat there, with his head bent against the wind and the mud splashing into his face, Sir James recollected too well the repeated warnings of the past five years, serious warnings by men who knew our shortcomings, but to which no attention had been paid. Both the Government and the public had remained apathetic, the idea of peril had been laughed to scorn, and the country had, ostrich-like, buried its head in the sand, and allowed Continental nations to supersede us in business, in armaments, in everything.

The danger of invasion had always been ridiculed as a mere alarmist's fiction; those responsible for the defence of the country had smiled, the Navy had been reduced, and the Army had remained in contented inefficiency.

If the blow had really been struck by Germany? If she had risked three or four, out of her twenty-three, army corps, and had aimed at the heart of the British Empire? What then? Ay! what then?

As the car glided down Regent Street into Pall Mall and towards Whitehall, Sir James saw on every side crowds discussing the vague but astounding reports now published in special editions of all the Sunday papers, and shouted wildly everywhere.

Boys bearing sheets fresh from the Fleet Street presses were seized, and bundles torn from them by excited Londoners eager to learn the latest intelligence.

Around both War Office and Admiralty great surging crowds were clamouring loudly for the truth. Was it the truth, or was it only a hoax? Half London disbelieved it. Yet from every quarter, from the north and from across the bridges, thousands were pouring in to ascertain what had really occurred, and the police had the greatest difficulty in keeping order.

In Trafalgar Square, where the fountains were plashing so calmly in the autumn sunlight, a shock-headed man mounted the back of one of the lions and harangued the crowd with much gesticulation, denouncing the Government in the most violent terms; but the orator was ruthlessly pulled down by the police in the midst of his fierce attack.

It was half-past two o'clock in the afternoon. The Germans had already been on English soil ten hours, yet London was in ignorance of where they had actually landed, and utterly helpless.

CHAPTER II

EFFECT IN THE CITY

MONDAY, 3RD SEPTEMBER, 1910, was indeed Black Monday for London.

By midnight on Sunday the appalling news had spread everywhere. Though the full details of the terrible naval disasters were not yet to hand, yet it was vaguely known that our ships had been defeated in the North Sea, and many of them sunk.

Before 7 a.m. on Monday, however, telegrams reaching London by the subterranean lines from the north gave thrilling stories of frightful disasters we had, while all unconscious, suffered at the hands of the German fleet.

With London, the great cities of the north, Liverpool, Manchester, Sheffield, and Birmingham, awoke utterly dazed. It seemed incredible. And yet the enemy had, by his sudden and stealthy blow, secured command of the sea and actually landed.

The public wondered why a formal declaration of war had not previously been made, ignorant of the fact that the declaration preceding the Franco-German War was the first made by any civilised nation prior to the commencement of hostilities for one hundred and seventy years. The peril of the nation was now recognised on every hand.

Eager millions poured into the City by every train from the suburbs and towns in the vicinity of the Metropolis, anxious to ascertain the truth for themselves, pale with terror, wild with excitement, indignant that our land forces were not already mobilised and ready to move eastward to meet the invader.

As soon as the banks were opened there was a run on them, but by noon the Bank of England had suspended all specie payments. The other banks, being thus unable to meet their engagements, simply closed the doors, bringing business to an abrupt standstill. Consols stood at 90 on Saturday, but by noon on Monday were down to 42—lower even than they were in 1798, when they stood at 47¼. Numbers of foreigners tried to speculate heavily, but were unable to do so, for banking being suspended they could not obtain transfers.

On the Stock Exchange the panic in the afternoon was indescribable. Securities of every sort went entirely to pieces, and there were no buyers. Financiers were surprised that no warning in London had betrayed the position of affairs, London being the money centre of the world. Prior to 1870 Paris shared with London the honour of being the pivot of the money market, but on the suspension of cash payments by the Bank of France during the Franco-German War, Paris lost that position. Had it not been that the milliards comprising the French War indemnity were intact in golden louis in the fortress of Spandau, Germany could never have hoped to wage sudden war with Great Britain before she had made Berlin independent of London in a money sense, or, at any rate, to accumulate sufficient gold to carry on the war for at least twelve months. The only way in which she could have done this was to raise her rate so as to offer better terms than London. Yet directly the Bank of England discovered the rate of exchange going against her, and her stock of gold diminishing, she would have responded by raising the English bank-rate in order to check the flow. Thus competition would have gone on until the rates became so high that all business would be checked, and people would have realised their securities to obtain the necessary money to carry on their affairs. Thus, no doubt, the coming war would have been forecasted had it not been for Germany's already prepared war-chest, which the majority of persons have nowadays overlooked. Its possession had enabled Germany to strike her sudden blow, and now the Bank of England, which is the final reserve of gold in the United Kingdom, found that as notes were cashed so the stock of gold diminished until it was in a few hours compelled to obtain from the Government suspension of the Bank charter. This enabled the Bank to suspend cash payment, and issue notes without a corresponding deposit of the equivalent in gold.

The suspension, contrary to increasing the panic, had, curiously enough, the immediate effect of somewhat allaying it. Plenty of people in the City were confident that the blow aimed could not prove an effective one, and that the Germans, however many might have landed, would quickly be sent back again. Thus many level-headed business men regarded the position calmly, believing that when our command of the sea was again re-established, as it must be in a day or two, the enemy would soon be non-existent.

Business outside the money market was, of course, utterly de-moralised. The buying of necessities was now uppermost in every-one's mind. Excited crowds in the streets caused most of the shops in the City and West End to close, while around the Admiralty were great crowds of eager men and women of all classes, tearful wives of bluejackets jostling with officers' ladies from Mayfair and Belgravia, demanding news of their loved ones—inquiries which, alas! the casualty office were unable to satisfy. The scene of grief, terror, and suspense was heartrending. Certain ships were known to have been sunk with all on board after making a gallant fight, and those who had husbands, brothers, lovers, or fathers on board wept loudly, calling upon the Government to avenge the ruthless murder of their loved ones.

In Manchester, in Liverpool, indeed, all through the great manufacturing centres of the north, the excitement of London was reflected.

In Manchester there was a panic "on 'Change," and the crowd in Deansgate coming into collision with a force of mounted police, some rioting occurred, and a number of shop windows broken, while several agitators who attempted to speak in front of the infirmary were at once arrested.

Liverpool was the scene of intense anxiety and excitement, when a report was spread that German cruisers were about the estuary of the Mersey. It was known that the coal staithes, cranes, and petroleum tanks at Penarth, Cardiff, Barry, and Llanelly had been destroyed; that Aberdeen had been bombarded; and there were rumours that, notwithstanding the mines and defences of the Mersey, the city of Liverpool, with all its crowd of valuable shipping, was to share the same fate.

The whole place was in a ferment. By eleven o'clock the stations were crowded by women and children sent by the men away into the country—anywhere from the doomed and defenceless city. The Lord Mayor vainly endeavoured to inspire confidence, but telegrams from London, announcing the complete financial collapse, only increased the panic.

In London all through the morning, amid the chaos of business in the City, the excitement had been steadily growing, until shortly after three o'clock the "Daily Mail" issued a special edition containing a copy of a German proclamation which, it was said, was now posted everywhere in East Norfolk, East Suffolk, and in Maldon in Essex, already occupied by the enemy.

The original proclamation had been found pasted by some unknown hand upon a barn door near the town of Billericay, and had been detached and brought to London in a motor-car by a correspondent.

It showed plainly the German intention was to deal a hard and crushing blow, and it struck terror into the heart of London, for it read as will be seen on next page.

Upon the walls of the Mansion House, the Guildhall, outside the Bank of England, the Royal Exchange, upon the various public buildings within the city wards, and westward beyond Temple Bar, proclamations were being posted. Indeed, upon all the hoardings in Greater London appeared various broadsheets side by side. One by the Chief Commissioner of Police, regulating the traffic in the streets, and appealing to the public to assist in the preservation

PROCLAMATION

WE, GENERAL COMMANDING THE 3RD GERMAN ARMY, HAVING SEEN the proclamation of His Imperial Majesty the Emperor William, King of Prussia, Chief of the Army, which authorises the generals commanding the different German Army Corps to establish special measures against all municipalities and persons acting in contradiction to the usages of war, and to take what steps they consider necessary for the well-being of the troops.

HEREBY GIVE PUBLIC NOTICE:

(1) THE MILITARY JURISDICTION is hereby established. It applies to all territory of Great Britain occupied by the German Army, and to every action endangering the security of the troops by rendering assistance to the enemy. The Military Jurisdiction will be announced and placed vigorously in force in every parish by the issue of this present proclamation.

(2) ANY PERSON OR PERSONS NOT BEING BRITISH SOLDIERS, or not showing by their dress that they are soldiers:

    (a) SERVING THE ENEMY as spies;

    (b) MISLEADING THE GERMAN TROOPS when charged to serve as guides;

    (c) SHOOTING, INJURING, OR ROBBING any person belonging to the German Army, or forming part of its personnel;

    (d) DESTROYING BRIDGES OR CANALS, damaging telegraphs, telephones, electric light wires, gasometers, or railways, interfering with roads, setting fire to munitions of war, provisions, or quarters established by German troops;

    (e) TAKING ARMS against the German troops,

WILL BE PUNISHED BY DEATH.

IN EACH CASE the officer presiding at the Council of War will be charged with the trial, and pronounce judgment. Councils of War may not pronounce ANY OTHER CONDEMNATION SAVE THAT OF DEATH.

THE JUDGMENT WILL BE IMMEDIATELY EXECUTED.

(3) TOWNS OR VILLAGES in the territory in which the contravention takes place will be compelled to pay indemnity equal to one year's revenue.

(4) THE INHABITANTS MUST FURNISH necessaries for the German troops daily as follows:—

1 lb. 10 oz. bread.	1 oz. tea.	1½ pints beer, or
13 oz. meat.	1½ oz. tobacco	1 wine-glassful of
3 lb. potatoes.	or 5 cigars.	brandy or whisky
		½ pint wine.

The ration for each horse:—

| 13 lb. oats. | 3 lb. 6 oz. hay. | 3 lb. 6 oz. straw. |

(ALL PERSONS WHO PREFER to pay an indemnity in money may do so at the rate of 2s. per day per man.)

(5) COMMANDERS OF DETACHED corps have the right to requisition all that they consider necessary for the well-being of their men, and will deliver to the inhabitants official receipts for goods so supplied.

WE HOPE IN CONSEQUENCE that the inhabitants of Great Britain will make no difficulty in furnishing all that may be considered necessary.

(6) AS REGARDS the individual transactions between the troops and the inhabitants, we give notice that one German mark shall be considered the equivalent to one English shilling.

THE GENERAL COMMANDING THE NINTH GERMAN ARMY CORPS,
VON KRONHELM

Beccles, September the Third, 1910

of order; and a Royal Proclamation, brief but noble, urging every Briton to do his duty, to take his part in the defence of King and country, and to unfurl the banner of the British Empire that had hitherto carried peace and civilisation in every quarter of the world. Germany, whose independence had been respected, had attacked us without provocation; therefore hostilities were, alas, inevitable.

When the great poster printed in big capitals and headed by the Royal Arms made its appearance it was greeted with wild cheering.

It was a message of love from King to people—a message to the highest and to the lowest. Posted in Whitechapel at the same hour as in Whitehall, the throngs crowded eagerly about it and sang "God Save our Gracious King," for if they had but little confidence in the War Office and Admiralty, they placed their trust in their Sovereign, the first diplomat in Europe. Therefore the loyalty was spontaneous, as it always is. They read the royal message, and cheered and cheered again.

As evening closed in yet another poster made its appearance in every city, town, and village in the country, a poster issued by military and police officers, and naval officers in charge of dockyards—the order for mobilisation.

The public, however, little dreamed of the hopeless confusion in the War Office, in the various regimental depôts throughout the country, at headquarters everywhere, and in every barracks in the kingdom. The armed forces of England were passing from a peace to a war footing; but the mobilisation of the various units—namely, its completion in men, horses, and material—was utterly impossible in the face of the extraordinary regulations which, kept a strict secret by the Council of Defence until this moment, revealed a hopeless state of things.

The disorder was frightful. Not a regiment was found fully equipped and ready to march. There was a dearth of officers, equipment, horses, provisions—of, indeed, everything. Men had guns without ammunition; cavalry and artillery were without horses; engineers only half equipped; volunteers with no transport whatever; balloon sections without balloons, and searchlight units vainly trying to obtain the necessary instruments.

Horses were being requisitioned everywhere. The few horses that, in the age of motor-cars, now remained on the roads in London were quickly taken for draught, and all horses fit to ride were commandeered for the cavalry.

During the turmoil daring German spies were actively at work south of London. The Southampton line of the London and South-Western Railway was destroyed—with explosives placed by unknown hands—by the bridge over the Wey, near Weybridge, being blown up; and again that over the Mole, between Walton and Esher, while the Reading line was cut by the great bridge over the Thames at Staines being destroyed. The line, too, between Guildford and Waterloo, was also rendered impassable by the wreck of the midnight train, which was blown up half-way between Wansborough and Guildford, while in several other places nearer London bridges were rendered unstable by dynamite, the favourite method apparently being to blow the crown out of an arch.

The well-laid plans of the enemy were thus quickly revealed. Among the thousands of Germans working in London, the hundred or so spies, all trusted soldiers, had passed unnoticed but, working in unison, each little group of two or three had been allotted its task, and had previously thoroughly reconnoitred the position and studied the most rapid or effective means.

The railways to the east and north-east coasts all reported wholesale damage done on Sunday night by the advance agents of the enemy, and now this was continued on the night of Monday in the south, the objective being to hinder troops from moving north from Aldershot. This was, indeed, effectual, for only by a long détour could the troops be moved to the northern defences of London, and while many were on Tuesday entrained, others were conveyed to London by the motor omnibuses sent down for that purpose.

Everywhere through London and its vicinity, as well as Manchester, Birmingham, Sheffield, Coventry, Leeds, and Liverpool, motor-cars and motor-omnibuses from dealers and private owners were being requisitioned by the military authorities, for they would, it was believed, replace cavalry to a very large extent.

Wild and extraordinary reports were circulated regarding the disasters in the north. Hull, Newcastle, Gateshead, and Tynemouth had, it was believed, been bombarded and sacked. The shipping in the Tyne was burning, and the Elswick works were held by the enemy. Details were, however, very vague, as the Germans were taking every precaution to prevent information reaching London.

CHAPTER III

NEWS OF THE ENEMY

TERROR AND EXCITEMENT reigned everywhere. The wildest rumours were hourly afloat. London was a seething stream of breathless multitudes of every class.

On Monday morning the newspapers throughout the kingdom had devoted the greater part of their space to the extraordinary intelligence from Norfolk and Suffolk, and Essex, and other places. Only the slow, old-fashioned *Globe* remained asleep, or pretended to know nothing of what was in progress.

That we were actually invaded was plain, but most of the newspapers happily preserved a calm, dignified tone, and made no attempt at sensationalism. The situation was far too serious.

Like the public, however, the Press had been taken entirely by surprise. The blow had been so sudden and so staggering that half the alarming reports were discredited.

In addition to the details of the enemy's operations, as far as could as yet be ascertained, the *Morning Post* on Monday contained an account of a mysterious occurrence at Chatham, which read as follows:

CHATHAM, SEPT. 1 (11.30 P.M.)

"An extraordinary accident took place on the Medway about eight o'clock this evening. The steamer *Pole Star*, 1,200 tons register, with a cargo of cement from Frindsbury, was leaving for Hamburg, and came into collision with the *Frauenlob*, of Bremen, a somewhat larger boat, which was inward bound, in a narrow part of the channel about half-way between Chatham and Sheerness. Various accounts of the mishap are current, but whichever of the vessels was responsible for the bad steering or neglect of the ordinary rules of the road, it is certain that the *Frauenlob* was cut into by the stem of the *Pole Star* on her port bow, and sank almost across the channel. The *Pole Star* swung alongside her after the collision, and very soon afterwards sank in an almost parallel position. Tugs and steamboats carrying a number of naval officers and the port authorities are about to proceed to the scene of the accident, and if, as seems probable, there is no chance of raising the vessels, steps will be at once taken to blow them up. In the present state of our foreign relations such an obstruction directly across the entrance to one of our principal war-ports is a national danger, and will not be allowed to remain a moment longer than can be helped."

SEPT. 2

"An extraordinary *dénouement* has followed the collision in the Medway reported in my telegram of last night, which renders it impossible to draw any other conclusion than that the affair is anything but an accident. Everything now goes to prove that the whole business was premeditated and was the result of an organised plot with the object of 'bottling up' the numerous men-of-war that are now being hurriedly equipped for service in Chatham Dockyard. In the words of Scripture, 'An enemy hath done this,' and there can be very little doubt as to the quarter from which the outrage was engineered. It is nothing less than an outrage to perpetrate what is in reality an overt act of hostility in a time of profound peace, however much the political horizon may be darkened by lowering war-clouds. We are living under a Government whose leader lost no time in announcing that no fear of being sneered at as a 'Little Englander' would deter him from seeking peace and ensuring it by a reduction of our naval and military armaments, even at that time known to be inadequate to the demands likely to be made upon them if our Empire is to be maintained. We trust, however, that even this parochially-minded statesman will lose no time in probing the conspiracy to its depths, and in seeking instant satisfaction from those personages, however highly placed and powerful, who have committed this outrage on the laws of civilisation.

"As soon as the news of the collision reached the dockyard the senior officer at Kethole Reach was ordered by wire to take steps to prevent any vessel from going up the river, and he at once despatched several picket-boats to the entrance to warn in-coming ships of the blocking of the channel, while a couple of other boats were sent up to within a short distance of the obstruction to make assurance doubly sure. The harbour signals ordering 'suspension of all movings' were also hoisted at Garrison Point.

"Among other ships which were stopped in consequence of these measures was the *Van Gysen*, a big steamer hailing from Rotterdam, laden, it was stated, with steel rails for the London, Chatham, and Dover Railway, which were to be landed at Port Victoria. She was accordingly allowed to proceed, and anchored, or appeared to anchor, just off the railway pier at that place. Ten minutes later the officer of the watch on board H.M.S. *Medici* reported that he thought she was getting under way again. It was then pretty dark. An electric searchlight being switched on, the *Van Gysen* was discovered steaming up the river at a considerable speed. The *Medici* flashed the news to the flagship, which at once fired a gun, hoisted the recall and the *Van Gysen's* number in the international code, and despatched her steam pinnace, with orders to overhaul the Dutchman and stop him at whatever cost. A number of the marines on guard were sent in her with their rifles.

"The *Van Gysen* seemed well acquainted with the channel, and continually increased her speed as she went up the river, so that she was within half a mile of the scene of the accident before the steamboat came up with her. The officer in charge called to the skipper through the megaphone to stop his engines and to throw him a rope, as he wanted to come on board. After pretending for some time not to understand him, the skipper slowed his engines and said, 'Ver vel, come 'longside gangway.' As the pinnace hooked on at the gangway, a heavy iron cylinder cover was dropped into her from the height of the *Van Gysen's* deck. It knocked the bowman overboard and crashed into the fore part of the boat, knocking a big hole in the port side forward. She swung off at an angle and stopped to pick up the man overboard. Her crew succeeded in rescuing him, but she was making water fast, and there was nothing for it but to run her into the bank. The lieutenant in charge ordered a rifle to be fired at the *Van Gysen* to bring her to, but she paid not the smallest attention, as might have been expected, and went on her way with gathering speed.

"The report, however, served to attract the attention of the two picket-boats which were patrolling up the river. As she turned a bend in the stream they both shot up alongside out of the darkness, and ordered her peremptorily to stop. But the only answer they received was the sudden extinction of all lights in the steamer. They kept alongside, or rather one of them did, but they were quite helpless to stay the progress of the big wall-sided steamer. The faster of the picket-boats shot ahead with the object of warning those who were busy examining the wrecks. But the *Van Gysen*, going all she knew, was close behind, an indistinguishable black blur in the darkness, and hardly had the officer in the picket-boat delivered his warning before she was heard close at hand. Within a couple of hundred yards of the two wrecks she slowed down, for fear of running right over them. On she came, inevitable as Fate. There was a crash as she came into collision with the central deckhouses of the *Frauenlob* and as her bows scraped past the funnel of the *Pole Star*. Then followed no fewer than half a dozen muffled reports. Her engines went astern for a moment, and down she settled athwart the other two steamers, heeling over to port as she did so. All was turmoil and confusion. None of the dockyard and naval craft present were equipped with searchlights. The harbour-master, the captain of the yard, even the admiral superintendent, who had just come down in his steam launch, all bawled out orders.

"Lights were flashed and lanterns swung up and down in the vain endeavour to see more of what had happened. Two simultaneous shouts of 'Man overboard!' came from tugs and boats at opposite sides of the river. When a certain amount of order was restored it was discovered that a big dockyard tug was settling down by the head. It seems she had been grazed by the *Van Gysen* as she came over the obstruction, and forced against some portion of one of the foundered vessels, which had pierced a hole in her below the water-line.

"In the general excitement the damage had not been discovered, and now she was sinking fast. Hawsers were made fast to her with the utmost expedition possible in order to tow her clear of the piled-up wreckage, but it was too late. There was only just time to rescue her crew before she too added herself to the underwater barricade. As for the crew of the *Van Gysen*, it is thought that all must have gone down in her, as no trace of them has as yet been discovered, despite a most diligent search, for it was considered that, in an affair which had been so carefully planned as this certainly must have been, some provision must surely have been made for the escape of the crew. Those who have been down at the scene of the disaster report that it will be impossible to clear the channel in less than a week or ten days, using every resource of the dockyard.

"A little later I thought I would go down to the dockyard on the off-chance of picking up any further information. The Metropolitan policeman at the gate would on no account allow me to pass at that hour, and I was just turning away when, by a great piece of good fortune, I ran up against Commander Shelley.

"I was on board his ship as correspondent during the manœuvres of the year before last. 'And what are you doing down here?' was his very natural inquiry after we had shaken hands. I told him that I had been down in Chatham for a week past as special correspondent, reporting on the half-hearted preparations being made for the possible mobilisation, and took the opportunity of asking him if he could give me any further information about the collision between the three steamers in the Medway. 'Well,' said he, 'the best thing you can do is to come right along with me. I have just been hawked out of bed to superintend the diving operations, which will begin the moment there is a gleam of daylight.' Needless to say, this just suited me, and I hastened to thank him and to accept his kind offer. 'All right,' he said, 'but I shall have to make one small condition.'

"'And that is?' I queried.

"'Merely to let me "censor" your telegrams before you send them,' he returned. 'You see, the Admiralty might not like to have too much said about this business, and I don't want to find myself in the dirt-tub.'

"The stipulation was a most reasonable one, and however I disliked the notion of having probably my best paragraphs eliminated, I could not but assent to my friend's proposition. So away we marched down the echoing spaces of the almost deserted dockyard till we arrived at the 'Thunderbolt' pontoon. Here lay a pinnace with steam up, and lighted down the sloping side of the old ironclad by the lantern of the policeman on duty, we stepped on board and shot out into the centre of the stream. We blew our whistles and the coxswain waved a lantern, whereupon a small tug that had a couple of dockyard lighters attached gave a hoarse 'toot' in response, and followed us down the river. We sped along in the darkness against a strong tide that was making upstream, past Upnor Castle, that quaint old Tudor fortress with its long line of modern powder magazines, and along under the deeper shadows beneath Hoo Woods till we came abreast of the medley of mud flats and grass-grown islets just beyond them. Here above the thud of the engines and the plash of the water, a thin, long-drawn-out cry wavered through the night. 'Some one hailing the boat, sir,' reported the lookout forward. We had all heard it. 'Ease down,' ordered Shelley, and hardly moving against the rushing tideway we listened for its repetition. Again the voice was raised in quavering supplication. 'What the dickens does he say?' queried the commander. 'It's German,' I answered. 'I know that language well. I think he's asking for help. May I answer him?'

"'By all means. Perhaps he belongs to one of those steamers.' The same thought was in my own mind. I hailed in return, asking where he was and what he wanted. The answer came back that he was a shipwrecked seaman, who was cold, wet, and miserable, and implored to be taken off from the islet where he found himself, cut off from everywhere by water and darkness. We ran the boat's nose into the bank, and presently succeeded in hauling aboard a miserable object, wet through, and plastered from head to foot with black Medway mud. The broken remains of a cork life-belt hung from his shoulders. A dram of whisky somewhat revived him. 'And now,' said Shelley, 'you'd better cross-examine him. We may get something out of the fellow.' The foreigner, crouched down shivering in the stern-sheets half covered with a yellow oilskin that some charitable bluejacket had thrown over him, appeared to me in the light of the lantern that stood on the deck before him to be not only suffering from cold, but from terror. A few moments' conversation with him confirmed my suspicions. I turned to Shelley and exclaimed, 'He says he'll tell us everything if we spare his life,' I explained. 'I'm sure I don't want to shoot the chap,' replied the commander. 'I suppose he's implicated in this "bottling up" affair. If he is, he jolly well deserves it, but I don't suppose anything will be done to him. Anyway, his information may be valuable, and so you may tell him that he is all right as far as I'm concerned, and I will do my best for him with the Admiral. I daresay that will satisfy him. If not, you might threaten him a bit. Tell him anything you like if you think it will make him speak.' To cut a long story short, I found the damp Dutchman amenable to reason, and the following is the substance of what I elicited from him.

"He had been a deck hand on board the *Van Gysen*. When she left Rotterdam he did not know that the trip was anything out of the way. There was a new skipper whom he had not seen before, and there were also two new mates with a new chief engineer. Another steamer followed them all the way till they arrived at the Nore. On the way over he and several other seamen were sent for by the captain, and asked if they would volunteer for a dangerous job, promising them £50 a-piece if it came off all right. He and five others agreed, as did two or three stokers, and were then ordered to remain aft and not communicate with any others of the crew. Off the Nore all the remainder were transferred to the following steamer, which steamed off to the eastward. After they were gone the selected men were told that the officers all belonged to the Imperial German Navy, and by orders of the Kaiser were about to attempt to block up the Medway.

"A collision between two other ships had been arranged for, one of which was loaded with a mass of old steel rails into which liquid cement had been run, so that her hold contained a solid impenetrable block. The *Van Gysen* carried a similar cargo, and was provided with an arrangement for blowing holes in her bottom. The crew were provided with life-belts, and the half of the money promised, and all except the captain, the engineer, and the two mates dropped overboard just before arriving at the sunken vessels.

They were advised to make their way to Gravesend, and then to shift for themselves as best they could. He had found himself on a small island, and could not muster up courage to plunge into the cold water again in the darkness.

"'By Jove! This means war with Germany, man!—War!' was Shelley's comment. At two o'clock this afternoon we knew that it did, for the news of the enemy's landing in Norfolk was signalled down from the dockyard. We also knew from the divers that the cargo of the sunken steamers was what the rescued seamen had stated it to be. Our bottle has been fairly well corked."

This amazing revelation showed how cleverly contrived was the German plan of hostilities. All our splendid ships at Chatham had, in that brief half-hour, been bottled up and rendered utterly useless. Yet the authorities were not blameless in the matter, for in November, 1905, a foreign warship actually came up the Medway in broad daylight, and was not noticed until she began to bang away her salutes, much to the utter consternation of every one.

This incident, however, was but one of the many illustrations of Germany's craft and cunning. The whole scheme had been years in careful preparation.

She intended to invade us, and regarded every stratagem as allowable in her sudden dash upon England, an expedition which promised to result in the most desperate war of modern times.

At that moment the *Globe*, at last aroused from its long and peaceful sleep, reproduced those plain, prophetic words of Lord Overstone, written some years before to the Royal Defence Commission: "Negligence alone can bring about the calamity under discussion. Unless we suffer ourselves to be surprised we cannot be invaded with success. It is useless to discuss what will occur or what can be done after London has fallen into the hands of an invading foe. The apathy which may render the occurrence of such a catastrophe possible will not afterwards enable the country, enfeebled, dispirited, and disorganised by the loss of its capital, to redeem the fatal error."

Was that prophecy to be fulfilled?

Some highly interesting information was given by the Ipswich correspondent of the *Central News*.

Repeated briefly, it was as follows:—

"Shortly before three o'clock on Sunday morning the coastguard at Lowestoft, Corton, and Beach End discovered that their telephonic communication was interrupted, and half an hour later, to the surprise of every one, a miscellaneous collection of mysterious craft were seen approaching the harbour: and within an hour many of them were high and dry on the beach, while others were lashed alongside the old dock, the new fish-docks of the Great Eastern Railway, and the wharves, disembarking a huge force of German infantry, cavalry, motor-infantry, and artillery. The town, awakened from its slumbers, was utterly paralysed, the more so when it was discovered that the railway to London was already interrupted, and the telegraph lines all cut. On landing, the enemy commandeered all provisions, including all motor-cars they could discover, horses and forage, while the banks were seized, and the infantry, falling in, marched up Old Nelson Street into High Street, and out upon the Beccles Road. The first care of the invaders was to prevent the people of Lowestoft damaging the Swing Bridge, a strong guard being instantly mounted upon it, and so quietly and orderly was the landing effected that it was plain the German plans of invasion were absolutely perfect in every detail.

"Few hitches seemed to occur. The mayor was summoned at six o'clock by General von Kronhelm, the generalissimo of the German Army, and briefly informed that the town of Lowestoft was occupied, and that all armed resistance would be punished by death. Then, ten minutes later, when the German war-flag was flying from several flagstaffs in various parts of the town, the people realised their utter helplessness.

"The Germans, of course, knew that, irrespective of the weather, a landing could be effected at Lowestoft, where the fish-docks and wharves, with their many cranes, were capable of dealing with a large amount of stores. The Denes, that flat, sandy plain between the upper town and the sea, they turned into a camping-ground, and large numbers were billeted in various quarters of the town itself.

"The people were terror-stricken. To appeal to London for help was impossible, as the place had been cut entirely off, and around it a strong chain of outposts had already been thrown, preventing any one from escaping. The town had, in a moment, as it seemed, fallen at the mercy of the foreigners. Even the important-looking police constables of Lowestoft, with their little canes, were crestfallen, sullen, and inactive.

"While the landing was continuing during all Sunday the advance guard moved rapidly over Mutford Bridge, along the Beccles Road, occupying a strong position on the west side of the high ground east of Lowestoft. Beccles, where von Kronhelm established his headquarters, resting as it does on the River Waveney, is strongly held. The enemy's main position appears to run from Windle Hill, one mile north-east of Gillingham, thence north-west through Bull's Green, Herringfleet Hill, over to Grove Farm and Hill House to Raveningham, whence it turns easterly to Haddiscoe, which is at present its northern limit. The total front from Beccles Bridge north is about five miles, and commands the whole of the flat plain west towards Norwich. It has its south flank resting on the River Waveney, and to the north on Thorpe Marshes. The chief artillery position is at Toft Monks—the highest point. Upon the high tower of Beccles Church is established a signal station, communication being made constantly with Lowestoft by helio by day, and acetylene lamps by night.

"The enemy's position has been most carefully chosen, for it is naturally strong, and, being well held to protect Lowestoft from any attack from the west, the landing can continue uninterruptedly, for Lowestoft beach and docks are now entirely out of the line of any British fire.

"March outposts are at Blythburgh, Wenhaston, Holton, Halesworth, Wissett, Rumburgh, Homersfield, and Bungay, and then north to Haddiscoe, while cavalry patrols watch by day, the line roughly being from Leiston through Saxmundham, Framlingham, and Tannington, to Hoxne.

"The estimate, gleaned from various sources in Lowestoft and Beccles, is that up to Monday at midday nearly a whole Army Corps,

PROCLAMATION

CITIZENS OF LONDON

THE NEWS OF THE BOMBARDMENT of the City of Newcastle and the landing of the German Army at Hull, Weybourne, Yarmouth, and other places along the East Coast is unfortunately confirmed.

THE ENEMY'S INTENTION is to march upon the City of London, which must be resolutely defended.

THE BRITISH NATION and the Citizens of London, in face of these great events, must be energetic in order to vanquish the invader.

The ADVANCE must be CHALLENGED FOOT BY FOOT. The people must fight for King and Country.

Great Britain is not yet dead, for indeed, the more serious her danger, the stronger will be her unanimous patriotism.

GOD SAVE THE KING.

HARRISON, LORD MAYOR
Mansion House, London, September 3rd, 1910

with stores, guns, ammunition, etc., had already landed, while there are also reports of a further landing at Yarmouth, and at a spot still farther north, but at present there are no details.

"The enemy," he concluded, "are at present in a position of absolute security."

CHAPTER IV

A PROPHECY FULFILLED

THIS AUTHENTIC NEWS of the position of the enemy, combined with the vague rumours of other landings at Yarmouth, along the coast at some unknown point north of Cromer, at King's Lynn, and other places, produced an enormous sensation in London, while the *Central News* account, circulated to all the papers in the Midlands and Lancashire, increased the panic in the manufacturing districts.

The special edition of the *Evening Star*, issued at about six o'clock on Tuesday evening, contained another remarkable story which threw some further light upon the German movements. It was, of course, known that practically the whole of the Norfolk and Suffolk coast was already held by the enemy, but with the exception of the fact that the enemy's cavalry vedettes and reconnoitring patrols were out everywhere at a distance about twenty miles from the shore, England was entirely in the dark as to what had occurred anywhere else but at Lowestoft. Attempts had been made to penetrate the cavalry screen at various points, but in vain. What was in progress was carefully kept a secret by the enemy. The veil was, however, now lifted. The story which the *Evening Star* had obtained exclusively, and which was eagerly read everywhere, had been related by a man named Scotney, a lobster-fisherman, of Sheringham, in Norfolk, who had made the following statement to the chief officer of coastguard at Wainfleet, in Lincolnshire:

"Just before dawn on Sunday morning I was in the boat with my son Ted off the Robin Friend, taking up the lobster pots, when we suddenly saw about three miles off shore a mixed lot of curious-looking craft strung out right across the horizon, and heading apparently for Cromer. There were steamers big and little, many of them towing queer flat-bottomed kind of boats, lighters, and barges, which, on approaching nearer, we could distinctly see were filled to their utmost capacity with men and horses.

"Both Ted and I stood staring at the unusual sight, wondering whatever it meant. They came on very quickly, however—so quickly, indeed, that we thought it best to move on. The biggest ships went along to Weybourne Gap, where they moored in the twenty-five feet of water that runs in close to the shore, while some smaller steamers and the flats were run high and dry on the hard shingle. Before this I noticed that there were quite a number of foreign warships in the offing, with several destroyers far away in the distance both to east and west.

"From the larger steamships all sorts of boats were lowered, including apparently many collapsible whaleboats, and into these, in a most orderly manner, from every gangway and accommodation-ladder, troops—Germans we afterwards discovered them to be, to our utter astonishment—began to descend.

"These boats were at once taken charge of by steam pinnaces and cutters and towed to the beach. When we saw this we were utterly dumbfounded. Indeed, at first I believed it to be a dream, for ever since I was a lad I had heard the ancient rhyme my old father was so fond of repeating:

'He who would Old England win,
Must at Weybourne Hoop begin.'

"As everybody knows, nature has provided at that lonely spot every advantage for the landing of hostile forces, and when the Spanish Armada was expected, and again when Napoleon threatened an invasion, the place was constantly watched. Yet nowadays, except for the coastguard, it has been utterly unprotected and neglected.

"The very first soldiers who landed formed up quickly, and under the charge of an officer ran up the low hill to the coastguard station, I suppose in order to prevent them signalling a warning. The funny thing was, however, that the coastguards had already been held up by several well-dressed men—spies of the Germans, I suppose. I could distinctly see one man holding one of the guards with his back to the wall, and threatening him with a revolver.

"Ted and I had somehow been surrounded by the crowd of odd craft which dodged about everywhere, and the foreigners now and then shouted to me words that unfortunately I could not understand.

"Meanwhile, from all the boats strung out along the beach, from Sheringham right across to the Rocket House at Salthouse, swarms of drab-coated soldiers were disembarking, the boats immediately returning to the steamers for more. They must have been packed as tightly as herrings in a barrel; but they all seemed to know where to go to, because all along at various places little flags were held by men, and each regiment appeared to march across and assemble at its own flag.

"Ted and I sat there as if we were watching a play. Suddenly we saw from some of the ships and bigger barges horses being lowered into the water and allowed to swim ashore. Hundreds seemed to gain the beach even as we were looking at them. Then, after the first lot of horses had gone, boats full of saddles followed them. It seemed as though the foreigners were too busy to notice us, and we—not wanting to share the fate of Mr. Gunter, the coastguard, and his mates—just sat tight and watched.

"From the steamers there continued to pour hundreds upon hundreds of soldiers, who were towed to land, and then formed up in solid squares, which got bigger and bigger. Horses innumerable—quite a thousand, I should reckon—were slung overboard from some of the smaller steamers which had been run high and dry on the beach, and as the tide had now begun to run down, they landed only knee-deep in water. Those steamers, it seemed to me, had big bilge keels, for as the tide ebbed they did not heel over. They had, no doubt, been specially fitted for the purpose. Out of some they began to hoist all sorts of things, wagons, guns, motor-cars, large bales of fodder, clothing, ambulances with big red crosses on them, flat-looking boats—pontoons I think they call them—and great piles of cooking pots and pans, square boxes of stores, or perhaps ammunition, and as soon as anything was landed it was hauled up above the high-water mark.

"In the meantime lots of men had mounted on horseback and ridden off up the lane which leads into Weybourne village. At first half a dozen started at a time; then, as far as I could judge, about fifty more started. Then larger bodies went forward, but more and more horses kept going ashore, as though their number was never-ending.

They must have been stowed mighty close, and many of the ships must have been specially fitted up for them.

"Very soon I saw cavalry swarming up over Muckleburgh, Warborough, and Telegraph Hills, while a good many trotted away in the direction of Runton and Sheringham. Then, soon after they had gone—that is, in about an hour and a half from their first arrival—the infantry began to move off, and, as far as I could see, they marched inland by every road, some in the direction of Kelling Street and Holt, others over Weybourne Heath towards Bodham, and still others skirting the woods over to Upper Sheringham. Large masses of infantry marched along the Sheringham Road, and seemed to have a lot of officers on horseback with them, while up on Muckleburgh Hill I saw frantic signalling in progress.

"By this time they had a quantity of carts and wagons landed, and a large number of motor-cars. The latter were soon started, and, manned by infantry, moved swiftly in procession after the troops. The great idea of the Germans was apparently to get the beach clear of everything as soon as landed, for all stores, equipment, and other tackle were pushed inland as soon as disembarked.

"The enemy kept on landing. Thousands of soldiers got ashore without any check, and all proceeding orderly and without the slightest confusion, as though the plans were absolutely perfect. Everybody seemed to know exactly what to do. From where we were we could see the coastguards held prisoners in their station, with German sentries mounted around; and as the tide was now setting strong to the westward, Ted and I just let our anchor off the ground and allowed ourselves to drift. It occurred to me that perhaps I might be able give the alarm at some other coastguard station if I could only drift away unnoticed in the busy scene now in progress.

"That the Germans had actually landed in England was now apparent; yet we wondered what our own fleet could be doing, and pictured to ourselves the jolly good drubbing that our cruisers would give the audacious foreigner when they did haul in sight. It was for us, at all costs, to give the alarm, so gradually we drifted off to the nor'-westward, in fear every moment lest we should be

noticed and fired at. At last we got around Blakeney Point successfully, and breathed more freely; then, hoisting our sail, we headed
for Hunstanton, but seeing numbers of ships entering the Wash, and
believing them to be also Germans, we put our helm down and ran
across into Wainfleet Swatchway to Gibraltar Point, where I saw the
chief officer of coastguards and told him all the extraordinary events
of that memorable morning."

The report added that the officer of coastguard in question had,
three hours before, noticed strange vessels coming up the Wash, and
had already tried to report by telegraph to his divisional inspecting
officer at Harwich, but could obtain no communication. An hour
later, however, it had become apparent that a still further landing
was being effected on the south side of the Wash, in all probability
at King's Lynn.

The fisherman Scotney's statement had been sent by special
messenger from Wainfleet on Sunday evening, but, owing to the
dislocation of the railway traffic north of London, the messenger
was unable to reach the offices of the coastguard in Victoria Street,
Westminster until Monday. The report received by the Admiralty
had been treated as confidential until corroborated, lest undue public
alarm should be caused.

It had then been given to the Press as revealing the truth of what
had actually happened.

The enemy had entered by the back door of England, and the
sensation it caused everywhere was little short of panic.

Some further very valuable information was also received by the
Intelligence Department of the War Office, revealing the military
position of the invaders who had landed at Weybourne Hoop.

The whole of the IVth German Army Corps, about 38,000 men,
had been landed at Weybourne, Sheringham, and Cromer. It consisted
of the 7th and 8th Divisions complete, commanded respectively by
Major-General Dickmann and Lieutenant-General von Mirbach. The
7th Division comprised the 13th and 14th Infantry Brigades, consisting of Prince Leopold of Anhalt-Dessau's 1st Magdeburg Regiment,
the 3rd Magdeburg Infantry Regiment, Prince Louis Ferdinand von
Preussen's 2nd Magdeburg Regiment, and the 5th Hanover Infantry

Regiment. Attached to this division were the Magdeburg Hussars No. 10, and the Uhlan Regiment of Altmärk No. 16.

In the 8th Division were the 15th and 16th Brigades, comprising a Magdeburg Fusilier Regiment, an Anhalt Infantry Regiment, the 4th and 8th Thuringen Infantry, with the Magdeburg Cuirassiers, and a regiment of Thuringen Hussars. The cavalry were commanded by Colonel Frölich, while General von Kleppen was in supreme command of the whole corps.

Careful reconnaissance of the occupied area showed that, immediately on landing, the German position extended from the little town of Holt, on the west, eastward, along the main Cromer road, as far as Gibbet Lane, slightly south of Cromer, a distance of about five miles. This constituted a naturally strong position; indeed, nature seemed to have provided it specially to suit the necessities of a foreign invader. The ground for miles to the south sloped gently away down to the plain, while the rear was completely protected, so that the landing could proceed until every detail had been completed.

Artillery were massed on both flanks, namely, at Holt and on the high ground near Felbrigg, immediately south of Cromer. This last-named artillery was adequately supported by the detached infantry close at hand. The whole force was covered by a strong line of outposts. Their advanced sentries were to be found along a line starting from Thornage village, through Hunworth, Edgefield, Barningham Green, Squallham, Aldborough, Hanworth, to Roughton. In rear of them lay their pickets, which were disposed in advantageous situations. The general line of these latter were at North Street, Pondhills to Plumstead, thence over to Matlash Hall, Aldborough Hall, and the rising ground north of Hanworth. These, in their turn, were adequately supplemented by the supports, which were near Hempstead Green, Baconsthorpe, North Narningham, Bessingham, Sustead, and Melton.

In case of sudden attack, reserves were at Bodham, West Beckham, East Beckham, and Aylmerton, but orders had been issued by Von Kleppen, who had established his headquarters at Upper Sheringham, that the line of resistance was to be as already indicated—namely, that having the Holt–Cromer Road for its crest. Cuirassiers, Hussars, and some motorists—commanded by Colonel von Dorndorf—were acting independently some fifteen miles to the south scouring the whole country, terrifying the villagers, commandeering all supplies, and posting Von Kronhelm's proclamation, which has already been reproduced.

From inquiries it was shown that on the night of the invasion six men, now known to have been advance agents of the enemy, arrived at the Ship Inn, at Weybourne. Three of them took accommodation for the night, while their companions slept elsewhere. At two o'clock the trio let themselves out quietly, were joined by six other men, and just as the enemy's ships hove in sight nine of them seized the coastguards and cut the wires, while the other three broke into the Weybourne Stores, and, drawing revolvers, obtained possession of the telegraph instrument to Sheringham and Cromer until they could hand it over to the Germans.

That the Fourth German Army Corps were in a position as strong as those who landed at Lowestoft could not be denied, and the military authorities could not disguise from themselves the extreme gravity of the situation.

BERLIN UM EINS!   BERLIN UM EINS!

Das Kleine Journal

MITTAGS AUSGABE.

BERLIN, MONTAG, DEN 3 SEPTEMBER 1910

Triumph der Deutschen Waffen.

Vernichtung der Englischen Flotte.

Von Kronhelm Auf Dem Vormarsche Nach London.

CHAPTER V

STATE OF SIEGE DECLARED

THAT OUR FLEET had been taken unawares was apparent. There were all sorts of vague rumours of a sudden attack upon the North Sea Fleet at Rosyth, and a fierce cruiser battle, in which we had been badly beaten by Germany. It is, however, the land campaign which we have here to record.

The authentic account of a further landing in Essex—somewhere near Maldon—was now published. The statement had been dictated by Mr. Henry Alexander, J.P.,—the Mayor of Maldon, who had succeeded in escaping from the town,—to Captain Wilfred Quare, of the Intelligence Department of the War Office. This Department had, in turn, given it to the newspapers for publication.

It read as follows:—

"On Sunday morning, September 2, I had arranged to play a round of golf with my friend Somers, of Beeleigh, before church. I met him at the Golf Hut at about 8.30. We played one round, and were at the last hole but three in a second round when we both thought we heard the sound of shots fired somewhere in the town. We couldn't make anything at all of it, and as we had so nearly finished the round, we thought we would do so before going to inquire about it. I was making my approach to the final hole when an exclamation from Somers spoilt my stroke. I felt annoyed, but as I looked around—doubtless somewhat irritably—my eyes turned in the direction in which I now saw my friend was pointing with every expression of astonishment in his countenance.

"'Who on earth are those fellows?' he asked. As for me, I was too dumbfounded to reply. Galloping over the links from the direction of the town came three men in uniform—soldiers, evidently. I had often been in Germany, and recognised the squat pickelhaubes and general get-up of the rapidly approaching horsemen at a glance.

BY THE KING

PROCLAMATION

FOR CALLING OUT THE ARMY RESERVE.

EDWARD R.

WHEREAS by the Reserve Forces Act, 1882, it is amongst other things enacted that in case of imminent national danger or of great emergency, it shall be lawful for Us, by Proclamation, the occasion being declared in Council and notified by the Proclamation, if Parliament be not then sitting, to order that the Army Reserve shall be called out on permanent service; and by any such Proclamation to order a Secretary of State from time to time to give, and when given, to revoke or vary such directions as may seem necessary or proper for calling out the forces or force mentioned in the Proclamation, or all or any of the men belonging thereto:

AND WHEREAS Parliament is not sitting, and whereas WE have declared in Council and hereby notify the present state of Public Affairs and the extent of the demands on Our Military Forces for the protection of the interests of the Empire constitute a case of great emergency within the meaning of the said Act:

NOW THEREFORE we do in pursuance of the said Act hereby order that Our Army Reserve be called out on permanent service, and We do hereby order the Right Honourable Charles Leonard Spencer Cotterell, one of our Principal Secretaries of State, from time to time to give, and when given, to revoke or vary such directions as may seem necessary or proper for calling out Our Army Reserve, or all or any of the men belonging thereto, and such men shall proceed to and attend at such places and at such times as may be respectively appointed by him to serve as part of Our Army until their services are no longer required.

Given at Our Court at James', this fourth day of September, in the year of our Lord, one thousand nine hundred and ten, and in the tenth year of Our Reign.

GOD SAVE THE KING.

"They were upon us almost as he spoke, pulling up their horses with a great spattering up of grass and mud, quite ruining one of our best greens. All three of them pointed big, ugly repeating pistols at us, and the leader, a conceited-looking ass in staff uniform, required us to 'surrender' in quite a pompous manner, but in very good English.

"'Do we look so very dangerous, Herr Lieutenant?' inquired I in German.

"He dropped a little of his frills when he heard me speak in his native language, asked which of us was the Mayor, and condescended to explain that I was required in Maldon by the officer at present in command of his Imperial Majesty the Kaiser's forces occupying that place.

"I looked at my captor in complete bewilderment. Could he be some fellow trying to take a rise out of me by masquerading as a German officer? But no, I recognised at once that he was the genuine article.

"He demanded my parole, which I made no difficulty about giving, since I did not see any way of escape, and in any case was only too anxious to get back to town to see how things were.

"'But you don't want my friend, do you—he lives out the other way?' I queried.

"'I don't want him, but he will have to come all the same,' rejoined the German. 'It isn't likely we're going to let him get away to give the alarm in Colchester, is it?'

"Obviously it was not, and without more ado we started off at a sharp walk, holding on to the stirrup leathers of the horsemen.

"As we entered the town there was on the bridge over the river a small picket of blue-coated German infantry. The whole thing was a perfect nightmare. It was past belief.

"'How on earth did you get here?' I couldn't help asking.

"'By water,' he answered shortly, pointing down the river as he spoke, where I was still further astonished—if it were possible after such a morning—to see several steam pinnaces and boats flying the black and white German ensign.

"I was conducted straight to the Moot Hall. There I found a grizzled veteran waiting on the steps, who turned round and entered the building as we came up. We followed him inside, and I was introduced to him. He appeared to be a truculent old ruffian.

"'Well, Mr. Mayor,' he said, pulling viciously at his white moustache, 'do you know that I've a great mind to take you out into the street and have you shot?'

"I was not at all inclined to be browbeated.

"'Indeed, Herr Hauptman?' I answered. 'And may I inquire in what way I have incurred the displeasure of the Hochwohlgeboren officer?'

"'Don't trifle with me, sir. Why do you allow your miserable Volunteers to come out and shoot my men?'

"'My Volunteers? I am afraid I don't understand what you mean,' I said. 'I'm not a Volunteer officer. Even if I were, I should have no cognisance of anything that has happened within the last two hours, as I have been down on the golf course. This officer will bear me out,' I added, turning to my captor. He admitted that he had found me there.

"'But, anyway, you are the Mayor,' persisted my interrogator. 'Why did you allow the Volunteers to come out?'

"'If you had been good enough to inform us of your visit, we might have made better arrangements,' I answered. 'But in any case you must understand that a mayor has little or no authority in this country. His job is to head subscription-lists, eat a dinner or two, and make speeches on public occasions.'

"He seemed to have some difficulty in swallowing this, but as another officer who was there, writing at a table, and who, it appears, had lived at some period in England, corroborated my statement, the choleric colonel seemed to be a little mollified, and contented himself with demanding my parole not to leave Maldon until he had reported the matter to the General for decision. I gave it without more ado, and then asked if he would be good enough to tell me what had happened. From what he told me, and what I heard afterwards, it seems that the Germans must have landed a few of their men about half an hour before I left home, down near the

Marine Lake. They had not entered the town at once, as their object was to work round outside and occupy all entrances, to prevent anyone getting away with the news of their presence. They had not noticed the little lane leading to the golf course, and so I had gone down without meeting any of them, although they had actually got a picket just beyond the railway arch at that time. They had completed their cordon before there was any general alarm in the town, but at the first reliable rumour it seems that young Shand, of the Essex Volunteers, had contrived to get together twenty or thirty of his men in their uniforms and foolishly opened fire on a German picket down by St. Mary's Church. They fell back, but were almost instantly reinforced by a whole company that had just landed, and our men, rushing forward, had been ridden into by some cavalry that came up a side street. They were dispersed, a couple of them were killed, and several wounded, among them poor Shand, who was hit in the right lung. They had bagged four Germans, however, and their commanding officer was furious. It was a pity that it happened, as it could not possibly have been of any use. But it seems that Shand had no idea that it was more than a very small detachment that had landed from a gun-boat that some one said they had seen down the river. Some of the Volunteers were captured afterwards and sent off as prisoners, and the Germans posted up a notice that all Volunteers were forthwith to surrender either themselves or their arms and uniforms, under pain of death. Most of them did the latter. They could do nothing after it was found that the Germans had a perfect army somewhere between Maldon and the sea, and were pouring troops into the town as fast as they could.

"That very morning a Saxon rifle battalion arrived from the direction of Mundon, and just afterwards a lot of spike-helmeted gentlemen came in by train from Wickford way. So it went on all day, until the whole town was in a perfect uproar. The infantry were billeted in the town, but the cavalry and guns crossed the river and canal at Heybridge, and went off in the direction of Witham.

"Maldon is built on a hill that slopes gradually towards the east and south, but rises somewhat abruptly on the west and north, humping up a shoulder, as it were, to the north-west. At this corner they started to dig entrenchments just after one o'clock, and soon officers and orderlies were busy all round the town, plotting, measuring, and setting up marks of one kind and another. Other troops appeared to be busy down in Heybridge, but what they were doing I could not tell, as no one was allowed to cross the bridge over the river.

"The German officer who had surprised me down on the golf course did not turn out to be a bad kind of youth on further acquaintance. He was a Captain von Hildebrandt, of the Guard Fusilier Regiment, who was employed on the Staff, though in what capacity he did not say. Thinking it was just as well to make the best of a bad job, I invited him to lunch. He said he had to be off. He, however, introduced me to three friends of his in the 101st Grenadiers, who, he suggested, should be billeted on me. I thought the idea a fairly good one, and Von Hildebrandt, having apparently arranged this with the billeting officer without any difficulty, I took them home with me to lunch.

"I found my wife and family in a great state of mind, both on account of the untoward happenings of the morning and my non-return from golf at the expected time. They had imagined all sorts of things which might have befallen me, but luckily seemed not to have heard of my adventure with the choleric colonel. Our three foreigners soon made themselves very much at home, but as they were undeniably gentlemen, they contrived to be about as agreeable as could be expected under the circumstances. Indeed, their presence was to a great extent a safeguard against annoyance, as the stable and back premises were stuffed full of soldiers, who might have been very troublesome had they not been there to keep them in order.

"Of what was happening up in London we knew nothing. Being Sunday, all the shops were shut; but I went out and contrived to lay in a considerable stock of provisions one way and another, and it was just as well I did, for I only just anticipated the Germans, who commandeered everything in the town, and put everybody on an allowance of rations. They paid for them with bills on the British Government, which were by no means acceptable to the shopkeepers. However, it was 'Hobson's choice'—that or nothing.

The Germans soothed them by saying that the British Army would be smashed in a couple of weeks, and the defrayment of such bills would be among the conditions of peace. The troops generally seemed to be well-behaved, and treated those inhabitants with whom they came in contact in an unexceptionable manner. They did not see very much of them, however, as they were kept hard at work all day with their entrenchments and were not allowed out of their billets after eight o'clock that evening. No one, in fact, was allowed to be about the streets after that hour. Two or three people were shot by the sentries as they tried to break out in one direction or the other. These affairs produced a feeling of horror and indignation in the town, as Englishmen, having such a long experience of peace in their own country, have always refused to realise what war really means.

"The German fortifications went on at a rapid rate. Trenches were dug all round the northern and western sides of the town before dark on the first evening, and the following morning I woke up to find three huge gun-pits yawning in my garden, which looked to the northward. During breakfast there was a great rattling and rumbling in the street without, and presently three big field howitzers were dragged in and planted in the pits. There they stood, their ugly snouts pointing skyward in the midst of the wreck of flowers and fruit.

"Afterwards I went out and found that other guns and howitzers were being put in position all along the north side of Beeleigh Road, and round the corner by the Old Barracks. The high tower of the disused Church of St. Peter's, now utilised for the safe custody of Dr. Plume's library, had been equipped as a lookout and signal station."

Such was the condition of affairs in the town of Maldon on Monday morning.

The excitement in London, and indeed all over the country, on Tuesday night was intense. Scotney's story of the landing at Weybourne was eagerly read everywhere.

As the sun sank blood-red into the smoke haze behind Nelson's Monument in Trafalgar Square, it was an ominous sign to the panic-stricken crowds that day and night were now assembled there.

The bronze lions facing the four points of the compass were now mere mocking emblems of England's departed greatness. The mobilisation muddle was known; for, according to the papers, hardly any troops had as yet assembled at their places of concentration. The whole of the east of England was helplessly in the invader's hands. From Newcastle had come terrible reports of the bombardment. Half the city was in flames, the Elswick works were held by the enemy, and whole streets in Newcastle, Gateshead, Sunderland, and Tynemouth were still burning fiercely.

The Tynemouth fort had proved of little or no use against the enemy's guns. The Germans had, it appeared, used petrol bombs with appalling results, spreading fire, disaster, and death everywhere. The inhabitants, compelled to fly with only the clothes they wore, had scattered all over Northumberland and Durham, while the enemy had seized a quantity of valuable shipping that had been in the Tyne, hoisted the German flag, and converted the vessels to their own uses.

Many had already been sent across to Wilhelmshaven, Emden, Bremerhaven, and other places to act as transports, while the Elswick works—which surely ought to have been properly protected—supplied the Germans with quantities of valuable material.

Panic and confusion were everywhere. All over the country the railway system was utterly disorganised, business everywhere was at a complete deadlock, for in every town and city all over the kingdom the banks were closed.

Lombard Street, Lothbury, and other banking centres in the City had all day on Monday been the scene of absolute panic. There, as well as at every branch bank all over the metropolis, had occurred a wild rush to withdraw deposits by people who foresaw disaster. Many, indeed, intended to fly with their families away from the country.

The price of the necessities of life had risen further, and in the East End and poorer districts of Southwark the whole population were already in a state of semi-starvation. But worst of all, the awful truth with which London was now face to face was that the metropolis was absolutely defenceless.

NOTICE

TO ALL GERMAN SUBJECTS RESIDENT IN ENGLAND.

WILHELM

To all OUR LOYAL SUBJECTS, GREETING.

We hereby COMMAND and enjoin that all persons born within the German Empire, or being German subjects, whether liable to military service or not, shall join our arms at any headquarters of either of our Army Corps in England within 24 hours of the date of this proclamation.

Any German subject failing to obey this our Command will be treated as an enemy.

By the EMPEROR'S Command.
Given at Beccles, Sept. 3rd, 1910.

VON KRONHELM,
Commanding the Imperial German Army in England.

Every hour the papers were appearing with fresh details of the invasion, for reports were so rapidly coming in from every hand that the Press had difficulty in dealing with them.

Hull and Goole were known to be in the hands of the invaders, and Grimsby, where the Mayor had been unable to pay the indemnity demanded, had been sacked. But details were not yet forthcoming.

Londoners, however, learnt late that night more authentic news from the invaded zone, of which Beccles was the centre, and it was to the effect that those who had landed at Lowestoft were the IXth German Army Corps, with General von Kronhelm, the Generalissimo of the German Army. This Army Corps, consisting of about 40,000 men, was divided into the 17th Division, commanded by Lieutenant-General Hocker, and the 18th by Lieutenant-General von Rauch. The cavalry was under the command of Major-General von Heyden, and the motor-infantry under Colonel Reichardt.

According to official information which had reached the War Office and been given to the Press, the 17th Division was made up of the Bremen and Hamburg Infantry Regiments, the Grand Duke of Mecklenburg's Grenadiers, the Grand Duke's Fusiliers, the Lübeck Regiment No. 162, the Schleswig-Holstein Regiment No. 163, while the cavalry brigade consisted of the 17th and 18th Grand Duke of Mecklenburg's Dragoons.

The 18th Division consisted of the Schleswig Regiment No. 84 and the Schleswig Fusiliers No. 86, the Thuringen Regiment, and the Duke of Holstein's Regiment, the two latter regiments being billeted in Lowestoft, while the cavalry brigade forming the screen across from Leiston by Wilby to Castle Hill were Queen Wilhelmina's Hanover Hussars and the Emperor of Austria's Schleswig-Holstein Hussars No. 16. These, with the smart motor infantry, held every communication in the direction of London.

As far as could be gathered, the German commander had established his headquarters in Beccles, and had not moved. It now became apparent that the telegraph cables between the East coast and Holland and Germany, already described in the first chapter, had never been cut at all. They had simply been held by the enemy's advance agents until the landing had been effected. And now Von Kronhelm had actually established direct communication between Beccles and Emden, and on to Berlin.

Reports from the North Sea spoke of the enemy's transports returning to the German coast, escorted by cruisers; therefore the plan was undoubtedly not to move until a very much larger force had been landed. Could England regain her command of the sea in time to prevent the completion of the blow?

That night the London streets presented a scene of panic indescribable. The theatres opened, but closed their doors again, as nobody would see plays while in that excited state. Every shop was closed, and every railway station was filled to overflowing with the exodus of terrified people fleeing to the country westward, or reserves on their way to join the colours.

The incredulous manner in which the country first received the news had now been succeeded by wild terror and despair. On that bright Sunday afternoon they laughed at the report as a mere journalistic sensation, but ere the sun set the hard, terrible truth was forced upon them, and now, on Tuesday night, the whole country, from Brighton to Carlisle, from Yarmouth to Aberystwyth, was utterly disorganised and in a state of terrified anxiety.

The eastern counties were already beneath the iron heel of the invader, whose objective was the world's great capital—London.

Would they reach it? That was the serious question upon every one's tongue that fevered, breathless night.

CHAPTER VI

HOW THE ENEMY DEALT THE BLOW

MEANWHILE, at the regimental depôts feverish excitement prevailed on Wednesday, September 5, now that every man was ordered on active service. All officers and men who had been on leave were recalled, and medical inspection of all ranks at once commenced. Rations and bedding, stores and equipment were drawn, but there was a great lack of uniforms. Unlike the German Army, where every soldier's equipment is complete even to the last button on the proverbial gaiter, and stowed away where the owner knows where to obtain it, our officers commanding depôts commenced indenting for clothing on the Royal Army Clothing Department and the Army Corps Clothing Department.

A large percentage of men were, of course, found medically unfit to serve, and were discharged to swell the mobs of hungry idlers. The plain clothes of the reservists coming in were disposed of, no man daring to appear in the ranks unless in uniform, Von Kronhelm's proclamation having forbidden the tactics of the Boers of putting mere armed citizens into the field.

Horse-collecting parties went out all over the country, taking with them head-collars, head-ropes, bits, reins, surcingles, numnahs, horse-blankets, and nose-bags. These scoured every county in search of likely animals, every farm, every livery stable, every hunting-box, all hound-kennels and private stables were visited, and a choice made. All this, however, took time. Precious hours were thus being wasted while the enemy were calmly completing their arrangements for the long-contemplated blow at the heart of the British Empire.

While the War Office refused any information, special editions of the papers during Wednesday printed sensational reports of the ruthless completion of the impenetrable screen covering the operations of the enemy on the whole of the East Coast.

News had, by some means, filtered through from Yarmouth that a similar landing to those at Lowestoft and Weybourne had been effected. Protected as such an operation was by its flanks being supported by the IVth and IXth Army Corps landing on either side, the Xth Army Corps, under General von Wilburg, had seized Yarmouth, with its many miles of wharves and docks, which were now crowded by the lighters' craft of flotilla from the Frisian Islands.

It was known that the landing had been effected simultaneously with that at Lowestoft. The large number of cranes at the fish-docks were of invaluable use to the enemy, for there they landed guns, animals, and stores, while the provisions they found at the various ship's chandlers, and in such shops as Blagg's, and the International Stores in King Street, Peter Brown's, Doughty's, Lipton's, Penny's and Barnes's, were at once commandeered. Great stores of flour were seized in Clarke's and Press's mills, while the horse-provender mills in the vicinity supplied them with valuable forage.

Beyond these few details, as far as regarded the fate of Yarmouth, nothing further was at present known.

The British division at Colchester, which comprised all the regular troops north of the Thames in the eastern command, was, no doubt, in a critical position, threatened so closely north and south by the enemy. None of the regiments—the Norfolks, the Leicestershire, and the King's Own Scottish Borderers of the 11th Infantry Brigade—were up to their strength. The 12th Infantry Brigade, which

CITY OF NORWICH

CITIZENS—

AS IS WELL KNOWN, a hostile army has landed upon the coast of Norfolk, and has already occupied Yarmouth and Lowestoft, establishing their headquarters at Beccles.

IN THESE GRAVE CIRCUMSTANCES our only thought is for England, and our duty as citizens and officials is to remain at our post and bear our part in the defence of Norwich, our capital now threatened.

YOUR PATRIOTISM, of which you have on so many occasions in recent wars given proof, will, I have no doubt, again be shown. By your resistance you will obtain the honour and respect of your enemies, and by the individual energy of each one of you the honour and glory of England may be saved.

CITIZENS OF NORWICH, I appeal to you to view the catastrophe calmly, and bear your part bravely in the coming struggle.

CHARLES CARRINGTON, Mayor

Norwich, September 4, 1910

also belonged to the division, possessed only skeleton regiments stationed at Hounslow and Warley. Of the 4th Cavalry Brigade, some were at Norwich, the 21st Lancers were at Hounslow, while only the 16th Lancers were at Colchester. Other cavalry regiments were as far away as Canterbury, Shorncliffe, and Brighton, and although there were three batteries of artillery at Colchester, some were at Ipswich, others at Shorncliffe, and others at Woolwich.

Therefore it was quite evident to the authorities in London that unless both Colchester and Norwich were instantly strongly supported, they would soon be simply swept out of existence by the enormous masses of German troops now dominating the whole eastern coast, bent upon occupying London.

Helpless though they felt themselves to be, the garrison at Colchester did all they could. All available cavalry had been pushed out past Ipswich, north to Wickham Market, Stowmarket, and across to Bury St. Edmunds, only to find on Wednesday morning that they were covering the hasty retreat of the small body of cavalry who had been stationed at Norwich. They, gallantly led by their officers, had done everything possible to reconnoitre and attempt to pierce the enemy's huge cavalry screen, but in every instance entirely in vain. They had been outnumbered by the squadrons of independent cavalry operating in front of the Germans, and had, alas! left numbers of their gallant comrades upon the roads, killed and wounded.

Norwich had, therefore, on Wednesday morning fallen into the hands of the German cavalry, utterly defenceless. From the Castle the German flag was now flying, the Britannia Barracks were being used by the enemy, food had all been seized, the streets were in a state of chaos, and a complete reign of terror had been created when a company of British Infantry, having fired at some Uhlans, were ruthlessly shot down in the street close by the Maid's Head.

In addition to this, the Mayor of Norwich was taken prisoner, lodged in the Castle, and held as surety for the well-behaviour of the town.

Everywhere Von Kronhelm's famous proclamation was posted, and as the invaders poured into the city the inhabitants looked on in sullen silence, knowing that they were now under German military discipline, the most rigorous and drastic in the whole world.

A special issue of *The Times* in the evening of the 3rd September contained the following vivid account—the first published—of the happenings in the town of Goole, in Yorkshire:

GOOLE, SEPTEMBER 3

"Shortly before five o'clock on Sunday morning the night operator of the telephone call-office here discovered an interruption on the trunk-line, and on trying the telegraphs was surprised to find that there was no communication in any direction. The railway station, being rung up, replied that their wires were also down.

"Almost immediately afterwards a well-known North Sea pilot rushed into the post office and breathlessly asked that he might telephone to Lloyd's. When told that all communication was cut off he wildly shouted that a most extraordinary sight was to be seen in the River Ouse, up which was approaching a continuous procession of tugs, towing flats, and barges filled with German soldiers.

"This was proved to be an actual fact, and the inhabitants of Goole, awakened from their Sunday morning slumbers by the shouts of alarm in the streets, found, to their abject amazement, foreign soldiers swarming everywhere. On the quay they found activity everywhere, German being spoken on all hands. They watched a body of cavalry, consisting of the 1st Westphalian Hussars, the Westphalian Cuirassiers, land with order and ease at the Victoria Pier, whence, after being formed up on the quay, they advanced at a sharp trot up Victoria Street, Ouse Street, and North Street to the railway stations, where, as is generally known, there are large sidings of the North-East Lancashire and Yorkshire lines in direct communication both with London and the great cities of the north. The enemy here found great quantities of engines and rolling stock, all of which was at once seized, together with huge stacks of coal at the new sidings.

"Before long the first of the infantry of the 13th Division, which was commanded by Lieutenant-General Doppschutz, marched up to the stations. They consisted of the 13th and 56th Westphalian Regiments, and the cavalry on being relieved advanced out of the town, crossing the Dutch River by the railway bridge, and pushed on as far as Thorne and Hensall, near which they at once strongly held the several important railway junctions.

"Meanwhile cavalry of the 14th Brigade, consisting of Westphalian Hussars and Uhlans, were rapidly disembarking at Old Goole, and, advancing southwards over the open country of Goole Moors and Thorne Waste, occupied Crowle. Both cavalry brigades were acting independently of the main body, and by their vigorous action both south and west they were entirely screening what was happening in the port of Goole.

"Infantry continued to pour into the town from flats and barges, arriving in endless procession. Doppschutz's Division landed at Aldan Dock, Railway Dock, and Ship Dock; the 14th Division at the Jetty and Basin, also in the Barge Dock and at the mouth of the Dutch

River; while some, following the cavalry brigade, landed at Old Goole and Swinefleet.

"As far as can be ascertained, the whole of the VIIth German Army Corps have landed, at any rate as far as the men are concerned. The troops, who are under the supreme command of General Baron von Bistram, appear to consist almost entirely of Westphalians, and include Prince Frederick of the Netherlands' 2nd Westphalians; Count Bulow von Dennewitz's 6th Westphalians; but one infantry brigade, the 79th, consisted of men from Lorraine.

"Through the whole day the disembarkation proceeded, the townsmen standing there helpless to lift a finger and watching the enemy's arrival. The Victoria Pleasure Grounds were occupied by parked artillery, which towards afternoon began to rumble through the streets. The German gunners, with folded arms, sat unconcernedly upon the ammunition boxes as the guns were drawn up to their positions. Horses were seized wherever found, the proclamation of Von Kronhelm was nailed upon the church doors, and the terrified populace read the grim threat of the German field-marshal.

"The wagons, of which there were hundreds, were put ashore mostly at Goole, but others up the river at Hook and Swinefleet. When the cavalry advance was complete, as it was soon after midday, and when reports had come in to Von Bistram that the country was clear of the British, the German infantry advance began. By nightfall they had pushed forward, some by road, some by rail, and others in the numerous motor-wagons that had accompanied the force, until march-outposts were established, south of Thorne, Askern, and Crowle, straddling the main road at Bawtry. These places, including Fishlake and the country between them, were at once strongly held, while ammunition and stores were pushed up by railway to both Thorne and Askern.

"The independent cavalry advance continued through Doncaster until dusk, when Rotherham was reached, during which advance scattered bodies of British Imperial Yeomanry were met and compelled to retreat, a dozen or so lives being lost. It appears that late in the afternoon of Sunday news was brought into Sheffield of what was in progress, and a squadron of Yeomanry donned their uniforms and rode forward to reconnoitre, with the disastrous results already mentioned.

"The sensation caused in Sheffield when it became known that German cavalry were so close as Rotherham was enormous, and the scenes in the streets soon approached a panic; for it was wildly declared that that night the enemy intended to occupy the town. The Mayor telegraphed to the War Office, appealing for additional defensive force, but no response was received to the telegram. The small force of military in the town, which consisted of the 2nd Battalion Yorkshire Light Infantry, some Royal Artillery, and the local Volunteers, were soon assembled, and going out occupied the strong position above Sheffield between Catcliffe and Tinsley, overlooking the valley of the Rother to the east.

"The expectation that the Germans intended an immediate descent on Sheffield was not realised, because the German tactics were merely to reconnoitre and report on the defences of Sheffield, if any existed. This they did by remaining to the eastward of the river Rother, whence the high ground rising before Sheffield could be easily observed.

"Before dusk one or two squadrons of Cuirassiers were seen to be examining the river to find fords and ascertain the capacity of the bridges, while others appeared to be comparing the natural features of the ground with the maps with which they all appeared to be provided.

"As night fell, however, the cavalry retired towards Doncaster, which town was occupied, the Angel being the cavalry headquarters. The reason the Germans could not advance at once upon Sheffield was that the cavalry was not strongly supported by infantry from their base, the distance from Goole being too great to be covered in a single day. That the arrangements for landing were in every detail perfect could not be doubted, but owing to the narrow channel of the Ouse time was necessary, and it is considered probable that fully three days must elapse from Sunday before the Germans are absolutely established.

"An attempt has been made by the Yorkshire Light Infantry and the York and Lancaster Regiment, with three battalions of Volunteers stationed at Pontefract, to discover the enemy's strength and position between Askern and Snaith, but so far without avail, the cavalry screen across the whole country being impenetrable.

"The people of the West Riding, and especially the inhabitants of Sheffield, are stupefied that they have received no assistance—not even a reply to the Mayor's telegram. This fact has leaked out, and has caused the greatest dissatisfaction. An enemy is upon us, yet we are in ignorance of what step, if any, the authorities are taking for our protection.

"There are wild rumours here that the enemy have burned Grimsby, but these are generally discredited, for telegraphic and telephonic communication has been cut off, and at present we are completely isolated. It has been gathered from the invaders that the VIIIth Army Corps of the Germans have landed and seized Hull, but at present this is not confirmed. There is, alas! no communication with the place, therefore the report may possibly be true.

"Dewsbury, Huddersfield, Wakefield, and Selby are all intensely excited over the sudden appearance of German soldiers, and were at first inclined to unite to stem their progress. But the German proclamation, showing the individual peril of any citizen taking arms against the invaders, having been posted everywhere, has held every one scared and in silent inactivity.

"'Where is our Army?' every one is asking. The whole country has run riot in a single hour, now that the Germans are upon us. On every hand it is asked: 'What will London do?'"

Reports now reached London that the VIIth German Army Corps had landed at Hull and Goole, and, taking possession of these towns, were moving upon Sheffield in order to paralyse our trade in the Midlands. Hull had been bombarded, and was in flames! Terrible scenes were taking place at that port.

On that memorable Sunday, when a descent had been made upon our shores, there were in German ports on the North Sea nearly a million tons gross of German shipping. Normally, in peace time, half a million tons is always to be found there, the second half having been quietly collected by ships putting in unobserved into such ports as Emden, Bremen, Bremerhaven, and Geestemunde, where

GOD SAVE THE KING

PROCLAMATION

To all whom it may concern.

In regard to the Decree of September 3rd of the present year, declaring a state of siege in the Counties of Norfolk and Suffolk.

In regard to the Decree of August 10th, 1906, regulating the public administration of all theatres of war and military servitude;

Upon the proposition of the Commander-in-Chief

It is decreed as follows:

(1)   There are in a state of war:

1st. In the Eastern Command, the counties of Northamptonshire, Rutlandshire, Cambridgeshire, Norfolk, Suffolk, Essex, Huntingdonshire, Bedfordshire, Hertfordshire, and Middlesex (except that portion included in the London Military District).

2nd. In the Northern Command, the counties of Northumberland, Durham, Cumberland, and Yorkshire, with the southern shore of the estuary of the Humber.

(2)   I, Charles Leonard Spencer Cotterell, his Majesty's Principal Secretary of State for War, am charged with the execution of this Decree.

War Office, Whitehall,
September the Fourth, 1910

there are at least ten miles of deep-sea wharves, with ample railway access. The arrival of these crafts caused no particular comment, but they had already been secretly prepared for the transport of men and horses while at sea.

Under the cover of the Frisian Islands, from every canal, river, and creek had been assembled a huge multitude of flats and barges, ready to be towed by tugs alongside the wharves and filled with troops. Of a sudden, in a single hour it seemed, Hamburg, Altona, Cuxhaven, and Wilhelmshaven were in excited activity, and, almost before the inhabitants themselves realised what was really in progress, the embarkation had well commenced.

At Emden, with its direct cable to the theatre of war in England, was concentrated the brain of the whole movement. Beneath the lee of the covering screen of Frisian Islands, Borkum, Juist, Norderney, Langebog, and the others, the preparations for the descent upon England rapidly matured.

Troop-trains from every part of the Fatherland arrived with the punctuality of clockwork. From Düsseldorf came the VIIth Army Corps, the VIIIth from Coblenz, the IXth were already assembled at their headquarters at Altona, while many of them being stationed at Bremen embarked from there; the Xth came up from Hanover, the XIVth from Magdeburg, and the Corps of German Guards, the pride and flower of the Kaiser's troops, arrived eagerly at Hamburg from Berlin and Potsdam, among the first to embark.

Each army corps consisted of about 38,000 officers and men, 11,000 horses, 144 guns, and about 2,000 motor-cars, wagons, and carts. But for this campaign—which was more of the nature of a raid than of any protracted campaign—the supply of wheeled transport, with the exception of motor-cars, had been somewhat reduced.

Each cavalry brigade attached to an army corps consisted of 1,400 horses and men, with some thirty-five light machine guns and wagons. The German calculation—which proved pretty correct—was that each army corps could come over to England in 100,000 tons gross of shipping, bringing with them supplies for twenty-seven days in another 3,000 tons gross. Therefore about 618,000 tons gross conveyed the whole of the six corps, leaving an ample margin still in German ports for any emergencies. Half this tonnage consisted of about 100 steamers, averaging 3,000 tons each, the remainder being the boats, flats, lighters, barges, and tugs previously alluded to.

The Saxons who, disregarding the neutrality of Belgium, had embarked at Antwerp, had seized the whole of the flat-bottomed craft in the Scheldt and the numerous canals, as well as the merchant ships in the port, finding no difficulty in commandeering the amount of tonnage necessary to convey them to the Blackwater and the Crouch.

As hour succeeded hour the panic increased.

It was now also known that, in addition to the various corps who had effected a landing, the German Guards had, by a sudden swoop into the Wash, got ashore at King's Lynn, seized the town, and united their forces with Von Kleppen's corps, who, having landed at Weybourne, were now spread right across Norfolk. This picked corps of Guards was under the command of that distinguished officer, the Duke of Mannheim, while the infantry divisions were under Lieutenant-Generals von Castein and Von Der Decken.

The landing at King's Lynn on Sunday morning had been quite a simple affair. There was nothing whatever to repel them, and they disembarked on the quays and in the docks, watched by the astonished populace. All provisions were seized at shops, while headquarters were established at the municipal buildings, and the German flag hoisted upon the old church, the tower of which was at once used as a signal station.

Old-fashioned people of Lynn peered out of their quiet respectable houses in King Street in utter amazement; but soon, when the German proclamation was posted, the terrible truth was plain.

In half an hour, even before they could realise it, they had been transferred from the protection of the British flag to the militarism of the German.

Ere sundown on Sunday, stalwart grey-coated sentries of the Guards Fusiliers from Potsdam and the Grenadiers from Berlin were holding the roads at Gayton, East Walton, Narborough, Markham, Fincham, Stradsett, and Stow Bardolph. Therefore on Sunday night, from Spalding on the east, Peterborough, Chatteris, Littleport, Thetford, Diss, and Halesworth, were faced by a huge cavalry screen protecting the landing and repose of the great German Army behind it.

Slowly but carefully the enemy were maturing their plans for the defeat of our defenders and the sack of London.

CHAPTER VII

DESPERATE FIGHTING IN ESSEX

LONDON WAS AT A STANDSTILL. Trade was entirely stopped. Shopkeepers feared to open their doors on account of the fierce, hungry mobs parading the street. Orators were haranguing the crowds in almost every open space. The police were either powerless, or feared to come into collision with the assembled populace. Terror and blank despair were everywhere.

There was unrest night and day. The banks, head offices, and branches, unable to withstand the run upon them when every one demanded to be paid in gold, had, by mutual arrangement, shut their doors, leaving excited and furious crowds of customers outside unpaid. Financial ruin stared every one in the face. Those who were fortunate enough to realise their securities on Monday were fleeing from London south and westward. Day and night the most extraordinary scenes of frantic fear were witnessed at Paddington, Victoria, Waterloo, and London Bridge. The southern railways were badly disorganised by the cutting of the lines by the enemy, but the Great Western system was, up to the present, intact, and carried thousands upon thousands to Wales, to Devonshire, and to Cornwall. In those three hot, breathless days the Red Hand of Ruin spread out upon London.

The starving East met the terrified West, but in those moments the bonds of terror united class with mass. Restaurants and theatres were closed; there was but little vehicular traffic in the streets, for of horses there were none, while the majority of the motor 'buses had been requisitioned, and the transit of goods had been abandoned. "The City," that great army of daily workers, both male and female, was out of employment, and swelled the idlers and gossips, whose temper and opinion were swayed each half-hour by the papers now constantly appearing night and day without cessation.

Cabinet Councils had been held every day, but their decisions, of course, never leaked out to the public. The King also held Privy Councils, and various measures were decided upon. Parliament, which had been hurriedly summoned, was due to meet, and every one speculated as to the political crisis that must now ensue.

In St. James's Park, in Hyde Park, in Victoria Park, on Hampstead Heath, in Greenwich Park—in fact, in each of the "lungs of London,"—great mass meetings were held, at which resolutions were passed condemning the Administration and eulogising those who, at the first alarm, had so gallantly died in defence of their country.

It was declared that by the culpable negligence of the War Office and the National Defence Committee we had laid ourselves open to complete ruin, both financially and as a nation.

The man-in-the-street already felt the strain, for the lack of employment and the sudden rise in the price of everything had brought him up short. Wives and families were crying for food, and those without savings and with only a few pounds put by looked grimly into the future and at the mystery it presented.

Most of the papers published the continuation of the important story of Mr. Alexander, the Mayor of Maldon, which revealed the extent of the enemy's operations in Essex and the strong position they occupied. It ran as below:

"Of the events of the early hours of the morning I have no very clear recollection. I was bewildered, staggered, dumbfounded by the sights and sounds which beset me. Of what modern war meant I had till then truly but a very faint idea. To witness its horrid realities enacted in this quiet, out-of-the-way spot where I had pitched my tent for so many years brought them home to me literally as well as metaphorically.

"I had run down Cromwell Hill, and, seeing the flames of Heybridge, was impelled to get nearer, if possible, to discover more particularly the state of affairs in that direction. But I was reckoning without the Germans. When I got to the bridge over the river at the foot of the hill, the officer in charge there absolutely prevented my crossing. Beyond the soldiers standing or kneeling behind whatever cover was offered by the walls and buildings abutting on the riverside, and a couple of machine guns placed so as to command the bridge and the road beyond, there was nothing much to see. A number of Germans were, however, very busy in the big mill just across the river, but what they were doing I could not make out. As I turned to retrace my step the glare of the conflagration grew suddenly more and more intense. A mass of dark figures came running down the brightly illuminated road towards the bridge, while the rifle fire became louder, nearer, and heavier than ever. Every now and again the air became alive with, as it were, the hiss and buzz of flying insects. The English must have fought their way through Heybridge, and these must be the bullets from their rifles. It was dangerous to stay down there any longer, so I took to my heels. As I ran I heard a thundering explosion behind me, the shock of which nearly threw me to the ground. Looking over my shoulder, I saw that the Germans had blown up the mill at the farther end of the bridge, and were now pushing carts from either side in order to barricade it. The two Maxims, too, began to pump lead with their hammering reports, and the men near them commenced to fall in twos and threes. I made off to the left, and passed into High Street by the end of St. Peter's Church, now disused. At the corner I ran against Mr. Clydesdale, the optician, who looks after the library which now occupies the old building. He pointed to the tower, which stood darkly up against the blood-red sky.

"'Look at those infernal Germans!' he said. 'They can't even keep out of that old place. I wish we could have got the books out before they came.'

"I could not see any of our invaders where he was pointing, but presently I became aware of a little winking, blinking light at the very summit of the tower.

"'That's them,' said Clydesdale. 'They're making signals, I think. My boy says he saw the same thing on Purleigh Church tower last night. I wish it would come down with them, that I do. It's pretty shaky, anyway.'

"The street was fairly full of people. The Germans, it is true, had ordered that no one should be out of doors between eight in the evening and six in the morning; but just now they appeared to have their hands pretty full elsewhere, and if any of the few soldiers that were about knew of or thought anything of the interdiction, they said nothing.

"The crash of a salvo of heavy guns from the direction of my own house interrupted him.

"'That'll be the guns in my garden,' I said.

"'Yes, sir, and they've got three monstrous great ones in the opening between the houses just behind the church there,' said Clydesdale.

"As he spoke, the guns in question bellowed out, one after the other.

"'Look—look at the tower!' I cried.

"The light at the top had disappeared and the lofty edifice was swaying slowly, slowly, over to the left.

"'She's gone at last!' exclaimed Clydesdale.

"It was true. Down came the old steeple that had pointed heavenward for so many generations, with a mighty crash and concussion that swallowed up even the noise of the battle, though cannon of all sorts and sizes were now joining in the hellish concert, and shell from the English batteries began to roar over the town. The vibration and shock of the heavy guns had been too much for the old tower, which, for years in a tottery condition, had been patched up so often.

"As soon as the cloud of dust cleared off we ran towards the huge pile of débris that filled the little churchyard. Several other people followed. It was very dark down there, in the shadow of the trees and houses, despite the fire-light overhead, and we began striking matches as we looked about among the heaps of bricks and beams to see if there were any of the German signal party among them. Why we should have taken the trouble under the circumstances I do not quite know. It was an instinctive movement of humanity on my part, and that of most of the others, I suppose.

"I caught sight of an arm in a light blue sleeve protruding from the débris, and took hold of it in a futile attempt to remove some of the bricks and rubbish which I thought were covering the body of its owner. To my horror, it came away in my hand. The body to which it belonged might be buried yards away in the immense heap of ruins. I dropped it with a cry, and fled from the spot.

"Dawn was now breaking. I do not exactly remember where I wandered to after the fall of St. Peter's Tower, but it must have been between half-past five and six when I found myself on the high ground at the north-western corner of the town, overlooking the golf links, where I had spent so many pleasant hours in that recent past that now seemed so far away. All around me were batteries, trenches, and gun-pits. But though the firing was still going on somewhere away to the right, where Heybridge poured black smoke skyward like a volcano, gun and howitzer were silent, and their attendant artillerymen, instead of being in cover behind their earthen parapets, were clustered on the top, watching intently something that was passing in the valley below them. So absorbed were they that I was able to creep up behind them, and also get a sight of what was taking place. And this is what I saw:

"Over the railway bridge which spanned the river a little to the left were hurrying battalion after battalion of green and blue clad German infantry. They moved down the embankment after crossing, and continued their march behind it. Where the railway curved to the right and left, about half a mile beyond the bridge, the top of the embankment was lined with dark figures lying down and apparently firing, while over the golf course from the direction of Beeleigh trotted squadron after squadron of sky-blue riders, their green and white lance pennons fluttering in the breeze. They crossed the Blackwater and Chelmer Canal, and cantered off in the direction of Langford Rectory.

"At the same time I saw line after line of the Germans massed behind the embankment spring over it and advance rapidly towards the lower portion of the town, just across the river. Hundreds fell under the fire from the houses, which must have been full of Englishmen, but one line after another reached the buildings. The firing was now heavier than ever—absolutely incessant and continuous—though, except for an occasional discharge from beyond Heybridge, the artillery was silent.

"I have but little knowledge of military matters, but it was abundantly evident, even to me, that what I had just seen was a very formidable counter-attack on the part of the Germans, who had brought up fresh troops either from the rear of the town or from farther inland, and launched them against the English under cover of the railway embankment. I was not able to see the end of the encounter, but bad news flies apace, and it soon became common knowledge in the town that our troops from Colchester had not only failed to cross the river at any point, but had been driven helter-skelter out of the lower town near the station and from the smoking ruins of Heybridge with great loss, and were now in full retreat.

"Indeed, some hundreds of our khaki-clad fellow-countrymen were marched through the town an hour or two later as prisoners, to say nothing of the numbers of wounded, who, together with those belonging to the Germans, soon began to crowd every available building suitable for use as an hospital. The wounded prisoners with their escort went off towards Mundon, and are reported to have gone in the direction of Steeple. It was altogether a disastrous day, and our hopes, which had begun to rise when the British had penetrated into the northern part of the town, now fell below zero.

"It was a black day for us, and for England. During the morning the same officer who had captured me on the golf course came whirling into Maldon on a 24-h.p. Mercedes car. He drove straight up to my house, and informed me that he had orders to conduct me to Prince Henry, who was to be at Purleigh early in the afternoon.

"'Was it in connection with the skirmish with the Volunteers?' I asked.

"'I don't know,' was the reply. 'But I don't fancy so. In the meantime, could I write here for an hour or two?' he asked politely. 'I have much to write to my friends in Germany, and have not had a minute up to now.'

"I was very glad to be able to oblige the young man in such a small way, and left him in my study till midday, very busy with pens, ink, and paper.

"After a makeshift of a lunch, the car came round, and we got into the back seat. In front sat his orderly and the chauffeur, a fierce-looking personage in a semi-military uniform. We ran swiftly down the High Street, and in a few minutes were spinning along the Purleigh Road, where I saw much that amazed me. I then for the first time realised how absolutely complete were the German plans."

TUESDAY, SEPTEMBER 4

"About six o'clock this morning I awoke rather suddenly. The wind had gone round to the northward, and I was certain that heavy firing was going on somewhere in that direction. I opened the window and looked out. The 'thud' and rumble of a cannonade, with the accompaniment of an occasional burst of musketry, came clearly and loudly on the wind from the hills by Wickham Bishops village. The church spire was in plain view, and little faint puffs and rings of grey smoke were just visible in its vicinity every now and again, sometimes high up in the air, at others among the trees at its base. They were exploding shells; I had no doubt of that. What was going on it was impossible to say, but I conjectured that some of our troops from Colchester had come into collision with the Germans, who had gone out in that direction the day of their arrival. The firing continued for about an hour, and then died away.

"Soon after eight, Count von Ohrendorff, the general officer commanding the 32nd Division, who appeared to be the supreme authority here, sent for me, and suggested that I should take steps to arrange for the manufacture of lint and bandages by the ladies living in the town. I could see no reason for objecting to this, and so promised to carry out his suggestion. I set about the matter at once, and, with the assistance of my wife, soon had a couple of score of more or less willing workers busily engaged in the National Schoolroom. In the meantime the roll of a terrible cannonade had burst forth again from Wickham Bishops. It seemed louder and more insistent than ever. As soon as I got away from the schools I hurried home and climbed out on the roof. The top of the Moot Hall and other coigns of vantage had all been occupied by the Germans. However, with the aid of a pair of field-glasses I was able to see a good bit. Black smoke was now pouring from Wickham Bishops in clouds, and every now and again I fancied I could see the forked tongues of flame shooting up above the surrounding trees. A series of scattered black dots now came out on the open ground to the south of the church. The trees of Eastland Wood soon hid them from my sight, but others followed, mingled with little moving black blocks which I took to be formed bodies of troops. After them came four or five guns, driven at breakneck pace towards the road that passes between Eastland and Captain's Woods, then more black dots, also in a desperate hurry. Several of these last tumbled, and lay still here and there all over the slope.

"Other dots followed at their heels. They were not quite so distinct. I looked harder. Hurrah! They were men in khaki. We were hustling these Germans at last. They also disappeared behind the woods. Then from the fringe of trees about Wickham half a dozen big brilliant flashes, followed after an interval by the loud detonation of heavy cannon. I could not distinguish much more, though the rattle of battle went on for some time longer. Soon after eleven four German guns galloped in from Heybridge. These were followed by a procession of maimed and limping humanity. Some managed to get along unaided, though with considerable difficulty. Others were supported by a comrade, some carried between two men, and others borne along on stretchers. A couple of ambulance carts trotted out and picked up more wounded. Our bandages and lint had not long to wait before being required. After this there was a cessation of firing.

"About one o'clock the German general sent word to me that he thought an attack quite possible during the afternoon, and that he strongly advised me to get all the women and children out of the town—for the time being at any rate. This was evidently well meant, but it was a pretty difficult matter to arrange for, to say nothing of raising a panic among the inhabitants. However, in an hour and a half's time I had contrived to marshal several hundred of them together, and to get them out on the road to Mundon. The weather was warm for the time of the year, and I thought, if the worst came to the worst, they could spend the night in the old church. I left the sad little column of exiles—old, bent women helped along by their daughters, tiny children dragged along through the dust, clutching their mothers' skirts; infants in arms; and other older and sturdier children staggering beneath the weight of the most precious home adornments—and made the best of my way back to arrange for the forwarding to them of their rations.

"At every step on my homeward way I expected to hear the cannonade begin again. But beyond the twittering of the birds in the trees and hedgerows, the creak and rumble of a passing cart, and the rush of a train along the railway on my left—just the usual sounds of the countryside—nothing broke the stillness. As I stepped out on the familiar highway, I could almost bring myself to believe that the events of the past twenty-four hours were but the phantasmagoria of a dream. After interviewing some of the town councillors who were going to undertake the transport of provisions to the women and children at Mundon, I walked round to my own house.

"My wife and family had driven over to Purleigh on the first alarm, and had arranged to stay the night with some friends, on whatever shake-downs could be improvised, since every house in the peninsula harboured some of the ubiquitous German officers and men. I wandered through the familiar rooms, and came out into the garden, or rather, what had been the garden. There I saw that the Saxon gunners were all standing to their pieces, and one of my none too welcome guests accosted me as I left the house.

"'If you'll take my advice, sare, you'll get away out of this,' he said in broken English.

"'What! are you going to fire?' I asked.

"'I don't fancy so. It wouldn't hurt you if we were. But I think your English friends from Colchester are about to see if they can draw us.'

"As he spoke I became aware of a sharp, hissing noise like a train letting off steam. It grew louder and nearer, passed over our heads, and was almost instantly followed by a terrible crash somewhere behind the house. A deeper and more muffled report came up from the valley beyond Heybridge.

"'Well, they've begun now, and the best thing you can do is to get down into that gun epaulment there,' said the German officer.

"I thought his advice was good, and I lost no time in following it.

"'Here comes another!' cried he, as he jumped down into the pit beside me. 'We'll have plenty of them now.'

"So we did. Shell after shell came hissing and screaming at us over the tree-tops in the gardens lower down the hill. Each one of them sounded to me as if it were coming directly at my head, but one after another passed over us to burst beyond. The gunners all crouched close to the earthen parapet—and so did I. I am not ashamed to say so. My German officer, however, occasionally climbed to the top of the embankment and studied the prospect through his field-glasses. At length there was a loud detonation, and a column of dirt and smoke in the garden next below us. Then two shells struck the parapet of the gun-pit on our left almost simultaneously. Their explosion was deafening, and we were covered with the dust and stones they threw up.

"Immediately afterwards another shell passed so close over our heads that I felt my hair lift. It just cleared the parapet and plunged into the side of my house. A big hole appeared just to the right of the dining-room window, and through it came instantaneously the loud bang of the explosion. The glass was shattered in all the windows, and thick smoke, white and black, came curling from every one of them.

"'The house is on fire!' I shouted, and sprang madly from the pit. Heedless of the bombardment, I rushed into the building. Another crash sounded overhead as I entered, and a blaze of light shone down the stairway for an instant. Another projectile had found a billet in my home. I tried to make my way to my study, but found the passage blocked with fallen beams and ceiling. What with the smoke and dust, and the blocking of some of the windows, it was very dark in the hall, and I got quite a shock when, as I looked about me to find my way, I saw two red, glittering specks shining over the top of a heap of débris. But the howl that followed told me that they were nothing but the eyes of miserable Tim, the cat, who, left behind, had been nearly frightened out of his senses by the noise and concussion of the bursting shell. As I gazed at him another projectile struck the house quite close to us. Tim was simply smashed by a flying fragment. I was thrown down, and half-buried under a shower of bricks and mortar. I think that I must have lost consciousness for a time.

"The next thing I recollect was being dragged out into the garden by a couple of Saxons. I had a splitting headache, and was very glad of a glass of water that one of them handed to me. Their officer, who appeared to be quite a decent fellow, offered me his flask.

"'The house is all right,' he said, with his strong accent. 'It caught fire once, but we managed to get it under control. Your friends have cleared off—at any rate for the present. They got too bold at last, and pushed their guns down till they got taken in the flank by the warship in the river. They had two of their pieces knocked to bits, and then cleared out. Best thing you can do is to do the same.'

"I was in two minds. I could not save the house by staying, and might just as well join my people at Purleigh Rectory. On the other hand, I felt that it would better become me, as Mayor, to stick to the town. Duty triumphed, and I decided to remain where I was—at least for the present. All was now quiet, and after an early supper I turned in, and, despite the excitement of the day and my aching head, was asleep the moment I touched the pillow."

WEDNESDAY, SEPTEMBER 5

"It must have been about three in the morning when I awoke. My head was much better, and for a minute or two I lay comfortably in the darkness, without any recollection of the events of the preceding day. Then I saw a bright reflection pass rapidly over the ceiling. I wondered vaguely what it was. Presently it came back again, paused a moment, and disappeared. By this time I was wide awake. I went to the window and looked out. It was quite dark, but from somewhere over beyond Heybridge a long white ray was sweeping all along this side of Maldon. Now the foliage of a tree in the garden below would stand out in pale green radiance against the blackness; now the wall of a house half a mile away would reflect back the moving beam, shining white as a sheet of notepaper.

"Presently another ray shone out, and the two of them, moving backwards and forwards, made the whole of our hillside caper in a dizzy dance. From somewhere far away to my right another stronger beam now streamed through the obscurity, directed apparently at the sources of the other two, and almost simultaneously came the crack of a rifle from the direction of Heybridge, sharp and ominous in the quiet darkness of the night. Half a dozen scattered shots followed; then a faint cheer. More and more rifles joined in, and presently the burring tap-tap-tap of a Maxim. I hurried on my clothes. The firing increased in volume and rapidity; bugles rang out here, there, and everywhere through the sleeping town, and above the rolling, rattling clamour of the drums I could distinguish the hurried tramp of hundreds of feet.

"I cast one glance from the window as I quitted the room. The electric searchlights had increased to at least half a dozen. Some reached out long, steady fingers into the vague spaces of the night, while others wandered restlessly up and down, hither and thither. Low down over the trees of the garden a dull red glare slowly increased in extent and intensity. The rattle of musketry was now absolutely continuous. As I ran out of the house into the street, I was nearly carried off my feet by the rush of a battalion that was pouring down Cromwell Hill at the double. Hardly knowing what I did, I followed in their wake. The glare in front got brighter and brighter. A few steps, and I could see the cause of it. The whole of Heybridge appeared to be on fire, the flames roaring skywards from a dozen different conflagrations."

England halted breathless. Fighting had commenced in real earnest.

The greatest consternation was caused by the publication in The Times of the description of the operations in Essex, written by Mr. Henry Bentley, the distinguished war correspondent, who had served that journal in every campaign since Kitchener had entered Khartum.

All other papers, without exception, contained various accounts of the British defence at the point nearest London, but they were mostly of the scrappy and sensational order, based more on report than upon actual fact. The Times account, however, had been written with calm impartiality by one of the most experienced correspondents at the front. Whether he had been afforded any special facilities was not apparent, but, in any case, it was the most complete and truthful account of the gallant attempt on the part of our soldiers to check the advance from Essex westward.

During the whole of that hot, stifling day it was known that a battle was raging, and the excitement everywhere was intense.

The public were in anxious terror as the hours crept by, until the first authentic news of the result of the operations was printed in a special evening edition of *The Times*, as follows:

(FROM OUR WAR CORRESPONDENT)
DANBURY, ESSEX, SEPTEMBER 8

"To-day has been a momentous one for England. The great battle has raged since dawn, and though just at present there seems to be a lull, during which the opposing forces are, so to speak, regaining their breath, it can be by no means over.

"Dead and living alike will lie out on the battlefield the whole night through, for we must hold on to the positions so hardly won, and be ready to press forward at the first glimmer of daylight. Our gallant troops, Regular and Volunteers alike, have nobly vindicated the traditions of our race, and have fought as desperately as ever did their forebears at Agincourt, Albuera, or Waterloo. But while a considerable success—paid for, alas! by the loss of thousands of gallant lives—has been achieved, it will take at least another day's hard fighting before victory is in our grasp. Nowadays a soldier need not expect to be either victorious or finally defeated by nightfall, and although this battle, fought as it is between much smaller forces, and extending over a much more limited area, than the great engagement between the Russians and Japanese at Liaoyang, will not take quite so long a time to decide, the end is not yet in sight. I wrote this after a hard day's travelling backwards and forwards behind our advancing line of battle.

"I took my cycle with me in my motor-car, and whenever opportunity offered mounted it, and pushed forward as near to the fighting as I could get. Frequently I had to leave the cycle also, and crawl forward on hands and knees, sheltering in some depression in the ground, while the enemy's bullets whined and whistled overhead. As reported in a previous issue, the Army which had assembled at Brentwood moved forward on the 5th.

"During the afternoon the advanced troops succeeded in driving the enemy out of South Hanningfield, and before sundown they were also in full retreat from the positions they had held at East Hanningfield and Danbury. There was some stiff fighting at the latter place, but after a pounding from the artillery, who brought several batteries into action on the high ground north-west of East Hanningfield, the Germans were unable to withstand the attack of the Argyll and Sutherlands and the London Scottish, who worked their way through Danbury Park and Hall Wood right into their position, driving them from their entrenchments by a dashing bayonet charge. Everything north and east of the enemy's main position, which is now known to lie north and south, between Maldon and the river Crouch, was now in our hands, but his troops still showed a stout front at Wickford, and were also reported to be at Rayleigh, Hockley, and Canewdon, several miles to the eastward. All preparations were made to assault the German position at Wickford at daybreak to-day, but our scouts found that the place had been evacuated. The news that Rayleigh and Hockley had also been abandoned by the enemy came in shortly afterwards. The German invaders had evidently completed their arrangements for the defence of their main position, and now said, in effect, 'Come on, and turn us out if you can.'

"It was no easy task that lay before our gallant defenders. Maldon, perched on a high knoll, with a network of river and canal protecting it from assault from the northward, fairly bristles with guns, many of them heavy field howitzers, and has, as we know to our cost, already repulsed one attack by our troops. Farther south there are said to be many guns on the knolls about Purleigh. Great Canney Hill, standing boldly up like an immense redoubt, is reported to be seamed with entrenchments mounting many heavy guns. The railway embankment south of Maldon forms a perfect natural rampart along part of the enemy's position, while the woods and enclosures south-west of Great Canney conceal thousands of sharpshooters. A sort of advanced position was occupied by the enemy at Edwin Hall, a mile east of

Woodham Ferrers, where a pair of high kopjes a quarter of a mile apart offered command and cover to some of their field batteries.

"Our scouts have discovered also that an elaborate system of wire entanglements and other military obstacles protects almost the whole front of the somewhat extensive German position. On its extreme left their line is said to be thrown back at an angle, so that any attempt to outflank it would not only entail crossing the river Crouch, but would come under the fire of batteries placed on the high ground overlooking it. Altogether, it is a very tough nut to crack, and the force at our disposal none too strong for the work that lies before it.

"Further detail regarding our strength would be inadvisable for obvious reasons, but when I point out that the Germans are supposed to be between thirty and forty thousand strong, and that it is laid down by competent military authorities that to attack troops in an entrenched position a superiority of six to one is advisable, my readers can draw their own conclusions.

"The repairs to the railway line between Brentwood and Chelmsford, that had been damaged by the enemy's cavalry on their first landing, were completed yesterday, and all night reinforcements had been coming in by way of Chelmsford and Billericay. The general headquarters had been established at Danbury, and, thither I made my way as fast as my car could get along the roads, blocked as they were by marching horse, foot, and artillery. I had spent the night at South Hanningfield, so as to be on the spot for the expected attack on Wickford; but as soon as I found it was not to come off, I considered that at Danbury would be the best chance of finding out what our next move was to be.

"Nor was I mistaken. As I ran up to the village I found the roads full of troops under arms, and everything denoted action of some kind. I was lucky enough to come across a friend of mine on the staff—Captain B——, I will call him—who spared a moment to give me the tip that a general move forward was commencing, and that a big battle was imminent. Danbury is situated on the highest ground for many miles round, and as it bid fair to be a fine, clear day, I thought I could not do better than try and get a general look round from the summit of the church tower before proceeding farther. But I was informed that the General was up there with some of his staff and a signalling party, so that I could not ascend.

"My pass, however, eventually procured me admission to the little platform, which, by the way, the General left a moment after my arrival. It was now eight o'clock, the sun was fairly high in the heavens, and the light mists that hung about the low ground in the vicinity of Maldon were fast fading into nothingness. The old town was plainly distinguishable as a dark silhouette against the morning light, which, while it illumined the panorama spread out before me, yet rendered observation somewhat difficult, since it shone almost directly into my eyes. However, by the aid of my glasses I was able to see something of the first moves on the fatal chess-board where so many thousands of lives are staked on the bloody game of war.

"I noticed among other things that the lessons of the recent war in the East had not passed unobserved, for in all the open spaces on the eastern slope of the hill, where the roads were not screened by trees or coppices, lofty erections of hurdles and greenery had been placed overnight to hide the preliminary movements of our troops from the glasses of the enemy. Under cover of these, regiment after regiment of khaki-clad soldiers, batteries of artillery and ammunition carts, were proceeding to their allotted posts down the network of roads and lanes leading to the lower ground towards the south-east. Two battalions stood in quarter column behind Thrift Wood. They were kilted corps, probably the Argylls and the London Scottish. Several field batteries moved off to the left towards Woodham Walter. Other battalions took up their position behind Hyde Woods, farther away to the right, the last of them, the Grenadier Guards, I fancy, passing behind them and marching still farther southward.

"Finally, two strong battalions, easily recognised as marines by their blue war-kit, marched rapidly down the main road and halted presently behind Woodham Mortimer Place. All this time there was neither sight nor sound of the enemy. The birds carolled gaily in the old elms round my eyrie, the sparrows and martins piped and twittered in the eaves of the old church, and the sun shone genially on hill and valley, field and wood. To all appearance, peace reigned over the countryside, though the dun masses of troops in the shadows of the woodlands were suggestive of the autumn manœuvres. But for all this the 'Real Thing' was upon us. As I looked, first one, then another long and widely scattered line of crouching men in khaki issued from the cover of Hyde Woods and began slowly to move away towards the east. Then, and not till then, a vivid violet-white flash blazed out on the dim grey upland five miles away to the south-east, which had been pointed out to me as Great Canney, and almost at once a spout of earth and smoke sprang up a little way ahead of the advancing British. A dull boom floated up on the breeze, but was drowned in an ear-splitting crash somewhere close to me. I felt the old tower rock under the concussion, which I presently discovered came from a battery of at least six big 4·7 guns established just outside the churchyard.

"They were manned by a party of bluejackets, who had brought them over from Chatham. The movement I saw developing below me was the first step towards what I eventually discovered was our main objective—Purleigh.

"Could we succeed in establishing ourselves there, we should be beyond effective range from Maldon, and should also take Great Canney in reverse, as well as the positions on the refused left flank of the enemy. Maldon, too, would be isolated. Purleigh, therefore, was the key of the position. Our first move was in this direction. The scouts were picked men from the Line battalions, but the firing lines were composed of Volunteers and, in some cases, Militiamen. It was considered more politic to reserve the Regulars for the later stages of the attack. The firing from Canney, and afterwards from Purleigh, was at first at rather too long a range to be effective, even from the heavy guns that were in use, and later on the heavy long-range fire from 'Bloody Mary' and her sisters at Danbury, and other heavy guns and howitzers in the neighbourhood of East Hanningfield, kept it down considerably, although the big, high-explosive shells were now and again most terribly destructive to the advancing British.

"When, however, the firing line—which as yet had not been near enough to fire a shot in reply—arrived in the neighbourhood of Loddard's Hill, its left came under a terrible rifle fire from Hazeleigh Wood, while its right and centre were all but destroyed by a tornado of shrapnel from some German field batteries to the north of Purleigh. Though dazed and staggered under the appalling sleet of projectiles, the Volunteers stuck doggedly to their ground, though unable to advance. Line after line was pushed forward, the men stumbling and falling over the thickly-scattered bodies of their fallen comrades.

"It was a perfect holocaust. Some other card must be played at once, or the attack must fail."

The second of Mr. Henry Bentley's descriptive articles in *The Times* told a terrible truth, and was as follows:

(FROM OUR WAR CORRESPONDENT)
CHELMSFORD, SEPTEMBER 7

"When I sent off my despatch by motor-car last night, it was with very different feelings to those with which I take my pen in hand this evening, in the Saracen's Head Hotel, which is the headquarters of my colleagues, the correspondents.

"Last night, despite the hard fighting and the heavy losses we had sustained, the promise of the morrow was distinctly a good one. But now I have little heart with which to commence the difficult and unpleasant task of chronicling the downfall of all our high hopes, the repulse—ay, and the defeat—it is no use mincing matters—of our heroic and sorely tried Army.

"Yes, our gallant soldiers have sustained a reverse which, but for their stubborn fighting qualities and a somewhat inexplicable holding back on the part of the Germans, might very easily have culminated in disaster. Defeat although it undoubtedly is, the darkness of the gloomy outlook is illuminated by the brilliancy of the conduct of our troops.

"From General down to the youngest Volunteer drummer boy, our brave soldiers did all, and more, than could be humanly expected of them, and on none of them can be laid the blame of our ill-success. The plan of attack is agreed on all hands to have been as good a one as could have been evolved; the officers led well, their men fought well, and there was no running short of ammunition at any period of the engagement.

"'Who, then, was responsible?' it may well be asked. The answer is simple. The British public, which, in its apathetic attitude towards military efficiency, aided and abetted by the soothing theories of the extremists of the 'Blue Water' school, had, as usual, neglected to provide an Army fitted to cope in numbers and efficiency with those of our Continental neighbours. Had we had a sufficiency of troops, more especially of regular troops, there is not the slightest doubt that the victory would have been ours. As it was, our General was obliged to attack the enemy's position with a force whose numbers, even if they had been all regular soldiers, were below those judged necessary by military experts for the task in hand.

"Having broken through the German lines, success was in his grasp had he had sufficient reinforcements to have established him in the position he had won, and to beat back the inevitable counter-attack. But it is best that I should continue my account of the fighting from the point at which I closed my letter of yesterday. I had arrived at the checking of our advance near Loddard's Hill by the blast of shrapnel from the German field batteries. It was plain that the Volunteer Brigade, though it held its ground, could not advance farther. But, unnoticed by them, the General had been preparing for this eventuality.

"On the left the two battalions of Marines that I noticed drawn up behind Woodham Mortimer Place suddenly debouched on Loddard's Hill, and, carrying forward with them the débris of the Volunteer firing line, hurled themselves into Hazeleigh Wood. There was a sanguinary hand-to-hand struggle on the wire-entangled border, but the newcomers were not to be denied, and, after a quarter of an hour's desperate mêlée, which filled the sylvan glades with moaning and writhing wounded and stark dead bodies, we remained masters of the wood, and even obtained a footing on the railway line where it adjoins it.

"Simultaneously a long line of our field batteries came into action near Woodham Mortimer, some trying to beat down the fire of the German guns opposite, while others replied to a battery which had been established near West Maldon Station to flank the railway, and which was now beginning to open on Hazeleigh Wood. The latter were assisted by a battery of 4·7 guns manned by Volunteers, which took up a position behind Woodham Walter. The firing on Great Canney from our batteries at East Hanningfield redoubled, the whole summit of the hill being at times obscured by the clouds of smoke and débris from the explosions of the big, high-explosive projectiles.

"The main firing line, continually fed from the rear, now began slowly to gain ground, and when the Grenadiers and the Irish Guards, who had managed to work up through the series of plantations that run eastwards for nearly two miles from Woodham Hall without drawing any particular attention from the busily engaged enemy, came into action on the right, there was a distinct move forward. But the defence was too stubborn, and about midday the whole line again came to a standstill, its left still in Hazeleigh Wood, its right at Prentice Farm. Orders were passed that the men should try to entrench themselves as best they could, and spades and other tools were sent forward to those corps who were not provided with them already.

"Here we must leave the main attack to notice what was going on elsewhere. On the north the Colchester Garrison again brought their heavy artillery into action on the slopes south of Wickham Bishops, while others of our troops made a show of advancing against Maldon from the west. These movements were, however, merely intended to keep the German garrison occupied. But on the right a rather important flanking movement was in progress.

"We had a considerable body of troops at East Hanningfield, which lies in a hollow between two little ridges, both running from south-west to north-east, and about a mile apart. The most easterly ridge is very narrow for the most part, and behind it were stationed several batteries of our field howitzers, which fired over it at Great Canney at a range of about 5,000 yards. A number of 4·7-inch guns, scattered over the western hill, were also concentrated on the same target. Although the range was an extremely long one, there is no doubt that they made a certain number of effective hits, since Great Canney offered a conspicuous and considerable target. But beyond this the flashes of their discharges drew off all attention from the howitzer batteries in front of them, and served to conceal their presence from the enemy. Otherwise, although invisible, their presence would have been guessed at. As it was, not a single German projectile came anywhere near them.

"When the fighting began, those troops who were not intended to be held in reserve or to co-operate with the right of the main attack moved off in the direction of Woodham Ferrers, and made a feint of attacking the German position astride the two kopjes at Edwin's Hall, their field guns coming into action on the high ground north of Rettendon, and engaging those of the enemy at long range. But the real attack on this salient of the German position came from a very different quarter.

"The troops detailed for this movement were those who had advanced against Wickford at daybreak, and had found it abandoned by the enemy. They consisted of the Oxfordshire Light Infantry, the Honourable Artillery Company, and the Inns of Court Volunteers, together with their own and three or four other machine-gun detachments, their Maxims being mounted on detachable legs instead of carriages. Co-operating with them were the Essex and the East Kent Yeomanry, who were scouting in the direction of Hockley.

"The troops had a long, wearisome march before them, the design being to take advantage of the time of low tide, and to move along out of sight of the enemy behind the northern bank of the river Crouch, as it had been discovered that the German line of defence turned back to the eastward at a mile or two north of the river at the point aimed at. Its guns still commanded it, and might be trusted to render abortive any attempt to throw a bridge across it. The Yeomanry had the task of occupying the attention of the enemy at Canewdon, and of preventing the passage of boats from the German warships. This part of our operations succeeded admirably. The long creeping lines of the Oxfordshires and the machine-gun detachments in their khaki uniforms were almost indistinguishable against the steep mud banks at any distance, and they escaped observation both from the German main lines and from their outpost at Canewdon until they had reached the entrances of the two branch creeks for which they were making.

"Then, and not till then, came the sound of artillery from the left rear of the German position. But it was too late. The Oxford companies pushed forward at the double. Five companies lined the embankments of Stow Creek, the easternmost of the two, while the remainder, ensconced in Clementsgreen Creek, aligned the whole of their machine-guns on the southern of the two kopjes against which the manœuvre had been directed. Their fire, which, coming from a little to the rear of the left flank of the southern kopje, completely enfiladed it, created such slaughter and confusion that the Honourable Artillery Company and the Inns of Court, who had been working up the railway line from Battle Bridge, had little difficulty in establishing themselves at Woodham Ferrers Station and in an adjacent farm. Being almost immediately afterwards reinforced by the arrival of two regular battalions who had been pushed forward from Rettendon, a determined assault was made on the southern kopje. Its defenders, demoralised by the pelting shower of lead from the machine-gun battery, and threatened also by the advance from Woodham Ferrers village, gave way, and our people, forcing their way over every obstacle, seized the position amid frantic cheering.

"Meanwhile the Oxfordshires had been subjected to a determined counter-attack from North Frambridge. Preceded by a pounding from the guns on Kit's Hill, but aided by the fire of the Yeomanry on the south bank of the river, who galloped up and lined the embankment, thus flanking the defenders of Stow Creek, it was beaten back with considerable loss. The machine-guns were transferred to the neighbourhood of South Kopje, and used with such effect that its defenders, after repulsing several counter-attacks from the adjoining German entrenchment, were able to make themselves masters of the North Kopje also.

"Elsewhere the fighting still continued strenuous and deadly. The main attack had contrived to make some little shelter for itself; but though three separate attempts were made to advance from this, all ended in failure, one nearly in disaster. This was the last of the three, when the advancing line was charged by a mass of cavalry which suddenly appeared from behind Great Canney Hill. I myself was a witness of this attack, the most picturesque incident of the day's fighting.

"I was watching the progress of the engagement through my glasses from the high ground about Wickham's Farm, when I saw line after line of the German horsemen in their sky-blue tunics and glittering helmets trot out into the open, canter, and one after another break into a mad gallop, as they bore down upon the advancing lines of our citizen soldiers. Staunchly as these had withstood the murderous fire which for hours had been directed upon them, this whirlwind of lance and sabre, the thunder of thousands of hoofs, and the hoarse cries of the riders, were rather more than such partially trained soldiers could stand. A scattering discharge from their rifles was followed by something very much approaching a *sauve qui peut*.

"A large number of Volunteers, however, sought shelter among the ruined houses of Cock Clarke's hamlet, from whence they opened a heavy fire on the adventurous horsemen. The Argyll and Sutherland Highlanders, who were by this time in Mosklyns Copse, and the Guards and other troops on the right, also opened a rapid and sustained fire on the German cavalry, which, seconded by the shrapnel from our guns on Loddard's Hill, caused them to turn and ride back for their lives. There was a tremendous outburst of firing from both sides after this, followed by quite a lull. One could well imagine that all the combatants were exhausted by the prolonged effort of the day. It was now between five and six in the evening. It was at this time that the news of the capture of the two kopjes reached me, and I made for Danbury to write my despatches.

"Shortly after my arrival I heard of the capture of Spar Hill, a detached knoll about 1,200 yards to the north-west of Purleigh. The Marines from Hazeleigh Wood and the Highlanders from Mosklyns Copse had suddenly and simultaneously assaulted it from opposite sides, and were now entrenching themselves upon it. What wonder, then, that I reported satisfactory progress, and reckoned—too confidently, as it proved—on a victory for the morrow?

"I spent a great part of that night under the stars on the hilltop near East Hanningfield, watching the weird play of the searchlights which swept over the country from a score of different positions, and listening to the crash of artillery and clatter of rifle fire which now and again told of some attempted movement under cover of the darkness. Just before daylight the continuous roar of battle began again, and when light dawned I found that our troops had cut right through the German lines, and had penetrated as far as Cop Kitchen's Farm, on the Maldon–Mundon road. Reinforcements were being hurried up, and an attack was being pushed towards the rear of Purleigh and Great Canney, which was being heavily bombarded by some of our large guns, which had been mounted during the night on the two kopjes.

"But the reinforcements were not enough. The Germans held fast to Purleigh and to some reserve positions they had established about Mundon. After two or three hours of desperate effort, costing the lives of thousands, our attack was at a standstill. At this critical moment a powerful counter-attack was made from Maldon, and, outnumbered and almost surrounded, our gallant warriors had to give ground. But they fell back as doggedly as they had advanced, the Argylls, Marines, and Grenadiers covering the retreat on Danbury.

"The guns at East Hanningfield and the two kopjes checked the pursuit to a great extent, and the Germans seemed unwilling to go far from their works. The kopjes had to be abandoned later in the day, and we now occupy our former line from Danbury to Billericay, and are busily engaged in entrenching ourselves."

CHAPTER VIII

DEFENCE AT LAST

LATE ON WEDNESDAY NIGHT came tardy news of the measures we were taking to mobilise.

The Aldershot Army Corps, so complete in the "Army List," consisted, as all the world knew, of three divisions, but of these only two existed, the other being found to be on paper. The division in question, located at Bordon, was to be formed on mobilisation, and this measure was now being proceeded with. The train service was practically suspended, owing to the damage done to the various lines south of London by the enemy's emissaries. Several of these men had been detected, and, being in plain clothes, were promptly shot out of hand. However, their work had, unfortunately for us, been accomplished, and trains could only run as far as the destroyed bridges, so men on their way to join their respective corps were greatly delayed in consequence.

All was confusion at Bordon, where men were arriving in hundreds on foot and by the service of motor omnibuses, which the War Office had on the day before established between Charing Cross and Aldershot. Perspiring staff officers strove diligently, without much avail, to sort out into their respective units this ever-increasing mass of reservists.

There was perfect chaos.

Before the chief constituent parts of the division—that is to say, regiments who were stationed elsewhere—had arrived little could be done with the reservists. The regiments in question were in many cases stationed at considerable distance, and, although they had received orders to start, were prevented from arriving owing to the universal interruptions of the railway traffic south. By this, whole valuable days were lost—days when at any hour the invaders might make a sudden swoop on London.

Reports were alarming and conflicting. Some said that the enemy meant to strike a blow upon the capital just as suddenly as they had landed, while others reassured the alarmists that the German plans were not yet complete, and that they had not sufficient stores to pursue the campaign.

Reservists, with starvation staring them in the face, went eagerly south to join their regiments, knowing that at least they would be fed with regularity; while, in addition, the true patriotic spirit of the Englishman had been roused against the aggressive Teuton, and everyone, officer and man, was eager to bear his part in driving the invader into the sea.

The public were held breathless. What would happen?

Arrivals at Aldershot, however, found the whole of the arrangements in such a complete muddle that Army Service Corps men, who ought to have been at Woolwich, were presenting themselves for enrolment at Bordon, and infantry of the line were conducted into the camp of the Dragoons. The Motor Volunteer Corps were at this moment of very great use. The cars were filled with staff officers and other exalted officials, who were settling themselves in various offices, and passing out again to make necessary arrangements for dealing with such a large influx of men.

There were activity and excitement everywhere. Men were rapidly drawing their clothing, or as much of it as they could get, and civilians were quickly becoming soldiers on every hand. Officers of the Reserve were driving up in motor-cars and cabs, many of them with their old battered uniform cases, that had seen service in the field in distant parts of the globe. Men from the "Junior" and the "Senior" wrung each other's hands on returning to active duty with their old regiments, and at once settled down into the routine work they knew so well.

The rumour, however, had now got about that a position in the neighbourhood of Cambridge had been selected by the General Staff as being the most suitable theatre of action where an effective stand could, with any hope of success, be made. It was evident that the German tactics were to strike a swift and rapid blow at London. Indeed, nothing at present stood in their way except the gallant little garrison at Colchester, who had been so constantly driven back by the enemy's cavalry on attempting to make any reconnaissance, and who might be swept out of existence at any hour.

During Tuesday and Wednesday large gangs of workmen had been busy repairing the damaged lines. The first regiment complete for the field was the 2nd Battalion of the 5th Fusiliers, who carried upon their colours the names of a score of battles, ranging from Corunna and Badajoz, all through the Peninsula, Afghanistan, and Egypt, down to the Modder River. This regiment left by train for London on Tuesday evening, and was that same night followed by the 2nd Battalion King's Liverpool Regiment and the 1st King's

Shropshire Light Infantry, while the Manchester Regiment got away soon after midnight.

These formed the second infantry brigade of the 1st Division, and were commanded by Brigadier-General Sir John Money. They were several hours getting up to London, whence from Clapham Junction their trains circled London on to the Great Eastern system to Braintree, where the Horn Hotel was made the headquarters. By other trains in the small hours of the morning the last of the Guards Brigade under Colonel (temporary Brigadier-General) Lord Wansford departed, and duly arrived at Saffron Walden, to join their comrades on the line of defence.

The divisional troops were also on the move early on Wednesday. Six batteries of artillery and the field company of Royal Engineers left by road. There was a balloon section accompanying this, and searchlights, wireless instruments, and cables for field-telegraphy were carried in the waggons.

The 2nd Division, under Lieutenant-General Morgan, C.B., was also active. The 3rd Infantry Brigade, commanded by Major-General Fortescue, composed of 2nd Battalion Northamptonshire Regiment, the 2nd Bedfordshire, the 1st Princess of Wales' Own, and the 1st Royal Welsh Fusiliers, were preparing, but had not yet moved. The 4th Infantry Brigade of the same division, consisting of the 3rd and 4th Battalions King's Royal Rifle Corps, the 2nd Sherwood Foresters, and the 2nd South Lancashire, with the usual smartness of those distinguished regiments, were quick and ready, now as ever, to go to the front. They were entrained to Baldock, slightly east of Hitchin, where they marched out on the Icknield Way. These were followed by Fortescue's Brigade, who were also bound for Baldock and the neighbourhood.

The bulk of the cavalry and field artillery of both divisions, together with the divisional troops, were compelled to set out by march-route from Aldershot for the line of defences. The single and all-sufficient reason of this delay in sending out the cavalry and artillery was owing to the totally inadequate accommodation on the railways for the transport of so many horses and guns. The troop-trains, which were of course necessary to transport the infantry, were not forthcoming in sufficient numbers, this owing to the fact that at several points the lines to London were still interrupted.

The orders to the cavalry who went by march-route were to get up to the line proposed to be taken up by the infantry as quickly as possible, and to operate in front of it to the east and north-east in screening and reconnoitring duties. The temporary deficiency of cavalry, who ought, of course, to have been the first to arrive at the scene, was made good as far as possible by the general employment of hordes of motor-cyclists, who scoured the country in large armed groups, in order to ascertain, if possible, the dispositions of the enemy. This they did, and very soon after their arrival reported the result of their investigations to the general officers commanding the 1st and 2nd Divisions.

Meanwhile both cavalry and artillery in great bodies, and strings of motor omnibuses filled with troops, were upon the white, dusty roads passing through Staines to Hounslow and Brentford, thence to London, St. Albans, en route to their respective divisions. Roughly, the distance was over fifty miles, therefore those marching were compelled to halt the night on the way, while those in the motor omnibuses got through to their destination.

The sight of British troops hurrying to the front swelled the hearts of the villagers and townsfolk with renewed patriotism, and everywhere, through the blazing, dusty day, the men were offered refreshment by even the poorest and humblest cottagers. In Bagshot, in Staines, and in Hounslow the people went frantic with excitement, as squadron after squadron rapidly passed along, with its guns, waggons, and ambulances rumbling noisily over the stones in the rear.

Following these came pontoon troops with their long grey waggons and mysterious-looking bridging apparatus, telegraph troops, balloon sections, supply columns, field bakery, and field hospitals, the last-named packed in waggons marked with the well-known red cross of the Geneva Convention.

No sooner was Aldershot denuded of its army corps, however, than battalions began to arrive from Portsmouth on their way north, while troops from the great camp on Salisbury Plain were rapidly being pushed to the front, which, roughly speaking, extended through Hitchin, Royston, to Saffron Walden, across to Braintree, and also the high ground commanding the valley of the Colne to Colchester.

The line chosen by the General Staff was the natural chain of hills which presented the first obstacle to the enemy advancing on London from the wide plain stretching eastward beyond Cambridge to the sea.

If this could be held strongly, as was intended, by practically the whole of the British forces located in the South of England, including the Yeomanry, Militia, and Volunteers—who were now all massing in every direction—then the deadly peril threatening England might be averted.

But could it be held?

This was the appalling question on every one's tongue all over the country, for it now became generally known that upon this line of defence four complete and perfectly equipped German army corps were ready to advance at any moment, in addition to the right flank being exposed to the attack of the XIIth Saxon Corps, entrenched on the Essex coast.

It was estimated that no fewer than two hundred thousand Germans were already upon English soil!

The outlook grew blacker every hour.

London was in a state of absolute stagnation and chaos. In the City, business was now at an entire standstill. The credit system had received a fatal blow, and nobody wanted to buy securities. Had people kept level heads in the crisis there would have been a moratorium, but, as it was, a panic had been created that nothing could allay. Even Consols were now unsaleable. Some of the smaller banks were known to have failed, and traders and manufacturers all over the country had been ruined on account of credit, the foundation of all trade, having been swept away. Only persons of the highest financial standing could have dealt with the banks, even if they had remained open.

The opinion held in banking circles was that if the invasion should unfortunately prove disastrous to England, and Germany

We, Wilhelm,

Give notice to the inhabitants of those provinces occupied by the German Imperial Army, that—

I make war upon the soldiers, and not upon English citizens. Consequently, it is my wish to give the latter and their property entire security, and as long as they do not embark upon hostile enterprise against the German troops they have a right to my protection.

Generals commanding the various corps in the various districts in England are ordered to place before the public the stringent measures which I have ordered to be adopted against towns, villages, and persons who act in contradiction to the usages of war. They are to regulate in the same manner all the operations necessary for the well-being of our troops, to fix the difference between the English and German rate of exchange, and to facilitate in every manner possible the individual transactions between our Army and the inhabitants of England.

Wilhelm

Given at Potsdam, September 4th, 1910

demand a huge indemnity, there was still hope, however small. The experience of the Franco-German war had proved that, though in such circumstances the Bank, for a considerable period, might not be able to resume cash payments, yet, with sound finance, there was no reason that the currency should greatly depreciate. During the period of suspension of cash payments by the Bank of France, the premium on gold never went above 1·5 per cent., and during most of the period was 5, 4, or even less per mille. Therefore what the French by sound banking had been able to do, there was no reason why English bankers could not also do.

At the outbreak of the war of 1870, on August 1, French Three per Cent. Rentes were at 60·85, and Four and a Half per Cent. at 98. On the memorable day of Sedan, September 2, they were at 50·80 and 88·50 respectively, and on January 2, 1871, Three per Cents. were down to 50·95. At the commencement of the Commune, on March 18, they were at 51·50 and 76·25, and on the 30th of that month down to 50·60 and 76·25 respectively.

With so little money in England as there now was, securities had fallen to the value at which holders would as soon not sell as sell at such a great discount. High rates and the heavy fall in the value of securities had brought business in every quarter all over London to a standstill. Firms all over the country were now hard put to in order to find the necessary money to carry on their various trades. Instantly after the report of the reverse at Sheffield, there was a wild rush to obtain gold, and securities dropped even a few more points.

Therefore there was little or nothing for the banks to do, and Lombard Street, Lothbury, and the other banking centres were closed, as though it had been Sunday or Bank Holiday. Despair was, alas! everywhere, and the streets presented strange scenes.

Most of the motor omnibuses had been taken off the road and pressed into the service of the military. The walls bore a dozen different broadsides and proclamations, which were read by the gaping, hungry crowds.

The Royal Standard was flying from St. Stephen's Tower, for Parliament had now met, and all members who were not abroad for their summer vacation had taken their places at the heated debates now hourly in progress. Over Buckingham Palace the Royal Standard also flew proudly, while upon every public building was displayed a Union Jack or a white ensign, many of which had done duty at the coronation of His Majesty King Edward. The Admiralty flew its own flag, and upon the War Office, the India Office, the Foreign Office, and all the dark, sombre Government buildings in Whitehall was bunting displayed.

The wild enthusiasm of Sunday and Monday, however, had given place to a dark, hopeless apprehension. The great mobs now thronging all the principal thoroughfares in London were already half-famished. Food was daily rising in price, and the East End was already starving. Bands of lawless men and women from the slums of Whitechapel were parading the West End streets and squares, and were camping out in Hyde Park and St. James's Park.

The days were stifling, for it was an unusually hot September following upon a blazing August, and as each breathless evening the sun sank, it shed its blood-red afterglow over the giant metropolis, grimly precursory of the ruin so surely imminent.

Supplies were still reaching London from the country, but there had been immediate panic in the corn and provision markets, with the result that prices had instantly jumped up beyond the means of the average Londoner. The poorer ones were eagerly collecting the refuse in Covent Garden Market and boiling it down to make soup in lieu of anything else, while wise fathers of families went to the shops themselves and made meagre purchases daily of just sufficient food to keep body and soul together.

For the present there was no fear of London being absolutely starved, at least the middle class and wealthier portion of it. At present it was the poor—the toiling millions now unemployed—who were the first to feel the pinch of hunger and its consequent despair. They filled the main arteries of London—Holborn, Oxford Street, the Strand, Regent Street, Piccadilly, the Haymarket, St. James's Street, Park Lane, Victoria Street, and Knightsbridge, overflowing northward into Grosvenor, Berkeley, Portman, and Cavendish Squares, Portland Place, and to the terraces around Regent's Park. The centre of London became congested. Day and night it was the same. There was no sleep. From across the river and from the East End the famished poor came in their bewildering thousands, the majority of them honest workers, indignant that by the foolish policy of the Government they now found themselves breadless.

Before the Houses of Parliament, before the fine new War Office and the Admiralty, before Downing Street, and before the houses of known members of the Government, constant demonstrations were being made, the hungry crowds groaning at the authorities, and singing "God Save the King." Though starving and in despair, they were nevertheless loyal, still confident that by the personal effort of His Majesty some amicable arrangement would be arrived at. The French *entente cordiale* was remembered, and our Sovereign had long ago been declared to be the first diplomat in Europe. Every Londoner believed in him, and loved him.

Many houses of the wealthy, especially those of foreigners, had their windows broken. In Park Lane, in Piccadilly, and in Grosvenor Square more particularly, the houses seemed to excite the ire of the crowds, who, notwithstanding special constables having been sworn in, were now quite beyond the control of the police. The German Ambassador had presented his letters of recall on Sunday evening, and together with the whole staff had been accorded a safe conduct to Dover, whence they had left for the Continent. The Embassy in Carlton House Terrace, and also the Consulate-General in Finsbury Square, had, however, suffered severely at the hands of the angry crowd, notwithstanding that both premises were under police protection.

All the German waiters employed at the Cecil, the Savoy, the Carlton, the Métropole, the Victoria, the Grand, and the other big London hotels, had already fled for their lives out into the country, anywhere from the vengeance of the London mob. Hundreds of them were trying to make their way within the German lines in Essex and Suffolk, and it was believed that many had succeeded—those, most probably, who had previously acted as spies. Others, it was reported, had been set upon by the excited populace, and more than one had lost his life.

Pandemonium reigned in London. Every class and every person in every walk of life was affected. German interests were being looked after by the Russian Ambassador, and this very fact caused a serious demonstration before Chesham House, the big mansion where lives the representative of the Czar. Audacious spies had, in secret, in the night actually posted copies of Von Kronhelm's proclamation upon the Griffin at Temple Bar, upon the Marble Arch, and upon the Mansion House. But these had been quickly torn down, and if the hand that had placed them there had been known, it would certainly have meant death to the one who had thus insulted the citizens of London.

Yet the truth was, alas! too plain. Spread out across Essex and Suffolk, making leisurely preparations and laughing at our futile defence, lay over one hundred thousand well-equipped, well-fed Germans, ready, when their plans were completed, to advance upon and crush the complex city which is the pride and home of every Englishman—London.

On Friday night an official communication from the War Office was issued to the Press, showing the exact position of the invaders. It was roughly this:

"The IXth German Corps, which had effected a landing at Lowestoft, had, after moving along the most easterly route, including the road through Saxmundham and Ipswich, at length arrived at a position where their infantry outposts had occupied the higher slopes of the rising ground overlooking the river Stour, near Manningtree, which town, as well as Ipswich, was held by them.

"The left flank of this corps rested on the river Stour itself, so that it was secure from any turning movement. Its front was opposed to and directly threatened Colchester, while its outposts, to say nothing of its independent cavalry, reached out in a northerly direction towards Stowmarket, where they joined hands with the left flank of the Xth Corps—those under Von Wilburg, who had landed at Yarmouth—whose headquarters were now at Bury St. Edmunds, their outposts being disposed south, overlooking the valley of the upper reaches of the Stour."

Nor was this all. From Newmarket there came information that the enemy who had landed at Weybourne and Cromer—viz., the IVth Corps under Von Kleppen—were now encamping on the race-course and being billeted in the town and villages about, including Exning, Ashley, Moulton, and Kentford. Frölich's cavalry brigade had penetrated south, covering the advance, and had now scoured the country, sweeping away the futile resistance of the British Yeomanry, and scattering cavalry squadrons which they found opposed to them, all the time maintaining communication with the Xth Corps on their left, and the flower of the German Army, the Guards Corps, from King's Lynn, on their right. Throughout the advance from Holt, Von Dorndorf's motorists had been of the greatest utility. They had taken constantly companies of infantry hither and thither. At any threatened point, so soon as the sound of firing was heard in any cavalry skirmish or little engagement of outposts, the smart motor infantry were on the spot with the promptness of a fire brigade proceeding to a call. For this reason the field artillery, who were largely armed with quick-firing guns, capable of pouring in a hail of shrapnel on any exposed point, were enabled to push on much further than would have been otherwise possible. They were always adequately supported by a sufficient escort of these up-to-date troops, who, although infantry, moved with greater rapidity than cavalry itself, and who, moreover, brought with them their Maxims, which dealt havoc far and near.

The magnificent troops of the Duke of Mannheim, in their service uniforms, who had landed at King's Lynn, had come across the wide, level roads, some by way of Downham Market, Littleport, and Ely, and arrived at Cambridge. The 2nd Division, under Lieutenant-General von Kasten, protecting the exposed flanks, had marched viâ Wisbech, March, Chatteris, and St. Ives, while the masses of the cavalry of the Guard, including the famous White Cuirassiers, had been acting independently around the flat fen country, Spalding and Peterborough, and away to quaint old Huntingdon, striking terror into the inhabitants, and effectively checking any possible offensive movement of the British that might have been directed upon the great German Army during its ruthless advance.

Beyond this, worse remained. It was known that the VIIth Corps, under Von Bristram, had landed at Goole, and that General Graf Haeseler had landed at Hull, New Holland, and Grimsby. This revealed what the real strategy of the Generalissimo had been. Their function seemed twofold. First and foremost their presence, as a glance at the map will show, effectually prevented any attack from the British troops gathered from the north and elsewhere, and who were, as shown, concentrated near Sheffield and Birmingham, until these two corps had themselves been attacked and repulsed, which we were, alas! utterly unable to accomplish.

These were two fine German army corps, complete to the pro-verbial last button, splendidly equipped, well fed, and led by officers who had had life-long training and were perfectly well acquainted with every mile of the country they occupied, by reason of years of

careful study given to maps of England. It was now entirely plain
that the function of these two corps was to paralyse our trade in
Yorkshire and Lancashire, to commit havoc in the big cities, to terrify
the people, and to strike a crushing blow at our industrial centres,
leaving the siege of London to the four other corps now so rapidly
advancing upon the metropolis.

Events meanwhile were marching quickly in the North.

The town of Sheffield throughout Tuesday and Wednesday was
the scene of the greatest activity. Day and night the streets were filled
with an excited populace, and hour by hour the terror increased.

Every train arriving from the North was crowded with Volunteers
and troops of the line from all stations in the Northern Command.
The 1st Battalion West Riding Regiment had joined the Yorkshire
Light Infantry, who were already stationed in Sheffield, as had also
the 19th Hussars, and from every regimental district and depôt
came battalions of Militia and Volunteers. From Carlisle came the
Reservists of the Border Regiment, from Richmond those of the
Yorkshire Regiment, from Newcastle came what was left of the
Reservists of the Durham Light Infantry, and the Northumberland
Fusiliers, from Lancaster the Royal Lancashires, while field artillery
came from Seaforth and Preston, and small bodies of Reservists
of the Liverpool and the South Lancashire Regiments came from
Warrington. Contingents of the East and North Lancashire Regiments arrived from Preston. The Militia, including battalions of the
Liverpool Regiment, the South Lancashire Regiment, the Lancashire
Fusiliers, and other regiments in the command, were hurried to the
scene of action outside Sheffield. From every big town in the whole
of the North of England and South of Scotland came straggling units
of Volunteers. The mounted troops were almost entirely Yeomanry,
and included the Duke of Lancaster's Own Imperial Yeomanry,
the East Riding of Yorks, the Lancashire Hussars, Northumberland
Yeomanry, Westmorland and Cumberland Yeomanry, the Queen's
Own Yorkshire Dragoons, and the York Hussars.

These troops, with their ambulances, their baggage, and all
their impedimenta, created the utmost confusion at both railway
stations. The great concourse of idlers cheered and cheered again,

the utmost enthusiasm being displayed when each battalion forming up was marched away out of the town to the position chosen for the defence, which now reached from Woodhouse on the south, overlooking and commanding the whole valley of the river Rother, through Catcliffe, Brinsworth, and Tinsley, previously alluded to, skirting Greasborough to the high ground north of Wentworth, also commanding the river Don and all approaches to it through Mexborough, and over the various bridges which spanned this stream—a total of about eight miles.

The south flank was thrown back another four miles to Norton, in an endeavour to prevent the whole position being turned, should the Germans elect to deliver their threatened blow from a more southerly point than was anticipated.

The total line, then, to be occupied by the defenders was about twelve miles, and into this front was crowded the heterogeneous mass of troops of all arms. The post of honour was at Catcliffe, the dominating key to the whole position, which was occupied by the sturdy soldiers of the 1st Battalion West Riding Regiment and the 2nd Battalion Yorkshire Light Infantry, while commanding every bridge crossing the rivers which lay between Sheffield and the invaders were concentrated the guns of the 7th Brigade Royal Horse Artillery, and of the Field Artillery, the 2nd, the 30th, the 37th, and 38th Brigades, the latter having hurriedly arrived from Bradford.

All along the crests of these slopes which formed the defence of Sheffield, rising steeply from the river at times up to five hundred feet, were assembled the Volunteers, all now by daybreak on Thursday morning busily engaged in throwing up shelter-trenches and making hasty earthwork defences for the guns. The superintendence of this force had merged itself into that of the Northern Command, which nominally had its headquarters in York, but which had now been transferred to Sheffield itself, for the best of reasons—that it was of no value at York, and was badly wanted farther south. General Sir George Woolmer, who so distinguished himself in South Africa, had therefore shifted his headquarters to the Town Hall in Sheffield, but as soon as he had begun to get the line of defence completed, he, with his staff, moved on to Handsworth, which was centrally situated.

In the command were to be found roughly twenty-three battalions of Militia and forty-eight of Volunteers; but, owing to the supineness and neglect of the Government, the former regiments now found themselves, at the moment when wanted, greatly denuded of officers, and, owing to any lack of encouragement to enlist, largely depleted in men. As regards the Volunteers, matters were even worse, only about fifteen thousand having responded to the call to arms. And upon these heroic men, utterly insufficient in point of numbers, Sheffield had to rely for its defence.

Away to the eastward of Sheffield—exactly where was yet unknown—sixty thousand perfectly equipped and thoroughly trained German horse, foot, and artillery, were ready at any moment to advance westward into our manufacturing districts!

CHAPTER IX

BRITISH SUCCESS AT ROYSTON

Arrests of alleged spies were reported from Manchester and other large towns. Most of the prisoners were, however, able to prove themselves naturalised British subjects; but several were detained pending investigation and examination of correspondence found at their homes. In Manchester, where there are always a number of Germans, it is known that many slipped away on Sunday night after the publication of the news of the invasion.

In most of the larger Midland towns notices had been issued by the mayors deprecating hostility towards residents of foreign origin, and stating that all suspicious cases were already receiving the attention of the police.

In Stafford the boot factories were idle. In the Potteries all work was at a standstill. At Stoke-on-Trent, at Hanley, at Burslem, Tunstall, and Congleton all was chaos, and thousands upon thousands were already wanting bread. The silk-thread industry at Leek was ruined, so was the silk industry at Macclesfield; the great breweries at Burton were idle, while the hosiery factories of Leicester and the boot factories of Northampton were all shut.

With the German troops threatening Sheffield, Nottingham was in a state of intense alarm. The lace and hosiery factories had with one accord closed on Tuesday, and the great Market Place was now filled day and night by thousands upon thousands of unemployed mill-hands of both sexes. On Friday, however, came the news of how Sheffield had built barricades against the enemy, and there ensued a frantic attempt at defence on the part of thousands of terrified and hungry men and women. In their frenzy they sacked houses in order to obtain material to construct the barricades, which were, however, built just where the fancy took the crowd.

The white, interminable North Road, that runs so straight from London through York and Berwick to Edinburgh, was, with its by-roads in the Midlands, now being patrolled by British cavalry, and here and there telegraphists around a telegraph post showed that those many wires at the roadside were being used for military communication.

At several points along the road between Wansford Bridge and Retford the wires had been cut and tangled by the enemy's agents, but by Friday all had been restored again. In one spot, between Weston and Sutton-on-Trent, eight miles south of Newark, a trench had actually been dug during the night, the tube containing the subterranean telegraph lines discovered, and the whole system to the North disorganised. Similar damage had been done by German spies to the line between London and Birmingham, two miles south of Shipston-on-Stour; and again the line between Loughborough and Nottingham had been similarly destroyed.

The Post Office linesmen had, however, quickly made good the damage everywhere in the country not already occupied by the enemy, and telegraph and telephone communication North and South was now practically again in its normal state.

Through Lincolnshire the enemy's advance patrols had spread South over every road between the Humber and the Wash, and in the city of Lincoln itself a tremendous sensation was caused when on Wednesday, market-day, several bodies of German motor-cyclists swept into the Stonebow and dismounted at the Saracen's Head, amid the crowd of farmers and dealers who had assembled there, not, alas! to do business, but to discuss the situation. In a moment the city was panic-stricken. From mouth to mouth the dread truth spread, that the Germans were upon them, and people ran indoors and barricaded themselves within their houses.

A body of Uhlans came galloping proudly through the Stonebow a quarter of an hour later, and halted in High Street as though awaiting orders. Then in rapid succession troops seemed to arrive from all quarters, many halting in the Cathedral Close and by Exchequer Gate, and others riding through the streets in order to terrify the inhabitants.

Von Kronhelm's famous proclamation was posted by German soldiers upon the police station, upon the Stonebow, and upon the door of the grand old Cathedral itself, and before noon a German officer accompanied by his staff called upon the Mayor, and warned him that Lincoln was occupied by the German troops, and that any armed resistance would be punished by death, as the Generalissimo's proclamation stated. An indemnity was demanded, and then the powerless people saw upon the Cathedral and upon several of the public buildings the German flag rise and float out upon the summer wind.

Boston was full of German infantry, and officers had taken up temporary quarters in the Peacock and other hotels in the market-place, while upon the "Stump" the enemy's colours were flying.

No news came from London. People in Norwich, Ipswich, Yarmouth, and other places heard vaguely of the invasion in the North, and of fighting in which the Germans were careful to report that they were always successful. They saw the magnificently equipped army of the Kaiser, and, comparing it with our mere apology for military force, regarded the issue as hopeless from the very first. In every town the German colours were displayed, and all kinds of placards in German and in English made their appearance.

The *Daily Chronicle*, on September 10, published the following despatch from one of its war correspondents:

ROYSTON, SEPTEMBER 9

"Victory at last. A victory due not only to the bravery and exertion of our troops, regular and auxiliary, but also to the genius of Field-Marshal Lord Byfield, our Commander-in-Chief, ably seconded by the energy and resource with which Sir William Packington, in command of the IVth Army Corps at Baldock, carried out that part of the programme entrusted to him.

"But though in this success we may hope that we are seeing the first glimmerings of dawn—of deliverance from the nightmare of German invasion that is now oppressing our dear old England—we must not be led into foolishly sanguine hopes. The snake has been scotched, and pretty badly into the bargain, but he is far from being killed. The German IVth Army Corps, under the famous General Von Kleppen, their magnificent Garde Corps commanded by the Duke of Mannheim, and Frölich's fine Cavalry Division, have been repulsed in their attack on our positions near Royston and Saffron Walden, and driven back with great loss and confusion. But we are too weak to follow up our victory as it should be followed up.

"The menace of the IXth and Xth Corps on our right flank ties us to our selected position, and the bulk of our forces being composed of indifferently trained Volunteers and Militia, is much more formidable behind entrenchments than when attempting to manœuvre in a difficult and intricate country such as it is about here. But, on the other hand, we have given pause to the invaders, and have certainly gained a few days' time, which will be invaluable to us.

"We shall be able to get on with the line of fortifications that are being constructed to bar the approaches to London, and behind which it will be necessary for us to make our final stand. I do not conceive that it is possible for such an agglomeration of amateur troops as ours are in the main to defeat in the open field such formidable and well-trained forces as the Germans have succeeded in throwing into this country. But when our Navy has regained command of the sea, we hope that we may, before very long, place our unwelcome visitors 'between the devil and the deep sea'—the part of the devil being played by our brave troops finally concentrated behind the strong defences of the metropolis. In short, that the Germans may run out of ammunition and provisions. For if communication with the Fatherland is effectively cut, they must starve, unless they have previously compelled our submission; for it is impossible for an army of the size that has invaded us to live on the country.

"No doubt hundreds, nay thousands, of our non-militant country-men—and, alas! women and children—will starve before the German troops are conquered by famine, that most terrible of enemies; but this issue seems to be the only possible one that will save the country.

"But enough of these considerations of the future. It is time that I should relate what I can of the glorious victory which our gallant defenders have torn from the enemy. I do not think that I am giving any information away if I state that the British position lay mainly between Saffron Walden and Royston, the headquarters respectively of the IInd and IIIrd Army Corps. The IVth Corps was at Baldock, thrown back to cover the left flank and protect our communications by the Great Northern Railway. A detached force, from what command supplied it is not necessary or advisable to say, was strongly entrenched on the high ground north-west of Helions Bumpstead, serving to strengthen our right. Our main line of defence—very thinly held in some parts—began a little to the south-east of Saffron Walden, and ran westwards along a range of high ground through Elmdon and Chrishall to Heydon. Here it turned south through Great Chrishall to Little Chrishall, where it again turned west, and occupied the high range south of Royston on which stands the village of Therfield.

"The night before the battle we knew that the greater portion of the German IVth and Garde Corps were concentrated, the former at Newmarket, the 1st Division of the latter at Cambridge, the 2nd on this side of St. Ives, while Frölich's Cavalry Division had been in constant contact with our outposts the greater part of the day previous. The Garde Cavalry Brigade was reported to be well away to the westward towards Kettering, as we suppose, on account of the reports which have been going about of a concentration of Yeomanry and Militia in the hilly country near Northampton. Our Intelligence Department, which appears to have been very well served by its spies, obtained early knowledge of the intention of the Germans to make an attack on our position. In fact, they talked openly of it, and stated at Cambridge and Newmarket that they would not manœuvre at all, and only hoped that we should hold on long enough to our position to enable them to smash up our IInd and IIIrd Corps by a frontal attack, and so clear the road to London. The main roads lent themselves admirably to such strategy, which rendered the reports of their intentions the more probable, for they all converged on our position from their main points of concentration.

"The letter 'W' will exactly serve to show the positions of the contending forces. St. Ives is at the top of the first stroke, Cambridge at the junction of the two shorter centre ones, Newmarket at the top of the last stroke, while the British positions at Royston and Saffron Walden are at the junctions of all four strokes at the bottom of the letter. The strokes also represent the roads, except that from Cambridge three good roads lead towards each of the British positions. The prisoners taken from the Germans in the various preliminary skirmishes also made no bones of boasting that a direct attack was imminent, and our Commander-in-Chief eventually, and rightly as it proved, determined to take the risk of all this information having been specially promulgated by the German Staff to cover totally different intentions, as was indeed quite probable, and to accept it as true. Having made up his mind, he lost no time in taking action. He ordered the IVth Corps under Sir William Packington to move on Potton, twelve miles to the north-west, as soon as it was dark. As many cavalry and mounted infantry as could possibly be spared from Royston were placed at his disposal.

"It ought to be stated that while the auxiliary troops had been busily employed ever since their arrival in entrenching the British position, the greater part of the regular troops had been occupying an advanced line two or three miles to the northward on the lower spurs of the hills, and every possible indication of a determination to hold this as long as possible was afforded to the German reconnoitrers. During the night these troops fell back to the position which had been prepared, the outposts following just before daylight. About 6 a.m. the enemy were reported to be advancing in force along the Icknield Way from Newmarket, and also by the roads running on either bank of the river Cam. Twenty minutes later considerable bodies of German troops were reported at Fowlmere and Melbourn on the two parallel Royston–Cambridge roads. They must have followed very close on the heels of our retiring outposts. It was a very misty morning—down in the low ground over which the enemy were advancing especially so—but at about seven a gust of wind from the westward dispelled the white fog-wreaths that hung about our left front, and enabled our lookouts to get a glimpse along the famous Ermine Street, which runs straight as an arrow from Royston for twenty or thirty miles to the N.N.W.

"Along this ancient Roman way, far as the eye could reach, poured a steady stream of marching men, horse, foot, and artillery. The wind dropped, the mists gathered again, and once more enveloped the invaders in an impenetrable screen. But by this time the whole British line was on the qui vive. Regulars, Militia, and Volunteers were marching down to their chin-deep trenches, while those who were already there busied themselves in improving their loopholes and strengthening their head cover. Behind the ridges of the hills the gunners stood grouped about their 'Long Toms' and heavy howitzers, while the field batteries waited, ready horsed, for orders to gallop under cover of the ridge to whichever set of emplacements should first require to be manned and armed. We had not enough to distribute before the movements of the enemy should, to a certain extent, show his hand.

"About seven o'clock a series of crackling reports from the outskirts of Royston announced that the detachment of Mounted Infantry, who now alone held it, was exchanging shots with the advancing enemy, and in a few minutes, as the morning mistiness cleared off, the General and his staff, who were established at the northern edge of the village of Therfield, three or four hundred feet higher up than the German skirmishers, were able to see the opening of the battle spread like a panorama before them. A thick firing line of drab-costumed Germans extended right across from Holland Hall to the Coach and Horses on the Fowlmere Road. On their left moved two or three compact masses of cavalry, while the infantry reserves were easily apparent in front of the village of Melbourn. Our Mounted Infantry in the village were indistinguishable, but away on the spur to the north-east of Royston a couple of batteries of Horse Artillery were unlimbered and were pushing their guns up to the brow of the hill by hand. In two minutes they were in action, and hard at work.

"Through the glasses the shrapnel could be seen bursting, half a dozen together, in front of the advancing Germans, who began to fall fast. But almost at once came an overwhelming reply from somewhere out of sight behind Melbourn. The whole hilltop around our guns was like a spouting volcano. Evidently big high-explosive shells were being fired from the German field-howitzers. In accordance with previous orders, our horse-gunners at once ran down their guns, limbered up, and started to gallop back towards our main position. Simultaneously a mass of German cavalry deployed into attack formation near the Coach and Horses, and swept down in their direction with the evident intention of cutting off and capturing them. But they reckoned without their escort of Mounted Infantry, who had been lying low behind the long, narrow line of copse north of Lowerfield Farm. Safely ensconced behind this—to cavalry—impassable barrier, the company, all good shots, opened a terrible magazine fire on the charging squadrons as they passed at close range. A Maxim they had with them also swept horses and men away in swathes. The charge was checked, and the guns saved, but we had not finished with the German reiters. Away to the north-east a battery of our 4·7 guns opened on the disorganised cavalry, firing at a range of four thousand yards. Their big shells turned the momentary check into a rout, both the attacking cavalry and their supports galloping towards Fowlmere to get out of range. We had scored the first trick!

"The attacking lines of German Infantry still pressed on, however, and after a final discharge the Mounted Infantry in Royston sprang on their horses and galloped back over Whitely Hill, leaving the town to be occupied by the enemy. To the eastward the thunder of heavy cannon, gradually growing in intensity, proclaimed that the IInd Corps was heavily attacked. Covered by a long strip of plantation, the German IVth Corps contrived to mass an enormous number of guns on a hill about two miles north of the village of Elmdon, and a terrific artillery duel began between them and our artillery entrenched along the Elmdon–Heydon ridge. Under cover of this the enemy began to work his infantry up towards Elmdon, obtaining a certain amount of shelter from the spurs which ran out towards the north-east of our line. Other German troops with guns put in an appearance on the high ground to the north-east of Saffron Walden, near Chesterton Park.

"To describe the fortunes of this fiercely contested battle, which spread along a front of nearly twenty miles, counting from the detached garrison of the hill at Helions Bumpstead—which, by the way, succeeded in holding its ground all day, despite two or three most determined assaults by the enemy—to Kelshall on the left of the British position, would be an impossibility in the space at my disposal. The whole morning it raged all along the northern slopes of the upland held by our gallant troops. The fiercest fighting was, perhaps, in the neighbourhood of Elmdon, where our trenches were more than once captured by the Magdeburg battalions, only to be themselves hurled out again by the rush of the 1st Coldstream Guards, who had been held in reserve near the threatened point. By noon the magnificent old palace at Audley End was in flames. Art treasures which were of inestimable value and absolutely unreplaceable perished in this shocking conflagration. Desperate fighting was going on in the streets of the little town of Saffron Walden, where a mingled mass of Volunteers and Militia strove hard to arrest the advance of a portion of the German Army which was endeavouring to work round the right of our position.

"On our left the Foot Guards and Fusiliers of the 1st German Guard Division, after receiving a terrible pounding from our guns when they poured into Royston at the heels of our Mounted Infantry, had fought their way up the heights to within fifteen hundred yards of our trenches on the upper slopes of the ridge. Farther than that they had been unable to advance. Their close formations offered an excellent target to the rifles of the Volunteers and Militia lining our entrenchments. The attackers had lost men in thousands, and were now endeavouring to dig themselves in as best they could under the hail of projectiles that continually swept the hillside. About noon, too, the 2nd Division of the Garde Corps, after some skirmishing with the Mounted Infantry away on our left front, got into attack formation along the line of the Hitchin and Cambridge Railway, and, after pouring a deluge of projectiles from field guns and howitzers upon our position, advanced upon Therfield with the greatest bravery and determination. They had succeeded by 2 p.m. in driving our men from the end of the spur running northward near Therfield Heath, and managed to get a number of their howitzers up there, and at once opened fire from the cover afforded by several copses out of which our men had been driven.

"In short, things were beginning to look very bad for Old England, and the watchers on the Therfield heights turned their glasses anxiously northward in search of General Sir William Packington's force from Potton. They had not long to wait. At 2.15 the winking flash of a heliograph away near Wendy Place, about eight miles up Ermine Street, announced that the advance guard, consisting of the 1st Royal Welsh Fusiliers, was already at Bassingbourn, and that the main body was close behind, having escaped detection by all the enemy's patrols and flank guards. They were now directly in the rear of the right of the German reserves, who had been pushed forward into the neighbourhood of Royston to support the attack of their main body on the British position. A few minutes later it was evident that the enemy had also become aware of their advent. Two or three regiments hurriedly issued from Royston and deployed to the north-west. But the guns of the Baldock Corps turned such a 'rafale' fire upon them that they hesitated and were lost.

"Every long-range gun in the British entrenchments that would bear was also turned upon them, leaving the infantry and field guns to deal with the troops assaulting their position. The three battalions, as well as a fourth that was sent to their assistance, were simply swept out of existence by this terrible cross-fire. Their remnants streamed away, a disorganised crowd of scattered stragglers, towards Melbourn; while, still holding on to Bassingbourn, the Baldock force moved down on Royston, driving everything before it.

"The most advanced German troops made a final effort to capture our position when they saw what was going on behind them, but it was half-hearted; they were brought to a standstill, and our men, fixing bayonets, sprang from their trenches and charged down upon them with cheers, which were taken up all along the line for miles. The Germans here and there made a partial stand, but in half an hour they were down on the low ground, falling back towards the north-east in the greatest confusion, losing men in thousands from the converging fire of our guns. Their cavalry made a gallant attempt to save the day by charging our troops to the north of Royston. It was a magnificent sight to see their enormous masses sweeping over the ground with an impetus which looked capable of carrying everything before it, but our men, clustering behind the hedges of Ermine Street, mowed them down squadrons at a time. Not one of them reached the roadway. The magnificent Garde Corps was routed."

BATTLE OF ROYSTON
SUNDAY SEPT. 9TH

"The combined IIIrd and IVth Corps now advanced on the exposed right flank of the German IVth Corps, which, fighting gallantly, fell back, doing its best to cover the retreat of its comrades, who, on their part, very much hampered its movements. By nightfall there was no unwounded German south of Whittlesford, except as a prisoner. By this time, too, we were falling back on our original position."

CHAPTER X

BRITISH ABANDON COLCHESTER

ON TUESDAY, 10th SEPTEMBER, the *Daily News* published the following telegram from its war correspondent, Mr. Edgar Hamilton:

CHELMSFORD, MONDAY, SEPT. 9

"I sit down, after a sleepless night, to indite the account of our latest move. We hear that Sheffield has fallen, and our troops are in flight. As, by the time this appears in print, the enemy will of necessity be aware of our abandonment of Colchester, the censor will not, I imagine, prevent the despatch of my letter.

"For our move has been made one of a retrograde nature, and I do not doubt that the cavalry of the German IXth Corps are close behind us and in touch with our own. But I must not, in using the word 'retrograde,' be supposed to criticise in any way the strategy of our generals. For every one here is, I am sure, fully persuaded of the wisdom of the step. Colchester, with its plucky little garrison, was altogether too much 'in the air,' and stood a great risk of being isolated by a converging advance of the IXth and Xth Corps of the German invaders, to say nothing of the XIIth (Saxon) Corps at Maldon, which since the unfortunate battle of Purleigh has shown itself very active to the north and east.

"The Saxons have refrained from attacking our Vth Corps since its repulse, and it has been left almost in peace to entrench its position from Danbury to the southward; but, on the other hand, while not neglecting to further strengthen their already formidable defences between the Blackwater and the Crouch, their cavalry have scoured the country up to the very gates of Colchester. Yesterday morning the 16th Lancers and the 17th Hussars—who had fallen back from Norwich—together with some of the local Yeomanry, moved out by the Tolleshunt d'Arcy and Great Totham roads, and drove in their patrols with some loss. At Tiptree Heath there was a sharp cavalry engagement between our red Lancers and several squadrons of a sky-blue hussar regiment. Our people routed them, but in the pursuit that followed would have fared badly, as they fell in with the four remaining squadrons supported by another complete regiment, had it not been for the opportune arrival of the Household Cavalry Brigade, which had moved north-east from Danbury to co-operate. This completely changed the aspect of affairs. The Germans were soundly beaten, with the loss of a large number of prisoners, and galloped back to Maldon in confusion. In the meantime, the 2nd King's Own Royal Lancaster Regiment and the 5th Battery R.F. Artillery had been sent down to Witham by train, whence they marched up to the high ground near Wickham Bishops. They and the Yeomanry were left there in a position to cover the main London Road and the Great Eastern Railway, and at the same time threaten any movement of the enemy by the Great Totham Road. When the news of our success reached Colchester, soon after midday, we were all very jubilant. In fact, I fear that a great many people spent the afternoon in a species of fool's paradise. And when towards the evening the announcement of our splendid victory at Royston was posted up on the red walls of the fine town hall, and outside the Cups, there was an incipient outbreak of that un-English excitement known as 'Mafficking.'

"But this exultation was fated to be but short-lived, even though the Mayor appeared on the balcony of the Town Hall and addressed the crowd, while the latest news was posted outside the offices of the *Essex Telegraph*, opposite the post office. The wind was in the north, and about 5.45 in the afternoon the sound of a heavy explosion was heard from the direction of Manningtree. I was in the Cups Hotel at the time arranging for an early dinner, and ran out into the street. As I emerged from the archway of the hotel I distinctly heard a second detonation from the same direction. A sudden silence, ominous and unnatural, seemed to fall on the yelping jingoes in the street, in the midst of which the rumble of yet another explosion rolled down on the wind, this time from a more westerly direction. Men asked their neighbours breathlessly as to what all this portended. I myself knew no more than the most ignorant of the crowd, till in an officer who rushed hastily by me in Head Street, on his way into the hotel, I recognised my friend Captain Burton, of the Artillery.

"I buttonholed him at once.

"'Do I know what those explosions were?' repeated he in answer to my inquiry. 'Well, I don't know, but I'm open to bet you five to one that it's the sappers blowing up the bridges over the Stour at Manningtree and Stratford St. Mary.'

"'Then the Germans will have arrived there?' I queried.

"'Most probably. And look here,' he continued, taking me aside by the arm, and lowering his voice, 'you take my tip. We shall be out of this to-night. So you'd best pack up your traps and get into marching order.'

"'Do you know this?' said I.

"'Not officially, or I shouldn't tell you anything about it. But I can put two and two together. We all knew that the General wouldn't be fool enough to try and defend an open town of this size with such a small garrison against a whole army corps, or perhaps more. It would serve no good purpose, and expose the place to destruction and bring all sorts of disaster on the civil population. You could have seen that for yourself, for no attempt whatever has been made to erect defences of any kind; neither have we received any reinforcements at all. If they had meant to defend it they could certainly have contrived to send us some Volunteers and guns at any rate. No, the few troops we have here have done their best in assisting the Danbury Force against the Saxons, and are much too valuable to be left here to be cut off without being able to do much to check the advance of the enemy. If we had been going to try anything of that kind, we should have now been holding the line of the river Stour; but I know we have only small detachments at the various bridges, sufficient only to drive off the enemy's cavalry patrols. By now, having blown up the bridges, I expect they are falling back as fast as they can get. Besides, look here,' he added, 'what do you think that battalion was sent to Wickham Bishops for this morning?'

"I told him my theories as set forth above.

"'Oh, yes, that's all right,' he answered. 'But you may bet your boots that there's more in it than that. In my opinion, the General has had orders to clear out as soon as the enemy are preparing to cross the Stour, and the Lancasters are planted there to protect our left flank from an attack from Maldon while we are retreating on Chelmsford.'

"'But we might fall back on Braintree?' I hazarded.

"'Don't you believe it. We're not wanted there—at least, I mean, not so much as elsewhere. Where we shall come in is to help to fill the gap between Braintree and Danbury. I think, myself, we might just as well have done it before. We have been sending back stores by rail for the last two days. Well, good-bye,' he said, holding out his hand. 'Keep all this to yourself, and mark my words, we'll be off at dusk.'

"Away he went, and convinced that his prognostications were correct—as, indeed, in the main they proved—I hastened to eat my dinner, pay my bill, and get my portmanteau packed and stowed away in my motor. As soon as the evening began to close in I started and made for the barracks, going easy. The streets were still full of people, but they were very quiet, and mostly talking together in scattered groups. A shadow seemed to have fallen on the jubilant crowd of the afternoon, though, as far as I could ascertain, there were no definite rumours of the departure of the troops and the close advent of the enemy.

"When I arrived at the barracks, I saw at once that there was something in the wind, and pulled up alongside the barrack railings, determined to watch the progress of events. I had not long to wait. In about ten minutes a bugle sounded, and the scattered assemblage of men on the barrack-square closed together and solidified into a series of quarter columns. At the same time the Volunteer battalion moved across from the other side of the road and joined the Regular troops. I heard a sharp clatter and jingling behind me, and, looking round, saw the General and his staff with a squad of cavalry canter up the road. They turned into the barrack gate, greeted by a sharp word of command and the rattle of arms from the assembled battalions. As far as I could make out, the General made them some kind of address, after which I heard another word of command, upon which the regiment nearest to the gate formed fours and marched out.

"It was the 2nd Dorsetshire. I watched anxiously to see which way they turned. As I more than expected, they turned in the direction of the London Road. My friend had been right so far, but till the troops arrived at Mark's Tey, where the road forked, I could not be certain whether they were going towards Braintree or Chelmsford. The Volunteers followed; then the Leicestershires, then a long train of artillery, field batteries, big 4·7 guns, and howitzers. The King's Own Scottish Borderers formed the rearguard. With them marched the General and his staff; I saw no cavalry. I discovered afterwards that the General, foreseeing that a retirement was imminent, had ordered the 16th Lancers and the 7th Hussars, after their successful morning performance, to remain till further orders at Kelvedon and Tiptree respectively, so that their horses were resting during the afternoon.

"During the night march the former came back and formed a screen behind the retiring column, while the latter were in a position to observe and check any movement northwards that might be made by the Saxons, at the same time protecting its flank and rear from a possible advance by the cavalry of Von Kronhelm's Army, should they succeed in crossing the river Stour soon enough to be able to press after us in pursuit by either of the two eastern roads leading from Colchester to Maldon. After the last of the departing soldiers had tramped away into the gathering darkness through the mud, which after yesterday's downpour still lay thick upon the roads, I bethought me that I might as well run down to the railway station to see if anything was going on there. I was just in time.

"The electric light disclosed a bustling scene as the last of the ammunition and a certain proportion of stores were being hurried into a long train that stood with steam up ready to be off. The police allowed none of the general public to enter the station, but my correspondent's pass obtained me admission to the departure platform. There I saw several detachments of the Royal Engineers, the Mounted Infantry—minus their horses, which had been already sent on—and some of the Leicestershire Regiment. Many of the men had their arms, legs, or heads bandaged, and bore evident traces of having been in action. I got into conversation with a colour-sergeant of the Engineers, and learned these were the detachments who had been stationed at the bridges over the Stour. It appears there was some sharp skirmishing with the German advance troops before the officers in command had decided that they were in sufficient force to justify them in blowing up the bridges. In fact, at the one at which my informant was stationed, and that the most important one of all, over which the main road from Ipswich passed at Stratford St. Mary, the officer in charge delayed just too long, so that a party of the enemy's cavalry actually secured the bridge, and succeeded in cutting the wires leading to the charges which had been placed in readiness to blow it up. Luckily, the various detachments present rose like one man to the occasion, and, despite a heavy fire, hurled themselves upon the intruders with the bayonet with such determination and impetus, that the bridge was swept clear in a moment. The wires were reconnected, and the bridge cleared of our men just as the Germans, reinforced by several of their supporting squadrons, who had come up at a gallop, dashed upon it in pursuit. The firing key was pressed at this critical moment, and, with a stunning report, a whole troop was blown into the air, the remaining horses, mad with fright, stampeding despite all that their riders could do. The road was cut, and the German advance temporarily checked, while the British detachment made off as fast as it could for Colchester.

"I asked the sergeant how long he thought it would be before the Germans succeeded in crossing it. 'Bless you, sir, I expect they're over by now,' he answered. 'They would be sure to have their bridging companies somewhere close up, and it would not take them more than an hour or two to throw a bridge over that place.' The bridges at Boxted Mill and Nayland had been destroyed previously.

"The railway bridge and the other one at Manningtree were blown up before the Germans could get a footing, and their defenders had come in by rail. But my conversation was cut short, the whistle sounded, the men were hustled on board the train, and it moved slowly out of the station. As for me, I hurried out to my car, and, putting on speed, was soon clear of the town, and spinning along for Mark's Tey. It is about five miles, and shortly before I got there I overtook the marching column. The men were halted, and in the act of putting on their greatcoats. I was stopped here by the rearguard, who took charge of me, and would not let me proceed until permission was obtained from the General.

"Eventually this officer ordered me to be brought to him, I presented my pass; but he said, 'I am afraid that I shall have to ask you either to turn back or to slow down and keep pace with us. In fact, you had better do the latter. I might, indeed, have to exercise my powers and impress your motor, should the exigencies of the Service require it.' I saw that it was best to make virtue of necessity, and replied that it was very much at his service, and that I was very well content to accompany the column. In point of fact, the latter was strictly true, for I wanted to see what was to be seen, and there were no points about going along with no definite idea of where I wanted to get to, with a possible chance of falling into the hands of the Saxons into the bargain. So a Staff officer, who was suffering from a slight wound, was placed alongside me, and the column, having muffled itself in its greatcoats, once more began to plug along through the thickening mire. My position was just in front of the guns, which kept up a monotonous rumble behind me. My companion was talkative, and afforded me a good deal of incidental and welcome information. Thus, just after we started, and were turning to the left at Mark's Tey, a bright glare followed by a loudish report came from the right of the road. 'What's that?' I naturally ejaculated. 'Oh, that will be the sappers destroying the junction with the Sudbury line,' he replied. 'There's the train waiting for them just beyond.'

"So it was. The train that I had seen leaving had evidently stopped after passing the junction, while the line was broken behind it. 'They will do the same after passing the cross line at Witham,' volunteered he.

"A mile or two further on we passed between two lines of horse-men, their faces set northwards and muffled to the eyes in their long cloaks. 'That's some of the 16th,' he said, 'going to cover our rear.'

"So we moved on all night through the darkness and rain, and with the first glimmer of dawn halted at Witham. We had about

NOTICE

CONCERNING WOUNDED BRITISH SOLDIERS

IN COMPLIANCE with an order of the Commander-in-Chief of the German Imperial Army, the Governor-General of East Anglia decrees as follows:—

(1) Every inhabitant of the counties of Norfolk, Suffolk, Essex, Cambridge, Lincolnshire, Yorkshire, Nottingham, Derby, Leicester, Northampton, Rutland, Huntingdon, and Hertford, who gives asylum to or lodges one or more ill or wounded British soldier, is obliged to make a declaration to the mayor of the town or to the local police within 24 hours, stating name, grade, place of birth, and nature of illness or injury.

Every change of domicile of the wounded is also to be notified within 24 hours.

In absence of masters, servants are ordered to make the necessary declarations.

The same order applies to the directors of hospitals, surgeries, or ambulance stations, who receive the British wounded within our jurisdiction.

(2) All mayors are ordered to prepare lists of the British wounded, showing the number, with their names, grade, and place of birth in each district.

(3) The mayor, or the superintendent of police, must send on the 1st and 15th of each month a copy of his lists to the headquarters of the Commander-in-Chief. The first list must be sent on the 15th September.

(4) Any person failing to comply with this order will, in addition to being placed under arrest for harbouring British troops, be fined a sum not exceeding £20.

(5) This decree is to be published in all towns and villages in the Province of East Anglia.

Count VON SCHONBURG-WALDENBURG,
Lieutenant-General, Governor of German East Anglia

IPSWICH, September 6, 1910

nine miles still to go to reach Chelmsford, which I learned was our immediate destination, and it was decided to rest here for an hour, while the men made the best breakfast they could from the contents of their haversacks. But the villagers brought out hot tea and coffee, and did the best they could for us, so we did not fare so badly after all. As for me, I got permission to go on, taking with me my friend the Staff officer, who had despatches to forward from Chelmsford. I pushed on at full speed. We were there in a very short space of time, and during the morning I learned that the Braintree Army was falling back on Dunmow, and that the Colchester garrison was to assist in holding the line of the river Chelmer."

CHAPTER XI

FIERCE FIGHTING AT CHELMSFORD

A despatch from Mr. Edgar Hamilton to the *Daily News*, as follows, was published on Saturday, 15th September:

"At Little Waltham I found myself close to the scene of action. About a mile ahead of me the hamlet of Howe Street was in flames and burning furiously. I could see the shells bursting in and all over it in perfect coveys. I could not make out where they were coming from, but an officer I met said he thought the enemy must have several batteries in action on the high ground about Littley Green, a mile and a half to the north on the opposite side of the river. I crossed over myself, and got up on the knoll where the Leicestershires and Dorsets had been stationed, together with a number of the 4·7-inch guns brought from Colchester.

"This piece of elevated ground is about two miles long, running almost north and south, and at the top of it I got an extensive view to the eastward right away to beyond Witham, as the ground fell all the way. The country was well wooded, and a perfect maze of trees and hedgerows. If there were any Germans down there in this plain they were lying very low indeed, for my glasses did not discover the least indication of their presence. Due east my view was bounded by the high wooded ground about Wickham Bishops and Tiptree Heath, which lay a long blue hummock on the horizon, while to the south-east Danbury Hill, with our big war-balloon floating overhead, was plainly discernible.

"While I gazed on the apparently peaceful landscape I was startled by a nasty, sharp hissing sound, which came momentarily nearer. It seemed to pass over my head, and was followed by a loud bang in the air, where now hung a ring of white smoke. It was a shell from the enemy. Just ahead of me was a somewhat extensive wood; and, urged by some insane impulse of seeking shelter, I left the car, which I ordered my chauffeur to take back for a mile and wait, and made for the close-standing trees. If I had stopped to think I should have realised that the wood gave me actually no protection whatever, and I had not gone far when the crashing of timber and noise of the bursting projectiles overhead and in the undergrowth around made me understand clearly that the Germans were making a special target of the wood, which, I imagine, they thought might conceal some of our troops. I wished heartily that I was seated beside my chauffeur in his fast-receding car.

"However, my first object was to get clear of the wood again, and after some little time I emerged on the west side, right in the middle of a dressing station for the wounded, which had been established in a little hollow. Two surgeons, with their assistants, were already busily engaged with a number of wounded men, most of whom were badly hit by shrapnel bullets about the upper part of the body. I gathered from one or two of the few most slightly wounded men that our people had been, and were, very hardly put to it to hold their own. 'I reckon,' said one of them, a bombardier of artillery, 'that the enemy must have got more than a hundred guns firing at us, and at Howe Street village. If we could only make out where the foreign devils were,' continued my informant, 'our chaps could have knocked a good many of them out with our four-point-sevens, especially if we could have got a go at them before they got within range themselves. But they must have somehow contrived to get them into position during the night, for we saw nothing of them coming up. They are somewhere about Chatley, Fairstead Lodge, and Little Leighs, but as we can't locate them exactly, and only have ten guns up here, it don't give us much chance, does it?' Later I saw an officer of the Dorsets, who confirmed the gunner's story, but added that our people were well entrenched and the guns well concealed, so that none of the latter had been put out of action, and he thought we should be able to hold on to the hill all right. I regained my car without further adventure, bar several narrow escapes from stray shell, and made my way back as quickly as possible to Chelmsford.

"The firing went on all day, not only to the northward, but also away to the southward, where the Saxons, while not making any determined attack, kept the Vth Corps continually on the alert, and there was an almost continuous duel between the heavy pieces. As it appeared certain that the knoll I had visited in the forenoon was the main objective of the enemy's attack, reinforcements had been more than once sent up there, but the German shell fire was so heavy that they found it almost impossible to construct the additional cover required. Several batteries of artillery were despatched to Pleshy and Rolphy Green to keep down, if possible, the fire of the Germans, but it seemed to increase rather than diminish. They must have had more guns in action than they had at first. Just at dusk their infantry had made the first openly offensive movement.

"Several lines of skirmishers suddenly appeared in the valley between Little Leighs and Chatley, and advanced towards Lyonshall Wood, at the north end of the knoll east of Little Waltham. They were at first invisible from the British gun positions on the other side of the Chelmer, and when they cleared the spur on which Hyde Hall stands they were hardly discernible in the gathering darkness. The Dorsetshire and the other battalions garrisoning the knoll manned their breastworks as they got within rifle range, and opened fire, but they were still subjected to the infernal rafale from the Hanoverian guns on the hills to the northward, and to make matters worse at this critical moment the Xth Corps brought a long line of guns into action between Flacks Green and Great Leighs Wood, in which position none of the British guns except a few on the knoll itself could reach them. Under this cross hurricane of projectiles the British fire was quite beaten down, and the Germans followed up their skirmishers by almost solid masses, which advanced with all but impunity save for the fire of the few British long-range guns at Pleshy Mount. There they were firing almost at random, as the gunners could not be certain of the exact whereabouts of their objectives. There was a searchlight on the knoll, but at the first sweep of its ray it was absolutely demolished by a blizzard of shrapnel. Every German gun was turned upon it. The Hanoverian battalions now swarmed to the assault, disregarding the gaps made in their ranks by the magazine fire of the defenders as soon as their close advance masked the fire of their own cannon.

BATTLE OF CHELMSFORD
POSITION ON THE EVENING OF SEPTEMBER 11

"The British fought desperately. Three several times they hurled back at the attackers, but, alas! we were overborne by sheer weight of numbers. Reinforcements summoned by telephone, as soon as the determined nature of the attack was apparent, were hurried up from every available source, but they only arrived in time to be carried down the hill again in the rush of its defeated defenders, and to share with them the storm of projectiles from the quick-firers of General von Kronhelm's artillery, which had been pushed forward during the assault. It was with the greatest difficulty that the shattered and disorganised troops were got over the river at Little Waltham. As it was, hundreds were drowned in the little stream, and hundreds of others killed and wounded by the fire of the Germans. They had won the first trick. This was indisputable, and as ill news travels apace, a feeling of gloom fell upon our whole force, for it was realised that the possession of the captured knoll would enable the enemy to mass troops almost within effective rifle range of our river line of defence. I believe that it was proposed by some officers on the staff that we should wheel back our left and take up a fresh position during the night. This was overruled, as it was recognised that to do so would enable the enemy to push in between the Dunmow force and our own, and so cut our general line in half. All that could be done was to get up every available gun and bombard the hill during the night in order to hamper the enemy in his preparations for further forward movement and in his entrenching operations.

"Had we more men at our disposal I suppose there is little doubt that a strong counter-attack would have been made on the knoll almost immediately; but in the face of the enormous numbers opposed to us, I imagine that General Blennerhasset did not feel justified in denuding any portion of our position of its defenders. So all through the dark hours the thunder of the great guns went on. In spite of the cannonade the Germans turned on no less than three searchlights from the southern end of the knoll about midnight. Two were at once put out by our fire, but the third managed to exist for over half an hour, and enabled the Germans to see how hard we were working to improve our defences along the river bank. I am afraid that they were by this means able to make themselves acquainted with the positions of a great number of our trenches. During the night our patrols reported being unable to penetrate beyond Pratt's Farm, Mount Maskell, and Porter's Farm on the Colchester Road. Everywhere they were forced back by superior numbers. The enemy were fast closing in upon us. It was a terrible night in Chelmsford.

"There was panic on every hand. A man mounted the Tindal statue and harangued the crowd, urging the people to rise and compel the Government to stop the war. A few young men endeavoured to load the old Crimean cannon in front of the Shire Hall, but found it clogged with rust and useless. People fled from the villa residences in Brentwood Road into the town for safety, now that the enemy were upon them. The banks in High Street were being barricaded, and the stores still remaining in the various grocers' shops, Luckin Smith's, Martin's, Cramphorn's, and Pearke's, were rapidly being concealed from the invaders. All the ambulance waggons entering the town were filled with wounded, although as many as possible were sent south by train. By one o'clock in

DECREE

CONCERNING THE POWER OF COUNCILS OF WAR

WE, GOVERNOR-GENERAL OF EAST ANGLIA, in virtue of the powers conferred upon us by His Imperial Majesty the German Emperor, Commander-in-Chief of the German Armies, order, for the maintenance of the internal and external security of the counties of the Government-General:—

ARTICLE I.—Any individual guilty of incendiarism or of wilful inundation, of attack, or of resistance with violence against the Government-General or the agents of the civil or military authorities, of sedition, of pillage, of theft with violence, of assisting prisoners to escape, or of exciting soldiers to treasonable acts, shall be PUNISHED BY DEATH.

In the case of any extenuating circumstances, the culprit may be sent to penal servitude with hard labour for twenty years.

ARTICLE II.—Any person provoking or inciting an individual to commit the crimes mentioned in Article I. will be sent to penal servitude with hard labour for ten years.

ARTICLE III.—Any person propagating false reports relative to the operations of war or political events will be imprisoned for one year, and fined up to £100.

In any case where the affirmation or propagation may cause prejudice against the German Army, or against any authorities or functionaries established by it, the culprit will be sent to hard labour for ten years.

ARTICLE IV.—Any person usurping a public office, or who commits any act or issues any order in the name of a public functionary, will be imprisoned for five years, and fined £150.

ARTICLE V.—Any person who voluntarily destroys or abstracts any documents, registers, archives, or public documents deposited in public offices, or passing through their hands in virtue of their functions as government or civic officials, will be imprisoned for two years, and fined £150.

ARTICLE VI.—Any person obliterating, damaging, or tearing down official notices, orders, or proclamations of any sort issued by the German authorities will be imprisoned for six months, and fined £80.

ARTICLE VII.—Any resistance or disobedience of any order given in the interests of public security by military commanders and other authorities, or any provocation or incitement to commit such disobedience, will be punished by one year's imprisonment, or a fine of not less than £150.

ARTICLE VIII.—All offences enumerated in ARTICLES I–VII are within the jurisdiction of the Councils of War.

ARTICLE IX.—It is within the competence of Councils of War to adjudicate upon all other crimes and offences against the internal and external security of the English provinces occupied by the German Army, and also upon all crimes against the military or civil authorities, or their agents, as well as murder, the fabrication of false money, of blackmail, and all other serious offences.

ARTICLE X.—Independent of the above, the military jurisdiction already proclaimed will remain in force regarding all actions tending to imperil the security of the German troops, to damage their interests, or to render assistance to the Army of the British Government.

Consequently, there will be PUNISHED BY DEATH, and we expressly repeat this, all persons who are not British soldiers and—

(a) Who serve the British Army or the Government as spies, or receive British spies, or give them assistance or asylum.
(b) Who serve as guides to British troops, or mislead the German troops when charged to act as guides.
(c) Who shoot, injure, or assault any German soldier or officer.
(d) Who destroy bridges or canals, interrupt railways or telegraph lines, render roads impassable, burn munitions of war, provisions, or quarters of the troops.
(e) Who take arms against the German troops.

ARTICLE XI.—The organisation of Councils of War mentioned in ARTICLES VIII. and IX. of the Law of May 2, 1870, and their procedure are regulated by special laws which are the same as the summary jurisdiction of military tribunals. In the case of Article X. there remains in force the Law of July 21, 1867, concerning the military jurisdiction applicable to foreigners.

ARTICLE XII.—The present order is proclaimed and put into execution on the morrow of the day upon which it is affixed in the public places of each town and village, The Governor-General of East Anglia,

COUNT VON SCHONBURG-WALDENBERG,
LIEUTENANT-GENERAL

Norwich, September 7th, 1910

the morning, however, most of the civilian inhabitants had fled. The streets were empty, but for the bivouacking troops and the never-ending procession of wounded men. The General and his staff were deliberating to a late hour in the Shire Hall, at which he had established his headquarters. The booming of the guns waxed and waned till dawn, when a furious outburst announced that the second act of the tragedy was about to open.

"I had betaken myself at once to the round tower of the church, next the Stone Bridge, from which I had an excellent view both east and north. The first thing that attracted my eye was the myriad flashings of rifle fire in the dimness of the breaking day. They reached in a continuous line of coruscations from Boreham Hall, opposite my right hand, to the knoll by Little Waltham, a distance of three or four miles, I should say. The enemy were driving in all our outlying and advanced troops by sheer weight of numbers. Presently the heavy batteries at Danbury began pitching shell over in the direction of the firing, but as the German line still advanced, it had not apparently any very great effect. The next thing that happened was a determined attack on the village of Howe Street made from the direction of Hyde Hall. This is about two miles north of Little Waltham. In spite of our incessant fire, the Germans had contrived to mass a tremendous number of guns and howitzers on and behind the knoll they captured last night, and there was any quantity more on the ridge above Hyde Hall. All these terrible weapons concentrated their fire for a few moments on the blackened ruins of Howe Street. Not a mouse could have lived there. The little place was simply pulverised.

"Our guns at Pleshy Mount and Rolphy Green, aided by a number of field batteries, in vain endeavoured to make head against them. They were outnumbered by six to one. Under cover of this tornado of iron and fire, the enemy pushed several battalions over the river, making use of the ruins of the many bridges about there which had been hastily destroyed, and which they repaired with planks and other materials they brought along with them. They lost a large number of men in the process, but they persevered, and by ten o'clock were in complete possession of Howe Street, Langley's Park, and Great Waltham, and moving in fighting formation against Pleshy Mount and Rolphy Green, their guns covering their advance with a perfectly awful discharge of shrapnel. Our cannon on the ridge at Partridge Green took the attackers in flank, and for a time checked their advance, but, drawing upon themselves the attention of the German artillery, on the south end of the knoll, were all but silenced.

"As soon as this was effected another strong column of Germans followed in the footsteps of the first, and deploying to the left, secured the bridge at Little Waltham, and advanced against the gun positions on Partridge Green. This move turned all our river bank entrenchments right down to Chelmsford. Their defenders were now treated to the enfilade fire of a number of Hanoverian batteries that galloped down to Little Waltham. They stuck to their trenches gallantly, but presently when the enemy obtained a footing on Partridge Green they were taken in reverse, and compelled to fall back, suffering terrible losses as they did so. The whole of the infantry of the Xth Corps, supported—as we understand—by a division which had joined them from Maldon, now moved down on Chelmsford. In fact, there was a general advance of the three combined armies stretching from Partridge Green on the west to the railway line on the east. The defenders of the trenches facing east were hastily withdrawn, and thrown back on Writtle. The Germans followed closely with both infantry and guns, though they were for a time checked near Scot's Green by a dashing charge of our cavalry brigade, consisting of the 16th Lancers and the 7th, 14th, and 20th Hussars, and the Essex and Middlesex Yeomanry. We saw nothing of their cavalry, for a reason that will be apparent later. By one o'clock fierce fighting was going on all round the town, the German hordes enveloping it on all sides but one. We had lost a great number of our guns, or at any rate had been cut off from them by the German successes around Pleshy Mount, and in all their assaults on the town they had been careful to keep out of effective range of the heavy batteries on Danbury Hill. These, by the way, had their own work cut out for them, as the Saxon artillery were heavily bombarding the hill with their howitzers. The British forces were in a critical situation. Reinforcements—such as could be spared—were hurried up from the Vth Army Corps, but they were not very many in numbers, as it was necessary to provide against an attack by the Saxon Corps. By three o'clock the greater part of the town was in the hands of the Germans, despite the gallant way in which our men fought them from street to street, and house to house. A dozen fires were spreading in every direction, and fierce fighting was going on at Writtle. The overpowering numbers of the Germans, combined with their better organisation, and the number of properly trained officers at their disposal, bore the British mixed Regular and Irregular forces back, and back again.

"Fearful of being cut off from his line of retreat, General Blenner-hasset, on hearing from Writtle soon after three that the Hanoverians were pressing his left very hard, and endeavouring to work round it, reluctantly gave orders for the troops in Chelmsford to fall back on Widford and Moulsham. There was a lull in the fighting for about half an hour, though firing was going on both at Writtle and Danbury. Soon after four a terrible rumour spread consternation on every side. According to this, an enormous force of cavalry and motor infantry was about to attack us in the rear. What had actually happened was not quite so bad as this, but quite bad enough. It seems, according to our latest information, that almost the whole of the cavalry belonging to the three German Army Corps with whom we were engaged—something like a dozen regiments, with a proportion of horse artillery and all available motorists, having with them several of the new armoured motors carrying light, quick-firing and machine guns—had been massed during the last thirty-six hours behind the Saxon lines extending from Maldon to the River Crouch. During the day they had worked round to the southward, and at the time the rumour reached us were actually attacking Billericay, which was held by a portion of the reserves of our Vth Corps. By the time this news was confirmed the Germans were assaulting Great Baddow, and moving on Danbury from east, north, and west, at the same time resuming the offensive all along the line. The troops at Danbury must be withdrawn or they would be isolated. This difficult manœuvre was executed by way of West Hanningfield. The rest of the Vth Corps conformed to the movement, the Guards Brigade at East Hanningfield forming the rearguard, and fighting fiercely all night through with the Saxon troops, who moved out on the left flank of our retreat. The wreck of the first Corps and the Colchester garrison was now also in full retirement. Ten miles lay between it and the lines at Brentwood, and had the Germans been able to employ cavalry in pursuit, this retreat would have been even more like a rout than it was. Luckily for us the Billericay troops mauled the German cavalry pretty severely, and they were beset in the close country in that neighbourhood by Volunteers, motorists, and every one that the officer commanding at Brentwood could get together in this emergency.

"Some of them actually got upon our line of retreat, but were driven off by our advance guard; others came across the head of the retiring Vth Corps, but the terrain was all against cavalry, and after nightfall most of them had lost their way in the maze of lanes and hedgerows that covered the countryside. Had it not been for this we should probably have been absolutely smashed. As it was, rather more than half our original numbers of men and guns crawled into Brentwood in the early morning, worn out and dead-beat."

Reports from Sheffield also showed the position to be critical.

BOOK II

THE SIEGE OF LONDON

CHAPTER I

THE LINES OF LONDON

THE GERMAN SUCCESSES were continued in the North and Midlands, and, notwithstanding the gallant defence of Sir George Woolmer before Manchester and Sir Henry Hibbard before Birmingham, both cities were captured and occupied by the enemy after terrible losses. London, however, was the chief objective of Von Kronhelm, and towards the Metropolis he now turned his attention.

After the defeat of the British at Chelmsford on that fateful Wednesday, Lord Byfield decided to evacuate his position at Royston and fall back on the northern section of the London defence line, which had been under construction for the last ten days. These hasty entrenchments, which would have been impossible to construct but for the ready assistance of thousands of all classes of the citizens of London and the suburbs, extended from Tilbury on the east to Bushey on the west, passing by the Laindon Hills, Brentwood, Kelvedon, North Weald, Epping, Waltham Abbey, Cheshunt, Enfield Chase, Chipping Barnet, and Elstree. They were more or less continuous, consisting for the most part of trenches for infantry, generally following the lines of existing hedgerows or banks, which often required but little improvement to transform them into well-protected and formidable cover for the defending troops. Where it was necessary to cross open ground they were dug deep and winding, after the fashion adopted by the Boers in the South African War, so that it would be difficult, if not impossible, to enfilade them.

Special bomb-proof covers for the local reserves were also constructed at various points, and the ground in front ruthlessly cleared of houses, barns, trees, hedges, and everything that might afford shelter to an advancing enemy. Every possible military obstacle was placed in front of the lines that time permitted, abattis, military pits, wire entanglements, and small ground mines. At the more important points along the fifty miles of entrenchments, field works and redoubts for infantry were built, most of them being armed with 4·7 or even 6 and 7·5 in. guns, which had been brought from Woolwich, Chatham, Portsmouth, and Devonport, and mounted on whatever carriages could be adapted or improvised for the occasion.

The preparation of the London lines was a stupendous undertaking, but the growing scarceness and dearness of provisions assisted in a degree, as no free rations were issued to any able-bodied man unless he went out to work at the fortifications. All workers were placed under military law. There were any number of willing workers who proffered their services in this time of peril. Thousands of men came forward asking to be enlisted and armed. The difficulty was to find enough weapons and ammunition for them, to say nothing of the question of uniform and equipment, which loomed very large indeed. The attitude of the Germans, as set forth in Von Kronhelm's proclamations, precluded the employment of fighting men dressed in civilian garb, and their attitude was a perfectly natural and justifiable one by all the laws and customs of war.

It became necessary, therefore, that all men sent to the front should be dressed as soldiers in some way or another. In addition to that splendid corps, the Legion of Frontiersmen, many new armed organisations had sprung into being, some bearing the most fantastic names, such as the "Whitechapel War-to-the-Knives," the "Kensington Cowboys," the "Bayswater Braves," and the "Southwark Scalphunters." All the available khaki and blue serge was used up in no time; even though those who were already in possession of ordinary lounge suits of the latter material were encouraged to have them altered into uniforms by the addition of stand-up collars and facings of various colours, according to their regiments and corps.

Only the time during which these men were waiting for their uniforms was spent in drill in the open spaces of the Metropolis. As soon as they were clothed, they were despatched to that portion of the entrenchments to which their corps had been allocated, and there, in the intervals of their clearing and digging operations, they were hustled through a brief musketry course, which consisted for the most part in firing. The question of the provision of officers and N.C.O.s was an almost insuperable one. Retired men came forward on every side, but the supply was by no means equal to the demand, and they themselves in many instances were absolutely out of date as far as knowledge of modern arms and conditions were concerned. However, every one, with but very few exceptions, did his utmost, and by the 11th or 12th of the month the entrenchments were practically completed, and manned by upwards of 150,000 "men with muskets" of stout heart and full of patriotism, but in reality nothing but an army *pour rire* so far as efficiency was concerned.

The greater part of the guns were also placed in position, especially on the north and eastern portions of the lines, and the remainder were being mounted as fast as it was practicable. They were well manned by Volunteer and Militia Artillerymen, drawn from every district which the invaders had left accessible. By the 13th the eastern section of the fortifications was strengthened by the arrival of the remnants of the Ist and Vth Army Corps, which had been so badly defeated at Chelmsford, and no time was lost in reorganising them and distributing them along the lines, thereby, to a certain extent, leavening the unbaked mass of their improvised defenders. It was generally expected that the enemy would follow up the success by an immediate attack on Brentwood, the main barrier between Von Kronhelm and his objective—our great Metropolis. But, as it turned out, he had a totally different scheme in hand. The orders to Lord Byfield to evacuate the position he had maintained with such credit against the German Garde and IVth Corps have already been referred to. Their reason was obvious. Now that there was no organised resistance on his right, he stood in danger of being cut off from London, the defences of which were now in pressing need of his men. A large amount of rolling stock was at once despatched to Saffron Walden and Buntingford by the G.E.R. and to Baldock by the G.N.R., to facilitate the withdrawal of his troops and stores, and he was given an absolutely free hand as to how these were to be used, all lines being kept clear and additional trains kept at his disposal at their London termini.

September 13 proved a memorable date in the history of England.

The evacuation of the Baldock–Saffron Walden position could not possibly have been carried out in good order on such short notice, had not Lord Byfield previously worked the whole thing out in readiness. He could not help feeling that, despite his glorious victory on the ninth, a turn of Fortune's wheel might necessitate a retirement on London sooner or later, and, like the good General that he was, he made every preparation both for this, and other eventualities. Among other details, he had arranged that the mounted infantry should be provided with plenty of strong light wire. This was intended for the express benefit of Frölich's formidable cavalry brigade, which he foresaw would be most dangerous to his command in the event of a retreat. As soon, therefore, as the retrograde movement commenced, the mounted infantry began to stretch their wires across every road, lane and byway leading to the north and north-east. Some wires were laid low, within a foot of the ground, others high up, where they could catch a rider about the neck or breast. This operation they carried out again and again, after the troops had passed, at various points on the route of the retreat. Thanks to the darkness, this device well fulfilled its purpose. Frölich's brigade was on the heels of the retreating British soon after midnight, but, as it was impossible for them to move over the enclosed country at night, his riders were confined to the roads, and the accidents and delays occasioned by the wires were so numerous and disconcerting that their advance had to be conducted with such caution that as a pursuit it was of no use at all. Even the infantry and heavy guns of the retiring British got over the ground nearly twice as fast. After two or three hours of this, only varied by occasional volleys from detachments of our mounted infantry, who sometimes waited in rear of their snares to let fly at the German cavalry before galloping back to lay others, the enemy recognised the fact, and, withdrawing their cavalry till daylight, replaced them by infantry, but so much time had been lost that the British had got several miles' start.

As has been elsewhere chronicled, the brigade of four regular battalions with their guns, and a company of Engineers which were to secure the passage of the Stort and protect the left flank of the retirement, left Saffron Walden somewhere about 10.30 p.m. The line was clear, and they arrived at Sawbridgeworth in four long trains in a little under an hour. Their advent did not arouse the sleeping village, as the station lies nearly three-quarters of a mile distant on the further side of the river. It may be noted in passing that while the Stort is but a small stream, easily fordable in most places, yet it was important, if possible, to secure the bridges to prevent delay in getting over the heavy guns and waggons of the retiring British. A delay and congestion at the points selected for passage might, with a close pursuit, easily lead to disaster. Moreover, the Great Eastern Railway crossed the river by a wooden bridge just north of the village of Sawbridgeworth, and it was necessary to ensure the safe passage of the last trains over it before destroying it to preclude the use of the railway by the enemy.

There were two road bridges on the Great Eastern Railway near the village of Sawbridgeworth, which might be required by the Dunmow force, which was detailed to protect the same flank rather more to the northward. The most important bridge, that over which the main body of the Saffron Walden force was to retire, with all the impedimenta it had had time to bring away with it, was between Sawbridgeworth and Harlow, about a mile north of the latter village, but much nearer its station. Thither, then, proceeded the leading train with the Grenadiers, four 4·7 guns, and half a company of Royal Engineers with bridging materials. Their task was to construct a second bridge to relieve the traffic over the permanent one. The Grenadiers left one company at the railway station, two in Harlow village, which they at once commenced to place in a state of defence, much to the consternation of the villagers, who had not realised how close to them were trending the red footsteps of war. The remaining five companies with the other four guns turned northward, and after marching another mile or so occupied the enclosures round Durrington House and the higher ground to its north. Here the guns were halted on the road. It was too dark to select the best position for them, for it was now only about half an hour after midnight. The three other regiments which detrained at Sawbridgeworth were disposed as follows, continuing the line of the Grenadiers to the northward. The Rifles occupied Hyde Hall, formerly the seat of the

Earls of Roden, covering the operations of the Engineers, who were preparing the railway bridge for destruction, and the copses about Little Hyde Hall on the higher ground to the eastward.

The Scots Guards with four guns were between them and the Grenadiers, and distributed between Sheering village and Gladwyns House, from the neighbourhood of which it was expected that the guns would be able to command the Chelmsford Road for a considerable distance. The Seaforth Highlanders for the time being were stationed on a road running parallel to the railway, from which branch roads led to both the right, left, and centre of the position. An advanced party of the Rifle Brigade was pushed forward to Hatfield Heath with instructions to patrol towards the front and flanks, and, if possible, establish communication with the troops expected from Dunmow. By the time all this was completed it was getting on for 3 a.m. on the 13th. At this hour the advanced guard of the Germans coming from Chelmsford was midway between Leaden Roding and White Roding, while the main body was crossing the small River Roding by the shallow ford near the latter village. Their few cavalry scouts were, however, exploring the roads and lanes some little way ahead. A collision was imminent. The Dunmow force had not been able to move before midnight, and, with the exception of one regular battalion, the 1st Leinsters, which was left behind to the last and crowded into the only train available, had only just arrived at the northern edge of Hatfield Forest, some four miles directly north of Hatfield Heath. The Leinsters, who left Dunmow by train half an hour later, had detrained at this point at one o'clock, and just about three had met the patrols of the Rifles. A Yeomanry corps from Dunmow was also not far off, as it turned to its left at the cross-roads east of Takely, and was by this time in the neighbourhood of Hatfield Broad Oak. In short, all three forces were converging, but the bulk of the Dunmow force was four miles away from the point of convergence.

It was still profoundly dark when the Rifles at Hatfield Heath heard a dozen shots cracking through the darkness to their left front. Almost immediately other reports resounded from due east. Nothing could be seen beyond a very few yards, and the men of the advanced company drawn up at the cross-roads in front of the village inn fancied they now and again saw figures dodging about in obscurity, but were cautioned not to fire till their patrols had come in, for it was impossible to distinguish friend from foe. Shots still rattled out here and there to the front. About ten minutes later the captain in command, having got in his patrols, gave the order to fire at a black blur that seemed to be moving towards them on the Chelmsford Road. There was no mistake this time. The momentary glare of the discharge flashed on the shiny "pickel-haubes" of a detachment of German infantry, who charged forward with a loud "Hoch!" The Riflemen, who already had their bayonets fixed, rushed to meet them, and for a few moments there was a fierce stabbing affray in the blackness of the night. The Germans, who were but few in number, were overpowered, and beat a retreat, having lost several of their men. The Rifles, according to their orders, having made sure of the immediate proximity of the enemy, now fell back to the rest of their battalion at Little Hyde Hall, and all along the banks and hedges which covered the British front, our men, rifle in hand, peered eagerly into the darkness ahead of them.

Nothing happened for quite half an hour, and the anxious watchers were losing some of their alertness, when a heavy outburst of firing re-echoed from Hatfield Heath. To explain this we must return to the Germans. Von der Rudesheim, on obtaining touch with the British, at once reinforced his advanced troops, and they, a whole battalion strong, advanced into the hamlet meeting with no resistance. Almost simultaneously two companies of the Leinsters entered it from the northward. There was a sudden and unexpected collision on the open green, and a terrible fire was exchanged at close quarters, both sides losing very heavily. The British, however, were borne back by sheer weight of numbers, and, through one of those unfortunate mistakes that insist on occurring in warfare, were charged as they fell back by the leading squadrons of the Yeomanry who were coming up from Hatfield Broad Oak. The officer commanding the Leinsters decided to wait till it was a little lighter before again attacking the village. He considered that, as he had no idea of the strength of the enemy, he had best wait till the arrival of the troops now marching through Hatfield Forest. Von der Rudesheim, on his part, mindful of his instructions, determined to try to hold the few scattered houses on the north side of the heath which constituted the village, with the battalion already in it, and push forward with the remainder of his force towards Harlow. His first essay along the direct road *via* Sheering was repulsed by the fire of the Scots Guards lining the copses about Gladwyns. He now began to have some idea of the British position, and made his preparations to assault it at daybreak.

To this end he sent forward two of his batteries into Hatfield Heath, cautiously moved the rest of his force away to the left, arranged his battalions in the valley of the Pincey Brook ready for attacking Sheering and Gladwyns, placed one battalion in reserve at Down Hall, and stationed his remaining battery near Newman's End. By this time there was beginning to be a faint glimmer of daylight in the east, and, as the growing dawn began to render vague outlines of the nearer objects dimly discernible, hell broke loose along the peaceful countryside. A star shell fired from the battery at Newman's End burst and hung out a brilliant white blaze that fell slowly over Sheering village, lighting up its walls and roofs and the hedges along which lay its defenders, was the signal for the Devil's Dance to begin. Twelve guns opened with a crash from Hatfield Heath, raking the Gladwyns enclosures and the end of Sheering village with a deluge of shrapnel, whilst an almost solid firing line advanced rapidly against it, firing heavily.

The British replied lustily with gun, rifle, and maxim, the big high-explosive shells bursting amid the advancing Germans and among the houses of Hatfield Heath with telling effect. But the German assaulting lines had but six or seven hundred yards to go. They had been trained above all things to ignore losses and to push on at all hazards. The necessity for this had not been confused in their minds by maxims about the importance of cover, so the south side of the village street was taken at a rush. Von der Rudesheim continued to pile on his men, and, fighting desperately, the Guards-men were driven from house to house and from fence to fence. All this time the German battery at Newman's End continued to fire star shells with rhythmical regularity, lighting up the inflamed countenances of the living combatants, and the pale up-turned faces of the dead turned to heaven as if calling for vengeance on their slayers. In the midst of this desperate fighting the Leinsters, supported by a Volunteer and a Militia regiment, which had just come up, assaulted Hatfield Heath. The Germans were driven out of it with the loss of a couple of their guns, but hung on to the little church, around which such a desperate conflict was waged that the dead above ground in that diminutive God's acre outnumbered the "rude forefathers of the hamlet" who slept below.

It was now past five o'clock in the morning, and by this time strong reinforcements might have been expected from Dunmow, but, with the exception of the Militia and Volunteer battalions just referred to, who had pushed on at the sound of the firing, none were seen coming up. The fact was that they had been told off to certain positions in the line of defence they had been ordered to take up, and had been slowly and carefully installing themselves therein. Their commanding officer, Sir Jacob Stellenbosch, thought that he must carry out the exact letter of the orders he had received from Lord Byfield, and paid little attention to the firing except to hustle his battalion commanders, to try to get them into their places as soon as possible. He was a pig-headed man into the bargain, and would listen to no remonstrance. The two battalions which had arrived so opportunely had been at the head of the column, and had pushed forward "on their own" before he could prevent them. At this time the position was as follows: One German battalion was hanging obstinately on to the outskirts of Hatfield Heath; two were in possession of the copses about Gladwyns; two were in Sheering village, or close up to it, and the sixth was still in reserve at Down Hall. On the British side the Rifles were in their original position at Little Hyde Hall where also were three guns, which had been got away from Gladwyns. The Seaforths had come up, and were now firing from about Quickbury, while the Scots Guards, after suffering fearful losses, were scattered, some with the Highlanders, others with the five companies of the Grenadiers, who with their four guns still fought gallantly on between Sheering and Durrington House.

CHAPTER II

REPULSE OF THE GERMANS

THE TERRIBLE FIRE of the swarms of Germans who now lined the edges of Sheering village became too much for the four 4·7 guns on the open ground to the south.

Their gunners were shot down as fast as they touched their weapons, and when the German field battery at Newman's End, which had been advanced several hundred yards, suddenly opened a flanking fire of shrapnel upon them, it was found absolutely impossible to serve them. A gallant attempt was made to withdraw them by the Harlow Road, but their teams were shot down as soon as they appeared. This enfilade fire, too, decimated the Grenadiers and the remnant of the Scots, though they fought on to the death, and a converging attack of a battalion from Down Hall and another from Sheering drove them down into the grounds of Durrington House, where fighting still went on savagely for some time afterwards.

Von der Rudesheim had all but attained a portion of his object, which was to establish his guns in such a position that they could fire on the main body of the British troops when they entered Sawbridgeworth by the Cambridge Road. The place where the four guns with the Grenadiers had been stationed was within 3,000 yards of any part of that road between Harlow and Sawbridgeworth. But this spot was still exposed to the rifle fire of the Seaforths, who held Quickbury. Von der Rudesheim therefore determined to swing forward his left, and either drive them back down the hill towards the river, or at least to so occupy them that he could bring up his field-guns to their chosen position without losing too many of his gunners.

By six o'clock, thanks to his enormous local superiority in numbers, he had contrived to do this, and now the opposing forces with the exception of the British Grenadiers, who still fought with a German battalion between Durrington House and Harlow, faced each other north and south, instead of east and west, as they were at the beginning of the fight. Brigadier-General Lane-Edgeworth, who was in command of the British, had been sending urgent messages for reinforcements to the Dunmow Force, but when its commanding officer finally decided to turn his full strength in the direction of the firing, it took so long to assemble and form up the Volunteer regiments who composed the bulk of his command that it was past seven before the leading battalion had deployed to assist in the attack which it was decided to make against the German right. Meantime, other important events had transpired.

Von der Rudesheim had found that the battalion which was engaged with the Grenadiers could not get near Harlow village, or either the river or railway bridge at that place, both of which he wished to destroy. But his scouts had reported a lock and wooden footbridge immediately to the westward between Harlow and Sawbridgeworth, just abreast of the large wooded park surrounding Pishobury House on the farther side. He determined to send two companies over by this, their movements being hidden from the English by the trees. After crossing, they found themselves confronted by a backwater, but, trained in crossing rivers, they managed to ford and swim over, and advanced through the park towards Harlow Bridge. While this was in progress, a large force was reported marching south on the Cambridge Road.

While Von der Rudesheim, who was at the western end of Sheering hamlet, was looking through his glasses at the new arrivals on the scene of action—who were without doubt the main body of the Royston command, which was retiring under the personal supervision of Lord Byfield—a puff of white smoke rose above the trees about Hyde Hall, and at top speed four heavily loaded trains shot into sight going south. These were the same ones that had brought down the Regular British troops, with whom he was now engaged. They had gone north again, and picked up a number of Volunteer battalions belonging to the retreating force just beyond Bishop's Stortford. But so long a time had been taken in entraining the troops in the darkness and confusion of the retreat that their comrades who had kept to the road arrived almost simultaneously.

Von der Rudesheim signalled, and sent urgent orders for his guns to be brought up to open fire on them, but by the time the first team had reached him the last of the trains had disappeared from sight into the cutting at Harlow Station. But even now it was not too late to open fire on the troops entering Sawbridgeworth.

Things were beginning to look somewhat bad for Von der Rudesheim's little force. The pressure from the north was increasing every moment, his attack on the retreating troops had failed, he had not so far been able to destroy the bridges at Harlow, and every minute the likelihood of his being able to do so grew more remote. To crown all, word was brought him that the trains which had just slipped by were disgorging men in hundreds along the railway west of Harlow Station, and that these troops were beginning to move forward as if to support the British Grenadiers, who had been driven back towards Harlow. In fact, he saw that there was even a possibility of his being surrounded. But he had no intention of discontinuing the fight. He knew he could rely on the discipline and mobility of his well-trained men under almost any conditions, and he trusted, moreover, that the promised reinforcements would not be very long in turning up. But he could not hold on just where he was. He accordingly, by various adroit manœuvres, threw back his right to Down Hall, whose copses and plantations afforded a good deal of cover, and, using this as a pivot, gradually wheeled back his left till he had taken up a position running north and south from Down Hall to Matching Tye. He had not effected this difficult manœuvre without considerable loss, but he experienced less difficulty in extricating his left than he had anticipated, since the newly arrived British troops at Harlow, instead of pressing forward against him, had been engaged in moving into a position between Harlow and the hamlet of Foster Street, on the somewhat elevated ground to the south of Matching, which would enable them to cover the further march of the main body of the retreating troops to Epping.

But he had totally lost the two companies he had sent across the river to attack Harlow Bridge. Unfortunately for them, their arrival on the Harlow–Sawbridgeworth Road synchronised with that of the advanced guard of Lord Byfield's command. Some hot skirmishing took place in and out among the trees of Pishobury, and finally the Germans were driven to earth in the big square block of the red-brick mansion itself.

Here they made a desperate stand, fighting hard as they were driven from one storey to another. The staircases ran with blood, the woodwork smouldered and threatened to burst into flame in a dozen places. At length the arrival of a battery of field guns, which unlimbered at close range, induced the survivors to surrender, and they were disarmed and carried off as prisoners with the retreating army.

By the time Von der Rudesheim had succeeded in taking up his new position it was past ten o'clock, and he had been informed by despatches carried by motor-cyclists that he might expect assistance in another hour and a half.

The right column, consisting of the 39th Infantry Brigade of five battalions, six batteries, and a squadron of Dragoons, came into collision with the left flank of the Dunmow force, which was engaged in attacking Von der Rudesheim's right at Down Hall, and endeavouring to surround it. Sir Jacob Stellenbosch, who was in command, in vain tried to change front to meet the advancing enemy. His troops were nearly all Volunteers, who were incapable of quickly manœuvring under difficult circumstances; they were crumpled up and driven back in confusion towards Hatfield Heath. Had Von Kronhelm been able to get in the bulk of his cavalry from their luckless pursuit of the Ist and Vth British Army Corps, who had been driven back on Brentwood the evening previous, and so send a proportion with the 20th Division, few would have escaped to tell the tale. As it was, the unfortunate volunteers were shot down in scores by the *feu d'enfer* with which the artillery followed them up, and lay in twos and threes and larger groups all over the fields, victims of a selfish nation that accepted these poor fellows' gratuitous services merely in order that its citizens should not be obliged to carry out what in every other European country was regarded as the first duty of citizenship—that of learning to bear arms in the defence of the Fatherland.

By this time the greater portion of the retreating British Army, with all its baggage, guns and impedimenta, was crawling slowly along the road from Harlow to Epping. Unaccustomed as they were to marching, the poor Volunteers, who had already covered eighteen or twenty miles of road, were now toiling slowly and painfully along the highway. The regular troops, who had been engaged since early morning, and who were now mostly in the neighbourhood of Moor Hall, east of Harlow, firing at long ranges on Von der Rudesheim's men to keep them in their places while Sir Jacob Stellenbosch attacked their right, were now hurriedly withdrawn and started to march south by a track running parallel to the main Epping Road, between it and that along which the covering force of Volunteers, who had come in by train, were now established in position. The 1st and 2nd Coldstreamers, who had formed Lord Byfield's rearguard during the night, were halted in Harlow village.

Immediately upon the success obtained by his right column, General Richel von Sieberg, who commanded the 20th Hanoverian Division, ordered his two centre and left columns, consisting respectively of the three battalions 77th Infantry and two batteries of Horse Artillery, then at Matching Green, and the three battalions 92nd Infantry, 10th Pioneer Battalion, and five batteries Field Artillery, then between High Laver and Tilegate Green, to turn to their left and advance in fighting formation in a south-westerly direction, with the object of attacking the sorely-harassed troops of Lord Byfield on their way to Epping.

The final phase of this memorable retreat is best told in the words of the special war correspondent of the *Daily Telegraph*, who arrived on the scene at about one o'clock in the afternoon:

EPPING, 5 P.M., SEPTEMBER 9

"Thanks to the secrecy preserved by the military authorities, it was not known that Lord Byfield was falling back from the Royston–Saffron Walden position till seven this morning. By eight, I was off in my car for the scene of action, for rumours of fighting near Harlow had already begun to come in. I started out by way of Tottenham and Edmonton, expecting to reach Harlow by 9.30 or 10. But I reckoned without the numerous military officials with whom I came in contact, who constantly stopped me and sent me out of my way on one pretext or another. I am sure I hope that the nation has benefited by their proceedings. In the end it was close on one before I pulled up at the Cock Inn, Epping, in search of additional information, because for some time I had been aware of the rumbling growl of heavy artillery from the eastward, and wondered what it might portend. I found that General Sir Stapleton Forsyth, who commanded the Northern section of the defences, had made the inn his headquarters, and there was a constant coming and going of orderlies and staff-officers at its portals. Opposite, the men of one of the new irregular corps, dressed in dark green corduroy, blue flannel cricketing caps, and red cummerbunds, sat or reclined in two long lines on either side of their piled arms on the left of the wide street. On inquiry I heard that the enemy were said to be bombarding Kelvedon Hatch, and also that the head of our retreating columns was only three or four miles distant.

"I pushed on, and, after the usual interrogations from an officer in charge of a picket, where the road ran through the entrenchments about a mile farther on, found myself spinning along through the country in the direction of Harlow. As I began to ascend the rising ground towards Potter Street I could hear a continuous roll of artillery away to my right. I could not distinguish anything except the smoke of shells bursting here and there in the distance, on account of the scattered trees which lined the maze of hedgerows on every side. Close to Potter Street I met the head of the retreating army. Very tired, heated and footsore looked the hundreds of poor fellows as they dragged themselves along through the heat. It was a sultry afternoon, and the roads inches deep in dust.

"Turning to the right of Harlow Common, I met another column of men. I noticed that these were all Regulars, Grenadiers, Scots Guards, a battalion of Highlanders, another of Riflemen, and, lastly, two battalions of the Coldstreamers. These troops stepped along with rather more life than the citizen soldiers I had met previously, but still showed traces of their hard marching and fighting. Many of them were wearing bandages, but all the more seriously wounded had been left behind to be looked after by the Germans. All this time the firing was still resounding heavy and constant from the north-east, and from one person and another whom I questioned I ascertained that the enemy were advancing upon us from that direction. Half a mile farther on I ran into the middle of the fighting. The road ran along the top of a kind of flat ridge or upland, whence I could see to a considerable distance on either hand.

"Partially sheltered from the view by its hedges and the scattered cottages forming the hamlet of Foster Street was a long, irregular line of guns facing nearly east. Beyond them were yet others directed north. There were field batteries and big 4·7s. All were hard at work, their gunners working like men possessed, and the crash of their constant discharge was ear-splitting. I had hardly taken this in when 'Bang! Bang! Bang! Bang!'—four dazzling flashes opened in the air overhead, and shrapnel bullets rattled on earth, walls, and roofs with a sound as of handfuls of pebbles thrown on a marble pavement. But the hardness with which they struck was beyond anything in my experience.

"It was not pleasant to be here, but I ran my car behind a little public-house that stood by the wayside, and, dismounting, unslung my glasses and determined to get what view of the proceedings I could from the corner of the house. All around khaki-clad Volunteers lined every hedge and sheltered behind every cottage, while farther off, in the lower ground, from a mile to a mile and a half away I could distinguish the closely-packed firing lines of the Germans advancing slowly but steadily, despite the gaps made in their ranks by the fire of our guns. Their own guns, I fancied, I could make out near Tilegate Green to the north-east. Neither side had as yet opened rifle fire. Getting into my car I motored back to the main road, but it was so blocked by the procession of waggons and troops of the retreating army that I could not turn into it. Wheeling round I made my way back to a parallel lane I had noticed, and turning to the left again at a smithy, found myself in a road bordered by cottages and enclosures. Here I found the Regular troops I had lately met lining every hedgerow and fence, while I could see others on a knoll further to their left. There was a little church here, and, mounting to the roof, I got a comparatively extensive view. To my right the long dusty column of men and waggons still toiled along the Epping Road. In front, nearly three miles off, an apparently solid line of woods stretched along the horizon, surmounting a long, gradual and open slope. This was the position of our lines near Epping, and the haven for which Lord Byfield's tired soldiery were making. To the left the serried masses of drab-clad German infantry still pushed aggressively forward, their guns firing heavily over their heads.

"As I watched them three tremendous explosions took place in their midst, killing dozens of them. Fire, smoke, and dust rose up twenty feet in the air, while three ear-splitting reports rose even above the rolling thunder of the gunfire. More followed. I looked again towards the woodland. Here I saw blaze after blaze of fire among the dark masses of trees. Our big guns in the fortifications had got to work, and were punishing the Germans most severely, taking their attack in flank with the big 6-inch and 7·5-inch projectiles. Cheers arose all along our lines, as shell after shell, fired by gunners who knew to an inch the distances to every house and conspicuous tree, burst among the German ranks, killing and maiming the invaders by hundreds. The advance paused, faltered and, being hurriedly reinforced from the rear, once more went forward.

"But the big high explosive projectiles continued to fall with such accuracy and persistence that the attackers fell sullenly back, losing heavily as they did so. The enemy's artillery now came in for attention, and also was driven out of range with loss. The last stage in the retreat of Lord Byfield's command was now secured. The extended troops and guns gradually drew off from their positions, still keeping a watchful eye on the foe, and by 4.30 all were within the Epping entrenchments. All, that is to say, but the numerous killed and wounded during the running fight that had extended along the last seven or eight miles of the retreat, and the bulk of the Dunmow force under Sir Jacob Stellenbosch, which with its commander had, it was believed, been made prisoners. They had been caught between the 39th German Infantry Brigade and several regiments of cavalry, that it was said had arrived from the northward soon after they were beaten at Hatfield Heath. Probably these were the advanced troops of General Frölich's Cavalry Brigade."

CHAPTER III

BATTLE OF EPPING

THE FOLLOWING is extracted from *The Times* of 15th September:

EPPING, 14TH SEPTEMBER, EVENING

"I have spent a busy day, but have no very important news to record. After the repulse of the German troops attacking Lord Byfield's retreating army and the arrival of our sorely harassed troops behind the Epping entrenchments, we saw no more of the enemy that evening. All through the night, however, there was the sound of occasional heavy gun firing from the eastward. I have taken up my quarters at the Bell, an inn at the south end of the village, from the back of which I can get a good view to the north-west for from two to four miles. Beyond that distance the high ridge known as Epping Upland limits the prospect. The whole terrain is cut up into fields of various sizes and dotted all over with trees. Close by is a lofty red brick water-tower, which has been utilised by Sir Stapleton Forsyth as a signal station. Away about a mile to my left front as I look from the back of the Bell a big block of buildings stands prominently out on a grassy spur of high ground. This is Copped Hall and Little Copped Hall.

"Both mansions have been transformed into fortresses, which, while offering little or no resistance to artillery fire, will yet form a tough nut for the Germans to crack, should they succeed in getting through our entrenchments at that point. Beyond, I can just see a corner of a big earthwork that has been built to strengthen the defence line, and which has been christened Fort Obelisk from a farm of that name, near which it is situated. There is another smaller redoubt on the slope just below this hostelry, and I can see the gunners busy about the three big khaki-painted guns which are mounted in it. There are a 6-inch and two 4·7-inch guns I believe. This morning our cavalry, consisting of a regiment of yeomanry and some mounted infantry, who had formed a portion of Lord Byfield's force, went out to reconnoitre towards the north and east. They were not away long, as they were driven back in every direction in which they attempted to advance, by superior forces of the enemy's cavalry, who seemed to swarm everywhere.

"Later on, I believe, some of the German reiters became so venturesome that several squadrons exposed themselves to the fire of the big guns in the fort at Skip's Corner, and suffered pretty severely for their temerity. The firing continued throughout the morning away to eastward. At noon I thought I would run down and see if I could find anything out about it. I therefore mounted my car and ran off in that direction. I found that there was a regular duel going on between our guns at Kelvedon Hatch and some heavy siege guns or howitzers that the enemy had got in the neighbourhood of the high ground about Norton Heath, only about 3,000 yards distant from our entrenchments. They did not appear to have done us much damage, but neither, in all probability, did we hurt them very much, since our gunners were unable to exactly locate the hostile guns.

"When I got back to Epping, about three o'clock, I found the wide single street full of troops. They were those who had come in the previous afternoon with Lord Byfield, and who, having been allowed to rest till midday after their long fighting march, were now being told off to their various sections of the defence line. The Guard regiments were allocated to the northernmost position between Fort Royston and Fort Skips. The rifles were to go to Copped Hall, and the Seaforths to form the nucleus of a central reserve of Militia and Volunteers, which was being established just north of Gaynes Park. Epping itself and the contiguous entrenchments were confided to the Leinster Regiment, which alone of Sir Jacob Stellenbosch's brigade had escaped capture, supported by two Militia battalions. The field batteries were distributed under shelter of the woods on the south, east, and north-east of the town.

"During the afternoon the welcome news arrived that the remainder of Lord Byfield's command from Baldock, Royston, and Elmdon had safely arrived within our entrenchments at Enfield and New Barnet. We may now hope that what with Regulars, Militia, Volunteers, and the new levies, our lines are fully and effectively manned, and will suffice to stay the further advance of even such a formidable host as is that at the disposal of the renowned Von Kronhelm. It is reported too, from Brentwood, that great progress has already been made in reorganising and distributing the broken remnants of the 1st and 5th Armies that got back to that town after the great and disastrous battle of Chelmsford. Victorious as they were, the Germans must also have suffered severely, which may give us some breathing time before their next onslaught."

The following are extracts from the diary picked up by a *Daily Telegraph* correspondent, lying near the body of a German officer after the fighting in the neighbourhood of Enfield Chase. It is presumed that the officer in question was Major Splittberger, of the Kaiser Franz Garde Grenadier Regiment, since that was the name written inside the cover of the diary.

From enquiries that have since been instituted, it is probable that the deceased officer was employed on the staff of the General commanding the IVth Corps of the invading Army, though it would seem from the contents of his diary that he saw also a good deal of the operations of the Xth Corps. Our readers will be able to gather from it the general course of the enemy's strategy and tactics during the time immediately preceding the most recent disasters which have befallen our brave defenders. The first extract is dated September 15, and was written somewhere north of Epping:

"SEPT. 15.—So far the bold strategy of our Commander-in-Chief, in pushing the greater part of the Xth Corps directly to the west immediately after our victory at Chelmsford, has been amply justified by results. Although we just missed cutting off Lord Byfield and a large portion of his command at Harlow, we gained a good foothold inside the British defences north of Epping, and I don't think it will be long before we have very much improved our position here. The IVth Corps arrived at Harlow about midday yesterday in splendid condition, after their long march from Newmarket, and the residue of the Xth joined us at about the same time. As there is nothing like keeping the enemy on the move, no time was lost in preparing to attack him at the very earliest opportunity. As soon as it was dark the IVth Corps got its heavy guns and howitzers into position along the ridge above Epping Upland, and sent the greater portion of its field batteries forward to a position from which they were within effective range of the British fortifications at Skip's Corner.

"The IXth Corps, which had arrived from Chelmsford that evening, also placed its field artillery in a similar position, from which its fire crossed that of the IVth Corps. This Corps also provided the assaulting troops. The Xth Corps, which had been engaged all day on Thursday, was held in reserve. The howitzers on Epping Upland opened fire with petrol shell on the belt of woods that lies immediately in rear of the position to be attacked, and with the assistance of a strong westerly wind succeeded in setting them on fire and cutting off the most northerly section of the British defences from reinforcement. This was soon after midnight. The conflagration not only did us this service, but it is supposed so attracted the attention of the partially-trained soldiers of the enemy that they did not observe the IXth Corps massing for the assault.

"We then plastered their trenches with shrapnel to such an extent that they did not dare to show a finger above them, and finally carried the northern corner by assault. To give the enemy their due, they fought well, but we outnumbered them five to one, and it was impossible for them to resist the onslaught of our well-trained soldiers. News came to-day that the Saxons have been making a demonstration before Brentwood with a view of keeping the British employed down there so that they cannot send any reinforcements up here. At the same time they have been steadily bombarding Kelvedon Hatch from Norton Heath.

"We hear, too, that the Garde Corps have got down south, and that their front stretches from Broxbourne to Little Berkhamsted, while Frölich's Cavalry Division is in front of them, spread all over the country, from the River Lea away to the westward, having driven the whole of the British outlying troops and patrols under the shelter of their entrenchments. Once we succeed in rolling up the enemy's troops in this quarter, it will not be long before we are entering London."

"SEPT. 16.—Fighting went on all yesterday in the neighbourhood of Skip's Corner. We have taken the redoubt at North Weald Basset and driven the English back into the belt of burnt woodland, which they now hold along its northern edge. All day long, too, our big guns, hidden away behind the groves and woods above Epping Upland, poured their heavy projectiles on Epping and its defences. We set the village on fire three times, but the British contrived to extinguish the blaze on each occasion.

"I fancy Epping itself will be our next point of attack."

"SEPT. 17.—We are still progressing, fighting is now all but continuous. How long it may last I have no idea. Probably there will be no suspension of the struggle until we are actually masters of the Metropolis. We took advantage of the darkness to push forward our men to within three thousand yards of the enemy's line, placing them as far as possible under cover of the numerous copses, plantations, and hedgerows which cover the face of this fertile country. At 4 a.m. the General ordered his staff to assemble at Latton Park, where he had established his headquarters. He unfolded to us the general outline of the attack, which, he now announced, was to commence at six precisely.

"I thought myself that it was a somewhat inopportune time, as we should have the rising sun right in our eyes; but I imagine that the idea was to have as much daylight as possible before us. For although we had employed a night attack against Skip's Corner, and successfully too, yet the general feeling in our Army has always been opposed to operations of this kind. The possible gain is, I think, in no way commensurable with the probable risks of panic and disorder. The principal objective was the village of Epping itself; but simultaneous attacks were to be carried out against Copped Hall, Fort Obelisk, to the west of it, and Fort Royston, about a mile north of the village. The IXth Corps was to co-operate by a determined attempt to break through the English lining the burnt strip of woodland and to assault the latter fort in rear. It was necessary to carry out both these flanking attacks in order to prevent the main attack from being enfiladed from right and left. At 5.30 we mounted, and rode off to

Rye Hill about a couple of miles distant, from which the General intended to watch the progress of the operations. The first rays of the rising sun were filling the eastern sky with a pale light as we cantered off, the long wooded ridge on which the enemy had his position standing up in a misty silhouette against the growing day.

"As we topped Rye Hill I could see the thickly-massed lines of our infantry crouching behind every hedge, bank, or ridge, their rifle-barrels here and there twinkling in the feeble rays of the early sun, their shadows long and attenuated behind them. Epping with its lofty red water-tower was distinctly visible on the opposite side of the valley, and it is probable that the movement of the General's cavalcade of officers, with the escort, attracted the attention of the enemy's lookouts, for half-way down the hillside on their side of the valley a blinding violet-white flash blazed out, and a big shell came screaming along just over our heads, the loud boom of a heavy gun following fast on its heels. Almost simultaneously another big projectile hurtled up from the direction of Fort Obelisk, and burst among our escort of Uhlans with a deluge of livid flame and thick volumes of greenish brown smoke. It was a telling shot, for no fewer than six horses and their riders lay in a shattered heap on the ground.

"At six precisely our guns fired a salvo directed on Epping village. This was the preconcerted signal for attack, and before the echoes of the thunderous discharge had finished reverberating over the hills and forest, our front lines had sprung to their feet and were moving at a racing pace towards the enemy. For a moment the British seemed stupefied by the suddenness of the advance. A few rifle shots crackled out here and there, but our men had thrown themselves to the ground after their first rush before the enemy seemed to wake up. But there was no mistake about it when they did. Seldom have I seen such a concentrated fire. Gun, pom-pom, machine gun, and rifle blazed out from right to left along more than three miles of entrenchments. A continuous lightning-like line of fire poured forth from the British trenches, which still lay in shadow. I could see the bullets raising perfect sand-storms in places, the little pom-pom shells sparkling about all over our prostrate men, and the shrapnel bursting all along their front, producing perfect swathes of white smoke, which hung low down in the still air in the valley.

"But our artillery was not idle. The field guns, pushed well forward, showered shrapnel upon the British position, the howitzer shells hurtled over our heads on their way to the enemy in constantly increasing numbers as the ranges were verified by the trial shots, while a terrible and unceasing reverberation from the north-east told of the supporting attack made by the IXth and Xth Corps upon the blackened woods held by the English. The concussion of the terrific cannonade that now resounded from every quarter was deafening; the air seemed to pulse within one's ears, and it was difficult to hear one's nearest neighbour speak. Down in the valley our men appeared to be suffering severely. Every forward move of the attacking lines left a perfect litter of prostrate forms behind it, and for some time I felt very doubtful in my own mind if the attack would succeed. Glancing to the right, however, I was encouraged to see the progress that had been made by the troops detailed for the assault on Copped Hall and Obelisk Fort, and seeing this, it occurred to me that it was not intended to push the central attack on Epping home before its flank had been secured from molestation from this direction. Copped Hall itself stood out on a bare down almost like some mediæval castle, backed by the dark masses of forest, while to the west of it the slopes of Fort Obelisk could barely be distinguished, so flat were they and so well screened by greenery.

"But its position was clearly defined by the clouds of dust, smoke, and débris constantly thrown up by our heavy high-explosive shells, while ever and anon there came a dazzling flash from it, followed by a detonation that made itself heard even above the rolling of the cannonade, as one of its big 7·5 guns was discharged. The roar of their huge projectiles, too, as they tore through the air, was easily distinguishable. None of our epaulments were proof against them, and they did our heavy batteries a great deal of damage before they could be silenced.

"To cut a long story short, we captured Epping after a tough fight, and by noon were in possession of everything north of the Forest, including the war-scarred ruins that now represented the mansion of Copped Hall, and from which our pom-poms and machine guns were firing into Fort Obelisk. But our losses had been awful. As for the enemy, they could hardly have suffered less severely, for, though partially protected by their entrenchments, our artillery fire must have been utterly annihilating."

"SEPT. 18.—Fighting went on all last night, the English holding desperately on to the edge of the Forest, our people pressing them close, and working round their right flank. When day broke the general situation was pretty much like this. On our left the IXth Corps were in possession of the Fort at Toothill, and a redoubt that lay between it and Skip's Fort. Two batteries were bombarding a redoubt lower down in the direction of Stanford Rivers, which was also subjected to a cross fire from their howitzers near Ongar.

"As for the English, their position was an unenviable one. From Copped Hall—as soon as we have cleared the edge of the Forest of the enemy's sharpshooters—we shall be able to take their entrenchments in reverse all the way to Waltham Abbey. They have, on the other hand, an outlying fort about a mile or two north of the latter place, which gave us some trouble with its heavy guns yesterday, and which it is most important that we should gain possession of before we advance further. The Garde Corps on the western side of the River Lea is now, I hear, in sight of the enemy's lines, and is keeping them busily employed, though without pushing its attack home for the present.

"At daybreak this morning I was in Epping and saw the beginning of the attack on the Forest. It is rumoured that large reinforcements have reached the enemy from London, but as these must be merely scratch soldiers they will do them more harm than good in their cramped position. The Xth Corps had got a dozen batteries in position a little to the eastward of the village, and at six o'clock these guns opened a tremendous fire upon the north-east corner of the Forest, under cover of which their infantry deployed down in the low ground about Coopersale, and advanced to the attack. Petrol shells were not used against the Forest, as Von Kronhelm had given orders that it was not to be burned if it could possibly be avoided.

The shrapnel was very successful in keeping down the fire from the edge of the trees, but our troops received a good deal of damage from infantry and guns that were posted to the east of the Forest on a hill near Theydon Bois. But about seven o'clock these troops were driven from their position by a sudden flank attack made by the IXth Corps from Theydon Mount. Von Kleppen followed this up by putting some of his own guns up there, which were able to fire on the edge of the Forest after those of the Xth Corps had been masked by the close advance of their infantry. To make a long story short, by ten the whole of the Forest, east of the London Road, as far south as the cross roads near Jack's Hill, was in our hands. In the meantime the IVth Corps had made itself master of Fort Obelisk, and our gunners were hard at work mounting guns in it with which to fire on the outlying fort at Monkham's Hall. Von Kleppen was at Copped Hall about this time, and with him I found General von Wilberg, commanding the Xth Corps, in close consultation. The once fine mansion had been almost completely shot away down to its lower storey. A large portion of this, however, was still fairly intact, having been protected to a certain extent by the masses of masonry that had fallen all around it, and also by the thick ramparts of earth that the English had built up against its exposed side.

"Our men were still firing from its loopholes at the edge of the woods, which were only about 1,200 yards distant, and from which bullets were continually whistling in by every window. Two of our battalions had dug themselves in in the wooded park surrounding the house, and were also exchanging fire with the English at comparatively close ranges. They had, I was told, made more than one attempt to rush the edge of the Forest, but had been repulsed by rifle fire on each occasion. Away to the west I could see for miles, and even distinguish our shells bursting all over the enemy's fort at Monkham's Hall, which was being subjected to a heavy bombardment by our guns on the high ground to the north of it. About eleven Frölich's Cavalry Brigade, whose presence was no longer required in front of the Garde Corps, passed through Epping, going south-east. It is generally supposed that it is either to attack the British at Brentwood in the rear, or, which I think is more probable, to intimidate the raw levies by its presence between them and London, and to attack them in flank should they attempt to retreat.

"Just after eleven another battalion arrived at Copped Hall from Epping, and orders were given that the English position along the edge of the Forest was to be taken at all cost. Just before the attack began there was a great deal of firing somewhere in the interior of the Forest, presumably between the British and the advanced troops of the Xth Corps. However this may have been, it was evident that the enemy were holding our part of the Forest much less strongly and our assault was entirely successful, with but small loss of men. Once in the woods, the superior training and discipline of our men told heavily in their favour. While the mingled mass of Volunteers and raw free-shooters, of which the bulk of their garrison was composed, got utterly disorganised and out of hand under the severe strain on them that was imposed by the difficulties of wood fighting, and hindered and broke up the regular units, our people were easily kept well in hand, and drove the enemy steadily before them without a single check. The rattle of rifle and machine gun was continuous through all the leafy dells and glades of the wood, but by two o'clock practically the whole Forest was in the hands of our Xth Corps. It was then the turn of the IVth Corps, who in the meantime, far from being idle, had massed a large number of their guns at Copped Hall, from which, aided by the fire from Fort Obelisk, the enemy's lines were subjected to a bombardment that rendered them absolutely untenable, and we could see company after company making their way to Waltham Abbey.

"At three the order for a general advance on Waltham Abbey was issued. As the enemy seemed to have few, if any, guns at this place, it was determined to make use of some of the new armoured motors that accompanied the Army. Von Kronhelm, who was personally directing the operations from Copped Hall, had caused each Corps to send its own motors to Epping, so that we had something like thirty at our disposal. These quaint, grey monsters came down through the Forest and advanced on Epping by two parallel roads, one passing by the south of Warlies Park, the other being the main road from Epping. It was a weird sight to see these shore-going armour-clads flying down upon the enemy. They got within 800 yards of the houses, but the enemy contrived to block their further advance by various obstacles which they placed on the roads.

"There was about an hour's desperate fighting in the village. The old Abbey Church was set on fire by a stray shell, the conflagration spreading to the neighbouring houses, and both British and Germans being too busy killing each other to put it out, the whole village was shortly in flames. The British were finally driven out of it, and across the river by five o'clock. In the meantime every heavy gun that could be got to bear was directed on the fort at Monkham's Hall, which, during the afternoon, was also made the target for the guns of the Garde Corps, which co-operated with us by attacking the lines at Cheshunt, and assisting us with its artillery fire from the opposite side of the river. By nightfall the fort was a mass of smoking earth, over which fluttered our black cross flag, and the front of the IVth Corps stretched from this to Gillwell Park, four miles nearer London.

"The Xth Corps was in support in the Forest behind us, and forming also a front to cover our flank, reaching from Chingford to Buckhurst Hill. The enemy was quite demoralised in this direction, and showed no indication of resuming the engagement. As for the IXth Corps, its advanced troops were at Lambourne End, in close communication with General Frölich, who had established his headquarters at Havering-atte-Bower. We have driven a formidable wedge right into the middle of the carefully elaborated system of defence arranged by the English generals, and it will now be a miracle if they can prevent our entry into the capital.

"We had not, of course, effected this without great loss in killed and wounded, but you can't make puddings without breaking eggs, and in the end a bold and forward policy is more economical of life and limb than attempting to avoid necessary losses, as our present opponents did in South Africa, thereby prolonging the war to an almost indefinite period, and losing many more men by sickness and in driblets than would have been the case if they had followed a more determined line in their strategy and tactics. Just before the sun sank behind the masses of new houses which the monster city spreads out to the northward I got orders to carry a despatch to

General von Wilberg, who was stated to be at Chingford, on our extreme left. I went by the Forest road, as the parallel one near the river was in most parts under fire from the opposite bank.

"He had established his headquarters at the Foresters' Inn, which stands high up on a wooded mound, and from which he could see a considerable distance and keep in touch with his various signal stations. He took my despatch, telling me that I should have a reply to take back later on. 'In the meanwhile,' said he, 'if you will fall in with my staff you will have an opportunity of seeing the first shots fired into the biggest city in the world.' So saying, he went out to his horse, which was waiting outside, and we started off down the hill with a great clatter. After winding about through a somewhat intricate network of roads and by-lanes we arrived at Old Chingford Church, which stands upon a species of headland, rising boldly up above the flat and, in some places, marshy land to the westward.

"Close to the church was a battery of four big howitzers, the gunners grouped around them silhouetted darkly against the blood-red sky. From up here the vast city, spreading out to the south and west, lay like a grey, sprawling octopus spreading out ray-like to the northward, every rise and ridge being topped with a bristle of spires and chimney-pots. An ominous silence seemed to brood over the teeming landscape, broken only at intervals by the dull booming of guns from the northward. Long swathes of cloud and smoke lay athwart the dull, furnace-like glow of the sunset, and lights were beginning to sparkle out all over the vast expanse which lay before us mirrored here and there in the canals and rivers that ran almost at our feet. 'Now,' said Von Wilberg at length, 'commence fire.' One of the big guns gave tongue with a roar that seemed to make the church tower quiver above us. Another and another followed in succession, their big projectiles hurtling and humming through the quiet evening air on their errands of death and destruction in I know not what quarter of the crowded suburbs. It seemed to me a cruel and needless thing to do, but I am told that it was done with the set purpose of arousing such a feeling of alarm and insecurity in the East End that the mob might try to interfere with any further measures for defence that the British military authorities might undertake. I got my despatch soon afterwards and returned with it to the General, who was spending the night at Copped Hall. There, too, I got myself a shakedown and slumbered soundly till the morning."

"SEPT. 19.—To-day we have, I think, finally broken down all organised military opposition in the field, though we may expect a considerable amount of street fighting before reaping the whole fruits of our victories. At daybreak we began by turning a heavy fire from every possible quarter on the wooded island formed by the river and various back-waters just north of Waltham Abbey. The poplar-clad islet, which was full of the enemy's troops, became absolutely untenable under this concentrated fire, and they were compelled to fall back over the river. Our Engineers soon began their bridging operations behind the wood, and our infantry, crossing over, got close up to a redoubt on the further side and took it by storm. Again we were able to take a considerable section of the enemy's lines in reverse, and as they were driven out by our fire, against which they had no protection, the Garde Corps advanced, and by ten were in possession of Cheshunt.

"In the meanwhile, covered by the fire of the guns belonging to the IXth and Xth Corps, other bridges had been thrown across the Lea at various points between Waltham and Chingford, and in another hour the crossing began. The enemy had no good positions for his guns, and seemed to have very few of them. He had pinned his faith upon the big weapons he had placed in his entrenchments, and those were now of no further use to him. He had lost a number of his field guns, either from damage or capture, and with our more numerous artillery firing from the high ground on the eastern bank of the river we were always able to beat down any attempt he made to reply to their fire.

"We had a day of fierce fighting before us. There was no manœuvring. We were in a wilderness of scattered houses and occasional streets, in which the enemy contested our progress foot by foot. Edmonton, Enfield Wash, and Waltham Cross were quickly captured; our artillery commanded them too well to allow the British to make a successful defence; but Enfield itself, lying along a steepish ridge, on which the British had assembled what artillery they could scrape together, cost us dearly. The streets of this not too lovely suburban town literally ran with blood when at last we made our way into it. A large part of it was burnt to ashes, including unfortunately the ancient palace of Queen Elizabeth, and the venerable and enormous cedar-tree that overhung it.

"The British fell back to a second position they had apparently prepared along a parallel ridge farther to the westward, their left being between us and New Barnet and their right at Southgate.

"We did not attempt to advance farther to-day, but contented ourselves in reorganising our forces and preparing against a possible counter-attack, by barricading and entrenching the farther edge of Enfield Ridge."

"*Sept.* 20.—We are falling in immediately, as it has been decided to attack the British position at once. Already the artillery duel is in progress. I must continue to-night, as my horse is at the door."

The writer, however, never lived to complete his diary, having been shot half-way up the green slope he had observed the day previous.

CHAPTER IV

BOMBARDMENT OF LONDON

DAY BROKE. The faint flush of violet away eastward beyond Temple Bar gradually turned rose, heralding the sun's coming, and by degrees the streets, filled by excited Londoners, grew lighter with the dawn. Fevered night thus gave place to day—a day that was, alas! destined to be one of bitter memory for the British Empire.

Alarming news had spread that Uhlans had been seen reconnoitring in Snaresbrook and Wanstead, had ridden along Forest Road

THE BOMBARDMENT AND DEFENCES OF
LONDON
on Sept. 20th & 21st

Reference
—o— German Artillery
Barricades built by the populace
— — — Extreme limit of the zone of
bombardment

and Ferry Lane at Walthamstow, through Tottenham High Cross, up
High Street, Hornsey, Priory Road, and Muswell Hill. The Germans
were actually upon London!

The northern suburbs were staggered. In Fortis Green, North End,
Highgate, Crouch End, Hampstead, Stamford Hill, and Leyton the
quiet suburban houses were threatened, and many people, in fear of
their lives, had now fled southward into central London. Thus the
huge population of greater London was practically huddled together
in the comparatively small area from Kensington to Fleet Street, and
from Oxford Street to the Thames Embankment.

People of Fulham, Putney, Walham Green, Hammersmith, and
Kew had, for the most part, fled away to the open country across
Hounslow Heath to Bedfont and Staines; while Tooting, Balham,
Dulwich, Streatham, Norwood, and Catford had retreated farther
south into Surrey and Kent.

For the past three days thousands of willing helpers had followed the example of Sheffield and Birmingham, and constructed enormous barricades, obstructing at various points the chief roads leading from the north and east into London. Detachments of Engineers had blown up several of the bridges carrying the main roads out eastwards—for instance, the bridge at the end of Commercial Road, East, crossing the Limehouse Canal, while the six other smaller bridges spanning the canal between that point and the Bow Road were also destroyed. The bridge at the end of Bow Road itself was shattered, and those over the Hackney Cut at Marshall Hill and Hackney Wick were also rendered impassable.

Most of the bridges across the Regent's Canal were also destroyed, notably those in Mare Street, Hackney, the Kingsland Road, and New North Road, while a similar demolition took place in Edgware Road and the Harrow Road. Londoners were frantic, now that the enemy were really upon them. The accounts of the battles in the newspapers had, of course, been merely fragmentary, and they had not yet realised what war actually meant. They knew that all business was at a standstill, that the City was in an uproar, that there was no work, and that food was at famine prices. But not until German cavalry were actually seen scouring the northern suburbs did it become impressed upon them that they were really helpless and defenceless.

London was to be besieged!

This report having got about, the people began building barricades in many of the principal thoroughfares north of the Thames. One huge obstruction, built mostly of paving stones from the footways, overturned tramcars, waggons, railway trollies, and barbed wire, rose in the Holloway Road, just beyond Highbury Station. Another blocked the Caledonian Road a few yards north of the police-station, while another very large and strong pile of miscellaneous goods, bales of wool and cotton stuffs, building material, and stones brought from the Great Northern Railway depôt, obstructed the Camden Road at the south corner of Hilldrop Crescent. Across High Street, Camden Town, at the junction of the Kentish Town and other roads, five hundred men worked with a will, piling together every kind of ponderous object they could pillage from the neighbouring shops—pianos, iron bedsteads, wardrobes, pieces of calico and flannel, dress stuffs, rolls of carpets, floorboards, even the very doors wrenched from their hinges—until, when it reached to the second storey window and was considered of sufficient height, a pole was planted on top, and from it hung limply a small Union Jack.

The Finchley Road, opposite Swiss Cottage Station; in Shoot Up-hill, where Mill Lane runs into it; across Willesden Lane where it joins the High Road in Kilburn; the Harrow Road close to Willesden Junction Station; at the junction of the Goldhawk and Uxbridge roads; across the Hammersmith Road in front of the Hospital, other similar obstructions were placed with a view to preventing the enemy from entering London. At a hundred other points, in the narrower and more obscure thoroughfares, all along the north of London, busy workers were constructing similar defences, houses and shops being ruthlessly broken open and cleared of their contents by the frantic and terrified populace.

London was in a ferment. Almost without exception the gun-makers' shops had been pillaged, and every rifle, sporting gun, and revolver seized. The armouries at the Tower of London, at the various barracks, and the factory out at Enfield had long ago all been cleared of their contents; for now, in this last stand, every one was desperate, and all who could obtain a gun did so. Many, however, had guns but no ammunition; others had sporting ammunition for service rifles, and others cartridges, but no gun.

Those, however, who had guns and ammunition complete mounted guard at the barricades, being assisted at some points by Volunteers who had been driven in from Essex. Upon more than one barricade in North London a Maxim had been mounted, and was now pointed, ready to sweep away the enemy should they advance.

Other thoroughfares barricaded, beside those mentioned, were the Stroud Green Road, where it joins Hanley Road; the railway bridge in the Oakfield Road in the same neighbourhood; the Wight-man Road, opposite Harringay Station, the junction of Archway Road and Highgate Hill; the High Road, Tottenham, at its junction with West Green Road, and various roads around the New River reservoirs, which were believed to be one of the objectives of the enemy. These latter were very strongly held by thousands of brave and patriotic citizens, though the East London reservoirs across at Walthamstow could not be defended, situated so openly as they were. The people of Leytonstone threw up a barricade opposite the schools in the High Road, while in Wanstead a hastily-constructed, but perfectly useless, obstruction was piled across Cambridge Park, where it joins the Blake Road.

Of course, all the women and children in the northern suburbs had now been sent south. Half the houses in those quiet, newly-built roads were locked up, and their owners gone; for as soon as the report spread of the result of the final battle before London, and our crushing defeat, people living in Highgate, Hampstead, Crouch End, Hornsey, Tottenham, Finsbury Park, Muswell Hill, Hendon, and Hampstead saw that they must fly southward, now the Germans were upon them.

Think what it meant to those suburban families of City men! The ruthless destruction of their pretty, long-cherished homes, flight into the turbulent, noisy, distracted, hungry city, and the loss of every-thing they possessed. In most cases the husband was already bearing his part in the defence of the Metropolis with gun or with spade, or helping to move heavy masses of material for the construction of the barricades. The wife, however, was compelled to take a last look at all those possessions that she had so fondly called "home," lock her front door, and, with her children, join in those long mournful processions moving ever southward into London, tramping on and on—whither she knew not where.

Touching sights were to be seen everywhere in the streets that day. Homeless women, many of them with two or three little ones, were wandering through the less frequented streets, avoiding the main roads with all their crush, excitement, and barricade-building, but making their way westward, beyond Kensington and Ham-mersmith, which was now become the outlet of the Metropolis.

All trains from Charing Cross, Waterloo, London Bridge, Victoria, and Paddington had for the past three days been crowded to excess. Anxious fathers struggled fiercely to obtain places for their wives, mothers, and daughters—sending them away anywhere out of the city which must in a few hours be crushed beneath the iron heel.

The South Western and Great Western systems carried thousands upon thousands of the wealthier away to Devonshire and Cornwall—as far as possible from the theatre of war; the South Eastern and Chatham took people into the already crowded Kentish towns and villages, and the Brighton line carried others into rural Sussex. London overflowed southward and westward until every village and every town within fifty miles was so full that beds were at a premium, and in various places, notably at Chartham, near Canterbury, at Willesborough, near Ashford, at Lewes, at Robertsbridge, at Goodwood Park, and at Horsham, huge camps were formed, shelter being afforded by poles and rick cloths. Every house, every barn, every school, indeed every place where people could obtain shelter for the night, was crowded to excess, mostly by women and children sent south, away from the horrors that it was known must come.

Central London grew more turbulent with each hour that passed. There were all sorts of wild rumours, but, fortunately, the Press still preserved a dignified calm. The Cabinet were holding a meeting at Bristol, whither the Houses of Commons and Lords had moved, and all depended upon its issue. It was said that Ministers were divided in their opinions whether we should sue for an ignominious peace, or whether the conflict should be continued to the bitter end.

Disaster had followed disaster, and iron-throated orators in Hyde and St. James's Parks were now shouting "Stop the war! Stop the war!" The cry was taken up but faintly, however, for the blood of Londoners, slow to rise, had now been stirred by seeing their country slowly yet completely crushed by Germany. All the patriotism latent within them was now displayed. The national flag was shown everywhere, and at every point one heard "God save the King" sung lustily.

Two gunmakers' shops in the Strand, which had hitherto escaped notice, were shortly after noon broken open, and every available arm and all the ammunition seized. One man, unable to obtain a revolver, snatched half a dozen pairs of steel handcuffs, and cried with grim humour as he held them up: "If I can't shoot any of the sausage-eaters, I can at least bag a prisoner or two!"

The banks, the great jewellers, the diamond merchants, the safe-deposit offices, and all who had valuables in their keeping, were extremely anxious as to what might happen. Below those dark buildings in Lothbury and Lombard Street, behind the black walls of the Bank of England, and below every branch bank all over London, were millions in gold and notes, the wealth of the greatest city the world has ever known. The strong rooms were, for the most part, the strongest that modern engineering could devise, some with various arrangements by which all access was debarred by an inrush of water, but, alas! dynamite is a great leveller, and it was felt that not a single strong room in the whole of London could withstand an organised attack by German engineers.

A single charge of dynamite would certainly make a breach in concrete upon which a thief might hammer and chip day and night for a month without making much impression. Steel doors must give to blasting force, while the strongest and most complicated locks would also fly to pieces.

The directors of most of the banks had met and an endeavour had been made to co-operate and form a corps of special guards for the principal offices. In fact, a small armed corps was formed, and were on duty day and night in Lothbury, Lombard Street, and the vicinity. Yet what could they do if the Germans swept into London? There was but little to fear from the excited populace themselves, because matters had assumed such a crisis that money was of little use, as there was practically very little to buy. But little food was reaching London from the open ports on the west. It was the enemy that the banks feared, for they knew that the Germans intended to enter and sack the Metropolis, just as they had sacked the other towns that had refused to pay the indemnity demanded.

Small jewellers had, days ago, removed their stock from their windows and carried it away in unsuspicious-looking bags to safe hiding in the southern and western suburbs, where people for the most part hid their valuable plate, jewellery, etc., beneath a floor-board, or buried them in some marked spot in their small gardens.

The hospitals were already full of wounded from the various engagements of the past week. The London, St. Thomas', Charing Cross, St. George's, Guy's, and Bartholomew's were overflowing; and the surgeons, with patriotic self-denial, were working day and night in an endeavour to cope with the ever-arriving crowd of suffering humanity. The field hospitals away to the northward were also reported full.

The exact whereabouts of the enemy was not known. They were, it seemed, everywhere. They had practically over-run the whole country, and the reports from the Midlands and the North showed that the majority of the principal towns had now been occupied.

The latest reverses outside London, full and graphic details of which were now being published hourly by the papers, had created an immense sensation. Everywhere people were regretting that Lord Roberts' solemn warnings in 1906 had been unheeded, for had we adopted his scheme for universal service such dire catastrophe could never have occurred. Many had, alas! declared it to be synonymous with conscription, which it certainly was not, and by that foolish argument had prevented the public at large from accepting it as the only means for our salvation as a nation. The repeated warnings had been disregarded, and we had, unhappily, lived in a fool's paradise, in the self-satisfied belief that England could not be successfully invaded.

Now, alas! the country had realised the truth when too late.

That memorable day, September 20, witnessed exasperated struggles in the northern suburbs of London, passionate and bloody collisions, an infantry fire of the defenders overwhelming every attempted assault; and a decisive action of the artillery, with regard to which arm the superiority of the Germans, due to their perfect training, was apparent.

A last desperate stand had, it appears, been made by the defenders on the high ridge north-west of New Barnet, from Southgate to near Potter's Bar, where a terrible fight had taken place. But from the very first it was utterly hopeless. The British had fought valiantly in defence of London, but here again they were outnumbered, and after one of the most desperate conflicts in the whole campaign—in which our losses were terrible—the Germans at length had succeeded in entering Chipping Barnet. It was a difficult movement, and a fierce contest, rendered the more terrible by the burning houses, ensued in the streets and away across the low hills southward—a struggle full of vicissitudes and alternating successes, until at last the fire of the defenders was silenced, and hundreds of prisoners fell into the German hands.

Thus the last organised defence of London had been broken, and the barricades alone remained.

The work of the German troops on the lines of communication in Essex had for the past week been fraught with danger. Through want of cavalry the British had been unable to make cavalry raids; but, on the other hand, the difficulty was enhanced by the bands of sharpshooters—men of all classes from London who possessed a gun and who could shoot. In one or two of the London clubs the suggestion had first been mooted a couple of days after the outbreak of hostilities, and it had been quickly taken up by men who were in the habit of shooting game, but had not had a military training.

Within three days about two thousand men had formed themselves into bands to take part in the struggle and assist in the defence of London. They were practically similar to the Francs-tireurs of the Franco-German War, for they went forth in companies and waged a guerilla warfare, partly before the front and at the flanks of the different armies, and partly at the communications at the rear of the Germans. Their position was one of constant peril in face of Von Kronhelm's proclamation, yet the work they did was excellent, and only proved that if Lord Roberts' scheme for universal training had been adopted the enemy would never have reached the gates of London with success.

These brave adventurous spirits, together with "The Legion of Frontiersmen," made their attacks by surprise from hiding-places or from ambushes. Their adventures were constantly thrilling ones. Scattered all over the theatre of war in Essex and Suffolk, and all along the German lines of communication, the "Frontiersmen" rarely ventured on an open conflict, and frequently changed scene and point of attack. Within one week their numbers rose to over

8,000, and, being well served by the villagers, who acted as scouts and spies for them, the Germans found them very difficult to get at. Usually they kept their arms concealed in thickets and woods, where they would lie in wait for the Germans. They never came to close quarters, but fired at a distance. Many a smart Uhlan fell by their bullets, and many a sentry dropped, shot by an unknown hand.

Thus they harassed the enemy everywhere. At need they concealed their arms and assumed the appearance of inoffensive noncombatants. But when caught red-handed the Germans gave them "short shrift," as the bodies now swinging from telegraph poles on various high-roads in Essex testified.

In an attempt to put a stop to the daring actions of the "Frontiersmen," the German authorities and troops along the lines of communication punished the parishes where German soldiers were shot, or where the destruction of railways and telegraphs had occurred, by levying money contributions, or by burning the villages.

The guerilla war was especially fierce along from Edgware up to Hertford, and from Chelmsford down to the Thames. In fact, once commenced, it never ceased. Attacks were always being made upon small patrols, travelling detachments, mails of the field post-office, posts or patrols at stations on the lines of communication, while field-telegraphs, telephones, and railways were everywhere destroyed.

In consequence of the railway being cut at Pitsea, the villages of Pitsea, Bowers Gifford, and Vange had been burned. Because a German patrol had been attacked and destroyed near Orsett, the parish was compelled to pay a heavy indemnity. Upminster, near Romford, Theydon Bois, and Fyfield, near High Ongar, had all been burned by the Germans for the same reason; while at the Cherrytree Inn, near Rainham, five "Frontiersmen," being discovered by Uhlans in a hayloft asleep, were locked in and there burned alive. Dozens were, of course, shot at sight, and dozens more hanged without trial. But they were not to be deterred. They were fighting in defence of London, and around the northern suburbs the patriotic members of the "Legion" were specially active, though they never showed themselves in large bands.

Within London every man who could shoot game was now anxious to join in the fray, and on the day that the news of the last disaster reached the Metropolis hundreds left for the open country out beyond Hendon.

The enemy having broken down the defence at Enfield and cleared the defenders out of the fortified houses, had advanced and occupied the northern ridges of London in a line stretching roughly from Pole Hill, a little to the north of Chingford, across Upper Edmonton, through Tottenham, Hornsey, Highgate, Hampstead, and Willesden, to Twyford Abbey. All the positions had been well reconnoitred, for at grey of dawn the rumbling of artillery had been heard in the streets of those places already mentioned, and soon after sunrise strong batteries were established upon all the available points commanding London.

These were at Chingford Green, on the left-hand side of the road opposite the inn at Chingford; on Devonshire Hill, Tottenham; on the hill at Wood Green; in the grounds of the Alexandra Palace; on the high ground about Churchyard Bottom Wood; on the edge of Bishop's Wood, Highgate; on Parliament Hill, at a spot close to the Oaks on the Hendon road; at Dollis Hill, and at a point a little north of Wormwood Scrubs, and at Neasden, near the railway works.

The enemy's chief object was to establish their artillery as near London as possible, for it was known that the range of their guns even from Hampstead—the highest point, 441 feet above London—would not reach into the actual city itself. Meanwhile, at dawn, the German cavalry, infantry, motor-infantry, and armoured motor-cars—the latter mostly 35–40 h.p. Opel–Darracqs, with three quick-firing guns mounted in each, and bearing the Imperial German arms in black—advanced up the various roads leading into London from the north, being met, of course, with a desperate resistance at the barricades.

On Haverstock Hill, the three Maxims, mounted upon the huge construction across the road, played havoc with the Germans, who were at once compelled to fall back, leaving piles of dead and dying in the roadway, for the terrible hail of lead poured out upon the invaders could not be withstood. Two of the German armoured motor-cars were presently brought into action by the Germans, who replied with a rapid fire, this being continued for a full quarter of an hour without result on either side. Then the Germans, finding the defence too strong, again retired into Hampstead, amid the ringing cheers of the valiant men holding that gate of London. The losses of the enemy had been serious, for the whole roadway was now strewn with dead; while behind the huge wall of paving-stones, overturned carts, and furniture, only two men had been killed and one wounded.

Across in the Finchley Road a struggle equally as fierce was in progress; but a detachment of the enemy, evidently led by some German who had knowledge of the intricate side-roads, suddenly appeared in the rear of the barricade, and a fierce and bloody hand-to-hand conflict ensued. The defenders, however, stood their ground, and with the aid of some petrol bombs which they held in readiness they destroyed the venturesome detachment almost to a man, though a number of houses in the vicinity were set on fire, causing a huge conflagration.

In Highgate Road the attack was a desperate one, the enraged Londoners fighting valiantly, the men with arms being assisted by the populace themselves. Here again deadly petrol bombs had been distributed, and men and women hurled them against the Germans. Petrol was actually poured from windows upon the heads of the enemy, and tow soaked in paraffin and lit flung in among them, when in an instant whole areas of the streets were ablaze, and the soldiers of the Fatherland perished in the roaring flames.

Every device to drive back the invader was tried. Though thousands upon thousands had left the northern suburbs, many thousands still remained bent on defending their homes as long as they had breath. The crackle of rifles was incessant, and ever and anon the dull roar of a heavy field gun and the sharp rattle of a Maxim mingled with the cheers, yells, and shrieks of victors and vanquished.

The scene on every side was awful. Men were fighting for their lives in desperation.

Around the barricade in Holloway Road the street ran with blood; while in Kingsland, in Clapton, in West Ham, and Canning Town the enemy were making an equally desperate attack, and were being repulsed everywhere. London's enraged millions, the Germans were well aware, constituted a grave danger. Any detachments who carried a barricade by assault—as, for instance, they did one in the Hornsey Road near the station—were quickly set upon by the angry mob and simply wiped out of existence.

Until nearly noon desperate conflicts at the barricades continued. The defence was even more effectual than was expected; yet, had it not been that Von Kronhelm, the German generalissimo, had given orders that the troops were not to attempt to advance into London before the populace were cowed, there was no doubt that each barricade could have been taken in the rear by companies avoiding the main roads and proceeding by the side streets.

Just before noon, however, it was apparent to Von Kronhelm that to storm the barricades would entail enormous losses, so strong were they. The men holding them had now been reinforced in many cases by regular troops, who had come in in flight, and a good many guns were now manned by artillerymen.

Von Kronhelm had established his headquarters at Jack Straw's Castle, from which he could survey the giant city through his field-glasses. Below lay the great plain of roofs, spires, and domes, stretching away into the grey mystic distance, where afar rose the twin towers and double arches of the Crystal Palace roof. London—the great London—the capital of the world—lay at his mercy at his feet.

The tall, thin-faced General, with the grizzled moustache and the glittering cross at his throat, standing apart from his staff, gazed away in silence and in thought. It was his first sight of London, and its gigantic proportions amazed even him. Again he swept the horizon with his glass, and knit his grey brows. He remembered the parting words of his Emperor as he backed out of that plainly-furnished little private cabinet at Potsdam—

"You must bombard London and sack it. The pride of those English must be broken at all costs. Go, Kronhelm—go—and may the best of fortune go with you!"

The sun was at the noon causing the glass roof of the distant Crystal Palace to gleam. Far down in the grey haze stood Big Ben, the Campanile, and a thousand church spires, all tiny and, from that distance, insignificant. From where he stood the sound of crackling fire at the barricades reached him, and a little behind him a member of his staff was kneeling on the grass with his ear bent to the field telephone. Reports were coming in fast of the desperate resistance in the streets, and these were duly handed to him.

He glanced at them, gave a final look at the outstretched city that was the metropolis of the world, and then gave rapid orders for the withdrawal of the troops from the assault of the barricades, and the bombardment of London.

In a moment the field-telegraphs were clicking, the telephone bell was ringing, orders were shouted in German in all directions, and next second, with a deafening roar, one of the howitzers of the battery in the close vicinity to him gave tongue and threw its deadly shell somewhere into St. John's Wood.

The rain of death had opened! London was surrounded by a semi-circle of fire.

The great gun was followed by a hundred others as, at all the batteries along the northern heights, the orders were received. Then in a few minutes, from the whole line from Chingford to Willesden, roughly about twelve miles, came a hail of the most deadly of modern projectiles directed upon the most populous parts of the metropolis.

Though the Germans trained their guns to carry as far as was possible, the zone of fire did not at first it seemed extend farther south than a line roughly taken from Notting Hill through Bays-water, past Paddington Station, along the Marylebone and Euston Roads, then up to Highbury, Stoke Newington, Stamford Hill and Walthamstow.

When, however, the great shells began to burst in Holloway, Kentish Town, Camden Town, Kilburn, Kensal Green, and other places lying within the area under fire, a frightful panic ensued. Whole streets were shattered by explosions, and fires were breaking out, the dark clouds of smoke obscuring the sunlit sky. Roaring flame shot up everywhere, unfortunate men, women, and children were being blown to atoms by the awful projectiles, while others, distracted, sought shelter in any cellar or underground place they could find, while their houses fell about them like packs of cards.

The scenes within that zone of terror were indescribable.

When Paris had been bombarded years ago, artillery was not at the perfection it now was, and there had been no such high explosive known as in the present day. The great shells that were falling everywhere, on bursting filled the air with poisonous fumes, as well as with deadly fragments. One bursting in a street would wreck the rows of houses on either side, and tear a great hole in the ground at the same moment. The fronts of the houses were torn out like paper, the iron railings twisted as though they were wire, and paving-stones hurled into the air like straws.

Anything and everything offering a mark to the enemy's guns was shattered. St. John's Wood and the houses about Regent's Park suffered seriously. A shell from Hampstead, falling into the roof of one of the houses near the centre of Sussex Place, burst and shattered nearly all the houses in the row; while another fell in Cumberland Terrace and wrecked a dozen houses in the vicinity. In both cases the houses were mostly empty, for owners and servants had fled southward across the river as soon as it became apparent that the Germans actually intended to bombard.

At many parts in Maida Vale shells burst with appalling effect. Several of the houses in Elgin Avenue had their fronts torn out, and in one, a block of flats, there was considerable loss of life in the fire that broke out, escape being cut off owing to the stairs having been demolished by the explosion. Abbey Road, St. John's Wood Road, Acacia Road, and Wellington Road, were quickly wrecked.

In Chalk Farm Road, near the Adelaide, a terrified woman was dashing across the street to seek shelter with a neighbour, when a shell burst right in front of her, blowing her to fragments; while in the early stage of the bombardment a shell bursting in the Midland Hotel at St. Pancras caused a fire which in half an hour resulted in the whole hotel and railway terminus being a veritable furnace of flame. Through the roof of King's Cross Station several shells fell, and burst close to the departure platform. The whole glass roof was shattered, but beyond that little other material damage resulted.

Shots were now falling everywhere, and Londoners were staggered. In dense, excited crowds they were flying southwards towards the Thames. Some were caught in the streets in their flight, and were flung down, maimed and dying. The most awful sights were to be witnessed in the open streets; men and women blown out of recognition, with their clothes singed and torn to shreds, and helpless, innocent children lying white and dead, their limbs torn away and missing.

Euston Station had shared the same fate as St. Pancras, and was blazing furiously, sending up a great column of black smoke that could be seen by all London. So many were the conflagrations now breaking out that it seemed as though the enemy were sending into London shells filled with petrol, in order to set the streets aflame. This, indeed, was proved by an eye-witness, who saw a shell fall in Liverpool Road, close to the Angel. It burst with a bright red flash, and next second the whole of the roadway and neighbouring houses were blazing furiously.

Thus the air became black with smoke and dust, and the light of day obscured in Northern London. And through that obscurity came those whizzing shells in an incessant hissing stream, each one, bursting in these narrow, thickly populated streets, causing havoc indescribable, and a loss of life impossible to accurately calculate. Hundreds of people were blown to pieces in the open but hundreds more were buried beneath the *débris* of their own cherished homes, now being so ruthlessly destroyed and demolished.

On every side was heard the cry: "Stop the war—stop the war!"

But it was, alas! too late—too late.

Never in the history of the civilised world were there such scenes of reckless slaughter of the innocent and peace-loving as on that never-to-be-forgotten day when Von Kronhelm carried out the orders of his Imperial master, and struck terror into the heart of London's millions.

CHAPTER V

THE RAIN OF DEATH

THROUGH THE WHOLE AFTERNOON the heavy German artillery roared, belching forth their fiery vengeance upon London.

Hour after hour they pounded away, until St. Pancras Church was a heap of ruins and the Foundling Hospital a veritable furnace, as well as the Parcel Post Offices and the University College in Gower Street. In Hampstead Road many of the shops were shattered, and in Tottenham Court Road both Maple's and Shoolbred's suffered severely, for shells bursting in the centre of the roadway had smashed every pane of glass in the fronts of both buildings.

The quiet squares of Bloomsbury were in some cases great yawning ruins—houses with their fronts torn out revealing the shattered furniture within. Streets were indeed filled with tiles, chimney pots, fallen telegraph wires, and débris of furniture, stone steps, paving stones, and fallen masonry. Many of the thoroughfares, such as the Pentonville Road, Copenhagen Street, and Holloway Road, were, at points, quite impassable on account of the ruins that blocked them. Into the Northern Hospital, in the Holloway Road, a shell fell, shattering one of the wards, and killing or maiming every one of the patients in the ward in question, while the church in Tufnell Park Road was burning fiercely. Upper Holloway, Stoke Newington, Highbury, Kingsland, Dalston, Hackney, Clapton, and Stamford Hill were being swept at long range by the guns on Muswell Hill and Churchyard Bottom Hill, and the terror caused in those densely populated districts was awful. Hundreds upon hundreds lost their lives, or else had a hand, an arm, a leg blown away, as those fatal shells fell in never-ceasing monotony, especially in Stoke Newington and Kingsland. The many side roads lying between Holloway Road and Finsbury Park, such as Hornsey Road, Tollington Park, Andover, Durham, Palmerston, Campbell, and Forthill Roads, Seven Sisters Road, and Isledon Road were all devastated, for the guns for a full hour seemed to be trained upon them.

The German gunners in all probability neither knew nor cared where their shells fell. From their position, now that the smoke of the hundreds of fires was rising, they could probably discern but little. Therefore the batteries at Hampstead Heath, Muswell Hill, Wood Green, Cricklewood, and other places simply sent their shells as far distant south as possible into the panic-stricken city below. In Mountgrove and Riversdale Roads, Highbury Vale, a number of people were killed, while a frightful disaster occurred in the church at the corner of Park Lane and Milton Road, Stoke Newington. Here a number of people had entered, attending a special service for the success of the British arms, when a shell exploded on the roof, bringing it down upon them and killing over fifty of the congregation, mostly women.

The air, poisoned by the fumes of the deadly explosives and full of smoke from the burning buildings, was ever and anon rent by explosions as projectiles frequently burst in mid-air. The distant roar was incessant, like the noise of thunder, while on every hand could be heard the shrieks of defenceless women and children, or the muttered curses of some man who saw his home and all he possessed swept away with a flash and a cloud of dust. Nothing could withstand that awful cannonade. Walthamstow had been rendered untenable in the first half-hour of the bombardment, while in Tottenham the loss of life had been very enormous, the German gunners at Wood Green having apparently turned their first attention upon that place. Churches, the larger buildings, the railway station, in fact, anything offering a mark, was promptly shattered, being assisted by the converging fire from the batteries at Chingford.

On the opposite side of London, Notting Hill, Shepherd's Bush, and Starch Green were being reduced to ruins by the heavy batteries above Park Royal Station, which, firing across Wormwood Scrubs, put their shots into Notting Hill, and especially into Holland Park, where widespread damage was quickly wrought.

A couple of shells falling into the generating station of the Central London Railway, or "Tube," as Londoners usually call it, unfortunately caused a disaster and loss of life which were appalling. At the first sign of the bombardment many thousands of people descended into the "Tube" as a safe hiding-place from the rain of shell. At first the railway officials closed the doors to prevent the inrush, but the terrified populace in Shepherd's Bush, Bayswater, Oxford Street, and Holborn, in fact, all along the subterranean line, broke open the doors and descending by the lifts and stairs found themselves in a place which at least gave them security against the enemy's fire.

The trains had long ago ceased running, and every station was crowded to excess, while many were forced upon the line itself, and actually into the tunnels. For hours they waited there in eager breathlessness, longing to be able to ascend and find the conflict over. Men and women in all stations of life were huddled together, while children clung to their parents in wonder; yet as hour after hour went by, the report from above was still the same—the Germans had not ceased.

Of a sudden, however, the light failed. The electric current had been cut off by the explosion of the shells in the generating station at Shepherd's Bush, and the lifts were useless! The thousands who, in defiance of the orders of the company, had gone below at Shepherd's Bush for shelter, found themselves caught like rats in a hole. True, there was the faint glimmer of an oil light here and there, but, alas! that did not prevent an awful panic.

Somebody shouted that the Germans were above and had put out the lights, and when it was found that the lifts were useless a panic ensued that was indescribable. The people could not ascend the stairs, as they were blocked by the dense crowd, therefore they pressed into the narrow semi-circular tunnels in an eager endeavour to reach the next station, where they hoped they might escape; but once in there women and children were quickly crushed to death, or thrown down and trampled upon by the press behind.

In the darkness they fought with each other, pressing on and becoming jammed so tightly that many were held against the sloping walls until life was extinct. Between Shepherd's Bush and Holland Park Stations the loss of life was worst, for being within the zone of the German fire the people had crushed in frantically in thousands, and with one accord a move had unfortunately been made into the tunnels, on account of the foolish cry that the Germans were waiting above.

The railway officials were powerless. They had done their best to prevent any one going below, but the public had insisted, therefore no blame could be laid upon them for the catastrophe.

At Marble Arch, Oxford Circus, and Tottenham Court Road Stations, a similar scene was enacted, and dozens upon dozens, alas! lost their lives in the panic. Ladies and gentlemen from Park Lane, Grosvenor Square, and Mayfair had sought shelter at the Marble Arch Station, rubbing shoulders with labourers' wives and costerwomen from the back streets of Marylebone. When the lights failed, a rush had been made into the tunnel to reach Oxford Circus, all exit by the stairs being blocked, as at Shepherd's Bush, on account of the hundreds struggling to get down.

As at Holland Park, the terrified crowd fighting with each other became jammed and suffocated in the narrow space. The catastrophe was a frightful one, for it was afterwards proved that over four hundred and twenty persons, mostly weak women and children, lost their lives in those twenty minutes of darkness before the mains at the generating station, wrecked by the explosions, could be repaired.

Then, when the current came up again, the lights revealed the frightful mishap, and people struggled to emerge from the burrows wherein they had so narrowly escaped death.

Upon the Baker Street and Waterloo and other "Tubes," every station had also been besieged. The whole of the first-mentioned line from north to south was the refuge of thousands, who saw in it a safe place for retreat. The tunnels of the District Railway, too, were filled with terror-stricken multitudes, who descended at every station and walked away into a subterranean place of safety. No trains had been running for several days, therefore there was no danger from that cause.

Meanwhile the bombardment continued with unceasing activity.

The Marylebone Station of the Great Central Railway, and the Great Central Hotel, which seemed to be only just within the line of fire, were wrecked, and about four o'clock it was seen that the hotel, like that at St. Pancras, was well alight, though no effort could be made to save it. At the first two or three alarms of fire the Metropolitan Fire Brigade had turned out, but now that fresh alarms were reaching the chief station every moment, the brigade saw themselves utterly powerless to even attempt to save the hundred buildings, great and small, now furiously blazing.

Gasometers, especially those of the Gas Light and Coke Company at Kensal Green, were marked by the German gunners, who sent them into the air; while a well-directed petrol bomb at Wormwood Scrubs Prison set one great wing of the place alight, and the prisoners were therefore released. The rear of Kensington Palace, and the fronts of a number of houses in Kensington Palace Gardens were badly damaged, while in the dome of the Albert Hall was a great, ugly hole.

Shortly after five o'clock occurred a disaster which was of national consequence. It could only have been a mishap on the part of the Germans, for they would certainly never have done such irreparable damage willingly, as they destroyed what would otherwise have been most valuable of loot.

Shots suddenly began to fall fast in Bloomsbury, several of them badly damaging the Hotel Russell and the houses near, and it was therefore apparent that one of the batteries which had been firing from near Jack Straw's Castle had been moved across to Parliament Hill, or even to some point south of it, which gave a wider range to the fire.

Presently a shell came high through the air and fell full upon the British Museum, striking it nearly in the centre of the front, and in exploding carried away the Grecian-Ionic ornament, and shattered a number of the fine stone columns of the dark façade. Ere people in the vicinity had realised that the national collection of antiques was within range of the enemy's destructive projectiles, a second shell crashed into the rear of the building, making a great gap in the walls. Then, as though all the guns of that particular battery had converged in order to destroy our treasure-house of art and antiquity, shell after shell crashed into the place in rapid succession.

Before ten minutes had passed, grey smoke began to roll out from beneath the long colonnade in front, and, growing denser, told its own tale. The British Museum was on fire.

Nor was that all. As though to complete the disaster—although it was certain that the Germans were in ignorance—there came one of those terrible shells filled with petrol, which, bursting inside the manuscript room, set the whole place ablaze. In a dozen different places the building seemed to be now alight, especially the library, and thus the finest collection of books, manuscripts, Greek and Roman and Egyptian antiques, coins, medals, and prehistoric relics, lay at the mercy of the flames.

The fire brigade was at once alarmed, and at imminent risk of their lives, for shells were still falling in the vicinity, they, with the Salvage Corps and the assistance of many willing helpers—some of whom, unfortunately, lost their lives in the flames—saved whatever could be saved, throwing the objects out into the railed-off quadrangle in front.

The left wing of the Museum, however, could not be entered, although, after most valiant efforts on the part of the firemen, the conflagrations that had broken out in other parts of the building were at length subdued. The damage was, however, irreparable, for many unique collections, including all the prints and drawings, and many of the mediæval and historic manuscripts had already been consumed.

Shots now began to fall as far south as Oxford Street, and all along that thoroughfare from Holborn as far as Oxford Circus widespread havoc was being wrought. People fled for their lives back towards Charing Cross and the Strand. The Oxford Music Hall was a hopeless ruin, while a shell crashing through the roof of Frascati's restaurant carried away a portion of the gallery and utterly wrecked the whole place. Many of the shops in Oxford Street had their roofs damaged or their fronts blown out, while a huge block of flats in Great Russell Street was practically demolished by three shells striking in rapid succession.

Then, to the alarm of all who realised it, shots were seen to be passing high over Bloomsbury, south towards the Thames. The range had been increased, for, as was afterwards known, some heavier guns had now been mounted upon Muswell Hill and Hampstead Heath, which, carrying to a distance of from six to seven miles, placed the City, the Strand, and Westminster within the zone of fire. The zone in question stretched roughly from Victoria Park through Bethnal Green and Whitechapel, across to Southwark, the Borough, Lambeth, and Westminster to Kensington, and while the fire upon the northern suburbs slackened, great shells now came flying through the air into the very heart of London.

The German gunners at Muswell Hill took the dome of St. Paul's as a mark, for shells fell constantly in Ludgate Hill, in Cheapside, in Newgate Street, and in the Churchyard itself. One falling upon the steps of the Cathedral tore out two of the columns of the front, while another, striking the clock tower just below the face, brought down much of the masonry and one of the huge bells, with a deafening crash, blocking the road with débris. Time after time the great shells went over the splendid Cathedral, which the enemy seemed bent upon destroying, but the dome remained uninjured, though about ten feet of the top of the second tower was carried away.

On the Cannon Street side of St. Paul's a great block of drapery warehouses had caught fire, and was burning fiercely, while the drapers and other shops on the Paternoster Row side all had their windows shattered by the constant detonations. Within the Cathedral two shells that had fallen through the roof had wrought havoc with the beautiful reredos and the choir-stalls, many of the fine windows being also wrecked by the explosions.

Whole rows of houses in Cheapside suffered, while both the Mansion House, where the London flag was flying, and the Royal Exchange were severely damaged by a number of shells which fell in the vicinity. The equestrian statue in front of the Exchange had been overturned, while the Exchange itself showed a great yawn-ing hole in the corner of the façade next Cornhill. At the Bank of England a fire had occurred, but had fortunately been extinguished by the strong force of Guards in charge, though they gallantly risked their lives in so doing. Lothbury, Gresham Street, Old Broad Street, Lombard Street, Gracechurch Street, and Leadenhall Street were all more or less scenes of fire, havoc, and destruction. The loss of life was not great in this neighbourhood, for most people had crossed the river or gone westward, but the high explosives used by the Germans were falling upon shops and warehouses with appalling effect.

Masonry was torn about like paper, ironwork twisted like wax, woodwork shattered to a thousand splinters as, time after time, a great projectile hissed in the air and effected its errand of destruction. A number of the wharves on each side of the river were soon alight, and both Upper and Lower Thames Streets were soon impassable on account of huge conflagrations. A few shells fell in Shoreditch, Houndsditch, and Whitechapel, and these, in most cases, caused loss of life in those densely populated districts.

Westward, however, as the hours went on, the howitzers at Hampstead began to drop high explosive shells into the Strand, around Charing Cross, and in Westminster. This weapon had a calibre of 4.14 inches, and threw a projectile of 35 lbs. The tower of St. Clement Dane's Church crashed to the ground and blocked the roadway opposite Milford Lane; the pointed roof of the clock-tower of the Law Courts was blown away, and the granite fronts of the two banks opposite the Law Courts entrance were torn out by a shell which exploded in the footpath before them.

Shells fell time after time, in and about the Law Courts themselves, committing immense damage to the interior, while a shell bursting upon the roof of Charing Cross Station, rendered it a ruin as picturesque as it had been in December, 1905. The National Liberal Club was burning furiously; the Hotel Cecil and the Savoy did not escape, but no material damage was done to them. The Garrick Theatre had caught fire; a shot carried away the globe above the Coliseum, and the Shot Tower beside the Thames crashed into the river.

The front of the Grand Hotel in Trafalgar Square showed, in several places, great holes where the shell had struck, and a shell bursting at the foot of Nelson's Monument turned over one of the lions—overthrowing the emblem of Britain's might!

The clubs in Pall Mall were, in one or two instances, wrecked, notably the Reform, the Junior Carlton, and the Athenæum, into each of which shells fell through the roof and exploded within.

From the number of projectiles that fell in the vicinity of the Houses of Parliament, it was apparent that the German gunners could see the Royal Standard flying from the Victoria Tower, and were making it their mark. In the west front of Westminster Abbey several shots crashed, doing enormous damage to the grand old pile. The hospital opposite was set alight, while the Westminster Palace Hotel was severely damaged, and two shells falling into St. Thomas's Hospital created a scene of indescribable terror in one of the overcrowded casualty wards.

Suddenly one of the German high explosive shells burst on the top of the Victoria Tower, blowing away all four of the pinnacles, and bringing down the flagstaff. Big Ben served as another mark for the artillery at Muswell Hill and several shots struck it, tearing out one of the huge clock faces and blowing away the pointed apex of the tower. Suddenly, however, two great shells struck it right in the centre, almost simultaneously, near the base, and made such a hole in the huge pile of masonry that it was soon seen to have been rendered unsafe, though it did not fall.

Shot after shot struck other portions of the Houses of Parliament, breaking the windows and carrying away pinnacles.

One of the twin towers of Westminster Abbey fell a few moments later, and another shell, crashing into the choir, completely wrecked Edward the Confessor's shrine, the Coronation Chair, and all the objects of antiquity in the vicinity.

The old Horse Guards escaped injury, but one of the cupolas of the new War Office opposite was blown away, while shortly afterwards a fire broke out in the new Local Government Board and Education Offices. Number 10, Downing Street, the chief centre of the Government, had its windows all blown in—a grim accident, no doubt—the same explosion shattering several windows in the Foreign Office.

Many shells fell in St. James's and Hyde Parks, exploding harmlessly, but others, passing across St. James's Park, crashed into that high building, Queen Anne's Mansions, causing fearful havoc. Somerset House, Covent Garden Market, Drury Lane Theatre, and the Gaiety Theatre and Restaurant all suffered more or less, and two of the bronze footguards guarding the Wellington Statue at Hyde Park Corner were blown many yards away. Around Holborn Circus immense damage was being caused, and several shells bursting on the Viaduct itself blew great holes in the bridge.

So widespread, indeed, was the havoc, that it is impossible to give a detailed account of the day's terrors. If the public buildings suffered, the damage to property of householders and the ruthless wrecking of quiet English homes may well be imagined. The people had been driven out from the zone of fire, and had left their possessions to the mercy of the invaders.

South of the Thames very little damage was done. The German howitzers and long-range guns could not reach so far. One or two shots fell in York Road, Lambeth, and in the Waterloo and Westminster Bridge Roads, but they did little damage beyond breaking all the windows in the vicinity.

When would it end? Where would it end?

Half the population of London had fled across the bridges, and from Denmark Hill, Champion Hill, Norwood, and the Crystal Palace they could see the smoke issuing from the hundred fires.

London was cowed. These northern barricades, still held by bodies of valiant men, were making a last desperate stand, though the streets ran with blood. Every man fought well and bravely for his country, though he went to his death. A thousand acts of gallant heroism on the part of Englishmen were done that day, but alas! all to no purpose. The Germans were at our gates, and were not to be denied.

As daylight commenced to fade the dust and smoke became suffocating. And yet the guns pounded away with a monotonous regularity that appalled the helpless populace. Overhead there was a quick whizzing in the air, a deafening explosion, and as the masonry came crashing down the atmosphere was filled with poisonous fumes that half asphyxiated all those in the vicinity.

Hitherto the enemy had treated us, on the whole, humanely, but finding that desperate resistance in the northern suburbs, Von Kronhelm was carrying out the Emperor's parting injunction. He was breaking the pride of our own dear London, even at the sacrifice of thousands of innocent lives.

The scenes in the streets within that zone of awful fire baffled description. They were too sudden, too dramatic, too appalling. Death and destruction were everywhere, and the people of London now realised for the first time what the horrors of war really meant.

Dusk was falling. Above the pall of smoke from burning buildings the sun was setting with a blood-red light. From the London streets, however, this evening sky was darkened by the clouds of smoke and dust. Yet the cannonade continued, each shell that came hurtling through the air exploding with deadly effect and spreading destruction on all hands.

Meanwhile the barricades at the north had not escaped Von Kronhelm's attention. About four o'clock he gave orders by field telegraph for certain batteries to move down and attack them.

This was done soon after five o'clock, and when the German guns began to pour their deadly rain of shell into those hastily improvised defences there commenced a slaughter of the gallant defenders that was horrible. At each of the barricades shell after shell was directed, and very quickly breaches were made. Then upon the defenders themselves the fire was directed—a withering, awful fire from quick-firing guns which none could withstand. The streets, with their barricades swept away, were strewn with mutilated corpses. Hundreds upon hundreds had attempted to make a last stand, rallied by the Union Jack they waved above, but a shell exploding in their midst had sent them to instant eternity.

Many a gallant deed was done that day by patriotic Londoners in defence of their homes and loved ones—many a deed that should have earned the V.C.—but in nearly all cases the patriot who had stood up and faced the foe had gone to straight and certain death.

Till seven o'clock the dull roar of the guns in the north continued, and people across the Thames knew that London was still being destroyed, nay, pulverised. Then with accord came a silence—the first silence since the hot noon.

Von Kronhelm's field telegraph at Jack Straw's Castle had ticked the order to cease firing.

All the barricades had been broken.

London lay burning—at the mercy of the German eagle.

And as the darkness fell the German Commander-in-Chief looked again through his glasses, and saw the red flames leaping up in dozens of places, where whole blocks of shops and buildings, public institutions, whole streets in some cases, were being consumed.

London—the proud capital of the world, the "home" of the Englishman—was at last ground beneath the iron heel of Germany!

And all, alas! due to one cause alone—the careless insular apathy of the Englishman himself!

CHAPTER VI

FALL OF LONDON

OUTSIDE LONDON the September night had settled down on the blood-stained field of battle. With a pale light the moon had risen, partly hidden by chasing clouds, her white rays mingling with the lurid glare of the fires down in the great terrified Metropolis below. Northward, from Hampstead across to Barnet—indeed, over that wide district where the final battle had been so hotly fought—the moonbeams shone upon the pallid faces of the fallen.

Along the German line of investment there had now followed upon the roar of battle an uncanny silence.

Away to the west, however, there was still heard the growling of distant conflict, now mounting into a low crackling of musketry fire, and again dying away in muffled sounds. The last remnant of the British Army was being hotly pursued in the direction of Staines.

London was invested and bombarded, but not yet taken.

For a long time the German Field Marshal had stood alone upon Hampstead Heath apart from his staff, watching the great tongues of flame leaping up here and there in the distant darkness. His grey, shaggy brows were contracted, his thin aquiline face thoughtful, his hard mouth twitching nervously, unable to fully conceal the strain of his own feelings as conqueror of the English. Von Kronhelm's taciturnity had long ago been proverbial. The Kaiser had likened him to Moltke, and had declared that "he could be silent in seven languages." His gaze was one of musing, and yet he was the most active of men, and perhaps the cleverest strategist in all Europe. Often during the campaign he had astonished his aides-de-camp by his untiring energy, for sometimes he would even visit the outposts in person. On many occasions he had actually crept up to the most advanced posts at great personal risk to himself, so anxious had he been to see with his own eyes. Such visits from the Field Marshal himself were not always welcome to the German outposts, who, as soon as they showed the least sign of commotion consequent upon the visit, were at once swept by a withering English fire.

Yet he now stood there the conqueror. And while many of his officers were installing themselves in comfortable quarters in houses about North End, North Hill, South Hill, Muswell Hill, Roslyn Hill, Fitzjohn's Avenue, Netherhall, and Maresfield Gardens, and other roads in that vicinity, the great Commander was still alone upon the Heath, having taken nothing save a nip from his flask since his coffee at dawn.

Time after time telegraphic despatches were handed to him from Germany, and telephonic reports from his various positions around London, but he received them all without comment. He read, he listened, but he said nothing.

For a full hour he remained there, strolling up and down alone in quick impatience. Then, as though suddenly making up his mind, he called three members of his staff, and gave orders for an entry into London.

This, as he knew, was the signal for a terrible and bloody encounter. Bugles sounded. Men and officers, who had believed that the storm and stress of the day were over, and that they were entitled to rest, found themselves called upon to fight their way into the city that they knew would be defended by an irate and antagonistic populace.

Still, the order had been given, and it must be obeyed. They had expected that the advance would be at least made at dawn, but evidently Von Kronhelm feared that six hours' delay might necessitate more desperate fighting. He intended, now that London was cowed, that she should be entirely crushed. The orders of his master the Kaiser were to that effect.

Therefore, shortly before nine o'clock the first detachments of German infantry marched along Spaniards Road, and down Roslyn Hill to Haverstock Hill, where they were at once fired upon from behind the *débris* of the great barricade across the junction of Prince of Wales Road and Haverstock Hill. This place was held strongly by British Infantry, many members of the Legion of Frontiersmen—distinguished only by the little bronze badge in their buttonholes—and also by hundreds of citizens armed with rifles.

Twenty Germans dropped at the first volley, and next instant a Maxim, concealed in the first floor of a neighbouring house, spat forth its fire upon the invaders with deadly effect. The German bugle sounded the "Advance rapidly," and the men emulously ran forward, shouting loud hurrahs. Major van Wittich, who had distinguished himself very conspicuously in the fighting round Enfield Chase, fell, being shot through the lung when just within a few yards of the half-ruined barricade. Londoners were fighting desperately, shouting and cheering. The standard-bearer of the 4th Battalion of the Brunswick Infantry Regiment, No. 92, fell severely wounded, and the standard was instantly snatched from him in the awful hand-to-hand fighting which that moment ensued.

Five minutes later the streets were running with blood, for hundreds, both Germans and British, lay dead and dying. Every Londoner struggled valiantly until shot down; yet the enemy, always reinforced, pressed forward, until ten minutes later the defenders were driven out of their position, and the house from which the Maxim was sending forth its deadly hail had been entered and the gun captured. Volley after volley was still, however, poured out on the heads of the storming party, but already the pioneers were at work clearing a way for the advance, and very soon the Germans had surmounted the obstruction and were within London.

For a short time the Germans halted, then, at a signal from their officers, they moved along both roads, again being fired upon from every house in the vicinity, many of the defenders having retired to continue their defence from the windows. The enemy therefore turned their attention to these houses, and after desperate struggles house after house was taken, those of the defenders not wearing uniform being shot down without mercy. To such no quarter was given.

The contest now became a most furious one. Britons and Germans fought hand to hand. A battalion of the Brunswick Infantry with some riflemen of the Guard took several houses by rush in Chalk Farm Road; but in many cases the Germans were shot by their own comrades. Quite a number of the enemy's officers were picked off by the Frontiersmen, those brave fellows who had seen service in every corner of the world, and who were now in the windows and upon roofs. Thus the furious fight from house to house proceeded.

This exciting conflict was practically characteristic of what was at that moment happening in fifty other spots along the suburbs of North London. The obstinate resistance which we made against the Germans was met with equally obstinate aggression. There was no surrender. Londoners fell and died fighting to the very last.

Against those well-trained Teutons in such overwhelming masses we, however, could have no hope of success. The rushes of the infantry and rifles of the Guards were made skilfully, and slowly but surely broke down all opposition.

The barricade in the Kentish Town Road was defended with valiant heroism. The Germans were, as in Chalk Farm Road, compelled to fight their way foot by foot, losing heavily all the time. But here, at length, as at other points, the barricade was taken, and the defenders chased, and either taken prisoner or else ruthlessly shot down. A body of citizens armed with rifles were, after the storming of the barricades in question, driven back into Park Street, and there, being caught between two bodies of Germans, slaughtered to a man. Through those unlit side streets between the Kentish Town and Camden Roads—namely, the Lawford, Bartholomew, Rochester, Caversham, and Leighton Roads—there was much skirmishing, and many on both sides fell in the bloody encounter. A thousand deeds of bravery were done that night, but were unrecorded. Before the barricade in Holloway Road—which had been strongly repaired after the breach made in it by the German shells—the enemy lost very heavily, for the three Maxims which had there been mounted did awful execution. The invaders, however, seeing the strong defence, fell back for full twenty minutes, and then, making another rush, hurled petrol bombs into the midst of our men.

A frightful holocaust was the result. Fully a hundred of the poor fellows were literally burned alive; while the neighbouring houses, being set in flames, compelled the citizen free-shooters to quickly evacuate their position. Against such terrible missiles even the best trained troops cannot stand, therefore no wonder that all opposition at that point was soon afterwards swept away, and the pioneers quickly opened the road for the victorious legions of the Kaiser.

And so in that prosaic thoroughfare, the Holloway Road, brave men fought gallantly and died, while a Scotch piper paced the pavement sharply, backwards and forwards, with his colours flying. Then, alas! came the red flash, the loud explosions in rapid succession, and the next instant the whole street burst into a veritable sea of flame.

High Street, Kingsland, was also the scene of several fierce conflicts; but here the Germans decidedly got the worst of it. The whole infuriated population seemed to emerge suddenly from the side streets of the Kingsland Road on the appearance of the detachment of the enemy, and the latter were practically overwhelmed, notwithstanding the desperate fight they made. Then ringing cheers went up from the defenders.

The Germans were given no quarter by the populace, all of whom were armed with knives or guns, the women mostly with hatchets, crowbars, or edged tools.

Many of the Germans fled through the side streets towards Mare Street, and were hotly pursued, the majority of them being done to death by the maddened mob. The streets in this vicinity were literally a slaughterhouse.

The barricades in Finchley Road, and in High Road, Kilburn, were also very strongly held, and at the first-named it was quite an hour before the enemy's pioneers were able to make a breach. Indeed, then only after a most hotly contested conflict, in which there were frightful losses on both sides. Petrol bombs were here also used by the enemy with appalling effect, the road being afterwards cleared by a couple of Maxims.

Farther towards Regent's Park the houses were, however, full of sharpshooters, and before these could be dislodged the enemy had again suffered severely. The entry into London was both difficult and perilous, and the enemy suffered great losses everywhere.

After the breaking down of the defences in High Road, Kilburn, the men who had held them retired to the Town Hall, opposite Kilburn Station, and from the windows fired at the passing battalions, doing much execution. All efforts to dislodge them proved unavailing, until the place was taken by storm, and a fearful hand to hand fight was the outcome. Eventually the Town Hall was taken, after a most desperate resistance, and ten minutes later wilfully set fire to and burned.

In the Harrow Road and those cross streets between Kensal Green and Maida Vale the advancing Germans shared much the same fate as about Hackney. Surrounded by the armed populace, hundreds upon hundreds of them were killed, struck down by hatchets, stabbed by knives, or shot with revolvers, the crowd shouting, "Down with the Germans! Kill them! Kill them!"

Many of the London women now became perfect furies. So incensed were they at the wreck of their homes and the death of their loved ones that they rushed wildly into the fray with no thought of peril, only of bitter revenge. A German whenever caught was at once killed. In those bloody street fights the Teutons got separated from their comrades and were quickly surrounded and done to death.

Across the whole of the northern suburbs the scenes of bloodshed that night were full of horror, as men fought in the ruined streets, climbing over the smouldering débris, over the bodies of their comrades, and shooting from behind ruined walls. As Von Kronhelm had anticipated, his Army was compelled to fight its way into London.

The streets all along the line of the enemy's advance were now strewn with dead and dying. London was doomed.

The Germans now coming on in increasing, nay, unceasing numbers, were leaving behind them everywhere the trail of blood. Shattered London stood staggered.

Though the resistance had been long and desperate, the enemy had again triumphed by reason of his sheer weight of numbers.

Yet, even though he were actually in our own dear London, our people did not mean that he should establish himself without any further opposition. Therefore, though the barricades had been taken, the Germans found in every unexpected corner men who shot at them, and Maxims which spat forth their leaden showers beneath which hundreds upon hundreds of Teutons fell.

Yet they advanced, still fighting. The scenes of carnage were awful and indescribable, no quarter being given to any armed citizens not in uniform, be they men, women, or children.

The German Army was carrying out the famous proclamation of Field Marshal von Kronhelm to the letter!

They were marching on to the sack of the wealthiest city of the world.

It wanted still an hour of midnight. London was a city of shadow, of fire, of death. The silent streets, whence all the inhabitants had fled in panic, echoed to the heavy tread of German infantry, the clank of arms, and the ominous rumble of guns. Ever and anon an order was shouted in German as the Kaiser's legions went forward to occupy the proud capital of the world. The enemy's plans appeared to have been carefully prepared. The majority of the troops coming from the direction of Hampstead and Finchley entered Regent's Park, whence preparations were at once commenced for encampment; while the remainder, together with those who came down the Camden, Caledonian, and Holloway Roads, turned along Euston Road and Oxford Street to Hyde Park, where a huge camp was formed, stretching from the Marble Arch right along the Park Lane side away to Knightsbridge.

Officers were very soon billeted in the best houses in Park Lane and about Mayfair—houses full of works of art and other valuables that had only that morning been left to the mercy of the invaders. From the windows and balconies of their quarters in Park Lane they could overlook the encampment—a position which had evidently been purposely chosen.

Other troops who came in never-ending procession by the Bow Road, Roman Road, East India Dock Road, Victoria Park Road, Mare Street, and Kingsland Road all converged into the City itself, except those who had come from Edmonton down the Kingsland Road, and who, passing along Old Street and Clerkenwell, occupied the Charing Cross and Westminster districts.

At midnight a dramatic scene was enacted when, in the blood-red glare of some blazing buildings in the vicinity, a large body of Prince Louis Ferdinand of Prussia's 2nd Magdeburg Regiment suddenly swept up Threadneedle Street into the great open space before the Mansion House, whereon the London flag was still flying aloft in the smoke-laden air. They halted across the junction of Cheapside with Queen Victoria Street when, at the same moment, another huge body of the Uhlans of Altmark and Magdeburg Hussars came clattering along Cornhill, followed a moment later by battalion after battalion of the 4th and 8th Thuringen Infantry out of Moorgate Street, whose uniforms showed plain traces of the desperate encounters of the past week.

The great body of Germans had halted before the Mansion House, when General von Kleppen, the commander of the IVth Army Corps—who, it will be remembered, had landed at Weybourne—accompanied by Lieutenant-General von Mirbach, of the 8th Division, and Frölich, commander of the cavalry brigade, ascended the steps of the Mansion House and entered.

Within, Sir Claude Harrison, the Lord Mayor, who wore his robes and jewel of office, received them in that great, sombre room wherein so many momentous questions concerning the welfare of the British Empire had been discussed. The representative of the City of London, a short, stout, gray-haired man, was pale and agitated. He bowed, but he could not speak.

Von Kleppen, however, a smart, soldierly figure in his service uniform and many ribbons, bowed in response, and in very fair English said:—

"I regret, my Lord Mayor, that it is necessary for us to thus disturb you, but as you are aware, the British Army has been defeated, and the German Army has entered London. I have orders from Field Marshal von Kronhelm to place you under arrest, and to hold you as hostage for the good behaviour of the City during the progress of the negotiations for peace."

"Arrest!" gasped the Lord Mayor. "You intend to arrest me?"

"It will not be irksome, I assure you," smiled the German commander grimly. "At least, we shall make it as comfortable as possible. I shall place a guard here, and the only restriction I place upon you is that you shall neither go out nor hold any communication with any one outside these walls."

"But my wife?"

"If her ladyship is here I would advise that she leave the place. It is better that, for the present, she should be out of London."

The civic officials, who had all assembled for the dramatic ceremonial, looked at each other in blank amazement. The Lord Mayor was a prisoner!

Sir Claude divested himself of his jewel of office, and handed it to his servant to replace in safe keeping. Then he took off his robe, and, having done so, advanced closer to the German officers, who, treating him with every courtesy, consulted with him, expressing regret at the terrible loss of life that had been occasioned by the gallant defence of the barricades.

Von Kleppen gave the Lord Mayor a message from Von Kronhelm, and urged him to issue a proclamation forbidding any further opposition on the part of the populace of London. With the three officers Sir Claude talked for a quarter of an hour, while into the Mansion House there entered a strong guard of men of the 2nd Magdeburg, who quickly established themselves in the most comfortable quarters. German double sentries stood at every exit and in every corridor, and when a few minutes later the flag was hauled down and the German Imperial Standard run up, wild shouts of triumph rang from every throat of the densely packed body of troops assembled outside.

The joyous "hurrahs!" reached the Lord Mayor, still in conversation with Von Kleppen, Von Mirbach, and Frölich, and in an instant he knew the truth. The Teutons were saluting their own standard.

The civic flag had, either accidentally or purposely, been flung down into the roadway below, and was trampled in the dust. A hundred enthusiastic Germans, disregarding the shouts of their officers, fought for the flag, and it was instantly torn to shreds, and little pieces preserved as souvenirs.

Shout after shout in German went up from the wildly excited troops of the Kaiser when the light wind caused their own flag to flutter out, and then, as with one voice, the whole body of troops united in singing the German National Hymn.

The scene was weird and most impressive. London had fallen.

Around were the wrecked buildings, some still smouldering, some emitting flame. Behind lay the Bank of England with untold wealth locked within: to the right the damaged façade of the Royal Exchange was illuminated by a flickering light, which also shone upon the piled arms of the enemy's troops, causing them to flash and gleam.

In those silent, narrow City streets not an Englishman was to be seen. Every one save the Lord Mayor and his official attendants had fled.

The Government Offices in Whitehall were all in the hands of the enemy. In the Foreign Office, the India Office, the War Office, the Colonial Office, the Admiralty, and other minor offices were German guards. Sentries stood at the shattered door of the famous No. 10, Downing Street, and all up Whitehall was lined with infantry.

German officers were in charge of all our public offices, and all officials who had remained on duty were firmly requested to leave. Sentries were stationed to guard the archives of every department, and precautions were taken to guard against any further outbreaks of fire.

Across at the Houses of Parliament, with their damaged towers, the whole great pile of buildings was surrounded by triumphant troops, while across at the fine old Abbey of Westminster was, alas! a different scene. The interior had been turned into a temporary hospital, and upon mattresses placed upon the floor were hundreds of poor maimed creatures, some groaning, some ghastly pale in the last moments of agony, some silent, their white lips moving in prayer.

On one side in the dim light lay the men, some in uniform, others inoffensive citizens, who had been struck by cruel shells or falling *débris*; on the other side lay the women, some mere girls, and even children.

Flitting everywhere in the half light were nurses, charitable ladies, and female helpers, with numbers of doctors, all doing their best to alleviate the terrible sufferings of that crowded place, the walls of which showed plain traces of the severe bombardment. In places the roof was open to the angry sky, while many of the windows were gaunt and shattered.

A clergyman's voice somewhere was repeating a prayer in a low, distinct voice, so that all could hear, yet above all were the sighs and groans of the sufferers, and as one walked through that prostrate assembly of victims more than one was seen to have already gone to that land that lies beyond the human ken.

The horrors of war were never more forcibly illustrated than in Westminster Abbey that night, for the grim hand of death was there, and men and women lying with their faces to the roof looked into Eternity. Every hospital in London was full, therefore the overflow had been placed in the various churches. From the battlefields along the northern defences, Epping, Edmonton, Barnet, Enfield, and other places where the last desperate stand had been made, and from the barricades in the northern suburbs ambulance waggons were continually arriving full of wounded, all of whom were placed in the churches and in any large public buildings which had remained undamaged by the bombardment.

St. George's, Hanover Square, once the scene of many smart weddings, was now packed with unfortunate wounded soldiers, British and German lying side by side, while in the Westminster Cathedral and the Oratory at Brompton the Roman Catholic priests made hundreds of poor fellows as comfortable as they could, many members of the religious sisterhoods acting as nurses. St. James's Church in Piccadilly, St. Pancras Church, Shoreditch Church, and St. Mary Abbotts', Kensington, were all improvised hospitals, and many grim and terrible scenes of agony were witnessed during that long eventful night.

The light was dim everywhere, for there were only paraffin lamps, and by their feeble illumination many a difficult operation had to be performed by those London surgeons who one and all had come forward, and were now working unceasingly. Renowned specialists from Harley Street, Cavendish Square, Queen Ann Street, and the vicinity were directing the work in all the improvised hospitals, men whose names were world-famous kneeling and performing operations upon poor unfortunate private soldiers or upon some labourer who had taken up a gun in defence of his home.

Of lady helpers there were hundreds. From Mayfair and Belgravia, from Kensington and Bayswater, ladies had come forward offering their services, and their devotion to the wounded was everywhere apparent. In St. Andrew's, Wells Street, St. Peter's, Eaton Square, in the Scottish Church in Crown Court, Covent Garden, in the Temple Church, in the Union Chapel in Upper Street, in the Chapel Royal, Savoy, in St. Clement Danes in the Strand, and in St. Martin's-in-the-Fields, there were wounded in greater or less numbers, but the difficulties of treating them were enormous owing to the lack of necessaries for the performance of operations.

Weird and striking were the scenes within those hallowed places, as, in the half darkness with the long, deep shadows, men struggled for life or gave to the women kneeling at their side their name, their address, or a last dying message to one they loved.

London that night was a city of shattered homes, of shattered hopes, of shattered lives.

The silence of death had fallen everywhere. The only sounds that broke the quiet within those churches were the sighs, groans, and faint murmurings of the dying.

CHAPTER VII

GERMANS SACKING THE BANKS

DAY DAWNED DISMALLY and wet on September the 21st.

Over London the sky was still obscured by the smoke-pall, though as the night passed many of the raging fires had spent themselves.

Trafalgar Square was filled with troops who had piled arms and were standing at their ease. The men were laughing and smoking, enjoying a rest after the last forward movement and the street fighting of that night of horrors.

The losses on both sides during the past three days had been enormous; of the number of London citizens killed and wounded it was impossible to calculate. There had, in the northern suburbs, been wholesale butchery everywhere, so gallantly had the barricades been defended.

Great camps had now been formed in Hyde Park, in the Green Park between Constitution Hill and Piccadilly, and in St. James's Park. The Magdeburg Fusiliers were being formed up on the Horse Guards Parade, and from the flagstaff there now fluttered the ensign of the commander of an army corps, in place of the British flag. A large number of Uhlans and Cuirassiers were encamped at the west end of the Park, opposite Buckingham Palace, and both the Wellington Barracks and the Cavalry Barracks at Knightsbridge were occupied by Germans.

Many officers were already billeted in the Savoy, the Cecil, the Carlton, the Grand, and Victoria hotels, while the British Museum, the National Gallery, the South Kensington Museum, the Tower, and a number of other collections of pictures and antiques were all guarded strongly by German sentries. The enemy had thus seized our national treasures.

London awoke to find herself a German city.

In the streets lounging groups of travel-worn sons of the Fatherland were everywhere, and German was heard on every hand. Every

ounce of foodstuff was being rapidly commandeered by hundreds
of foraging parties, who went to each grocer's, baker's, or provision
shop in the various districts, seized all they could find, valued it,
and gave official receipts for it.

The price of food in London that morning was absolutely prohibitive, as much as two shillings being asked for a twopenny loaf.
The Germans had, it was afterwards discovered, been all the time,
since the Sunday when they landed, running over large cargoes of
supplies of all sorts to the Essex, Lincolnshire, and Norfolk coasts,
where they had established huge supply bases, well knowing that
there was not sufficient food in the country to feed their armed
hordes in addition to the population.

Shops in Tottenham Court Road, Holborn, Edgware Road, Oxford
Street, Camden Road, and Harrow Road were systematically visited
by the foraging parties, who commenced their work at dawn. Those
places that were closed and their owners absent were at once broken
open, and everything seized and carted to either Hyde Park or St.
James's Park, for though Londoners might starve, the Kaiser's troops
intended to be fed.

In some cases a patriotic shopkeeper attempted to resist. Indeed,
in more than one case a tradesman wilfully set his shop on fire rather
than its contents should fall into the enemy's hands. In other cases
the tradesmen who received the official German receipts burned
them in contempt before the officer's eyes.

The guidance of these foraging parties was, in very many cases,
in the hands of Germans in civilian clothes, and it was now
seen how complete and helpful the enemy's system of espionage
had been in London. Most of these men were Germans who,
having served in the army, had come over to England and obtained
employment as waiters, clerks, bakers, hairdressers, and private
servants, and being bound by their oath to the Fatherland had
served their country as spies. Each man, when obeying the Imperial command to join the German arms, had placed in the lapel
of his coat a button of a peculiar shape, with which he had long
ago been provided, and by which he was instantly recognised as
a loyal subject of the Kaiser.

This huge body of German soldiers, who for years had passed in England as civilians, was, of course, of enormous use to Von Kronhelm, for they acted as guides not only on the march and during the entry to London, but materially assisted in the victorious advance in the Midlands. Indeed, the Germans had for years kept a civilian army in England, and yet we had, ostrich-like, buried our heads in the sand, and refused to turn our eyes to the grave peril that had for so long threatened.

Systematically, the Germans were visiting every shop and warehouse in the shopping districts, and seizing everything eatable they could discover. The enemy were taking the food from the mouths of the poor in East and South London, and as they went southward across the river, so the populace retired, leaving their homes at the mercy of the ruthless invader.

Upon all the bridges across the Thames stood German guards, and none were allowed to cross without permits.

Soon after dawn Von Kronhelm and his staff rode down Haverstock Hill with a large body of cavalry, and made his formal entry into London, first having an interview with the Lord Mayor, and an hour afterwards establishing his headquarters at the new War Office in Whitehall, over which he hoisted his special flag as Commander-in-Chief. It was found that, though a good deal of damage had been done externally to the building, the interior had practically escaped, save one or two rooms. Therefore the Field Marshal installed himself in the private room of the War Minister, and telegraphic and telephonic communication was quickly established, while a wireless telegraph apparatus was placed upon the ruined summit of Big Ben for the purpose of communicating with Germany, in case the cables were interrupted by being cut at sea.

The day after the landing a similar apparatus had been erected on the Monument at Yarmouth, and it had been daily in communication with the one at Bremen. The German left nothing to chance.

The clubs in Pall Mall were now being used by German officers, who lounged in easy chairs, smoking and taking their ease, German soldiers being on guard outside. North of the Thames seemed practically deserted, save for the invaders who swarmed everywhere. South of the Thames the cowed and terrified populace were asking what the end was to be. What was the Government doing? It had fled to Bristol and left London to its fate, they complained.

What the German demands were was not known until the *Daily Telegraph* published an interview with Sir Claude Harrison, the Lord Mayor, which gave authentic details of them.

They were as follows:—

1. Indemnity of £300,000,000, paid in ten annual instalments.
2. Until this indemnity is paid in full, German troops to occupy Edinburgh, Rosyth, Chatham, Dover, Portsmouth, Devonport, Pembroke, Yarmouth, Hull.
3. Cession to Germany of the Shetlands, Orkneys, Bantry Bay, Malta, Gibraltar, and Tasmania.
4. India, north of a line drawn from Calcutta to Baroda, to be ceded to Russia.
5. The independence of Ireland to be recognised.

Of the claim of £300,000,000, fifty millions was demanded from London, the sum in question to be paid within twelve hours.

The Lord Mayor had, it appeared, sent his secretary to the Prime Minister at Bristol bearing the original document in the handwriting of Von Kronhelm. The Prime Minister had acknowledged its receipt by telegraph both to the Lord Mayor and to the German Field Marshal, but there the matter had ended.

The twelve hours' grace was nearly up, and the German Commander, seated in Whitehall, had received no reply.

In the corner of the large, pleasant, well-carpeted room sat a German telegraph engineer with a portable instrument, in direct communication with the Emperor's private cabinet at Potsdam, and over that wire messages were continually passing and repassing.

The grizzled old soldier paced the room impatiently. His Emperor had only an hour ago sent him a message of warm congratulation, and had privately informed him of the high honours he intended to bestow upon him. The German Eagle was victorious, and London—the great unconquerable London—lay crushed, torn, and broken.

The marble clock upon the mantelpiece shelf chimed eleven upon its silvery bells, causing Von Kronhelm to turn from the window to glance at his own watch.

"Tell His Majesty that it is eleven o'clock, and that there is no reply to hand," he said sharply in German to the man in uniform seated at the table in the corner.

The instrument clicked rapidly, and a silence followed.

The German Commander waited anxiously. He stood bending slightly over the green tape in order to read the Imperial order the instant it flashed from beneath the sea.

Five minutes—ten minutes passed. The shouting of military commands in German came up from Whitehall below. Nothing else broke the quiet.

Von Kronhelm, his face more furrowed and more serious, again paced the carpet.

Suddenly the little instrument whirred, and clicked as its thin green tape rolled out.

In an instant the Generalissimo of the Kaiser's army sprang to the telegraphist's side and read the Imperial command.

For a moment he held the piece of tape between his fingers, then crushed it in his hand and stood motionless.

He had received orders which, though against his desire, he was compelled to obey.

Summoning several members of his staff who had installed themselves in other comfortable rooms in the vicinity, he held a long consultation with them.

In the meantime telegraphic despatches were received from Sheffield, Manchester, Birmingham, and other German headquarters, all telling the same story—the complete investment and occupation of the big cities and the pacification of the inhabitants.

One hour's grace was, however, allowed to London—till noon.

Then orders were issued, bugles rang out across the parks, and in the main thoroughfares, where arms were piled, causing the troops to fall in, and within a quarter of an hour large bodies of infantry and engineers were moving along the Strand, in the direction of the City.

At first the reason of all this was a mystery, but very shortly it was realised what was intended when a detachment of the 5th Hanover Regiment advanced to the gate of the Bank of England opposite the Exchange, and, after some difficulty, broke it open and entered, followed by some engineers of Von Mirbach's Division. The building was very soon occupied, and, under the direction of General Von Kleppen himself, an attempt was made to open the strong rooms, wherein was stored that vast hoard of England's wealth. What actually occurred at that spot can only be imagined, as the commander of the IVth Army Corps and one or two officers and men were the only persons present. It is surmised, however, that the strength of the vaults was far greater than they had imagined, and that, though they worked for hours, all was in vain.

While this was in progress, however, parties of engineers were making organised raids upon the banks in Lombard Street, Lothbury, Moorgate Street, and Broad Street, as well as upon branch banks in Oxford Street, the Strand, and other places in the West End.

At one bank on the left-hand side of Lombard Street, dynamite being used to force the strong room, the first bullion was seized, while at nearly all the banks sooner or later the vaults were opened, and great bags and boxes of gold coin were taken out and conveyed in carefully guarded carts to the Bank of England, now in the possession of Germany.

In some banks—those of more modern construction—the greatest resistance was offered by the huge steel doors and concrete and steel walls and other devices for security. But nothing could, alas! resist the high explosives used, and in the end breaches were made, in all cases, and wealth uncounted and untold extracted and conveyed to Threadneedle Street for safe keeping.

Engineers and infantry handled those heavy boxes and those big bundles of securities gleefully, officers carefully counting each box or bag or packet as it was taken out to be carted or carried away by hand.

German soldiers under guard struggled along Lothbury beneath great burdens of gold, and carts, requisitioned out of the East End, rumbled heavily all the afternoon, escorted by soldiers.

Hammersmith, Camberwell, Hampstead, and Willesden yielded up their quota of the great wealth of London; but though soon after four o'clock a breach was made in the strong rooms of the Bank of England by means of explosives, nothing in the vaults was touched. The Germans simply entered there and formally took possession.

The coin collected from other banks was carefully kept, each separate from another, and placed in various rooms under strong guards, for it seemed to be their intention simply to hold London's wealth as security.

That afternoon very few banks—except the German ones— escaped notice. Of course, there were a few small branches in the suburbs which remained unvisited, yet by six o'clock Von Kronhelm was in possession of enormous quantities of gold.

In one or two quarters there had been opposition on the part of the armed guards established by the banks at the first news of the invasion. But any such resistance had, of course, been futile, and the man who had dared to fire upon the German soldiers had in every case been shot down.

Thus, when darkness fell, Von Kronhelm, from the corner of his room in the War Office, was able to report to his Imperial Master that not only had he occupied London, but that, receiving no reply to his demand for indemnity, he had sacked it and taken possession not only of the Bank of England, but of the cash deposits in most of the other banks in the metropolis.

That night the evening papers described the wild happenings of the afternoon, and London saw herself not only shattered, but ruined. The frightened populace across the river stood breathless. What was now to happen?

Though London lay crushed and occupied by the enemy, though the Lord Mayor was a prisoner of war and the banks in the hands of the Germans, though the metropolis had been wrecked and more than half its inhabitants had fled southward and westward into the country, yet the enemy received no reply to their demand for an indemnity and the cession of British territory.

Von Kronhelm, ignorant of what had occurred in the House of Commons at Bristol, sat in Whitehall and wondered. He knew well that the English were no fools, and their silence, therefore, caused him considerable uneasiness. He had lost in the various engagements over 50,000 men, yet nearly 200,000 still remained. His army of invasion was no mean responsibility, especially when at any moment the British might regain command of the sea. His supplies and reinforcements would then be at once cut off. It was impossible for him to live upon the country, and his food bases in Suffolk and Essex were not sufficiently extensive to enable him to make a prolonged campaign. Indeed, the whole scheme of operations which had been so long discussed and perfected in secret in Berlin was more of the nature of a raid than a prolonged siege.

The German Field Marshal sat alone and reflected. Had he been aware of the true state of affairs he would certainly have had considerable cause for alarm. True, though Lord Byfield had made such a magnificent stand, considering the weakness of the force at his disposal, and London was occupied, yet England was not conquered.

No news had leaked out from Bristol. Indeed, Parliament had taken every precaution that its deliberations were in secret.

The truth, however, may be briefly related. On the previous day the House had met at noon in the Colston Hall—a memorable sitting, indeed. The Secretary of State for War had, after prayers, risen in the hall and read an official despatch he had just received from Lord Byfield, giving the news of the last stand made by the British north of Enfield, and the utter hopelessness of the situation. It was received by the assembled House in ominous silence.

During the past week through that great hall the Minister's deep voice, shaken by emotion, had been daily heard as he was compelled to report defeat after defeat of the British arms. Both sides of the House had, after the first few days, been forced to recognise Germany's superiority in numbers, in training, in organisation—in fact in everything appertaining to military power. Von Kronhelm's strategy had been perfect. He knew more of Eastern England than the British Commander himself, and his marvellous system of spies and advance agents—Germans who had lived for years in England—had assisted him forward, until he had now occupied London, the city declared to be impregnable.

CITIZENS OF LONDON

WE, the GENERAL COMMANDING the German Imperial Army occupying London, give notice that:

(1) THE STATE OF WAR AND OF SIEGE continues to exist, and all categories of crime, more especially the contravention of all orders already issued, will be judged by Councils of War, and punished in conformity with martial law.

(2) THE INHABITANTS OF LONDON and its suburbs are ordered to instantly deliver up all arms and ammunition of whatever kind they possess. The term arms includes firearms, sabres, swords, daggers, revolvers, and sword-canes. Landlords and occupiers of houses are charged to see that this order is carried out, but in the case of their absence the municipal authorities and officials of the London County Council are charged to make domiciliary visits, minute and searching, being accompanied by a military guard.

(3) ALL NEWSPAPERS, JOURNALS, GAZETTES, AND PROCLAMATIONS, of whatever description, are hereby prohibited, and until further notice nothing further must be printed, except documents issued publicly by the military commander.

(4) ANY PRIVATE PERSON OR PERSONS taking arms against the German troops after this notice will be EXECUTED.

(5) ON THE CONTRARY, the Imperial German troops will respect private property, and no requisition will be allowed to be made unless it bears the authorisation of the Commander-in-Chief.

(6) ALL PUBLIC PLACES are to be closed at 8 P.M. All persons found in the streets of London after 8 P.M. will be arrested by the patrols. There is no exception to this rule except in the case of German Officers, and also in the case of doctors visiting their patients. Municipal officials will also be allowed out, providing they obtain a permit from the German headquarters.

(7) MUNICIPAL AUTHORITIES MUST provide for the lighting of the streets. In cases where this is impossible, each householder must hang a lantern outside his house from nightfall until 8 A.M.

> (8) AFTER TO-MORROW morning, at 10 o'clock, the women and children of the population of London will be allowed to pass without hindrance.
>
> (9) MUNICIPAL AUTHORITIES MUST, with as little delay as possible, provide accommodation for the German troops in private dwellings, in fire-stations, barracks, hotels, and houses that are still habitable.
>
> VON KRONHELM, Commander-in-Chief
>
> German Military Headquarters,
> WHITEHALL, London, September 21, 1910

Through the whole of September 20 the Minister constantly received despatches from the British Field Marshal and from London itself, yet each telegram communicated to the House seemed more hopeless than its predecessor.

The debate, however, proceeded through the afternoon. The Opposition were bitterly attacking the Government and the Blue Water School for its gross negligence in the past, and demanding to know the whereabouts of the remnant of the British Navy. The First Lord of the Admiralty flatly refused to make any statement. The whereabouts of our Navy at that moment was, he said, a secret, which must, at all hazards, be withheld from our enemy. The Admiralty were not asleep, as the country believed, but were fully alive to the seriousness of the crisis. He urged the House to remain patient, saying that as soon as he dared he would make a statement.

This was greeted by loud jeers from the Opposition, from whose benches, members, one after another, rose, and, using hard epithets, blamed the Government for the terrible disaster. The cutting down of our defences, the meagre naval programmes, the discouragement of the Volunteers and of recruiting, and the disregard of Lord Roberts' scheme in 1906 for universal military training were, they declared, responsible for what had occurred. The Government had been culpably negligent, and Mr. Haldane's scheme had been all insufficient. Indeed, it had been nothing short of criminal to mislead the Empire into a false sense of security which did not exist.

For the past three years Germany, while sapping our industries, had sent spies into our midst, and laughed at us for our foolish insular superiority. She had turned her attention from France to ourselves, notwithstanding the *entente cordiale*. She remembered how the much-talked-of Franco-Russian alliance had fallen to pieces, and relied upon a similar outcome of the friendship between France and Great Britain.

The aspect of the House, too, was strange; the Speaker in his robes looked out of place in his big uncomfortable chair, and members sat on cane-bottomed chairs instead of their comfortable benches at Westminster. As far as possible the usual arrangement of the House was adhered to, except that the Press were now excluded, official reports being furnished to them at midnight.

The clerks' table was a large plain one of stained wood, but upon it was the usual array of despatches, while the Serjeant-at-Arms, in his picturesque dress, was still one of the most prominent figures. The lack of committee rooms, of an adequate lobby, and of a refreshment department caused much inconvenience, though a temporary post and telegraph office had been established within the building, and a separate line connected the Prime Minister's room with Downing Street.

If the Government were denounced in unmeasured terms, its defence was equally vigorous. Thus, through that never-to-be-forgotten afternoon the sitting continued past the dinner hour on to late in the evening.

Time after time the despatches from London were placed in the hands of the War Minister, but, contrary to the expectation of the House, he vouchsafed no further statement. It was noticed that just before ten o'clock he consulted in an earnest undertone with the Prime Minister, the First Lord of the Admiralty, and the Home Secretary, and that a quarter of an hour later all four went out and were closeted in one of the smaller rooms with other members of the Cabinet for nearly half an hour.

Then the Secretary of State for War re-entered the House and resumed his seat in silence.

A few minutes afterwards Mr. Thomas Askern, member of one of the Metropolitan boroughs, and a well-known newspaper proprietor, who had himself received several private despatches, rose and received leave to put a question to the War Minister.

"I would like to ask the Right Honourable the Secretary of State for War," he said, "whether it is not a fact that soon after noon to-day the enemy, having moved his heavy artillery to certain positions commanding North London, and finding the capital strongly barricaded, proceeded to bombard it? Whether that bombardment, according to the latest despatches, is not still continuing at this moment; whether it is not a fact that enormous damage has already been done to many of the principal buildings of the metropolis, including the Government Offices at Whitehall, and whether great loss of life has not been occasioned?"

The question produced the utmost sensation. The House during the whole afternoon had been in breathless anxiety as to what was actually happening in London; but the Government held the telegraphs and telephone, and the only private despatches that had come to Bristol were the two received by some roundabout route known only to the ingenious journalists who had despatched them. Indeed, the despatches had been conveyed the greater portion of the way by motor-car.

A complete silence fell. Every face was turned towards the War Minister, who, seated with outstretched legs, was holding a fresh despatch he had just received.

He rose, and, in his deep bass voice, said:—

"In reply to the honourable member for South-East Brixton, the statement he makes appears, from information which has just reached me, to be correct. The Germans are, unfortunately, bombarding London. Von Kronhelm, it is reported, is at Hampstead, and the zone of the enemy's artillery reaches, in some cases, as far south as the Thames itself. It is true, as the honourable member asserts, an enormous amount of damage has already been done to various buildings, and there has undoubtedly been great loss of life. My latest information is that the non-combatant inhabitants—old persons, women, and children—are in flight across the Thames, and that the barricades in the principal roads leading in from the north are held strongly by the armed populace, driven back into London."

He sat down without further word.

A tall, thin, white-moustached man rose at that moment from the Opposition side of the House. Colonel Farquhar, late of the Royal Marines, was a well-known military critic, and represented West Bude.

"And this," he said, "is the only hope of England! The defence of London by an armed mob, pitted against the most perfectly equipped and armed force in the world! Londoners are patriotic, I grant. They will die fighting for their homes, as every Englishman will when the moment comes; yet, what can we hope, when patriotism is ranged against modern military science? There surely is patriotism in the savage negro races of Central Africa, a love of country perhaps as deep as in the white man's heart; yet a little strategy, a few Maxims, and all defence is quickly at an end. And so it must inevitably be with London. I contend, Mr. Speaker," he went on, "that by the ill-advised action of the Government from the first hour of their coming into power, we now find ourselves conquered. It only remains for them now to make terms of peace as honourable to themselves as the unfortunate circumstances will admit. Let the country itself judge their actions in the light of events of to-day, and let the blood of the poor murdered women and children of London be upon their heads. (Shame.) To resist further is useless. Our military organisation is in chaos, our miserably weak army is defeated and in flight. I declare to this House that we should sue at this very moment for peace—a dishonourable peace though it be; but the bitter truth is too plain—England is conquered!"

As he sat down amid the "hear, hears," and the loud applause of the Opposition there rose a keen-faced, dark-haired, clean-shaven man of thirty-seven or so. He was Gerald Graham, younger son of an aristocratic house, the Yorkshire Grahams, who sat for North-East Rutland. He was a man of brilliant attainments at Oxford, a splendid orator, a distinguished writer and traveller, whose keen brown eye, lithe upright figure, quick activity, and smart appearance, rendered him a born leader of men. For the past five years he had been marked out as a "coming man."

As a soldier he had seen hard service in the Boer War, being mentioned twice in despatches; as an explorer he had led a party through the heart of the Congo and fought his way back to civilisation through an unexplored land with valiant bravery that had saved the lives of his companions. He was a man who never sought notoriety. He hated to be lionised in society, refused the shoals of cards of invitation which poured in upon him, and stuck to his Parliamentary duties, and keeping faith with his constituents to the very letter.

As he stood up silent for a moment, gazing around him fearlessly, he presented a striking figure and in his navy serge suit he possessed the unmistakable cut of the smart, well-groomed Englishman who was also a man of note.

The House always listened to him, for he never spoke without he had something of importance to say. And the instant he was up a silence fell.

"Mr. Speaker," he said, in a clear, ringing voice, "I entirely disagree with my honourable friend the member for West Bude. England is not conquered! She is not beaten!"

The great hall rang with loud and vociferous cheers.

"London may be invested and bombarded. She may even be sacked, but Englishmen will still fight for their homes and fight valiantly. If we have a demand for indemnity let us refuse to pay it. Let us civilians—let the civilians in every corner of England—arm themselves and unite to drive out the invader! (Loud cheers.) I contend, Mr. Speaker, that there are millions of able-bodied men in this country who, if properly organised, will be able to gradually exterminate the enemy. Organisation is all that is required. Our vast population will rise against the Germans, and before the tide of popular indignation and desperate resistance the power of the invader must soon be swept away. Do not let us sit calmly here in security, and acknowledge that we are beaten. Remember, we have at this moment to uphold the ancient tradition of the British race, the honour of our forefathers, who have never been conquered. Shall we acknowledge ourselves conquered in this the twentieth century?"

"No!" rose from hundreds of voices, for the House was now carried away by young Graham's enthusiasm.

"Then let us organise!" he urged. "Let us fight on. Let every man who can use a sword or gun come forward, and we will commence hostilities against the Kaiser's forces that shall either result in their total extermination or in the power of England being extinguished. Englishmen will die hard. I myself will, with the consent of this House, head the movement, for I know that in the country we have millions who will follow me and will be equally ready to die for our country if necessary. Let us withdraw this statement that we are conquered. The real, earnest fight is now to commence," he shouted, his voice ringing clearly through the hall. "Let us bear our part, each one of us. If we organise and unite, we shall drive the Kaiser's hordes into the sea. They shall sue us for peace, and be made to pay us an indemnity, instead of us paying one to them. I will lead!" he shouted; "who will follow me?"

In London the Lord Mayor's patriotic proclamations were now obliterated by a huge bill bearing the German Imperial arms, the text of which told its own grim tale.

In the meantime the news of the fall of London was being circulated by the Germans to every town throughout the kingdom, their despatches being embellished by lurid descriptions of the appalling losses inflicted upon the English. In Manchester, a great poster, headed by the German Imperial arms, was posted up on the Town Hall, the exchange, and other places, in which Von Kronhelm announced the occupation of London; while in Leeds, Bradford, Stockport, and Sheffield similarly worded official announcements were also posted. The Press in all towns occupied by the Germans had been suppressed, papers only appearing in order to publish the enemy's orders. Therefore this official intelligence was circulated by proclamation, calculated to impress upon the inhabitants of the country how utterly powerless they were.

While Von Kronhelm sat in that large sombre room in the War Office, with his telegraph instrument to Potsdam ever ticking, and the wireless telegraphy constantly in operation, he wondered, and still wondered, why the English made no response to his demands.

NOTICE AND ADVICE

TO THE CITIZENS OF LONDON

I ADDRESS YOU SERIOUSLY.

We are neighbours, and in time of peace cordial relations have always existed between us. I therefore address you from my heart in the cause of humanity.

Germany is at war with England. We have been forced to penetrate into your country.

But each human life spared, and all property saved, we regard as in the interests of both religion and humanity.

We are at war, and both sides have fought a loyal fight.

Our desire is, however, to spare disarmed citizens and the inhabitants of all towns and villages.

We maintain a severe discipline, and we wish to have it known that punishment of the severest character will be inflicted upon any who are guilty of hostility to the Imperial German arms, either open or in secret.

To our regret any incitements, cruelties, or brutalities we must judge with equal severity.

I therefore call upon all local mayors, magistrates, clergy, and schoolmasters to urge upon the populace, and upon the heads of families, to urge upon those under their protection, and upon their domestics, to refrain from committing any act of hostility whatsoever against my soldiers.

All misery avoided is a good work in the eye of our Sovereign Judge, who sees all men.

I earnestly urge you to heed this advice, and I trust in you.

Take notice!

VON KRONHELM,
Commanding the Imperial German Army

German Military Headquarters,
WHITEHALL, London, September 20, 1910

He was in London. He had carried out his Emperor's instructions to the letter, he had received the Imperial thanks, and he held all the gold coin he could discover in London as security. Yet, without some reply from the British Government, his position was an insecure one. Even his thousand and one spies who had served him so well ever since he had placed foot upon English soil could tell him nothing. The deliberations of the House of Commons at Bristol were a secret.

In Bristol the hot, fevered night had given place to a gloriously sunny morning with a blue and cloudless sky. Above Leigh Woods the lark rose high in the sky, trilling his song, and the bells of Bristol rang out as merrily as they ever did, and above the Colston Hall still floated the Royal Standard—a sign that the House had not yet adjourned.

While Von Kronhelm held London, Lord Byfield and the remnant of the British Army, who had suffered such defeat in Essex and north of London, had, four days later, retreated to Chichester and Salisbury, where reorganisation was in rapid progress. One division of the defeated troops had encamped at Horsham. The survivors of those who had fought the battle of Charnwood Forest, and had acted so gallantly in the defence of Birmingham, were now encamped on the Malvern Hills, while the defenders of Manchester were at Shrewsbury. Speaking roughly, therefore, our vanquished troops were massing at four points, in an endeavour to make a last attack upon the invader. The Commander-in-Chief, Lord Byfield, was near Salisbury, and at any hour he knew that the German legions might push westward from London to meet him and to complete the coup.

The League of Defenders formed by Gerald Graham and his friends was, however, working independently. The wealthier classes, who, driven out of London, were now living in cottages and tents in various parts of Berks, Wilts, and Hants, worked unceasingly on behalf of the League, while into Plymouth, Exmouth, Swanage, Bristol, and Southampton more than one ship had already managed to enter laden with arms and ammunition of all kinds, sent across by the agents of the League in France. The cargoes were of a very miscellaneous character, from modern Maxims to old-fashioned rifles that had seen service in the war of 1870. There were hundreds of modern rifles, sporting guns, revolvers, swords—in fact, every weapon imaginable, modern and old-fashioned. These were at once taken charge of by the local branches of the League, and to those men who presented their tickets of identification the arms were served out, and practice conducted in the open fields. Three shiploads of rifles were known to have been captured by German warships, one off Start Point, another a few miles outside Padstow, and a third within sight of the coastguard at Selsey Bill. Two other ships were blown up in the Channel by drifting mines. The running of arms across from France and Spain was a very risky proceeding; yet the British skipper is nothing if not patriotic, and every man who crossed the Channel on those dangerous errands took his life in his hand.

Into Liverpool, Whitehaven, and Milford weapons were also coming over from Ireland, even though several German cruisers, who had been up to Lamlash to cripple the Glasgow trade, had now come south, and were believed still to be in the Irish Sea.

CHAPTER VIII

DEFENCES OF SOUTH LONDON

PREPARATIONS WERE BEING CONTINUED night and day to place the working-class districts in Southwark and Lambeth in a state of strong defence, and the constant meetings convened in public halls and chapels by the newly-formed League of Defenders incited the people to their work. Everybody lent a willing hand, rich and poor alike. People who had hitherto lived in comfort in Regent's Park, Hampstead, or one or other of the better-class northern suburbs, now found themselves herded among all sorts and conditions of men and women, and living as best they could in those dull, drab streets

THE DEFENCES OF
SOUTH LONDON
on Sept 26th

References
British Artillery
Barricades of the populace
Headquarters of the
League of Defenders

of Lambeth, Walworth, Battersea, and Kennington. It was, indeed, a strange experience for them. In the sudden flight from the north, parents had become separated from their children and husbands from their wives, so that in many cases haggard and forlorn mothers were in frantic search of their little ones, fearing that they might have already died of starvation or been trampled underfoot by the panic-stricken multitudes. The dense population of South London had already been trebled. They were penned in by the barricades in many instances, for each district seemed to be now placing itself in a state of defence, independent of any other.

Kennington, for instance, was practically surrounded by barricades, tons upon tons of earth being dug from the "Oval" and the "Park." Besides the barricades in Harleyford Road and Kennington Lane, all the streets converging on the "Oval" were blocked up, a huge defence arm just being completed across the junction of Kennington and Kennington Park Roads, and all the streets running into the latter thoroughfare from that point to the big obstruction at the

"Elephant" were blocked by paving-stones, bags of sand, barrels of cement, bricks, and such-like odds and ends impervious to bullets. In addition to this, there was a double fortification in Lambeth Road—a veritable redoubt—as well as the barricade at Lambeth Bridge, while all the roads leading from Kennington into the Lambeth Road, such as St. George's Road, Kennington Road, High Street, and the rest, had been rendered impassable and the neighbouring houses placed in a state of defence. Thus the whole district of Kennington became therefore a fortress in itself.

This was only a typical instance of the scientific methods of defence now resorted to. Mistakes made in North London were not now repeated. Day and night every able-bodied man, and woman too, worked on with increasing zeal and patriotism. The defences in Haverstock Hill, Holloway Road, and Edgware Road, which had been composed of overturned tramcars, motor 'buses, household furniture, etc., had been riddled by the enemy's bullets. The lesson had been heeded, and now earth, sand, tiles, paving-stones, and bricks were used.

From nearly all the principal thoroughfares south of the river the paving-stones were being rapidly torn up by great gangs of men, and whenever the artillery brought up a fresh Maxim or field-gun the wildest demonstrations were made. The clergy held special services in churches and chapels, and prayer meetings for the emancipation of London were held twice daily in the Metropolitan Tabernacle at Newington. In Kennington Park, Camberwell Green, the Oval, Vauxhall Park, Lambeth Palace Gardens, Camberwell Park, Peckham Rye and Southwark Park a division of Lord Byfield's army was encamped. They held the Waterloo terminus of the South-Western Railway strongly, the Chatham Railway from the Borough Road Station—now the terminus—the South-Eastern from Bricklayers' Arms, which had been converted into another terminus, as well as the Brighton line, at Battersea Park and York Road.

The lines destroyed by the enemy's spies in the early moments of the invasion had long ago been repaired, and up to the present railway and telegraphic communication south and west remained uninterrupted. The *Daily Telegraph* had managed to transfer some of its staff to the offices of a certain printer's in Southwark, and there, under difficulties, published several editions daily despite the German censorship. While northern London was without any news except that supplied from German sources, South London was still open to the world, the cables from the south coast being, as yet, in the hands of the British, and the telegraphs intact to Bristol and to all places in the West.

Thus, during those stifling and exciting days following the occupation, while London was preparing for its great uprising, the *South London Mirror*, though a queer, unusual-looking sheet, still continued to appear, and was read with avidity by the gallant men at the barricades.

Contrary to expectation, Von Kronhelm was leaving South London severely alone. He was, no doubt, wise. Full well he knew that his men, once within those narrow, tortuous streets beyond the river, would have no opportunity to manœuvre, and would, as in the case of the assault of Waterloo Bridge, be slaughtered to a man. His spies reported that each hour that passed rendered the populace the stronger, yet he did nothing, devoting his whole time, energy, and attention to matters in that half of London he was now occupying.

Everywhere the walls of South London were placarded with manifestoes of the League of Defenders. Day after day fresh posters appeared, urging patience and courage, and reporting upon the progress of the League. The name of Graham was now upon every one's lips. He had, it seemed, arisen as saviour of our beloved country. Every word of his inspired enthusiasm, and this was well illustrated at the mass meeting on Peckham Rye, when, beneath the huge flag of St. George, the white banner with the red cross—the ancient standard of England—which the League had adopted as theirs, he made a brilliant and impassioned appeal to every Londoner and every Englishman.

Report had it that the Germans had set a price upon his head, and that he was pursued everywhere by German spies—mercenaries who would kill him in secret if they could. Therefore he was compelled to go about with an armed police guard, who arrested any suspected person in his vicinity. The Government, who had at first laughed Graham's enthusiasm to scorn, now believed in him. Even Lord Byfield, after a long council, declared that his efforts to inspire enthusiasm had been amazingly successful, and it was now well known that the "Defenders" and the Army had agreed to act in unison towards one common end—the emancipation of England from the German thraldom.

Some men of the Osnabrück Regiment, holding Canning Town and Limehouse, managed one night, by strategy, to force their way through the Blackwall Tunnel and break down its defences on the Surrey side in an attempt to blow up the South Metropolitan Gas Works. The men holding the tunnel were completely overwhelmed by the number that pressed on, and were compelled to fall back, twenty of their number being killed. The assault was a victorious one, and it was seen that the enemy were pouring out, when, of a sudden, there was a dull, heavy roar, followed by wild shouts and terrified screams, as there rose from the centre of the river a great column of water, and next instant the tunnel was flooded, hundreds of the enemy being drowned like rats in a hole.

The men of the Royal Engineers had, on the very day previous, made preparations for destroying the tunnel if necessary, and had done so ere the Germans were aware of their intention. The exact loss of life is unknown, but it is estimated that over 400 men must have perished in that single instant, while those who had made the sudden dash towards the Gas Works were all taken prisoners, and their explosives confiscated.

The evident intention of the enemy being thus seen, General Sir Francis Bamford, from his headquarters at the Crystal Palace, gave orders for the tunnels at Rotherhithe and that across Greenwich Reach, as well as the several "tube" tunnels and subways, to be destroyed, a work which was executed without delay, and was witnessed by thousands, who watched for the great disturbances and upheavals in the bed of the river.

In the Old Kent Road the bridge over the canal, as well as the bridges in Wells Street, Sumner Road, Glengall Road, and Canterbury Road, were all prepared for demolition in case of necessity, the canal from the Camberwell Road to the Surrey Dock forming a moat behind which the defenders might, if necessary, retire. Clapham Common and Brockwell Park were covered with tents, for General Bamford's force, consisting mostly of auxiliaries, were daily awaiting reinforcements.

Lord Byfield, now at Windsor, was in constant communication by wireless telegraphy with the London headquarters at the Crystal Palace, as well as with Hibbard on the Malvern Hills and Woolmer at Shrewsbury. To General Bamford at Sydenham came constant news of the rapid spread of the national movement of defiance, and Lord Byfield, as was afterwards known, urged the London commander to remain patient, and invite no attack until the League were strong enough to act on the offensive. Affairs of outpost were, of course, constantly recurring along the river bank between Windsor and Egham, and the British Free-shooters and Frontiersmen were ever harassing the Saxons.

Very soon Von Kronhelm became aware of Lord Byfield's intentions, but his weakness was apparent when he made no counter-move. The fact was that the various great cities he now held required all his attention and all his troops. From Manchester, from Birmingham, from Leeds, Bradford, Sheffield, and Hull came similar replies. Any withdrawal of troops from either city would be the signal for a general rising of the inhabitants. Therefore, having gained possession, he could only now sit tight and watch.

From all over Middlesex, and more especially from the London area, came sensational reports of the drastic measures adopted by the Germans to repress any sign of revolt. In secret, the agents of the League of Defenders were at work, going from house to house, enrolling men, arranging for secret meeting-places, and explaining in confidence the programme as put forward by the Bristol committee. Now and then, however, these agents were betrayed, and their betrayal was in every case followed by a court-martial at Bow Street, death outside in the yard of the police station, and the publication in the papers of their names, their offence, and the hour of the execution.

Yet, undaunted and defiantly, the giant organisation grew as no other society had ever grown, and its agents and members quickly developed into fearless patriots. It being reported that the Saxons were facing Lord Byfield with the Thames between them, the people of West London began in frantic haste to construct barricades. The building of obstructions had, indeed, now become a mania north of the river as well as south. The people, fearing that there was to be more fighting in the streets of London, began to build huge defences all across West London. The chief were across King Street, Hammersmith, where it joins Goldhawk Road, across the junction of Goldhawk and Uxbridge Roads, in the Harrow Road where it joins Admiral Road, and Willesden Lane, close to the Paddington Cemetery, and the Latimer Road opposite St. Quintin Park Station. All the side streets leading into the Goldhawk Road, Latimer Road, and Ladbroke Grove Road were also blocked up, and hundreds of houses placed in a state of strong defence.

With all this Von Kronhelm did not interfere. The building of such obstructions acted as a safety-valve to the excited populace, therefore he rather encouraged than discountenanced it. The barricades might, he thought, be of service to his army if Lord Byfield really risked an attack upon London from that direction.

Crafty and cunning though he was, he was entirely unaware that those barricades were being constructed at the secret orders of the League of Defenders, and he never dreamed that they had actually been instigated by the British Commander-in-Chief himself.

Thus the Day of Reckoning hourly approached, and London, though crushed and starving, waited in patient vigilance.

At Enfield Chase was a great camp of British prisoners in the hands of the Germans, amounting to several thousands. Contrary to report, both officers and men were fairly well treated by the Germans, though with his limited supplies Von Kronhelm was already beginning to contemplate releasing them. Many of the higher-grade officers who had fallen into the hands of the enemy, together with the Lord Mayor of London, the Mayors of Hull, Goole, Lincoln, Norwich, Ipswich, and the Lord Mayors of Manchester and Birmingham, had been sent across to Germany, where, according to their own reports, they were being detained in Hamburg and treated with every consideration. Nevertheless, all this greatly incensed

Englishmen. Lord Byfield, with Hibbard and Woolmer, was leaving no stone unturned in order to reform our shattered Army, and again oppose the invaders. All three gallant officers had been to Bristol, where they held long consultation with the members of the Cabinet, with the result that the Government still refused to entertain any idea of paying the indemnity. The Admiralty were confident now that the command of the sea had been regained, and in Parliament itself a little confidence was also restored.

Yet we had to face the hard facts that nearly two hundred thousand Germans were upon British soil, and that London was held by them. Already parties of German commissioners had visited the National Gallery, the Wallace Collection, the Tate Gallery, and the British and South Kensington Museums, deciding upon and placing aside certain art treasures and priceless antiques ready for shipment to Germany. The Raphaels, the Titians, the Rubenses, the Fra Angelicos, the Velasquezes, the Elgin Marbles, the best of the Egyptian, Assyrian, and Roman antiques, the Rosetta Stone, the early Biblical and classical manuscripts, the historic charters of England, and such-like treasures which could never be replaced, were all catalogued and prepared for removal. The people of London knew this; for though there had been no newspapers, information ran rapidly from mouth to mouth. German sentries guarded our world-famous collections, which were now indeed entirely in the enemy's hands, and which the Kaiser intended should enrich the German galleries and museums.

One vessel flying the British flag had left the Thames laden with spoil, in an endeavour to reach Hamburg, but off Harwich she had been sighted and overhauled by a British cruiser, with the result that she had been steered to Dover. Therefore our cruisers and destroyers, having thus obtained knowledge of the enemy's intentions, were keeping a sharp lookout about the coast for any vessels attempting to leave for German ports.

Accounts of fierce engagements in the Channel between British and German ships went the rounds, but all were vague and unconvincing. The only solid facts were that the Germans held the great cities of England, and that the millions of Great Britain were slowly but surely preparing to rise in an attempt to burst asunder the fetters that now held them.

Government, Army, Navy, and Parliament had all proved rotten reeds. It was now every man for himself—to free himself and his loved ones—or to die in the attempt.

Through the south and west of England Graham's clear, manly voice was raised everywhere, and the whole population were now fast assembling beneath the banner of the Defenders, in readiness to bear their part in the most bloody and desperate encounter of the whole war.

The swift and secret death being meted out to the German sentries—or, in fact, to any German caught alone in a side street—having been reported to Von Kronhelm, he issued another of his now famous proclamations, which was posted upon half the hoardings in London; but the populace at once amused themselves by tearing it down wherever it was discovered. Von Kronhelm was the arch-enemy of London, and it is believed that there were at that moment no fewer than five separate conspiracies to encompass his death. Londoners detested the Germans, but with a hatred twenty times the more intense did they regard those men who, having engaged in commercial pursuits in England, had joined the colours and were now acting as spies.

CHAPTER IX

REVOLTS IN SHOREDITCH AND ISLINGTON

ON THE NIGHT of September 27, a very serious conflict, entailing much loss of life on both the London civilian and German side, occurred at the point where Kingsland Road joins Old Street, Hackney Road, and High Street. Across both Hackney and Kingsland Roads the barricades built before the bombardment still remained in a half-ruined state, any attempt at clearing them away being repulsed by the angry inhabitants. Dalston, Kingsland, Bethnal Green, and Shoreditch were notably antagonistic to the invaders, and several sharp encounters had taken place. Indeed, those districts were discovered by the enemy to be very unsafe.

The conflict in question, however, commenced at the corner of Old Street at about 9.30 in the evening, by three German tailors from Cambridge Road being insulted by two men, English labourers. The tailors appealed in German to four Westphalian infantrymen who chanced to be passing, and who subsequently fired and killed one of the Englishmen. This was the signal for a local uprising. The alarm given, hundreds of men and women rushed from their houses, many of them armed with rifles and knives, and, taking cover behind the ruined barricades, opened fire upon a body of fifty Germans, who very quickly ran up. The fire was returned, when from the neighbouring houses a perfect hail of lead was suddenly rained upon the Germans, who were then forced to retire down High Street towards Liverpool Street Station, leaving many dead.

Very quickly news was sent over the telephone, which the Germans had now established in many quarters of London, and large reinforcements were soon upon the scene. The men of Shoreditch had, however, obtained two Maxim guns, which had been secreted ever since the entry of the Germans into the Metropolis, and as the enemy endeavoured to storm their position they swept the street with a deadly fire. Quickly the situation became desperate, but the fight lasted over an hour. The sound of firing brought hundreds upon hundreds of Londoners upon the scene. All these took arms against the Germans, who, after many fruitless attempts to storm the defences, and being fired upon from every side, were compelled to fall back again.

They were followed along High Street into Bethnal Green Road, up Great Eastern Street into Hoxton Square and Pitfield Street, and there cut up, being given no quarter at the hands of the furious populace. In those narrow thoroughfares they were powerless, and were therefore simply exterminated.

The victory for the men of Shoreditch was complete, over three hundred and fifty Germans being killed, while our losses were only about fifty.

The conflict was at once reported to Von Kronhelm, and the very fact that he did not send exemplary punishment into that quarter was sufficient to show that he feared to arouse further the hornets' nest in which he was living, and more especially that portion of the populace north of the City.

News of the attack, quickly spreading, inspired courage in every other part of the oppressed Metropolis.

The successful uprising against the Germans in Shoreditch incited Londoners to rebel, and in various other parts of the Metropolis there occurred outbreaks.

Von Kronhelm had found to his cost that London was not to be so easily cowed after all. The size and population of the Metropolis had not been sufficiently calculated upon. It was as a country in itself, while the intricacies of its by-ways formed a refuge for the conspirators, who were gradually completing their preparations to rise en masse and strike down the Germans wherever found. In the open country his great army could march, manœuvre, and use strategy, but here in the maze of narrow London streets it was impossible to know in one thoroughfare what was taking place in the next.

Supplies, too, were now running very short. The distress among our vanquished populace was most severe; while Von Kronhelm's own army was put on meagre rations. The increasing price of food and consequent starvation had not served to improve the relations between the invaders and the citizens of London, who, though they were assured by various proclamations that they would be happier and more prosperous under German rule, now discovered that they were being slowly starved to death.

Their only hope, therefore, was in the efforts of that now gigantic organisation, the League of Defenders.

A revolt occurred in Pentonville Road, opposite King's Cross Underground Station, which ended in a fierce and terrible fray. A company of the Bremen Infantry Regiment No. 75, belonging to the IXth Corps, were marching from the City Road towards Regent's

Park, when several shots were fired at them from windows of shops almost opposite the station. Five Germans fell dead, including one lieutenant, a very gorgeous person who wore a monocle. Another volley rang out before the infantrymen could realise what was happening, and then it was seen that the half-ruined shops had been placed in such a state of defence as to constitute a veritable fortress.

The fire was returned, but a few moments later a Maxim spat its deadly fire from a small hole in a wall, and a couple of dozen of the enemy fell upon the granite setts of the thoroughfare. The rattle of musketry quickly brought forth the whole of that populous neighbourhood—or all, indeed, that remained of them—the working-class district between Pentonville Road and Copenhagen Street.

Quickly the fight became general. The men of Bremen endeavoured to take the place by assault, but found that it was impossible. The strength of the defences was amazing, and showed only too plainly that Londoners were in secret preparing for the great uprising that was being planned. In such a position were the houses held by the Londoners, that their fire commanded both the Pentonville and King's Cross Roads; but very soon the Germans were reinforced by another company of the same regiment, and these being attacked in the rear from Rodney Street, Cumming Street, Weston Street, York Street, Winchester Street, and other narrow turnings leading into the Pentonville Road, the fighting quickly became general.

The populace came forth in swarms, men and women, armed with any weapon or article upon which they could lay their hands, and all fired with the same desire.

Hundreds of men who came forth were armed with rifles which had been carefully secreted on the entry of the enemy into the Metropolis. The greater part of those men, indeed, had fought at the barricades in North London, and had subsequently taken part in the street fighting as the enemy advanced. Some of the arms had come from the League of Defenders, smuggled into the Metropolis nobody exactly knew how.

Up and down the King's Cross, Pentonville, and Caledonian Roads the crowd swayed and fought. The Germans against that overwhelming mass of angry civilians seemed powerless. Small bodies of the troops were cornered in the narrow by-streets, and then given no quarter. Brave-hearted Londoners, though they knew well what dire punishment they must inevitably draw upon themselves, had taken the law into their own hands, and were shooting or stabbing every German who fell into their hands.

The scene of carnage in that hour of fighting was awful. The *Daily Chronicle* described it as one of the most fiercely contested encounters in the whole history of the siege. Shoreditch had given courage to King's Cross, for, unknown to Von Kronhelm, houses in all quarters were being put in a state of defence, their position being carefully chosen by those directing the secret operations of the League of Defenders.

For over an hour the houses in question gallantly held out, sweeping the streets constantly with their Maxim. Presently, however, on further reinforcements arriving, the German colonel directed his men to enter the houses opposite. In an instant a door was broken in, and presently glass came tumbling down as muzzles of rifles were poked through the panes, and soon sharp crackling showed that the Germans had settled down to their work.

The defence of the Londoners was most obstinate. In the streets, Londoners attacked the enemy with utter disregard for the risks they ran. Women, among them many young girls, joined in the fray, armed with pistols and knives.

After a while a great body of reinforcements appeared in the Euston Road, having been sent hurriedly along from Regent's Park. Then the option was given to those occupying the fortified house to surrender, the colonel promising to spare their lives. The Londoners peremptorily refused. Everywhere the fighting became more desperate and spread all through the streets leading out of St. Pancras, York, and Caledonian Roads, until the whole of that great neighbourhood became the scene of a fierce conflict, in which both sides lost heavily. Right across Islington the street fighting spread, and many were the fatal traps set for the unwary German who found himself cut off in that maze of narrow streets between York Road and the Angel. The enemy, on the other hand, were shooting down women and girls as well as the men, even the non-combatants—those who came out of their homes to ascertain what was going on—being promptly fired at and killed.

In the midst of all this somebody ignited some petrol in a house a few doors from the chapel in Pentonville Road, and in a few moments the whole row of buildings were blazing furiously, belching forth black smoke and adding to the terror and confusion of those exciting moments. Even that large body of Germans now upon the scene were experiencing great difficulty in defending themselves. A perfect rain of bullets seemed directed upon them on every hand, and to-day's experience certainly proves that Londoners are patriotic and brave, and in their own districts they possess a superiority over the trained troops of the Kaiser.

At length, after a most sanguinary struggle, the Londoners' position was carried, the houses were entered, and twenty-two brave patriots, mostly of the working-class, taken prisoners. The populace now realising that the Germans had, after all, overpowered their comrades, in their fortress, fell back; but being pursued northward towards the railway line between Highbury and Barnsbury stations, many of them were despatched on the spot.

What followed was indeed terrible. The anger of the Germans now became uncontrollable. Having in view Von Kronhelm's proclamation—which sentenced to death all who, not being in uniform, fired upon German troops—they decided to teach the unfortunate populace a lesson. As a matter of fact, they feared that such revolts might be repeated in other quarters.

So they seized dozens of prisoners, men and women, and shot them down. Many of these summary executions took place against the wall of the St. Pancras Station at the corner of Euston Road. Men and women were pitilessly sent to death. Wives, daughters, fathers, sons were ranged up against that wall, and, at signal from the colonel, fell forward with bullets through them.

Of the men who so gallantly held the fortified house not a single one escaped. Strings of men and women were hurried to their doom in one day, for the troops were savage with the lust of blood, and Von Kronhelm, though he was aware of it by telephone, lifted not a finger to stop those arbitrary executions.

But enough of such details. Suffice it to say that the stones of Islington were stained with the blood of innocent Londoners, and that those who survived took a fierce vow of vengeance. Von Kronhelm's legions had the upper hand for the moment, yet the conflict and its bloody sequel had the effect of arousing the fiercest anger within the heart of every Briton in the Metropolis.

What was in store for us none could tell. We were conquered, oppressed, starved; yet hope was still within us. The League of Defenders were not idle, while South London was hourly completing her strength.

It seems that after quelling the revolt at King's Cross wholesale arrests were made in Islington. The guilt or innocence of the prisoners did not seem to matter. Von Kronhelm dealing out to them summary punishment.

Terror reigns in London. One newspaper correspondent—whose account is published this morning in South London, having been sent across the Thames by carrier pigeon, many of which were now being employed by the newspapers—had an opportunity of witnessing the wholesale executions which took place yesterday afternoon outside Dorchester House, where Von Kleppen has established his quarters. Von Kleppen seems to be the most pitiless of the superior officers. The prisoners, ranged up for inspection in front of the big mansion, were mostly men from Islington, all of whom knew only too well the fate in store for them. Walking slowly along and eyeing the ranks of these unfortunate wretches, the German General stopped here and there, tapping a man on the shoulder or beckoning him out of the rear ranks. In most cases, without further word, the individual thus selected was marched into the Park at Stanhope Gate, where a small supplementary column was soon formed.

Those chosen knew that their last hour had come. Some clasped their hands and fell upon their knees, imploring pity, while others remained silent and stubborn patriots. One man, his face covered with blood and his arm broken, sat down and howled in anguish, and others wept in silence. Some women—wives and daughters of the condemned men—tried to get within the Park to bid them adieu and to urge courage, but the soldiers beat them back with their

---

LEAGUE OF DEFENDERS

DAILY BULLETIN

The League of Defenders of the British Empire publicly announce to Englishmen, although the North of London is held by the enemy:

(1) That England will soon entirely regain command of the sea, and that a rigorous blockade of the German ports will be established.

(2) That three of the vessels of the North German Lloyd Transatlantic passenger service have been captured, together with a number of minor German ships in the Channel and Mediterranean.

(3) That four German cruisers and two destroyers have fallen into the hands of the British.

(4) That
ENGLAND'S MILLIONS ARE READY TO RISE!
Therefore
WE ARE NOT YET BEATEN!
BE PREPARED, AND WAIT.

LEAGUE OF DEFENDERS
Central Office: Bristol

---

rifles. Some of the men laughed defiantly, others met death with a stony stare. The eye-witness saw the newly-dug pit that served as a common grave, and he stood by and saw them shot and their corpses afterwards flung into it.

One young fair-haired woman, condemned by Von Kleppen, rushed forward to that officer, threw herself upon her knees, imploring mercy, and protested her innocence wildly. But the officer, callous and pitiless, simply motioned to a couple of soldiers to take her within the Park, where she shared the same fate as the men.

How long will this awful state of affairs last? We must die, or conquer. London is in the hands of a legion of assassins—Bavarians, Saxons, Würtembergers, Hessians, Badeners—all now bent upon prolonging the reign of terror, and thus preventing the uprising that they know is, sooner or later, inevitable.

Terrible accounts are reaching us of how the Germans are treating their prisoners on Hounslow Heath, at Enfield, and other places; of the awful sufferings of the poor unfortunate fellows, of hunger, of thirst, and of inhuman disregard for either their comfort or their lives.

At present we are powerless, hemmed in by our barricades. Behind us, upon Sydenham Hill, General Bamford is in a strong position, and his great batteries are already defending any attack upon London from the south. From the terrace in front of the Crystal Palace his guns can sweep the whole range of southern suburbs. Through Dulwich, Herne Hill, Champion Hill, and Denmark Hill are riding British cavalry, all of whom show evident traces of the hard and fierce campaign. We see from Sydenham constant messages being heliographed, for General Bamford and Lord Byfield are in hourly communication by wireless telegraphy or by other means.

What is transpiring at Windsor is not known, save that every night there are affairs of outposts with the Saxons, who on several occasions have attempted to cross the river by pontoons, and have on each occasion been driven back.

It was reported to Parliament at its sitting at Bristol yesterday that the Cabinet had refused to entertain any idea of paying the indemnity demanded by Germany, and that their reply to Von Kronhelm is one of open defiance. The brief summary of the speeches published shows that the Government are hopeful, notwithstanding the present black outlook. They believe that when the hour comes for the revenge, London will rise as a man, and that Socialists, Nonconformists, Labour agitators, Anarchists, and demagogues will unite with us in one great national patriotic effort to exterminate our conquerors as we would exterminate vermin.

Mr. Gerald Graham has made another great speech in the House, in which he reported the progress of the League of Defenders and its wide-spread ramifications. He told the Government that there were over seven millions of able-bodied men in the country ready to revolt the instant the word went forth. That there would be terrible bloodshed he warned them, but that the British would eventually prove the victors he was assured. He gave no details of the organisation, for to a great measure it was a secret one, and Von Kronhelm was already taking active steps to combat its intentions; but he declared that there was still a strong spirit of patriotism in the country, and explained how sturdy Scots were daily making their way south, and how men from Wales were already massing in Oxford.

The speech was received on both sides of the House with ringing cheers when, in conclusion, he promised them that, within a few days, the fiat would go forth, and the enemy would find himself crushed and powerless.

"South London," he declared, "is our stronghold, our fortress. To-day it is impregnable, defended by a million British patriots, and I defy Von Kronhelm—indeed, I dare him to attack it!"

Von Kronhelm was, of course, well aware of the formation of the Defenders, but treated the League with contempt. If there was any attempt at a rising, he would shoot down the people like dogs. He declared this openly and publicly, and he also issued a warning to the English people in the German official *Gazette*, a daily periodical printed in one of the newspaper offices in Fleet Street in both German and English.

The German commander fully believed that England was crushed; yet, as the days went on, he was puzzled that he received no response to his demand for indemnity. Twice he had sent special despatch-bearers to Bristol, but on both occasions the result was the same.

Diplomatic representations had been made in Berlin through the Russian Ambassador, who was now in charge of British interests in Germany, but all to no purpose. Our Foreign Minister simply acknowledged receipt of the various despatches. On the Continent the keenest interest was manifested at what was apparently a dead-lock. The British had, it was known, regained command of the sea. Von Kronhelm's supplies were already cut off. The cables in direct communication between England and Germany had been severed, and the Continental Press, especially the Paris journals, gleefully recounted how two large Hamburg–American liners attempting to reach Hamburg by passing north of Scotland had been captured by British cruisers.

In the Channel, too, a number of German vessels had been seized, and one that showed fight off the North Foreland was fired upon and sunk. The public at home, however, were more interested in

ENGLISHMEN!

YOUR HOMES ARE DESECRATED!
YOUR CHILDREN ARE STARVING!
YOUR LOVED ONES ARE DEAD!

WILL YOU REMAIN IN COWARDLY INACTIVITY?

The German Eagle flies over London. Hull, Newcastle and Birmingham are in ruins. Manchester is a German City. Norfolk, Essex, and Suffolk form a German colony.

The Kaiser's troops have brought death, ruin, and starvation upon you.

WILL YOU BECOME GERMANS?

NO!

Join THE DEFENDERS and fight for England.

You have England's Millions beside you.

LET US RISE!

Let us drive back the Kaiser's men.

Let us shoot them at sight.

Let us exterminate every single man who has desecrated English soil.

Join the New League of Defenders.

Fight for your homes. Fight for your wives. Fight for England.

FIGHT FOR YOUR KING!

THE NATIONAL LEAGUE OF DEFENDERS' Head Offices
Bristol, September 21st, 1910

supremacy on land. It was all very well to have command of the sea, they argued, but it did not appear to alleviate perceptibly the hunger and privations on land. The Germans occupied London, and while they did so all freedom in England was at an end.

A great poster headed "Englishmen," here reproduced, was seen everywhere. The whole country was flooded with it, and thousands upon thousands of heroic Britons, from the poorest to the wealthiest, clamoured to enrol themselves. The movement was an absolutely national one in every sense of the word. The name of Gerald Graham, the new champion of England's power, was upon every one's tongue. Daily he spoke in the various towns in the West of England, in Plymouth, Taunton, Cardiff, Portsmouth, and Southampton, and, assisted by the influential committee among whom were many brilliant speakers and men whose names were as household words, he aroused the country to the highest pitch of hatred against the enemy. The defenders, as they drilled in various centres through the whole of the West of England, were a strange and incongruous body. Grey-bearded Army pensioners ranged side by side with keen, enthusiastic youths, advised them and gave them the benefit of their expert knowledge. Volunteer officers in many cases assumed command, together with retired drill sergeants. The digging of trenches and the making of fortifications were assigned to navvies, bricklayers, platelayers, and agricultural labourers, large bodies of whom were under railway gangers, and were ready to perform any excavation work.

The Maxims and other machine guns were mostly manned by Volunteer artillery; but instruction in the working of the Maxim was given to select classes in Plymouth, Bristol, Portsmouth, and Cardiff. Time was of utmost value, therefore the drilling was pushed forward day and night. It was known that Von Kronhelm was already watchful of the movements of the League, and was aware daily of its growth.

In London, with the greatest secrecy, the defenders were banding together. In face of the German proclamation posted upon the walls, Londoners were holding meetings in secret and enrolling themselves.

Though the German eagle flew in Whitehall and from the summit of St. Stephen's Tower, and though the heavy tramp of German sentries echoed in Trafalgar Square, in the quiet, trafficless streets in the vicinity, England was not yet vanquished.

The valiant men of London were still determined to sell their liberty dearly, and to lay down their lives for the freedom of their country and honour of their King.

BOOK III

THE REVENGE

CHAPTER I

A BLOW FOR FREEDOM

DAILY TELEGRAPH OFFICE
OCT. 1, 2 P.M.

"THREE DAYS have passed since the revolt at King's Cross, and each day, both on the Horse Guards' Parade and in the Park, opposite Dorchester House, there have been summary executions. Von Kronhelm is in evident fear of the excited London populace, and is endeavouring to cow them by his plain-spoken and threatening proclamations, and by these wholesale executions of any person found with arms in his or her possession. But the word of command does not abolish the responsibility of conscience, and we are now awaiting breathlessly for the word to strike the blow in revenge.

"The other newspapers are reappearing, but all that is printed each morning is first subjected to a rigorous censorship, and nothing is allowed to be printed before it is passed and initialled by the two gold-spectacled censors who sit and smoke their pipes in an office to themselves. Below, we have German sentries on guard, for our journal is one of the official organs of Von Kronhelm, and what now appears in it is surely sufficient to cause our blood to boil.

"To-day, there are everywhere signs of rapidly increasing unrest. Londoners are starving, and are now refusing to remain patient any longer. The *Daily Bulletin* of the League of Defenders, though the posting of it is punishable by imprisonment, and it is everywhere torn down where discovered by the Germans, still gives daily brief news of what is in progress, and still urges the people to wait in patience, for 'the action of the Government,' as it is sarcastically put.

"Soon after eleven o'clock this morning a sudden and clearly premeditated attack was made upon a body of the Bremen infantry, who were passing along Oxford Street from Holborn to the Marble Arch. The soldiers were suddenly fired upon from windows of a row of shops between Newman Street and Rathbone Place, and before they could halt and return the fire they found themselves surrounded by a great armed rabble, who were emerging from all the streets leading into Oxford Street.

"While the Germans were manœuvring, some unknown hand launched from a window a bomb into the centre of them. Next second there was a red flash, a loud report, and twenty-five of the enemy were blown to atoms. For a few moments the soldiers were demoralised, but orders were shouted loudly by their officers, and they began a most vigorous defence. In a few seconds the fight was as fierce as that at King's Cross; for out of every street in that working-class district lying between the Tottenham Court Road and Great Portland Street on the north, and out of Soho on the South, poured thousands upon thousands of fierce Londoners, all bent upon doing their utmost to kill their oppressors. From almost every window along Oxford Street a rain of lead was now being poured upon the troops, who vainly strove to keep their ground. Gradually, however, they were, by slow degrees, forced back into the narrow side-turnings up Newman Street, and Rathbone Place into Mortimer Street, Foley Street, Goodge Street, and Charlotte Street; and there they were slaughtered almost to a man.

"Two officers were captured by the armed mob in Tottenham Street and, after being beaten, were stood up and shot in cold blood as vengeance for those shot during the past three days at Von Kleppen's orders at Dorchester House.

"The fierce fight lasted quite an hour; and though reinforcements were sent for, yet curiously none arrived.

"The great mob, however, were well aware that very soon the iron hand of Germany would fall heavily upon them; therefore, in frantic haste, they began soon after noon to build barricades and block up the narrow streets in every direction. At the end of Rathbone Place, Newman Street, Berners Street, Wells Street, and Great Tichfield Street, huge obstructions soon appeared, while on the east all by-streets leading into Tottenham Court Road were blocked up, and the same on the west in Great Portland Street, and on the north where the district was flanked by the Euston Road. So that by two o'clock the populous neighbourhood bounded by the four great thoroughfares was rendered a fortress in itself.

"Within that area were thousands of armed men and women from Soho, Bloomsbury, Marylebone, and even from Camden Town. There they remained in defiance of Von Kronhelm's newest proclamation, which stared one in the face from every wall."

LATER

"The enemy were unaware of the grave significance of the position of affairs, because Londoners betrayed no outward sign of the truth. Now, however, nearly every man and woman wore pinned upon their breasts a small piece of silk about two inches square, printed as a miniature Union Jack—the badge adopted by the League of Defenders. Though Von Kronhelm was unaware of it, Lord Byfield, in council with Greatorex and Bamford, had decided that, in order to demoralise the enemy and give him plenty of work to do, a number of local uprisings should take place north of the Thames. These would occupy Von Kronhelm, who would experience great difficulty in quelling them, and would no doubt eventually recall the Saxons from West Middlesex to assist. If the latter retired upon London they would find the barricades held by Londoners in their rear and Lord Byfield in their front, and be thus caught between two fires.

"In each district of London there is a chief of the Defenders, and to each chief these orders had been conveyed in strictest confidence. Therefore, to-day, while the outbreak occurred in Oxford Street, there were fully a dozen others in various parts of the metropolis, each of a more or less serious character. Every district has already prepared its own secret defences, its fortified houses, and its bar-ricades in hidden by-ways. Besides the quantity of arms smuggled into London, every dead German has had his rifle, pistol, and ammunition stolen from him. Hundreds of the enemy have been surreptitiously killed for that very reason. Lawlessness is everywhere, Government and Army have failed them, and Londoners are now taking the law into their own hands.

"In King Street, Hammersmith; in Notting Dale, in Forest Road, Dalston; in Wick Road, Hackney; in Commercial Road East, near

Stepney Station; and in Prince of Wales Road, Kentish Town, the League of Defenders this morning—at about the same hour—first made their organisation public by displaying our national emblem, together with the white flags, with the scarlet St. George's Cross, the ancient battle flag of England.

"For that reason, then, no reinforcements were sent to Oxford Street. Von Kronhelm was far too busy in other quarters. In Kentish Town, it is reported, the Germans gained a complete and decisive victory, for the people had not barricaded themselves strongly; besides, there were large reinforcements of Germans ready in Regent's Park, and these came upon the scene before the Defenders were sufficiently prepared. The flag was captured from the barricade in Prince of Wales Road, and the men of Kentish Town lost over four hundred killed and wounded.

"At Stepney, the result was the reverse. The enemy, believing it to be a mere local disturbance and easily quelled, sent but a small body of men to suppress it. But very quickly, in the intricate by-streets off Commercial Road, these were wiped out, not one single man surviving. A second and third body were sent, but so fiercely was the ground contested that they were at length compelled to fall back and leave the men of Stepney masters of their own district. In Hammersmith and in Notting Dale the enemy also lost heavily, though in Hackney they were successful after hard fighting.

"Every one declares that this secret order issued by the League means that England is again prepared to give battle, and that London is commencing by her strategic movement of local rebellions. The gravity of the situation cannot now, for one moment, be concealed. London north of the Thames is destined to be the scene of the fiercest and most bloody warfare ever known in the history of the civilised world. The Germans will, of course, fight for their lives, while we shall fight for our homes and for our liberty. But right is on our side, and right will win.

"Reports from all over the metropolis tell the same tale. London is alert and impatient. At a word she will rise to a man, and then woe betide the invader! Surely Von Kronhelm's position is not a very enviable one. Our two censors in the office are smoking their pipes very gravely. Not a word of the street fighting is to be published. They will write their own account of it."

10 P.M.

"There has been a most frightful encounter at the Oxford Street and Tottenham Court Road barricades—a most stubborn resistance and gallant defence on the part of the men of Marylebone and Bloomsbury.

"From the lips of one of our correspondents who was within the barricade I have just learned the details. It appears that just about four o'clock General Von Wilberg sent from the City a large force of the 19th Division under Lieutenant General Frankenfeld, and part of these, advancing through the squares of Bloomsbury into Gower Street, attacked the Defenders' position from the Tottenham Court Road, while others coming up Holborn and New Oxford Street entered Soho from Charing Cross Road and threw up counter-barricades at the end of Dean Street, Wardour Street, Berwick, Poland, Argyll, and the other streets, all of which were opposite the defences of the populace. In Great Portland Street, too, they adopted a similar line, and without much ado the fight, commenced in a desultory fashion, soon became a battle.

"Within the barricades was a dense body of armed and angry citizens, each with his little badge, and every single one of them was ready to fight to the death. There is no false patriotism now, no mere bravado. Men make declarations, and carry them out. The gallant Londoners, with their several Maxims, wrought havoc among the invaders, especially in the Tottenham Court Road, where hundreds were maimed or killed.

"In Oxford Street, the enemy being under cover of their counter-barricades, little damage could be done on either side. The wide, open, deserted thoroughfare was every moment swept by a hail of bullets, but no one was injured. On the Great Portland Street side the populace made a feint of giving way at the Mortimer Street barricade, and a body of the enemy rushed in, taking the obstruction by storm. But next moment they regretted it, for they were set upon by a thousand armed men and wild haired women, so that every man paid for his courage with his life. The women, seizing the weapons and ammunition of the dead Germans, now returned to the barricade to use them.

"The Mortimer Street defences were at once repaired, and it was resolved to relay the fatal trap at some other point. Indeed, it was repeated at the end of Percy Street, where about fifty more Germans, who thought themselves victorious, were set upon and exterminated.

"Until dusk the fight lasted. The Germans, finding their attack futile, began to hurl petrol bombs over the barricades and these caused frightful destruction among our gallant men, several houses in the vicinity being set on fire. Fortunately, there was still water in the street hydrants, and two fire engines had already been brought within the beleaguered area in case of necessity.

"At last, about seven o'clock, the enemy, having lost very heavily in attempting to take the well-chosen position by storm, brought down several light field-guns from Regent's Park; and, placing them at their counter-barricades—where, by the way, they had lost many men in the earlier part of the conflict while piling up their shelters—suddenly opened fire with shell at the huge obstructions before them.

"At first they made but little impression upon the flagstones, etc., of which the barricades were mainly composed. But before long their bombardment began to tell; for slowly, here and there, exploding shells made great breaches in the defences that had been so heroically manned. More than once a high explosive shell burst right among the crowd of riflemen behind a barricade, sweeping dozens into eternity in a single instant. Against the fortified houses each side of the barricades the German artillery trained their guns, and very quickly reduced many of those buildings to ruins. The air now became thick with dust and smoke; and mingled with the roar of artillery at such close quarters came the screams of the injured and the groans of the dying. The picture drawn by the eye-witness who described this was a truly appalling one. Gradually the Londoners were being overwhelmed, but they were selling their lives dearly, fully proving themselves worthy sons of grand old England.

"At last the fire from the Newman Street barricade of the Defenders was silenced, and ten minutes later, a rush being made across from Dean Street, it was taken by storm. Then ensued fierce and bloody hand-to-hand fighting right up to Cleveland Street, while almost at the same moment the enemy broke in from Great Portland Street.

"A scene followed that is impossible to describe. Through all those narrow, crooked streets the fighting became general, and on either side hundreds fell. The Defenders in places cornered the Germans, cut them off, and killed them. Though it was felt that now the barricades had been broken the day was lost, yet every man kept courage, and fought with all his strength.

"For half an hour the Germans met with no success. On the contrary, they found themselves entrapped amid thousands of furious citizens, all wearing their silken badges, and all sworn to fight to the death.

"While the Defenders still struggled on, loud and ringing cheers were suddenly raised from Tottenham Court Road. The people from Clerkenwell, joined by those in Bloomsbury, had arrived to assist them. They had risen, and were attacking the Germans in the rear.

"Fighting was now general right across from Tottenham Court Road to Gray's Inn Road, and by nine o'clock, though Von Wilberg sent reinforcements, a victory was gained by the Defenders. Over two thousand Germans are lying dead and wounded about the streets and squares of Bloomsbury and Marylebone. The League had struck its first blow for Freedom.

"What will the morrow bring us? Dire punishment—or desperate victory?"

DAILY CHRONICLE OFFICE,
OCT. 4, 6 P.M.

"The final struggle for the possession of London is about to commence. Through all last night there were desultory conflicts between the soldiers and the people, in which many lives have, alas! been sacrificed.

"Von Wilberg still holds the City proper, with the Mansion House as his headquarters. Within the area already shown upon

---

LEAGUE OF DEFENDERS

CITIZENS OF LONDON AND LOYAL PATRIOTS

The hour has come to show your strength, and to wreak your vengeance.

TO-NIGHT, OCT. 4, AT 10 P.M., rise, and strike your blow for freedom.

A MILLION MEN are with Lord Byfield, already within striking distance of London; a million follow them, and yet another million are ready in South London.

RISE, FEARLESS AND STERN. Let "England for Englishmen" be your battle-cry, and avenge the blood of your wives and your children.

**AVENGE THIS INSULT TO YOUR NATION.
REMEMBER: TEN O'CLOCK TO-NIGHT!**

---

the map there are no English, all the inhabitants having been long ago expelled. The great wealth of London is in German hands, it is true, but it is Dead Sea fruit. They are unable either to make use of it or to deport it to Germany. Much has been taken away to the base at Southminster and other bases in Essex, but the greater part of the bullion still remains in the Bank of England.

"The most exciting stories have been reaching us during the last twenty-four hours, none of which, however, have passed the censor. For that reason I, one of the sub-editors, am keeping this diary, as a brief record of events during the present dreadful times.

"After the terrific struggle in Marylebone three days ago, Von Kronhelm saw plainly that if London were to rise *en masse* she would at once assume the upper hand. The German Commander-in-Chief had far too many points to guard. On the west of London he was threatened by Lord Byfield and hosts of auxiliaries, mostly sworn members of the National League of Defenders; on the south, across the river, Southwark, Lambeth, and Battersea formed an impregnable fortress, containing over a million eager patriots ready to burst forth and sweep away the vain, victorious army; while within central London itself the people were ready to rise.

"Reports reaching us to-day from Lord Byfield's headquarters at Windsor are numerous, but conflicting. As far as can be gathered, the authentic facts are as follows: Great bodies of the Defenders, including many women, all armed, are massing at Reading, Sonning, Wokingham, and Maidenhead. Thousands have arrived, and are hourly arriving by train, from Portsmouth, Plymouth, Exeter, Bristol, Gloucester, and, in fact, all the chief centres of the West of England, where Gerald Graham's campaign has been so marvellously successful. Sturdy Welsh colliers are marching shoulder to shoulder with agricultural labourers from Dorset and Devon, and clerks and citizens from the towns of Somerset, Cornwall, Gloucestershire, and Oxfordshire are taking arms beside the riff-raff of their own neighbourhoods. Peer and peasant, professional man and pauper, all are now united with one common object—to drive back the invader, and to save our dear old England.

"Oxford has, it seems, been one of the chief points of concentration, and the undergraduates who re-assembled there to defend their colleges now form an advance-guard of a huge body of Defenders on the march, by way of Henley and Maidenhead, to follow in the rear of Lord Byfield. The latter holds Eton and the country across to High Wycombe, while the Saxon headquarters are still at Staines. Frölich's Cavalry Division are holding the country across from Pinner through Stanmore and Chipping Barnet to the prison camp at Enfield Chase. These are the only German troops outside West London, the Saxons being now barred from entering by the huge barricades which the populace of West London have during the past few days been constructing. Every road leading into London from West Middlesex is now either strongly barricaded or entirely blocked up. Kew, Richmond, and Kingston Bridges have been destroyed, and Lord Byfield, with General Bamford at the Crystal Palace, remains practically in possession of the whole of the south of the Thames.

"The conflict which is now about to begin will be one to the death. While, on the one hand, the Germans are bottled up among us, the fact must not be overlooked that their arms are superior, and that they are trained soldiers. Yet the two or three local risings of yesterday and the day previous have given us courage, for they show that the enemy cannot manœuvre in the narrow streets, and soon become demoralised. In London we fail because we have so few riflemen. If every man who now carries a gun could shoot, we could compel the Germans to fly a flag of truce within twenty-four hours. Indeed, if Lord Roberts' scheme of universal training in 1906 had been adopted, the enemy would certainly never have been suffered to approach our capital.

"Alas! apathy has resulted in this terrible and crushing disaster, and we have only now to bear our part, each one of us, in the blow to avenge this desecration of our homes and the massacre of our loved ones.

"To-day I have seen the white banners with the red cross—the ensign of the Defenders—everywhere. Till yesterday it was not openly displayed, but to-day it is actually hung from windows or flown defiantly from flagstaffs in full view of the Germans.

"In Kilburn, or, to be more exact, in the district lying between the Harrow Road and the High Road, Kilburn, there was another conflict this morning between some of the German Garde Corps and the populace. The outbreak commenced by the arrest of some men who were found practising with rifles in Paddington Recreation Ground. One man who resisted was shot on the spot, whereupon the crowd who assembled attacked the German picket, and eventually killed them to a man. This was the signal for a general outbreak in the neighbourhood, and half an hour later, when a force was sent to quell the revolt, fierce fighting became general all through the narrow streets of Kensal Green, especially at the big barricade that blocks the Harrow Road where it is joined by Admiral Road. Here the bridges over the Grand Junction Canal have already been destroyed, for the barricades and defences have been scientifically constructed under the instruction of military engineers.

"From an early hour to-day it has been apparent that all these risings were purposely ordered by the League of Defenders to cause Von Kronhelm's confusion. Indeed, while the outbreak at Kensal Green was in progress, we had another reported from Dalston, a third from Limehouse, and a fourth from Homerton. Therefore, it is quite certain that the various centres of the League are acting in unison upon secret orders from headquarters.

"Indeed, South London also took part in the fray this morning, for the Defenders at the barricade at London Bridge have now mounted several field guns, and have started shelling Von Wilberg's position in the City. It is said that the Mansion House, where the General had usurped the apartments of the deported Lord Mayor, has already been half reduced to ruins. This action is, no doubt, only to harass the enemy, for surely General Bamford has no desire to destroy the City proper any more than it has already been destroyed. Lower Thames Street, King William Street, Gracechurch Street, and Cannon Street have, at any rate, been found untenable by the enemy, upon whom some losses have been inflicted.

"South London is every moment anxious to know the truth. Two days after the bombardment we succeeded at night in sinking a light telegraph cable in the river across from the Embankment at the bottom of Temple Avenue, and are in communication with our temporary office in Southwark Street.

"An hour ago there came, through secret sources, information of another naval victory to our credit, several German warships being sunk and captured. Here we dare not print it, so I have just wired it across to the other side, where they are issuing a special edition.

"Almost simultaneously with the report of the British victory, namely, at five o'clock, the truth—the great and all-important truth—became revealed. The mandate has gone forth from the headquarters of the League of Defenders that London is to rise in her might at ten o'clock to-night, and that a million men are ready to assist us. Placards and bills on red paper are everywhere.

"Frantic efforts are being made by the Germans all over London to suppress both posters and handbills.

"It is now six o'clock. In four hours it is believed that London will be one huge seething conflict. Night has been chosen, I suppose, in order to give the populace the advantage. The by-streets are for the most part still unlit, save for oil-lamps, for neither gas nor electric light are yet in proper working order after the terrible dislocation of everything. The scheme of the Defenders is, as already proved, to lure the Germans into the narrower thoroughfares, and then exterminate them. Surely in the history of the world there has never been such a bitter vengeance as that which is now inevitable. London, the greatest city ever known, is about to rise!"

MIDNIGHT

"London has risen! How can I describe the awful scenes of panic, bloodshed, patriotism, brutality, and vengeance that are at this moment in progress? As I write, through the open window I can hear the roar of voices, the continual crackling of rifles, and the heavy booming of guns. I walked along Fleet Street at nine o'clock, and I found, utterly disregarding the order that no unauthorised persons are to be abroad after nightfall, hundreds upon hundreds of all classes, all wearing their little silk Union Jack badges pinned to their coats, on the way to join in their particular districts. Some carried rifles, others revolvers, while others were unarmed. Yet not a German did I see in the streets. It seemed as though, for the moment, the enemy had vanished. There was only the strong cordon across the bottom of Ludgate Hill, men who looked on in wonder, but without bestirring themselves.

"Is it possible that Von Kronhelm's strategy is to remain inactive, and refuse to fight?

"The first shot I heard fired, just after ten o'clock, was at the Strand end of Fleet Street, at the corner of Chancery Lane. There, I afterwards discovered, a party of forty German infantrymen had been attacked, and all of them killed. Quickly following this, I heard the distant booming of artillery, and then the rattle of musketry and pom-poms became general, but not in the neighbourhood where I was. For nearly half an hour I remained at the corner of Aldwych; then, on going farther along the Strand, I found that the Defenders from the Waterloo Road had made a wild sortie into the Strand, but could find no Germans there.

"The men who had for a fortnight held that barricade at the bridge were more like demons than human beings; therefore I retired, and in the crush made my way back to the office to await reports.

"They were not long in arriving. I can only give a very brief *résumé* at the moment, for they are so numerous as to be bewildering.

"Speaking generally, the whole of London has obeyed the mandate of the League, and, rising, are attacking the Germans at every point. In the majority of cases, however, the enemy hold strong positions, and are defending themselves, inflicting terrible losses upon the unorganised populace. Every Londoner is fighting for himself, without regard for orders or consequences. In Bethnal Green the Germans, lured into the maze of by-streets, have suffered great losses, and again in Clerkenwell, St. Luke's, Kingsland, Hackney and Old Ford. Whitechapel too, devoid of its alien population, who have escaped into Essex, has held its own, and the enemy have had some great losses in the streets off Cable and Leman Streets.

"With the exception of the sortie across Waterloo Bridge, South London is, as yet, remaining in patience, acting under the orders of General Bamford.

"News has come in ten minutes ago of a fierce and sudden attack upon the Saxons by Lord Byfield from Windsor, but there are, as yet, no details.

"From the office across the river I am being constantly asked for details of the fight, and how it is progressing. In Southwark the excitement is evidently most intense, and it requires all the energy of the local commanders of the Defenders to repress another sortie across that bridge.

"There has just occurred an explosion so terrific that the whole of this building has been shaken as though by an earthquake.

"London has struck her first blow of revenge. What will be its sequel?"

CHAPTER II

SCENES AT WATERLOO BRIDGE

THE FOLLOWING is the personal narrative of a young chauffeur named John Burgess, who assisted in the defence of the barricade at Waterloo Bridge.

The statement was made to a reporter at noon on October 5, while he was lying on a mattress in the Church of St. Martin's-in-the-Fields, so badly wounded in the chest that the surgeons had given him up.

He related his story in the form of a farewell letter to his sister. The reporter chanced to be passing, and, hearing him asking for some one to write for him, volunteered to do so.

"We all did our best," he said, "every one of us. Myself, I was at the barricade for thirteen days—thirteen days of semi-starvation, sleeplessness, and constant tension, for we knew not, from one moment to another, when a sudden attack might be made upon us. At first our obstruction was a mere ill-built pile of miscellaneous articles, half of which would not stop bullets; but on the third day our men, superintended by several non-commissioned officers in uniform, began to put the position in a proper state of defence, to mount Maxims in the neighbouring houses, and to place explosives in the crown of two of the arches of the bridge, so that we could instantly demolish it if necessity arose.

"Fully a thousand men were holding the position, but unfortunately few of them had ever handled a rifle. As regards myself, I had learned to shoot rooks when a boy in Shropshire, and now that I had obtained a gun I was anxious to try my skill. When the League of Defenders was started, and a local secretary came to us, we all eagerly joined, each receiving, after he had taken his oath and signed his name, a small silk Union Jack, the badge of the League, not to be worn till the word went forth to rise.

"Then came a period—long, dreary, shadeless days of waiting— when the sun beat down upon us mercilessly and our vigilance was required to be constant both night and day. So uncertain were the movements of the enemy opposite us that we scarcely dared to leave our positions for a moment. Night after night I spent sleeping in a neighbouring doorway, with an occasional stretch upon somebody's bed in some house in the vicinity. Now and then, whenever we saw Germans moving in Wellington Street, we sent a volley into them, in return receiving a sharp reply from their pom-poms. Constantly our sentries were on the alert along the wharves, and in the riverside warehouses, watching for the approach of the enemy's spies in boats. Almost nightly some adventurous spirits among the Germans would try and cross. On one occasion, while doing sentry duty in a warehouse backing on Commercial Road, I was sitting with a comrade at a window overlooking the river. The moon was shining, for the night was a balmy and beautiful one, and all was quiet. It was about two o'clock in the morning, and as we sat smoking our pipes, with our eyes fixed upon the glittering water, we suddenly saw a small boat containing three men stealing slowly along in the shadow.

"For a moment the rowers rested upon their oars, as if undecided, then pulled forward again in search of a landing-place. As they passed below our window I shouted a challenge. At first there was no response. Again I repeated it, when I heard a muttered imprecation in German.

"'Spies!' I cried to my comrade, and with one accord we raised our rifles and fired. Ere the echo of the first shot had died away I saw one man fall into the water, while at the next shot a second man half rose from his seat, threw up his hands, and staggered back wounded.

"The firing gave the alarm at the barricade, and ere the boat could approach the bridge, though the survivor pulled for dear life, a Maxim spat forth its red fire, and both boat and oarsman were literally riddled.

"Almost every night similar incidents were reported. The enemy were doing all in their power to learn the exact strength of our defences, but I do not think their efforts were very successful. The surface of the river, every inch of it, was under the careful scrutiny of a thousand watchful eyes.

"Each day the *Bulletin* of our national association brought us tidings of what was happening outside.

"At last, however, the welcome word came to us on the morning of October 4, that at ten that night we were to make a concerted attack upon the Germans. A scarlet bill was thrust into my hand, and as soon as the report was known we were all highly excited, and through the day prepared ourselves for the struggle.

"A gun sounded from the direction of Westminster. We looked at our watches, and found it was ten o'clock. Our bugles sounded and we sprang to our positions, as we had done dozens, nay hundreds, of times before. I felt faint, for I had only had half a pint of weak soup all day, for the bread did not go round. Nevertheless, the knowledge that we were about to strike the blow inspired me with fresh life and strength. Our officer shouted a brief word of command, and next moment we opened a withering fire upon the enemy's barricade in Wellington Street.

"In a moment a hundred rifles and several Maxims spat their red fire at us, but as usual the bullets flattened themselves harmlessly before us. Then the battery of artillery which Sir Francis Bamford had sent us three days before got into position, and in a few moments began hurling great shells upon the German defences.

"Behind us was a great armed multitude ready and eager to get at the foe, a huge, unorganised body of fierce, irate Londoners, determined upon having blood for blood. From over the river the sound of battle was rising, a great roaring like the sound of a distant sea, with ever and anon the crackling of rifles and the boom of guns, while above the night sky grew a dark blood-red with the glare of a distant conflagration.

"For half an hour we pounded away at the barricade in Wellington Street with our siege guns, Maxims, and rifles, until a well-directed shell exploded beneath the centre of the obstruction, blowing open a great gap and sending fragments high into the air. Then it seemed that all resistance suddenly ceased. At first we were surprised at this; but on further scrutiny we found that it was not our fire that had routed the enemy, but that they were being attacked in their rear by hosts of armed citizens surging down from Kingsway and the Strand.

"We could plainly discern that the Germans were fighting for their lives. Into the midst of them we sent one or two shells; but fearing to cause casualties among our own comrades, we were compelled to cease firing.

"The armed crowd behind us, finding that we were again inactive, at once demanded that our barricade should be opened, so that they might cross the bridge and assist their comrades by taking the Germans in the rear. For ten minutes our officer in charge refused, for the order of General Greatorex, Commander-in-Chief of the League, was that no sortie was to be made at present. However, the South Londoners became so infuriated that our commander was absolutely forced to give way, though he knew not into what trap we might fall, as he had no idea of the strength of the enemy in the neighbourhood of the Strand. A way was quickly opened in the obstruction, and two minutes later we were pouring across Waterloo Bridge in thousands, shouting and yelling in triumph as we passed the ruins of the enemy's barricade, and fell upon him with merciless revenge. With us were many women, who were, perhaps, fiercer and more unrelenting than the men. Indeed, many a woman that night killed a German with her own hands, firing revolvers in their faces, striking with knives, or even blinding them with vitriol.

"The scene was both exciting and ghastly. At the spot where I first fought—on the pavement outside the Savoy—we simply slaughtered the Germans in cold blood. Men cried for mercy, but we gave them no quarter. London had risen in its might, and as our comrades fought all along the Strand and around Aldwych, we gradually exterminated every man in German uniform. Soon the roadways of the Strand, Wellington Street, Aldwych, Burleigh Street, Southampton Street, Bedford Street, and right along to Trafalgar Square, were covered with dead and dying. The wounded of both nationalities were trodden underfoot and killed by the swaying, struggling thousands. The enemy's loss must have been severe in our particular quarter, for of the great body of men from Hamburg and Lübeck holding their end of Waterloo Bridge I do not believe a single one was spared, even though they fought for their lives like veritable devils.

"Our success intoxicated us, I think. That we were victorious at that point cannot be doubted, but with foolish disregard for our own safety, we pressed forward into Trafalgar Square, in the belief that our comrades were similarly making an attack upon the enemy there. The error was, alas! a fatal one for many of us. To fight an organised force in narrow streets is one thing, but to meet him in a large open space with many inlets, like Trafalgar Square, is another.

"The enemy were no doubt awaiting us, for as we poured out from the Strand at Charing Cross we were met with a devastating fire from German Maxims on the opposite side of the square. They were holding Whitehall—to protect Von Kronhelm's head-quarters—the entrances to Spring Gardens, Cockspur Street, and Pall Mall East, and their fire was converged upon the great armed multitude which, being pressed on from behind, came out into the open square only to fall in heaps beneath the sweeping hail of German lead.

"The error was one that could not be rectified. We all saw it when too late. There was no turning back now, I struggled to get into the small side-street that runs down by the bar of the Grand Hotel, but it was blocked with people already in refuge there.

"Another instant and I was lifted from my legs by the great throng going to their doom, and carried right in the forefront to the square. Women screamed when they found themselves facing the enemy's fire.

"The scene was awful—a massacre, nothing more or less. For every German's life we had taken, a dozen of our own were now being sacrificed.

"A woman was pushed close to me, her grey hair streaming down her back, her eyes starting wildly from her head, her bony hands smeared with blood. Suddenly she realised that right before her red fire was spitting from the German guns.

"Screaming in despair, she clung frantically to me.

"I felt next second a sharp burning pain in my chest.... We fell forward together upon the bodies of our comrades.... When I came to myself I found myself here, in this church, close to where I fell."

On that same night desperate sorties were made from the London, Southwark, and Blackfriars Bridges, and terrible havoc was committed by the Defenders.

The German losses were enormous, for the South Londoners fought like demons and gave no quarter.

CHAPTER III

GREAT BRITISH VICTORY

THE FOLLOWING DESPATCH from the war correspondent of *The Times* with Lord Byfield was received on the morning of October 5, but was not published in that journal till some days later, owing to the German censorship, which necessitated its being kept secret:—

WILLESDEN, OCTOBER 4 (EVENING)

"After a bloody but successful combat lasting from early dawn till late in the afternoon, the country to the immediate west of the metropolis has been swept clear of the hated invaders, and the masses of the 'League of Defenders' can be poured into the West of London without let or hindrance. In the desperate street fighting which is now going on they will be much more formidable than they were ever likely to be in the open field, where they were absolutely incapable of manœuvring. As for the Saxons—what is left of them—and Frölich's Cavalry Division, with whom we have been engaged all day, they have now fallen back on Harrow and Hendon, it is said; but it is currently reported that a constant movement towards the high ground near Hampstead is going on. These rumours come by way of London, since the enemy's enormous force of cavalry is still strong enough to prevent us getting any first-hand intelligence of his movements.

"As has been previously reported, the XIIth Saxon Corps, under the command of Prince Henry of Würtemberg, had taken up a position intended to cover the metropolis from the hordes of 'Defenders' which, supported by a small leaven of Regulars, with a proportion of cavalry and guns, were known to be slowly rolling up from the west and south. Their front, facing west, extended from Staines on the south, to Pinner on the north, passing through Stanwell, West Drayton, and Uxbridge. In addition they had a strong reserve in the neighbourhood of Hounslow, whose business it was to cover their left flank by keeping watch along the line of the Thames. They had destroyed all bridges over the river between Staines and Hammersmith. Putney Bridge, however, was still intact, as all attacks on it had been repulsed by the British holding it on the south side. Such was the general state of affairs when Lord Byfield, who had established his headquarters at Windsor, formed his plan of attack.

"As far as I have been able to ascertain, its general idea was to hold the Saxons to their position by the threat of 300,000 Defenders that were assembled and were continually increasing along a roughly parallel line to that occupied by the enemy at about ten miles' distance from it, while he attacked their left flank with what Regular and Militia regiments he could rapidly get together near Esher and Kingston. By this time the southern lines in the neighbourhood of London were all in working order, the damage that had been done here and there by small parties of the enemy who had made raids across the river having been repaired. It was, therefore, not a very difficult matter to assemble troops from Windsor and various points on the South of London at very short notice.

"General Bamford, to whom had been entrusted the defence of South London, and who had established his headquarters at the Crystal Palace, also contributed every man he could spare from the remnant of the Regular troops under his command.

"It was considered quite safe now that the Germans in the City were so hard pressed to leave the defence of the Thames bridges to the masses of Irregulars who had all along formed the bulk of their defenders. The risk that Prince Henry of Würtemberg would take the bull by the horns, and by a sudden forward move attack and scatter the inert and invertebrate mass of 'Defenders' who were in his immediate front had, of course, to be taken; but it was considered that in the present state of affairs in London he would hardly dare to increase the distance between the Saxon Corps and the rest of the German Army. Events proved the correctness of this surmise; but owing to unforeseen circumstances, the course of the battle was somewhat different from that which had been anticipated.

"Despite the vigilance of the German spies our plans were kept secret till the very end, and it is believed that the great convergence of Regular troops that began as soon as it was dark from Windsor and from along the line occupied by the Army of the League on the west, right round to Greenwich on the east, went on without any news of the movement being carried to the enemy.

"Before dawn this morning every unit was in the position to which it had been previously detailed, and, everything being in readiness, the Royal Engineers began to throw a pontoon bridge over the Thames at the point where it makes a bend to the south just above the site of Walton Bridge. The enemy's patrols and pickets in the immediate neighbourhood at once opened a heavy fire on the workers, but it was beaten down by that which was poured upon them from the houses in Walton-on-Thames, which had been quietly occupied during the night. The enemy in vain tried to reinforce them, but in order to do this their troops had to advance into a narrow peninsula which was swept by a cross-fire of shells from batteries which had been placed in position on the south side of the river for this very purpose.

"By seven o'clock the bridge was completed, and the troops were beginning to cross over covered by the fire of the artillery and by an advance guard which had been pushed over in boats. Simultaneously very much the same thing had been going on at Long Ditton, and fierce fighting was going on in the avenues and gardens round Hampton Court. Success here, too, attended the British arms. As a matter of fact, a determined attempt to cross the river in force had not at all been anticipated by the Germans. They had not credited their opponents with the power of so rapidly assembling an army and assuming an effective and vigorous offensive so soon after their terrible series of disasters.

"What they had probably looked for was an attempt to overwhelm them by sheer force of numbers. They doubtless calculated that Lord Byfield would stiffen his flabby masses of 'Defenders' with what trained troops he could muster, and endeavour to attack their lines along their whole length, overlapping them on the flank.

"They realised that to do this he would have to sacrifice his men in thousands upon thousands, but they knew that to do so would be his only possible chance of success in this eventuality, since the bulk of his men could neither manœuvre nor deploy. Still they reckoned that in the desperate situation of the British, he would make up his mind to do this.

"On their part, although they fully realised the possibility of being overwhelmed by such tactics, they felt pretty confident that, posted as they were behind a perfect network of small rivers and streams which ran down to join the Thames, they would at least succeed in beating off the attack with heavy loss, and stood no bad chance of turning the repulse into a rout by skilful use of Frölich's Cavalry Division, which would be irresistible when attacking totally untrained troops after they had been shattered and disorganised by artillery fire. This, at least, is the view of those experts with whom I have spoken.

"What, perhaps, tended rather to confirm them in their theories as to the action of the British was the rifle firing that went on along the whole of their front all night through. The officers in charge of the various units which conglomerated together formed the forces facing the Saxons, had picked out the few men under their command who really had some little idea of using a rifle, and, supplied with plenty of ammunition, had sent them forward in numerous small parties with general orders to approach as near the enemy's picket line as possible, and as soon as fired on to lie down and open fire in return. So a species of sniping engagement went on from dark to dawn. Several parties got captured or cut up by the German outlying troops and many others got shot by neighbouring parties of snipers. But, although they did not in all probability do the enemy much damage, yet they kept them on the alert all night, and led them to expect an attack in the morning. One way and another luck was entirely on the side of the patriots that morning.

"When daylight came the British massed to the westward of Staines had such a threatening appearance from their immense numbers, and their fire from their batteries of heavy guns and howitzers on the south side of the river, which took the German left flank in, was so heavy that Prince Henry, who was there in person, judged an attack to be imminent, and would not spare a man to reinforce his troops at Shepperton and Halliford, who were, numerically, totally inadequate to resist the advance of the British once they got across the river.

"He turned a deaf ear to the most imploring requests for assistance, but ordered the officer in command at Hounslow to move down at once and drive the British into the river. So it has been reported by our prisoners. Unluckily for him this officer had his hands quite full enough at this time; for the British, who had crossed at Long Ditton, had now made themselves masters of everything east of the Thames Valley branch of the London and South-Western Railway, were being continually reinforced, and were fast pushing their right along the western bank of the river.

"Their left was reported to be at Kempton Park, where they joined hands with those who had effected a crossing near Walton-on-Thames. More bridges were being built at Platt's Eyot, Tagg's Eyot, and Sunbury Lock, while boats and wherries in shoals appeared from all creeks and backwaters and hiding-places as soon as both banks were in the hands of the British.

"Regulars, Militia, and, lastly, Volunteers, were now pouring across in thousands. Forward was still the word. About noon a strong force of Saxons was reported to be retreating along the road from Staines to Brentford. They had guns with them, which engaged the field batteries which were at once pushed forward by the British to attack them. These troops, eventually joining hands with those at Hounslow, opposed a more determined resistance to our advance than we had hitherto encountered.

"According to what we learned subsequently from prisoners and others, they were commanded by Prince Henry of Würtemberg in person. He had quitted his position at Staines, leaving only a single battalion and a few guns as a rearguard to oppose the masses of the 'Defenders' who threatened him in that direction, and had placed his troops in the best position he could to cover the retreat of the rest of his corps from the line they had been occupying. He had, it would appear, soon after the fighting began, received the most urgent orders from Von Kronhelm to fall back on London and assist him in the street fighting that had now been going on without intermission for the best part of two days. Von Kronhelm probably thought that he would be able to draw off some of his numerous foes to the westward. But the message was received too late. Prince Henry did his best to obey it, but by this time the very existence of the XIIth Corps was at stake on account of the totally unexpected attack on his left rear by the British regular troops.

"He opposed such a stout resistance with the troops under his immediate command that he brought the British advance to a temporary standstill, while in his rear every road leading Londonward was crowded with the rest of his army as they fell back from West Drayton, Uxbridge, Ruislip and Pinner. Had they been facing trained soldiers they would have found it most difficult, if not impossible, to do this; but as it was the undisciplined and untrained masses of the League of Defenders lost a long time in advancing, and still longer in getting over a series of streams and dykes that lay between them and the abandoned Saxon position.

"They lost heavily, too, from the fire of the small rearguards that had been left at the most likely crossing-places. The Saxons were therefore able to get quite well away from them, and when some attempt was being made to form up the thousands of men who presently found themselves congregated on the heath east of Uxbridge, before advancing farther, a whole brigade of Frölich's heavy cavalry suddenly swept down upon them from behind Ickenham village. The débâcle that followed was frightful. The unwieldy mass of 'Leaguers' swayed this way and that for a moment in the panic occasioned by the sudden apparition of the serried masses of charging cavalry that were rushing down on them with a thunder of hoofs that shook the earth. A few scattered shots were fired, without any perceptible effect, and before they could either form up or fly the German Reiters were upon them. It was a perfect massacre. The 'Leaguers' could oppose no resistance whatever. They were ridden down and slaughtered with no more difficulty than if they had been a flock of sheep. Swinging their long, straight swords, the cavalrymen cut them down in hundreds and drove thousands into the river. The 'Defenders' were absolutely pulverised and fled westwards in a huge scattered crowd. But if the Germans had the satisfaction of scoring a local victory in this quarter, things were by no means rosy for them elsewhere. Prince Henry, by desperate efforts, contrived to hold on long enough in his covering position to enable the Saxons from the central portion of his abandoned line to pass through Hounslow and move along the London road, through Brentford.

"Here disaster befell them. A battery of 4.7 guns was suddenly unmasked on Richmond Hill, and, firing at a range of 5,000 yards, played havoc with the marching column. The head of it also suffered severe loss from riflemen concealed in Kew Gardens, and the whole force had to extend and fall back for some distance in a northerly direction. Near Ealing they met the Uxbridge brigade, and a certain delay and confusion occurred. However, trained soldiers such as these are not difficult to reorganise, and while the latter continued its march along the main road the remainder moved in several small parallel columns through Acton and Turnham Green. Before another half-hour had elapsed there came a sound of firing from the advanced guard. Orders to halt followed, then orders to send forward reinforcements.

"During all this time the rattle of rifle fire waxed heavier and heavier. It soon became apparent that every road and street leading into London was barricaded and that the houses on either side were crammed with riflemen. Before any set plan of action could be determined on, the retiring Saxons found themselves committed to a very nasty bout of street fighting. Their guns were almost useless, since they could not be placed in positions from which they could fire on the barricades except so close as to be under effective rifle fire. They made several desperate assaults, most of which were repulsed. In Goldhawk Road a Jäegar battalion contrived to rush a big rampart of paving-stones which had been improvised by the British; but, once over, they were decimated by the fire from the houses on either side of the street. Big high explosive shells from Richmond Hill, too, began to drop among the Saxons. Though the range was long, the gunners were evidently well informed of the whereabouts of the Saxon troops and made wonderfully lucky shooting.

"For some time the distant rumble of the firing to the south-west had been growing more distinct in their ears, and about four o'clock it suddenly broke out comparatively near by. Then came an order from Prince Henry to fall back on Ealing at once. What had happened? It will not take long to relate this. Prince Henry's covering position had lain roughly between East Bedfont and Hounslow, facing south-east. He had contrived to hold on to the latter place long enough to allow his right to pivot on it and fall back to Cranford Bridge. Here they were, to a certain extent, relieved from the close pressure they had been subjected to by the constantly advancing British troops, by the able and determined action of Frölich's Cavalry Brigade.

"But in the meantime his enemies on the left, constantly re-inforced from across the river—while never desisting from their so far unsuccessful attack on Hounslow—worked round through Twickenham and Isleworth till they began to menace his rear. He must abandon Hounslow, or be cut off. With consummate general-ship he withdrew his left along the line of the Metropolitan and District Railway, and sent word to the troops on his right to retire and take up a second position at Southall Green. Unluckily for him, there was a delay in transmission, resulting in a considerable number of these troops being cut off and captured. Frölich's cavalry were unable to aid them at this juncture, having their attention drawn away by the masses of 'Leaguers' who had managed to get over the Colne and were congregating near Harmondsworth.

"They cut these up and dispersed them, but afterwards found that they were separated from the Saxons by a strong force of British regular troops who occupied Harlington and opened fire on the Reiters that emptied numerous saddles. They, therefore, made off to the northward. From this forward nothing could check the steady advance of the English, though fierce fighting went on till dark all through Hanwell, Ealing, Perivale, and Wembley, the Saxons struggling gamely to the last, but getting more and more disorganised. Had it not been for Frölich's division on their right they would have been surrounded. As it was, they must have lost half their strength in casualties and prisoners.

"At dark, however, Lord Byfield ordered a general halt of his tired though triumphant troops, and bivouacked and billeted them along a line reaching from Willesden on the right through Wembley to Greenford. He established his headquarters at Wembley.

"I have heard some critics say that he ought to have pushed on his freshest troops towards Hendon to prevent the remnant of our opponents from re-entering London; but others, with reason, urge that he is right to let them into the metropolis, which they will now find to be merely a trap."

Extracts from the diary of General Von Kleppen, Commander of the IVth German Army Corps, occupying London:—

DORCHESTER HOUSE, PARK LANE, OCT. 6

"We are completely deceived. Our position, much as we are attempting to conceal it, is a very grave one. We believed that if we reached London the British spirit would be broken. Yet the more drastic our rule, the fiercer becomes the opposition. How it will end I fear to contemplate. The British are dull and apathetic, but, once roused, they fight like fiends.

"Last night we had an example of it. This League of Defenders, which Von Kronhelm has always treated with ridicule, is, we have discovered too late, practically the whole of England. Von Bistram, commanding the VIIth Corps, and Von Haeslen, of the VIIIth Corps, have constantly been reporting its spread through Manchester, Leeds, Bradford, Sheffield, Birmingham and the other great towns we now occupy; but our Commander-in-Chief has treated the matter lightly, declaring it to be a kind of offshoot of some organisation they have in England, called the Primrose League...

"Yesterday, at the Council of War, however, he was compelled to acknowledge his error when I handed him a scarlet handbill calling upon the British to make a concerted attack upon us at ten o'clock. Fortunately, we were prepared for the assault, otherwise I verily believe that the honours would have rested with the populace in London. As it is, we suffered considerable reverses in various districts, where our men were lured into the narrow side-streets and cut up. I confess I am greatly surprised at the valiant stand made everywhere by the Londoners. Last night they fought to the very end. A disaster to our arms in the Strand was followed by a victory in Trafalgar Square, where Von Wilberg had established defences for the purpose of preventing the joining of the people of the East End with those of the West..."

CHAPTER IV

MASSACRE OF GERMANS IN LONDON

DAILY TELEGRAPH OFFICE,
OCT. 12, 6 P.M.

"THROUGH the whole of last week the Germans occupying London suffered great losses. They are now hemmed in on every side.

"At three o'clock this morning, Von Kronhelm, having withdrawn the greater part of the troops from the defence of the bridges, in an attempt to occupy defensive positions in North London, the South Londoners, impatient with long waiting, broke forth and came across the river in enormous multitudes, every man bent upon killing a German wherever seen.

"The night air was rent everywhere by the hoarse, exultant shouts as London—the giant, all-powerful city—fell upon the audacious invader. Through our office windows came the dull roar of London's millions swelled by the 'Defenders' from the west and south of England, and by the gallant men from Canada, India, the Cape, and other British colonies who had come forward to fight for the Mother Country as soon as her position was known to be critical.

"In the streets are to be seen Colonial uniforms side by side with the costermonger from Whitechapel or Walworth, and dark-faced Indians in turbans are fighting out in Fleet Street and the Strand. In the great struggle now taking place many of our reporters and correspondents have unfortunately been wounded, and, alas! four of them killed.

"In these terrible days a man's life is not safe from one moment to another. Both sides seem to have now lost their heads completely. Among the Germans all semblance of order has apparently been thrown to the winds. It is known that London has risen to a man, and the enemy are therefore fully aware of their imminent peril. Already they are beaten. True, Von Kronhelm still sits in the War Office directing operations—operations he knows too well are foredoomed to failure.

"The Germans have, it must be admitted, carried on the war in a chivalrous spirit, until those drastic executions exasperated the people. Then neither side gave quarter, and now to-day, all through Islington, Hoxton, Kingsland, and Dalston, right out eastwards to Homerton, a perfect massacre of Germans is in progress.

"Lord Byfield has issued two urgent proclamations, threatening the people of London with all sorts of penalties if they kill instead of take an enemy prisoner, but they seem to have no effect. London is starved and angered to such a pitch that her hatred knows no bounds, and only blood will atone for the wholesale slaughter of the innocent since the bombardment of the metropolis began.

"The Kaiser has, we hear, left the 'Belvedere,' at Scarborough, where he has been living incognito. A confidential report, apparently well founded, has reached us that he embarked upon the steam-trawler Morning Star at Scarborough yesterday, and set out across the Dogger, with Germany, of course, as his destination. Surely he must now regret his ill-advised policy of making an attack upon England. He had gauged our military weakness very accurately, but he had not counted upon the patriotic spirit of our Empire. It may be that he has already given orders to Von Kronhelm, but it is nevertheless a very significant fact that the German wireless telegraph apparatus on the summit of Big Ben is in constant use by the German Commander-in-Chief. He is probably in hourly communication with Bremen, or with the Emperor himself upon the trawler *Morning Star.*

"Near Highbury Fields about noon to-day some British cavalry surprised a party of Germans, and attempted to take them prisoner. The latter showed fight, whereupon they were shot down to a man. The British held as prisoners by the Germans near Enfield have now been released, and are rejoining their comrades along the northern heights. Many believe that another and final battle will be fought north of London, but military men declare that the German power is already broken. Whether Von Kronhelm will still continue to lose his men at the rate he is now doing, or whether he will sue for peace, is an open question. Personally, he was against the bombardment of London from the very first, yet he was compelled to carry out the orders of his Imperial master. The invasion, the landing, and the successes in the north were, in his opinion, quite sufficient to have paralysed British trade and caused such panic that an indemnity would have been paid. To attack London was, in his opinion, a proceeding far too dangerous, and his estimate is now proved to have been the correct one. Now that they have lost command of the sea, and are cut off from their bases in Essex, the enemy's situation is hopeless. They may struggle on, but assuredly the end can only be an ignominious one.

"Yet the German eagle still flies proudly over the War Office, over St. Stephen's, and upon many other public buildings, while upon others British Royal Standards and Union Jacks are commencing to appear, each one being cheered by the excited Londoners, whose hearts are now full of hope. Germany shall be made to bite the dust. That is the war-cry everywhere. Many a proud Uhlan and Cuirassier has to-day ridden to his death amid the dense mobs, mad with the lust of blood. Some of the more unfortunate of the enemy have been lynched, and torn limb from limb, while others have died deaths too horrible to here describe in detail.

"Each hour brings to us further news showing how, by slow degrees, the German army of occupation is being wiped out. People are jeering at the audacious claim for indemnity presented to the British Government when the enemy entered London, and are asking whether we will not now present a claim to Germany. Von Kronhelm is not blamed so much as his Emperor. He has been the cat's paw, and has burned his fingers in endeavouring to snatch the chestnuts from the fire.

"As a commander, he has acted justly, fully observing the international laws concerning war. It was only when faced by the problem of a national uprising that he countenanced anything bordering upon capital punishment. An hour ago our censors were withdrawn. They came and shook hands with many members of the staff, and retired. This surely is a significant fact that Von Kronhelm hopes to regain the confidence of London by appearing to treat her with a fatherly solicitude. Or is it that he intends to sue for peace at any price?

"An hour ago another desperate attempt was made on the part of the men of South London, aided by a large body of British regulars, to regain possession of the War Office. Whitehall was once more the scene of a bloody fight, but so strongly does Von Kronhelm hold the place and all the adjacent thoroughfares—he apparently regarding it as his own fortress—that the attack was repulsed with heavy loss on our side.

"All the bridges are now open, the barricades are in most cases being blown up, and people are passing and repassing freely for the first time since the day following the memorable bombardment. London streets are, however, in a most deplorable condition. On every hand is ruin and devastation. Whole streets of houses rendered gaunt and windowless by the now spent fires meet the eye everywhere. In certain places the ruins were still smouldering, and in one or two districts the conflagrations spread over an enormous area. Even if peace be declared, can London ever recover from this present wreck? Paris recovered, and quickly too. Therefore we place our faith in British wealth, British industry, and British patriotism.

"Yes. The tide has turned. The great revenge now in progress is truly a mad and bloody one. In Kilburn this afternoon there was a wholesale killing of a company of German infantry, who, while marching along the High Road, were set upon by the armed mob, and practically exterminated. The smaller thoroughfares, Brondesbury Road, Victoria Road, Glendall Road, and Priory Park Road, across to Paddington Cemetery, were the scene of a frightful slaughter. The Germans died hard, but in the end were completely wiped out. German-baiting is now, indeed, the Londoner's pastime, and on this dark and rainy afternoon hundreds of men of the Fatherland have died upon the wet roads.

"Sitting here, in a newspaper office, as we do, and having fresh reports constantly before us, we are able to review the whole situation impartially. Every moment, through the various news-agencies and our own correspondents and contributors, we are receiving fresh facts—facts which all combine to show that Von Kronhelm cannot hold out much longer. Surely the Commander-in-Chief of a civilised army will not allow his men to be massacred as they are now being! The enemy's troops, mixed up in the maze of London streets as they are, are utterly unable to cope with the oncoming multitudes, some armed with rifles, and others with anything they can lay their hands upon.

"Women—wild, infuriated women—have now made their re-appearance north of the Thames. In more than one instance, where German soldiers have attempted to take refuge in houses, these women have obtained petrol, and, with screams of fiendish delight, set the houses in question on fire. Awful dramas are being enacted in every part of the metropolis. The history of to-day is written in German blood.

"Lord Byfield has established temporary headquarters at Jack Straw's Castle, where Von Kronhelm was during the bombardment, and last night we could see the signals exchanged between Hampstead and Sydenham Hill, from whence General Bamford has not yet moved. Our cavalry in Essex are, it is said, doing excellent work. Lord Byfield has also sent a body of troops across from Gravesend to Tilbury, and these have regained Maldon and Southminster after some hard fighting. Advices from Gravesend state that further reinforcements are being sent across the river to operate against the East of

London and hem in the Germans on that side. So confident is London of success that several of the railways are commencing to reorganise their traffic. A train left Willesden this afternoon for Birmingham, the first since the bombardment—while another has left Finsbury Park for Peterborough, to continue to York if possible. So wrecked are the London termini, however, that it must be some weeks before trains can arrive or be despatched from either Euston, King's Cross, Paddington, Marylebone, or St. Pancras. In many instances the line just north of the terminus is interrupted by a blown-up tunnel or a fallen bridge, therefore the termination of traffic must, for the present, be at some distance north on the outskirts of London.

"Shops are also opening in South London, though they have but little to sell. Nevertheless, this may be regarded as a sign of renewed confidence. Besides, supplies of provisions are now arriving, and the London County Council and the Salvation Army are distributing free soup and food in the lower-class districts. Private charity, everywhere abundant during the trying days of dark despair, is doing inestimable good among every class. The hard, grasping employer and the smug financier, who had hitherto kept scrupulous accounts, and have been noteworthy on account of their uncharitableness, have now, in the hour of need, come forward and subscribed liberally to the great Mansion House Fund, opened yesterday by the Deputy Lord Mayor of London. The subscription list occupies six columns of the issue of to-morrow's paper, and this, in itself, speaks well for the openheartedness of the moneyed classes of Great Britain.

"No movement has yet been made in the financial world. Bankers still remain with closed doors. The bullion seized at Southminster and other places is now under strong British guard, and will, it is supposed, be returned to the Bank immediately. Only a comparatively small sum has yet been sent across to Germany. Therefore all Von Kronhelm's strategy has utterly failed. By the invasion, Germany has, up to the present moment, gained nothing. She has made huge demands at which we can afford to jeer. True, she has wrecked London, but have we not sent the greater part of her fleet to the bottom of the North Sea, and have we not created havoc in German ports?

THE REVENGE 269

"The leave-taking of our two gold-spectacled censors was almost pathetic. We had come to regard them as necessities to puzzle and to play practical jokes of language upon. To-day for the first time we have received none of those official notices in German, with English translations, which of late have appeared so prominently in our columns. The German Eagle is gradually disentangling his talons from London, and means to escape us—if he can."

10.30 P.M.

"Private information has just reached us from a most reliable source that a conference has been arranged between Von Kronhelm and Lord Byfield. This evening the German Field Marshal sent a messenger to the British headquarters at Hampstead under a flag of truce. He bore a despatch from the German Commander asking that hostilities should be suspended for twenty-four hours, and that they should make an appointment for a meeting during that period.

"Von Kronhelm has left the time and place of meeting to Lord Byfield, and has informed the British Commander that he has sent telegraphic instruction to the German military governors of Birmingham, Sheffield, Manchester, Bradford, Leeds, Northampton, Stafford, Oldham, Wigan, Bolton, and other places, giving notice of his suggestion to the British, and ordering that for the present hostilities on the part of the Germans shall be suspended.

"It seems more than likely that the German Field Marshal has received these very definite instructions by wireless telegraph from the Emperor at Bremen or Potsdam.

"We understand that Lord Byfield, after a brief consultation by telegraph with the Government at Bristol, has sent a reply. Of its nature, however, nothing is known, and at the moment of writing hostilities are still in progress.

"In an hour's time we shall probably know whether the war is to continue, or a truce is to be proclaimed."

MIDNIGHT

"Lord Byfield has granted a truce, and hostilities have now been suspended.

"London has gone mad with delight, for the German yoke is cast off. Further information which has just reached us from private sources states that thousands of prisoners have been taken by Lord Byfield to-day, and that Von Kronhelm has acknowledged his position to be absolutely hopeless.

"The great German Army has been defeated by our British patriots, who have fought so valiantly and so well. It is not likely that the war will be resumed. Von Kronhelm received a number of British officers at the War Office half an hour ago, and it is said that he is already making preparations to vacate the post he has usurped.

"Lord Byfield has issued a reassuring message to London, which we have just received with instructions to print. It declares that although for the moment only a truce is proclaimed, yet this means the absolute cessation of all hostilities.

"The naval news of the past few days may be briefly summarised. The British main fleet entered the North Sea, and our submarines did most excellent work in the neighbourhood of the Maas Lightship. Prince Stahlberger had concentrated practically the whole of his naval force off Lowestoft, but a desperate battle was fought about seventy miles from the Texel, full details of which are not yet to hand. All that is known is that, having now regained command of the sea, we were enabled to inflict a crushing defeat upon the Germans, in which the German flagship was sunk. In the end sixty-one British ships were concentrated against seventeen German, with the result that the German fleet has practically been wiped out, there being 19,000 of the enemy's officers and men on the casualty list, the greatest recorded in any naval battle.

"Whatever may be the demands for indemnity on either side, one thing is absolutely certain, namely, that the invincible German Army and Navy are completely vanquished. The Eagle's wings are trailing in the dust."

CHAPTER V

HOW THE WAR ENDED

DAYS PASSED—WEARY, WAITING, ANXIOUS DAYS. A whole month went by. What had really happened at sea was unknown. After the truce, London very gradually began to resume her normal life, though the gaunt state of the streets was indescribably weird.

Shops began to open, and as each day passed, food became more plentiful and consequently less dear. The truce meant the end of the war, therefore thanksgiving services were held in every town and village throughout the country.

There were great prison-camps of Germans at Hounslow, Brentwood, and Barnet, while Von Kronhelm and his chief officers were also held as prisoners until some decision through diplomatic channels could be arrived at. Meanwhile a little business began to be done; thousands began to resume their employment, bankers reopened their doors, and within a week the distress and suffering of the poor became perceptibly alleviated. The task of burying the dead after the terrible massacre of the Germans in the London streets had been a stupendous one, but so quickly had it been accomplished that an epidemic was happily averted.

Parliament moved back to Westminster, and daily meetings of the Cabinet were being held in Downing Street. These resulted in the resignation of the Ministry, and with a fresh Cabinet, in which Mr. Gerald Graham, the organiser of the Defenders, was given a seat, a settlement was at last arrived at.

To further describe the chaotic state of England occasioned by the terrible and bloody war would serve no purpose. The loss and suffering which it had caused the country had been incalculable; statisticians estimated that in one month of hostilities it had amounted to £500,000,000, a part of which represented money transferred from British pockets to German, as the enemy had carried off some of the securities upon which the German troops had laid their hands in London.

Let us for a moment take a retrospective glance. Consols were at 50; bread was still 1s. 6d. per loaf; and the ravages of the German commerce-destroyers had sent up the cost of insurance on British shipping sky-high. Money was almost unprocurable; except for the manufacture of war material, there was no industry; and the suffering and distress among the poor could not be exaggerated. In all directions men, women, and children had been starving.

The mercantile community were loud in their outcry for "peace at any price," and the pro-German and Stop-the-War Party were equally vehement in demanding a cessation of the war. They found excuses for the enemy, and forgot the frightful devastation and loss which the invasion had caused to the country.

They insisted that the working class gained nothing, even though the British fleet was closely blockading the German coast, and their outcry was strengthened when a few days after the blockade of the Elbe had begun, two British battleships were so unfortunate as to strike German mines, and sink with a large part of their crews. The difficulty of borrowing money for the prosecution of the war was a grave obstacle in the way of the party of action, and preyed upon the mind of the British Government.

Socialism, with its creed of "Thou shalt have no other god but Thyself," and its doctrine, "Let us eat and drink, for to-morrow we die," had replaced the religious beliefs of a generation of Englishmen taught to suffer and to die sooner than surrender to wrong. In the hour of trial, amidst smoking ruins, among the holocausts of dead which marked the prolonged, bloody, and terrible battles on land and at sea, the spirit of the nation quailed, and there was really no great leader to recall it to ways of honour and duty.

The wholesale destruction of food, and particularly of wheat and meat, removed from the world's market a large part of its supplies, and had immediately sent up the cost of food everywhere, outside the United Kingdom as well as in it. At the same time, the attacks upon shipping laden with food increased the cost of insurance to prohibitive prices upon vessels freighted for the United Kingdom.

The underwriters after the first few captures by the enemy would not insure at all except for fabulous rates.

The withdrawal of all the larger British cruisers for the purpose of defeating the main German fleets in the North Sea left the commerce-destroyers a free hand, and there was no force to meet them. The British liners commissioned as commerce-protectors were too few and too slow to be able to hold their adversaries in check.

Neutral shipping was molested by the German cruisers. Whenever raw cotton or food of any kind was discovered upon a neutral vessel bound for British ports, the vessel was seized and sent into one or other of the German harbours on the West Coast of Africa.

The United Kingdom, indeed, might have been reduced to absolute starvation had it not been for the fact that the Canadian Government interfered in Canada to prevent similar German tactics from succeeding, and held the German contracts for the cornering of Canadian wheat, contrary to public policy.

The want of food, the high price of bread and meat in England, and the greatly increased cost of the supplies of raw material sent up the expenditure upon poor relief to enormous figures. Millions of men were out of employment, and in need of assistance. Mills and factories in all directions had closed down, either because of the military danger from the operations of the German armies, or because of the want of orders, or, again, because raw materials were not procurable.

Unfortunately, when the invasion began, many rich foreigners who had lived in England collected what portable property they possessed and retired abroad to Switzerland, Italy, and the United States. Their example was followed by large numbers of British subjects who had invested abroad, and now, in the hour of distress, were able to place their securities in a handbag and withdraw them to happier countries.

They may justly be blamed for this want of patriotism, but their reply was that they had been unjustly and mercilessly taxed by men who derided patriotism, misused power, and neglected the real interests of the nation in the desire to pander to the mob. Moreover, with the income-tax at 3s. 6d. in the pound, and with the cost of living enormously enhanced, they declared that it was a positive impossibility to live in England, while into the bargain their lives were exposed to danger from the enemy.

As a result of this wholesale emigration, in London and the country the number of empty houses inordinately increased, and there were few well-to-do people left to pay the rates and taxes. The fearful burden of the extravagant debts which the British municipalities had heaped up was cruelly felt, since the nation had to repudiate the responsibility which it had incurred for the payment of interest on the local debts. The Socialist dream, in fact, might almost be said to have been realised. There were few rich left, but the consequences to the poor, instead of being beneficial, were utterly disastrous.

Under the pressure of public opinion, constrained by hunger and financial necessities, and with thousands of German prisoners in their hands, the British Government acceded to the suggested conference to secure peace.

Peace was finally signed on January 13, 1911. The British Empire emerged from the conflict outwardly intact, but internally so weakened that only the most resolute reforms accomplished by the ablest and boldest statesmen, could have restored it to its old position.

Germany, on the other hand, emerged with an additional 21,000 miles of European territory, with an extended seaboard on the North Sea, fronting the United Kingdom at Rotterdam and the Texel, and, it was calculated, with a slight pecuniary advantage. Practically the entire cost of the war had been borne by England.

As is always the case, the poor suffered most. The Socialists, who had declared against armaments, were faithless friends of those whom they professed to champion. Their dream of a golden age proved utterly delusive. But the true authors of England's misfortunes escaped blame for the moment, and the Army and Navy were made the scapegoats of the great catastrophe.

When success did come, it came too late, and could not be utilised without a great British Army capable of carrying the war into the enemy's country, and thus compelling a satisfactory peace.

THE END.